White Trash in a Trailer Park

by Randal Patrick

EGGMAN PUBLISHING

Editor:
  Craig Owensby and Currey Copple

Front Cover Designed by:
  Brad Talbot

Design, typography, and text production:
  TypeByte Graphix

Library of Congress: 95–60650

ISBN: 1–886371–15–6

Eggman Publishing
3012 Hedrick Street
Nashville, Tennessee 37203
(800) 396-4626

everybody knows somebody who's white trash . . . but nobody thinks they are

Introduction

In the opening pages of Randal Patrick's "white trash in a trailer park," Evelyn Sewell awakens to another morning of existence in the Captain's Point Trailer Park, nestled on the bank of the Tennessee River. She imagines God looking down, is grateful for God's tolerance and for the possibilities of God's ever-present power to finger-snap trouble away.

It could happen, Evelyn believes wearily.

Today it could happen.

And then the alarm rings.

And trouble is still there.

For the rest of the residents of Captain's Point Trailer Park, another day is just another day. Trouble for them is a daily ritual, a monotonous, offensive, on-going Way of Living. To speak of hope is to yammer senselessly. Hope is as fragile as the supply-and-demand operation of the Big Sandy Auto Accessories Plant, and as empty as a beer bottle at midnight on the cluttered tables of the Dew Drop Inn.

Bluntly, God and Evelyn are heavily outnumbered.

But they are not deterred.

So what is this "white trash in a trailer park" all about anyway?

Evelyn and God, yes, but it's also about Clifford, Becky, Jimmie Clifford, Verdale, Nancy, Jerry, Wanda, Fat Ethel, Benny, Cecil, Toby, Jack, Joe, Ed, Ernistine, Shelia, Lloyd, Gerald—and others equally as fascinating. All characters.

And that is what is important about this book. It is very close to being the quintessential Southern story—background characters of society playing foreground characters in literature. As comparison, the works of Erskine Caldwell pop to mind.

Southern literature is not plot-driven; it's character-driven. Plot matters, of course, but it matters mostly as a thing to dangle characters from, much as a backyard clothesline holds the weekly wash. (How many people ever pause to look at a clothesline? Put the right kind of wash on it—from dingy sheets to skimpy panties —and it's bound to be seen and, perhaps, talked about.)

Randal Patrick knows all of this from his Paris, Tennessee roots.

He also knows (intuitively, I suspect) that the voice of Southern literature is not found on the tongue, but in the ear.

Patrick hears the South, and what he hears is not an accent, as they suspect in Los Angeles or in New York, but a way of speaking —phraseology. Phraseology that is warm, funny, profound, obscene, truthful, hurtful, revealing, concealing. It is language.

"white trash in a trailer park" is a leaping, scene-rich motion picture of a book, which is natural to Patrick. An actor and writer in film and television, he understands clearly the intricate weaving of fragments to make the whole. And the whole, in this case, is majestically achieved.

Take a chance. Get on the side of God and Evelyn and watch with them the goings-on of a community bumbling about in union activities at the Big Sandy Auto Accessories plant, or hailing the heroics of a championship high school football team. Enjoy their lusting, their pride, their failure, the gentle lies they tell themselves about who they are or what they may become.

When you finish, you may even understand why God looks in on Captain's Point Trailer Park every morning.

Terry Kay
author of
*To Dance With
The White Dog*
and
Shadow Song

To my grandmother, Ethel Johnson.

God sent us an angel

Author's Notes

The reader should be aware that I make no claims to being an authority on "white trash." Having been white trash all my life, I can only speak and write from personal experience and imagination. Like Clifford Sewell, I am stubborn as a mule and twice as opinionated. Like Clifford's daughter Becky, I grew up wanting to be an artist and escape what I believed to be the boring life of small town Tennessee—I was wrong. Like Nancy Calloway, I continually make that classic error of basing the crucial decisions of my life on the need to be loved and accepted by everyone except my family—the very people who love and accept me no matter what decision I make. Like Wesley Tubbs, I look at the world through beveled glass, questioning what others take for granted and always threatening to do something really big and very important—the first chance I get. Like Verdale Calloway, Nancy's mother, I drink too much, play Elvis records too loud, cry and feel sorry for my lot in life—always forgetting how good I actually have it. Like Jerry Burnette, I love my family and friends more than anything in this world, and I think about the ones who have passed on every day, wishing I could tell 'em one last time how much they mean to me. Like Evelyn Sewell, Clifford's wife and Becky's mother, I am a dreamer. I dream of a day when everybody'll have plenty of food on the table and a safe warm place to sleep, when all our families'll be happy and healthy and their lives filled with kindness and respect. And like Evelyn, once in a while I allow myself to dream of a brand new double-wide trailer with a dishwasher, a disposal, its very own septic tank, sitting on a good-size lot with plenty of trees—not too far from work and not too far from the river.

All characters in this book are fiction and in no way, shape, or form are based on any persons, living or dead. But I hope by the time you turn that last page you'll think of these folks as living, breathing, hard-working, beer-drinking, fist-fighting, woman-chasing, overtaxed, underpaid, God-fearing, human beings—I hope you'll think of 'em as your friends.

BOOK ONE

from your mouth to God's ears

1

Each morning when she awoke, the same image blinked to light in the dark, inner eye of Evelyn Sewell.

The image was of God.

God looking down.

God seeing the Captain's Point Trailer Park, snuggled close along the bank of the Tennessee River.

What God saw was the frosted tops of trailers—mobile homes—like eggs in a thick nest of Tennessee trees.

Evelyn believed God had a tender spot in His heart for these egg-trailers.

And then Evelyn Sewell would sigh—a long, deep, sad sigh. "If God only knew," she would think. "If he only knew."

But maybe he did know, she reasoned each morning. Of course he knew. He is all-knowing and all-seeing. And from such a great distance away as heaven, eggs must look pretty, and even strong, resting in this nest of green Tennessee oaks. But since he made eggs, as well as every other thing on this earth, God would surely know how easy it was for egg-trailers, and everyone in them, to break.

Each morning, Evelyn thought she would break.

She would break, and the yolk of her soul would spill out into the dark Tennessee clay and disappear.

Evelyn thought all of these things each morning, only moments before the soft orange light of dawn skimmed the mile across the churning waters of the Tennessee River. Only seconds before the alarm clock spit its mechanical ring across the room, across Captain's Point Trailer Park, across Tennessee, across the Southeastern United States, the Atlantic Ocean, the Earth, and finally the Universe. Evelyn knew the alarm had the power to reach the ears of God, even if it did not awaken anyone else in the trailer.

The clock sprang to life.

Evelyn swept at it with her hand and swatted the cut-off button with God's aim.

She took a last peaceful breath, her last moment suspended in the vision of God looking down on the egg-trailers of Captain's

Point Trailer Park, then she punched her heel across the sheets at her husband, Clifford.

"Clifford, honey? Get up."

Evelyn rolled from the bed and flipped on the lamp on the night stand.

She looked to Clifford. He did not move. If his chest did not rise and fall with his breathing, she would have thought him dead, maybe gone to God. Maybe not. With Clifford it would be a toss-up, and it would depend on how tolerant God was at the moment.

"Clifford?" Evelyn said wearily.

Clifford did not move.

"Clifford!" she barked.

Clifford's eyes snapped open like a blinking doll's.

"I'm awake, gotdamn it," Clifford growled.

Evelyn leaned toward him. "Don't you take the Lord's name in vain in this house, and I mean it," she hissed.

Clifford blinked into consciousness from his dream. A dream of plenty. A dream where everyone had all they needed for themselves and their families. He took a deep morning breath and scratched his fingers through his coarse, dark beard. Reality was setting in.

"Clifford, come on, get up," Evelyn encouraged.

"Evelyn, I'm up. Hush!"

Each morning it was the same, Evelyn thought as she moved down the narrow, paneled hallway of the trailer. The hallway in the morning always seemed to close in on her, its walls pushing against her, squeezing her, until her breathing was hard and labored.

Each morning, it was the same.

It began with God, moved to Clifford, and then down the narrow hall to Becky's room.

She open her daughter's bedroom door and flipped the light on. "Becky," she said, softly. "It's five-thirty baby." She saw Becky's body unroll from the pillow she hugged. "Lord, she's pretty to be sixteen," Evelyn thought. "Never knew I'd have me a baby so pretty."

"You awake, honey?" she asked. Becky twisted to the side of the bed and sat up. She yawned, stretched, nodded.

"Time to get up, baby."

As Evelyn moved to leave the room she noticed a new half-finished canvas on the easel in the corner, a corner filled with a young artist's paintings, sketches and supplies. She paused for a moment as she studied her daughter's latest work. She looked back at Becky wiping the sleep from her eyes and she wondered where this talent came from. Not from her side of the family. Certainly not from Clifford's. From God, of course. Evelyn smiled at the thought of her daughter being singled out by God with such a special gift. She closed the door and Becky fell back into bed, burying her face in the pillow.

God and Clifford and Becky and finally—God help us—Jimmie Clifford. Maybe Jimmie was last on Evelyn's morning route of life because Jimmie would have been last on God's list.

She pushed open the door to his room. Her hand found the light switch in a habit of years, but stopped. The bulb had been burned out for more than a week. Evelyn had sworn in a prayer to God that she would not change that bulb; if Jimmie wanted light in his room, let Jimmie change it. She crossed the room and pulled back the curtain. From outside, she could hear the muted voice of Elvis Presley coming from Verdale Calloway's trailer. She thought: "Oh dear Jesus, Verdale's at it again." She shook her head sadly, thinking of Verdale, knowing that Verdale was probably passed out again from drinking, knowing that a stack of Elvis records were on the record player.

A soft morning hue—like a dull pewter cloud tinted with the fading of the harvest moon—billowed into the room. And that, too, was sad to Evelyn. Such lovely light—God's own light—falling over the dirty clothes, motor parts and hot rod magazines that cluttered Jimmie's room.

"Jimmie Clifford, get up son," Evelyn ordered.

She heard a tired moan and stepped to the bed. In the bed, she saw the shadowy outline of Jimmie. He was naked. All six feet three inches, two hundred and forty pounds of Jimmie was naked. His feet hung off the end of the twin bed. I hope God's eyes are somewhere else, she thought.

"Jimmie Clifford, what have I told you about sleepin' butt nekkid?" she growled. "What if there was a fire or something?" She stepped to Jimmie and, with God's help and God's aim, she threw the palm of her hand at his ass. She heard it slap, felt the sting in her fingers.

"Mama, quit! What're you doing?"

"I want this room cleaned up and I mean it, Jimmie Clifford."

"Just get outta here," Jimmie snapped.

"You hush. Looks like a pig sty in here. Now get up and get ready to go to school!" God aimed and released Evelyn's hand again.

2

Toby Johnson was old, and as dark as the dark smoky room where he was sitting listening to the pleading voice of a Pentecostal preacher shouting from the old radio across the small room. His old brown fingers nimbly worked the makings of a roll-your-own cigarette. Beside him on the floor, his great-granddaughter Sudie played with a bird dog. The old dog wanted to sleep, but was patient with the baby girl. Her diaper was damp with urine. Toby listened intently to the preacher. He wanted to hear the preacher's voice, not the voices, the soft cries of pleasure, that slid from the bedroom behind him.

In the bedroom, Toby's granddaughter Janice rose from the bed. She glanced at the cloudy mirror that hung above the old dresser. She saw her reflection. Her ebony body—her small breasts with the erect nipples, the roped muscles of her abdomen, the dark, triangled hair at her legs—it surprised her and yet pleased her. It was always that way after lovemaking, the confusion of feelings racing through her in a quick glance.

She slipped from the bed and pulled a cotton dress over her head, then turned back to watch Jerry Burnette get dressed. He smiled at her as he sat up on the edge of the bed and reached for the camouflage hunting pants that he had hung over the ladder-back chair. His white chest and shoulders seemed ghostly to her, almost lifeless at times. His neck and arms were a reddish brown. "A farmer's tan," she thought. But Jerry was no farmer. She knew he was somewhere in his thirties, but he seemed older. Janice liked the way Jerry looked without his clothes. The way he felt. The way he tasted. She liked being with an older man. A man who knew how to be gentle during lovemaking. She pulled a cigarette from a package on the dresser and lit it.

Jerry tucked his camouflage shirt into his camouflage pants. He moved to the mirror and inspected himself, combing his fingers through his straight brown hair. He reached into his pocket and pulled out some money. He flipped through the bills, found the ones he wanted, and laid them on the dresser.

"Don't do that, Jerry," Janice insisted.

Jerry smiled that perfect, toothy smile, winked, took the cigarette from her lips, pulled on it, then gave it back to her. He slipped on his well-worn canvas field coat and walked out of the room. Janice picked up the money from the dresser, quickly counted it, then slipped it into the pocket of her dress.

The Pentecostal preacher was intoning a frightening call for donations to save God's kingdom when Jerry knelt beside Toby and stroked the head of the sleeping bird dog.

"Give you twenty dollars for this dog, Mr. Johnson," Jerry offered.

Toby smiled peacefully at Jerry.

"That dog ain't no count for huntin', son," Toby replied.

"I know it," Jerry said. "I just like him."

Toby laughed a deep rasp.

"Naw, I better not," he said. "That dog ain't never been nowhere but here. He might get lonesome for me."

Jerry grinned and stroked the dog again. He stood, walked into the kitchen and took the water dipper from its nail above the sink. The old pipes rattled as he ran himself a dipperful of water from the faucet. Janice leaned in the doorway behind him, holding Sudie. She was watching him closely, like a person trying to memorize someone's features. Jerry turned to her as he drank. He looked into her eyes. She could feel a shudder, something cold at her throat, and yet she believed the distance between them was warm, and somehow tender.

Jerry hooked the dipper back on its nail and walked out of the kitchen and onto the back porch of the shack. He picked up the rifle he had leaned against the door jamb, hopped down off the porch, and walked the old gray planks that had been placed across the soft muck of the back yard. Chickens protested and darted out of his way as Jerry reached the deep creek at the edge of the woods. From the door, holding Sudie, Janice watched as Jerry jumped the creek and disappeared up the hill and into the trees. She could feel his stain on her legs.

3

Nancy Calloway knew she was late. She could see the dull lights from the trailers bobbing on the slick surface of the Tennessee River.

She could imagine what her mother would say if she caught her coming in this late, or early. "What have I told you about staying out all night. What about school? A sixteen-year-old girl ain't got no business staying out all night. You think you're twenty-five, don'tchu?" Nancy cringed at the thought of hearing the high-pitched whine her mother always used in these situations.

Nancy touched the leg of the boy driving the white Ford pickup.

"Cut the lights off and let me out over there." She pointed to a large water oak near the river.

The boy did as instructed. He killed the motor and reached for Nancy, his hand pushing hard against her breast. She pushed him away.

"Got another smoke?" she asked as she pushed in the cigarette lighter.

"Shit," the boy sighed. He slid back under the steering wheel, reached into his shirt pocket, and shook a cigarette free from its pack. He gave it to Nancy, then pulled the lighter from the dash and held it for her. Nancy playfully blew smoke into his face. He reached for her again, running his hand along her thigh and under her short skirt. She kissed him, then pulled away.

"I gotta go, really," she said. "'I'm late as hell." She opened the door of the truck.

"Then go, I don't give a shit," the boy complained.

Nancy stopped, then looked back at the boy with a pained expression. She knew the game he was playing—that control game that boys always seemed to play with her.

"I'll see ya at school, okay?" She leaned quickly to him, brushed a kiss over his lips, and then slipped from the truck.

"We can get together tomorrow night again, if you want to?" she said as a peace offering.

"Maybe," the boy muttered as he leaned forward and turned the key in the ignition. The engine jumped to life.

The boy watched as Nancy ran down the hill toward the trailer park. He touched his groin. It ached from having her, and from wanting her again. "Jesus," he whispered. He shifted the truck into gear and pulled away.

Nancy paused at the edge of the trailer park. She drew hard on the cigarette, then flipped it away like a veteran smoker. She could see the dull glazed lights of her trailer, and she could hear the deep mellow voice of Elvis. "Oh, shit," she moaned. She crossed the park, slipping quietly passed the trailers that were just beginning to tremble to life. She could hear voices—harsh, soft, begging. A child was crying. A radio played a news report. A commode flushed in a rush of water. She could smell the thick odor of brewing coffee, the sweet cooking bacon and biscuits. She rushed on to her own trailer, took the steps in a clean jump, and eased open the door.

Nancy saw what she knew she would see: her mother Verdale on the living room floor, sleeping the sleep of the drunk. A plant stand—the stand Nancy had given her mother for Christmas—had been pulled over, the plants and dirt spilled across Verdale and the floor. Elvis was singing from the stacked records on the record player, which sat on a small table underneath a framed black velvet portrait of Elvis.

"Shit, mother," Nancy mumbled as she shook her head.

She stepped over her mother and hurried down the narrow hallway of the trailer, undressing. In a few moments she returned, slipping her nightgown over her surprisingly full body.

"Come on, Mama, get up!" Nancy said impatiently.

Verdale Calloway stirred awake. She stared up at her daughter, nodded, and permitted herself to be pulled from the floor. She did not speak as Nancy led her down the hallway to the bathroom. Verdale leaned wearily against the wall as Nancy prepared the shower. She did not protest as Nancy undressed her and guided her into the hot stream of water.

4

The only moments of peace in the morning for Evelyn Sewell were behind the locked door of the bathroom. "First up, first in," she reasoned. But even the bathroom seemed to close in on her in the early morning.

She wet a washcloth and then opened the mirrored medicine chest above the small sink. She fumbled through several brown plastic medicine bottles with her prescription typed on the label. Some of the bottles were empty, and had been for a long time. "I should clean this cabinet out," she thought. But Evelyn knew which pills had cured which ailment, and she felt if she threw the empties away she might forget which prescription had cured her. She chose two brown plastic bottles, twisted the child-proof top and dropped a couple of pills from each bottle into her hand, then popped the pills onto her tongue. Evelyn cupped her palms to take water from the faucet. She sipped from her hands and swallowed the pills two at a time. Then she replaced the caps on the medicine bottles and returned them to the cabinet. When she closed the medicine chest she caught a glimpse of herself in the mirror. She gently examined the crows' feet at the corners of her green eyes. She was only thirty-nine, but she believed she looked fifty. She wondered if God thought her vain, being worried about the aging of her face.

Evelyn open the door to the bathroom and moved down the hallway to the kitchen.

"Get up! Y'all get up!" she called. Her voice echoed down the hallway.

5

The morning sun had caught the mountain ridge with its fingers of light and was pulling itself up on the horizon. Jerry stepped from the woods and moved slowly through the tombstones of a small cemetery that nudged the back of a white, woodframed church. The church and the cemetery were very old.

Jerry looked once at the sun streaming through the trees on the ridge, then knelt beside a marble headstone in the shape of a heart. He read the marker:

> *Jerry Clayton Burnette, Jr.*
> *Born June 29, 1986*
> *Died July 16, 1990*
> *Asleep with the Angels*

He reached absently to a vase of plastic flowers that had been knocked over by a roving dog and righted the vase, pushing it into the soft, wet mound of grass and dirt. Jerry stood and inhaled slowly, feeling the hurt that was always with him at his son's grave. Behind him, deep in the woods, two gunshots exploded like rapid firecrackers. He looked toward the sound, lifted his rifle, and started for the trees that bordered the church's property to the west. He glanced back at the heart-shaped marker with its small mound of earth and noticed his own bootprint left in the grass and mud. "That's right about where I'll be buried," he thought. "Me and little Clayton right next to each other. That's the way it oughta be with a father and his only son." Jerry turned and walked from the cemetery with long, deliberate strides.

6

Clifford, in a fit of anger, had once described the interior of the Sewells' trailer perfectly: "If the Pope shopped at Wal-Mart, this is how his trailer would look." The look, especially in Evelyn's domain of the living room and kitchen, was a plastic and ceramic Bible Belt shrine to God and Jesus—a collection of cheap artifacts, with Jesus on the cross, Jesus in the garden at Gethsemane, Jesus and the apostles at the Last Supper. These artifacts annoyed Clifford, but they calmed Evelyn.

When she cooked—as she was doing now, preparing a breakfast that would be gobbled down without appreciation by her family—Evelyn's eyes scanned the images of Jesus. Each meant something to her. Each represented an offering begged for by a television evangelist who promised a healing of body, mind, and soul from a television studio located somewhere in the Bible Belt of the midwest and southeast. Evelyn was not prejudiced against any one particular religious organization. She listened to anyone who had something positive to say about God. Unless, of course, she was boycotting that particular TV channel for airing programs that good Christians believed undermined the morality of the family and ultimately the country. She did have her favorite, though, and she watched him every morning, boycott or not, as she cooked breakfast.

A tall, handsome man with a salt-and-pepper, country-western hairdo was telling of Jesus turning the water into wine. Evelyn watched, trying to feel what he was feeling as he cried for the lost souls of the world. As hard as she tried she could never quite get the feeling she thought she should have, the feeling she thought God wanted her to have, the feeling she thought others must be having. She wondered if God knew that she was at least trying to empathize. She wondered if it really mattered to God. She watched as the preacher reached out his hand to the camera and begged, with tears streaming down his face for the Christians at home to place their hands on his hands on their television screens.

She flipped the sizzling bacon in the frying pan and shot a look at the clock.

"Clifford, get up! Clifford!" Evelyn yelled toward the back of the trailer.

Clifford stepped from the shadows of the back bedroom, dressed only in his boxer shorts. He looked like a bear with a bad temper emerging from hibernation.

"Evelyn, shut the hell up!" He growled in his crackling morning voice.

"Hush Clifford. You're gonna be late for work," she called over her shoulder.

"You say that every gotdamn morning, and I ain't never been late for work." Clifford snapped as he stepped into the bathroom.

"Always a first time. And stop taking the Lord's name in vain in this house." she warned.

In her bedroom, Becky lay staring at the ceiling and listening to the argument. The daily ritual of argument. She crawled from bed, opened her door, and stumbled down the hall toward the bathroom.

"Will y'all quit yellin'?" she said.

She reached the bathroom. The door was open and her father was peeing in a loud, thick pouring. Becky stopped in her tracks.

"Daddy! Gross!" Becky sighed, rolled her eyes, then quickly turned back up the hallway.

"Mama!"

Her father kicked at the door. It half-closed. He mumbled, "Can't even take a piss in my own house anymore without somebody giving me a buncha shit about it."

Becky stormed up the hall of the trailer past Jimmie Clifford's room. He was still in bed. He was still naked.

"Jimmie Clifford, Daddy's up," she said with warning.

"Shut up," Jimmie mumbled from beneath his pillow.

Becky sighed another of her morning sighs and shuffled up the hall, through the living room, and into the kitchen.

"Mama, Daddy's in there peeing with the door open again." Becky opened the refrigerator and poured herself a glass of orange juice.

"You can't tell him nothin'," Evelyn said as she busily moved from stove to sink and back. "Set the table for me, honey."

Becky finished the juice and set the glass on the counter. "Mama, I've gotta wash my hair this morning." She turned and headed back through the living room toward the hall.

Evelyn looked at the empty glass on the counter, then looked at Becky as she walked away. She just shook her head as she picked up the glass and dropped it in the dishwater in the sink.

"Becky, you're gonna set this table for me now," Evelyn called after her. "I don't ask you to do much around—"

"Okay, Mama," Becky interrupted. "Wait just a minute." She stalked back down the hall. Her father, stretching and yawning and scratching, staggered out of the bathroom.

"Jimmie Clifford, you better be up, boy," Clifford said in a loud voice.

Clifford stepped back into his bedroom when he heard Becky's muffled call from the bathroom: "Daddy, gross!" He smiled. He knew she had sat on the toilet without looking. He had left the seat down.

"Daddy, did it ever occur to you to put the seat up when you're using the bathroom?" she snapped as she charged into his room.

"It occurred to me. I just didn't feel like leaning over and putting it up," he said. "You're starting to sound just like your mother, and if I was you I'd do damn near anything I could to avoid that."

Becky glared at him and stomped out. She could hear her mother calling. "Becky, get in here and do what I told you."

"I'm coming, Mother," Becky shouted. "Do you mind if I pee?"

She made a turn for the bathroom, then stopped and stepped back when she saw her brother, still naked, moving like a large animal from his room and down the hall toward her. "Gross!" she cried as she hugged the wall to keep from touching him as he passed. "Jimmie Clifford, you make me sick. Mama!"

"Shut up," Jimmie snarled as he entered the bathroom and started to urinate, leaving the door open.

Becky, rolled her eyes, turned, and started for the kitchen. "I'm obviously adopted. I don't even look like these people."

7

The breakfast that Nancy Calloway was cooking—sausage for a sausage-and-egg biscuit—made her feel queasy. She could taste the cigarette that she had quickly smoked as her mother showered and dressed. She was tender and sore from the fury of the night's sex, and she was tired. "Got to take a nap this afternoon," she thought. Or maybe she would skip school. Tell her mother she was having her period and had cramps. "No, shit, I can't do that," she remembered. "I've missed too many days this quarter already." Mr. Phillips, the high school principal, had warned her about being absent and sent a note home for her mother to sign. Nancy signed it. She had gotten good over the years at forging her mother's name on things like report cards and checks. If Verdale didn't remember, Nancy would tell her she had been drunk when she wrote the check. Verdale would always pitch a fit, but what was done was done. Well, whatever. She needed to sleep, and Nancy reckoned she could sleep in class as well as anywhere.

Then she remembered—today, the senior rings would be ordered. She wanted her name on the list. She had struggled through eleven years of school and she aimed to have that ring to show for it, even if she didn't have the education. She called out to Verdale: "Mama, can I borrow enough money to get my senior ring? We gotta turn the order in today."

Verdale entered the kitchen, her hair in a towel. A faded cotton robe was wrapped to her body. Her hangover coated her face like bad makeup. She looked much older than thirty-three.

"What's that smell?" she asked bitterly.

"Sausage," Nancy said. "I thought I'd make some sausage biscuits like they got at McDonald's."

Verdale lit a cigarette and sat at the table. She looked out the kitchen window at the morning mist moving eerily across the river. Nancy stepped from the stove to the table and poured her mother a cup of hot coffee.

"See if there's some of that brandy left," Verdale said. "It helps me with these headaches."

Nancy opened the pantry door. Verdale kept the booze right behind the Cheerios. "There's a little bit left." Nancy said stiffly.

She emptied the bottle into Verdale's cup, then dropped it heavily into the trash can. Nancy could feel the disgusted look Verdale was giving her, but she refused to look. If she made eye contact with her mother there would be an argument, and this morning she needed Verdale's help.

"Can I, Mama? Can I borrow enough money to finish out what I need for my ring?"

"How much?"

"I already got most of it. My baby-sitting money. I'll pay you back."

"How much do you need?" Verdale asked again.

"Oh, about—well, around ninety-five dollars, I guess."

"Damn. How much *is* the thang?"

"Altogether?" Nancy stalled. "About a hundred'n ninety dollars, I guess."

"You guess?" Verdale drew hard on her cigarette. "Shit. Do you know how much them things were when I was your age?"

Nancy slid a plate with a sausage-and-egg biscuit on it in front of her mother.

"Mama, you say that about ever'thing," she countered. "You didn't go to school long enough to get a senior ring."

"By the time I was your age, I already had you, Miss Smart Aleck," Verdale snapped.

Nancy rolled her eyes and turned back to the stove. She grabbed the frying pan she had cooked the sausage and eggs in, dropped it in the sink, and filled it with a quick burst of water from the faucet. She was determined not to fight with her mother. Not just yet anyway. That ring was too important to let her quick temper get in the way of the loan she needed. She stared out the small window above the sink and began to gnaw subconsciously on her thumbnail.

"I don't know why you don't ask your daddy to do something for you once in a while." Verdale said. "It's always left up to me to do everything."

"I called Daddy," Nancy replied quietly. She continued to stare out the kitchen window.

Verdale looked up from her coffee surprised. A small sting of jealousy shot through her. "What'd he say?" She questioned.

"What do you think?" Nancy replied sarcastically. "He said he didn't have it."

"Of course not," Verdale chuckled with relief. "He can't ever do anything for you."

Verdale sipped the coffee and brandy and stared out the window, remembering her ex-husband. She fought the good memories, trying hard to replace them with the bad. "Why do the good memories always come?" she thought. It made it hard to remind herself that she was not in love with him anymore. She pictured his face in her mind. She remembered the strong good looks, the dark hair and eyes, the stout body. She had always thought he looked like Elvis Presley. But not her mother, she recalled. "He's nearly fifteen years older than you," her mother had warned. "What's a thirty-year-old man want with a sixteen-year-old girl?"

"Mama, are you gonna eat? Your food's getting cold," Nancy said, snapping Verdale back to reality.

"What'd your daddy have to say?" Verdale asked.

"He didn't say nothing about you, so just eat." Nancy sighed.

"Don'tchu get smart with me, young lady," Verdale hissed.

"I'm not getting smart with you. I just get tired of you talking about Daddy all the time."

"Who answered when you called over there?" Verdale asked. "Did *she* answer?"

"Yes, Mama, *she* answered."

"Of course she answered." Verdale pouted. "Ever'time I have to call over there for something *she* answers. Like he can't answer his own damn phone." She paused and crushed her cigarette out in the ashtray. "What'd she say?"

"Nothing," Nancy sighed.

"Nothing? She didn't say a word, not hello, not kiss my ass, nothing?"

"Mama, she said, 'hello.' Then I said, 'Helen, can I speak to my daddy?' And then *she* said, 'Honey, it's Nancy on the phone for you.' "

"She said honey? She called him honey?" Verdale asked.

"Mother, they're married. She can call him anything she wants to."

"They're not married," Verdale argued. "Not really. Not in the eyes of God. They're not married. In the eyes of the Lord, it's adultery, pure and simple, and that's all it is."

"Well it may be adultery in the eyes of the Lord," Nancy said, "but in the eyes of the state of Tennessee, it's marriage and she can call him anything she wants to."

"Don't you take up for that slut," Verdale threatened.

"Mama, just eat and hush, okay?"

"I ain't hungry."

Nancy whirled toward her mother. She crossed to the table in two steps, picked up the plate with the uneaten sausage-and-egg biscuit on it, whirled again, and scraped the food into the trash can. Verdale watched in surprise as Nancy tossed the dish into the sink, stormed down the hall to her room, and slammed the door.

"You little bitch," Verdale called after her. She lit another cigarette and stared out the window down at the river. A barge was churning through the morning fog. Verdale wondered where it was going.

8

Wesley Tubbs struggled under the weight of the deer he carried over his shoulders. He was sweating and his breathing was labored, but he didn't care. He had left his trailer early this morning, long before dawn, with his mind on the deer, on the prize. He found it at the salt lick that was hidden just the other side of the old railroad bridge, and dropped it with his second shot. A clean strike to the heart. He could feel the perspiration sticking to his camouflage pants and shirt. His hair was wet, and it curled from under the band of his bright orange University of Tennessee Volunteers cap. He was tired and his thigh muscles ached in the cool morning air, but he felt good. He knew Jerry would be envious.

When he staggered from the brush at the edge of the woods, Wesley was surprised to see Jerry sitting on the hood of his truck smoking a cigarette. Wesley laughed as he walked past and rolled the deer into the bed of his truck. He drew a deep, pleased breath.

"I told 'chu, you should'a gone down there to that salt lick with me," he said to Jerry. "I saw two more big'uns down there on my way out."

"Wesley, you better quit hunting down at that salt lick. The game warden catches you, he'll take this truck," Jerry warned.

Wesley laughed as he pulled a small, round can of chewing tobacco from his rear pants pocket. "Well, I hope he has an easier time making the payments on it than I do." Wesley reached to touch the deer and petted it like a sleeping dog. "Feel that, Jerry. Now that's a beautiful animal. That's about the prettiest deer I nearly ever killed."

Jerry shook his head at Wesley, and sighed with a smile as he slammed shut the tailgate on the pickup.

Wesley took a pinch of tobacco from the can and placed it firmly on the inside of his bottom lip, then returned the can to his back pocket. "That's the problem with this country today, there's just too many goddamn rules and regulations. They're about to take all the fun outta huntin'. I mean, if a man can't go out in the woods and kill a wild animal without the government pitching a damn fit about it—well, shit—what can you do that's any fun. I don't know what this country's coming to, Jerry," Wesley said.

"Yeah, I guess." Jerry said, as the two men climbed into the pickup. Wesley drove slowly through the tall grass of the clearing, then turned down the dirt trail that led to the gravel road. He glanced in the rearview mirror at his prize in the bed of the pickup.

"You know what's funny about deer huntin'?" Wesley said after a few minutes. "We wear a camouflage coat and camouflage pants and an orange hat. That don't make a whole hell of a lotta sense, does it?"

"Deer's colorblind, Wesley." Jerry pointed out. "They can't tell if your hat's orange or not."

"Then what difference does it make if we wear camouflage pants then, if the deer can't tell what color it is. What good does it do to camouflage something if they ain't gonna see it anyway." Wesley objected. "We might as well hunt in a Sunday suit, for that matter."

Jerry swallowed a laugh as he shot a disbelieving look at Wesley.

"I wonder about stuff like that." Wesley said, as he turned his truck onto the two lane blacktop and headed toward the river road that led to the Captain's Point Trailer Park.

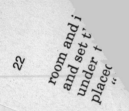

Clifford Sewell lumbered into the kitchen. He was ca~
work boots, and he dropped them on the table as he sat and pu~
on his socks. His big toe peeked through a hole in one of his socks,
and he doubled the end over to hide the toe.

"Clifford, don't put your nasty boots on the breakfast table.
Good grief," Evelyn protested.

Clifford frowned, then put his boots on the floor and wiggled
his feet into them one at a time. He bent to tie them.

The TV evangelist was begging for people to kneel in their living rooms and their kitchens, in their bathrooms and their bedrooms, and in their places of business. The evangelist was saying
that people who were bowed to God at this moment were the people that God had called as His Christian soldiers. Clifford felt
awkward, bending as he was to tie his boots. He sat up quickly
and propped one leg across the other to finish.

"Evelyn, what have I told you about that?" He pointed at the
television. "It's too early to have to listen to that son of a bitch."

"Don't start on me this morning, now," Evelyn grumbled. "I've
got cramps." She pulled a pan of biscuits from the oven, then
placed Clifford's lunchbox on the Formica-topped counter. She
opened it, cleaned out a Twinkie wrapper and banana peel, and
tossed them into the garbage.

"Why you gotta tell me when it's that time of the month?" he
asked. "I don't want to hear about ever' twenty-eight days."

"Shut up, Clifford," Evelyn said wearily. "What do you want in
your lunch, tuna fish or Spam?"

"Spam."

Evelyn shook the Spam from its can and began to cut it.
"Juanita said Billy told her some of 'em down at the plant had
started talking about trying to get a union in there again," she
said.

"Yeah, they circulatin' them petitions again," Clifford replied
dryly. "But it don't amount to nothing."

"Becky!" Evelyn shouted. "Clifford, make her get in here."

"Becky, get your butt in here and help your Mama!"

Becky, with her hair in curlers, stomped through the living

nto the kitchen. She pulled the plates from the cabinet
hem heavily onto the table. She jerked open the drawer
he sink, grabbed a handful of silverware, and quickly
it around the plates.

What's your damn problem?" Clifford asked sternly.

I am *trying* to get ready to go to school." she whined.

"You're gonna help your mother around here too," he said. "So
you can either get up earlier and wash your hair and primp, or
you can sleep later and go to school with dirty hair. It don't make
no difference to me. But you *will* help your mother, do you understand?" Clifford said as he stood.

Becky nodded, straightened the silverware, then pulled some
paper napkins from a ceramic holder in the shape of praying
hands and began to lay one at each plate.

Clifford unlocked the trailer door, stepped down the small
metal steps, and picked up the newspaper lying in the damp
grass. The morning air was crisp with the smells of autumn. Clifford waved to Lloyd Pinkerton as he pulled past on his way to work
at the Piggly Wiggly. He returned inside, wiping the dew off the
paper as he unrolled it.

"It don't seem like it's been a year since they voted the union
down last time," Evelyn continued.

"Nearly three," Clifford said as he sat. "Some of them old boys
down there ain't satisfied just to have a job. That ain't good
enough for 'em. Got to always be stirring up some shit down
there."

Evelyn cracked another egg and slipped it into the pan. "It
looks to me like if they keep voting it down, sooner or later they'd
just forget about it," she said.

"Hell, half them boys wouldn't even come to work if they didn't
have something to bitch about," Clifford sighed. He rubbed his
eyes with the knuckles of his hand, then turned through the paper to the sports. "They come over here from Nashville and light a
fire under everybody's ass. Tell us how bad we got it and what-all
they gonna do for us."

Becky filled the small glasses with orange juice as she set
them around the table. "Why don't they vote a union in?" She
asked. "What difference would it make?"

"'Cause old man Moss says he'll shut the plant down if they
bring a union in there," Clifford answered. "That scares the shit
out of ever'body and they vote it down, and that's all there is to it."

"We studied about unions in social studies," Becky replied. "In
Mrs. Graham's class. And some of 'em do a lot of good."

"Well, this one won't," Clifford snapped.

"You don't reckon there's a chance they'll get it passed this time, do you?" Evelyn said. She broke the yolk of the eggs as she turned them.

"Naw, hell, I hope not, 'cause after I get this promotion, I'll be same as management, and I don't want to have to deal with the damn union's bellyaching all the time."

"What kind of promotion you going to get, Daddy?" asked Becky.

"Shift foreman," Clifford answered confidently, as he turned the page of the paper and folded it to the article he was reading.

"Is that a good job, Daddy?" Becky asked. She noticed Jimmie Clifford ambling up the hall toward the kitchen. He was wearing only his boxer shorts. His great weight vibrated through the trailer.

"What job?" Jimmie mumbled.

"The one Daddy's gonna get." Becky said. "Shift foreman."

"Is that a good job?" Jimmie asked. He moved into the kitchen, picked up a few pieces of crisp bacon off a paper towel and crammed them into his mouth.

"Hell, yeah, it's a good job," Clifford announced. "I shoulda been promoted ten years ago, but they couldn't find anybody that could run that radial front press like I can."

"You gonna get a big raise, Daddy?" Becky inquired.

"We ain't gonna get rich, but it's a few more dollars a month," her father answered.

Becky slid into a chair next to Clifford. She said, "Well, I been looking at cars over at Owell's lot, the used side, and I saw a—"

Clifford did not look up from the paper. "I done told 'chu, I ain't buying you no gotdamn car."

"Clifford? Hush!" Evelyn growled.

"How come you bought Jimmie Clifford one then?" Becky asked angrily.

"He didn't buy me no car," Jimmie said, with his mouth full. "He gave me his old truck, and it's a piece of shit."

"Jimmie Clifford? Hush!" Evelyn ordered.

"It's the same difference," Becky quarreled. "Daddy, there's a used Toyota over there that don't cost much, and I could—"

Clifford dropped the paper on the table and leaned to Becky. "If I was gonna buy you a car—which I ain't—I wouldn't buy you a Japanese car if it hare-lipped the devil. So you can just forget it." He returned to reading the paper. "You don't need a car," he added.

"Oh, and Jimmie Clifford *does*, I guess?" Becky sighed and crossed her arms.

"Becky, just shut up," Jimmie barked. He pulled a hot biscuit from the pan, gingerly tore it apart and blew on it, then stuffed it in his mouth. "Shit! That's hot!"

Evelyn spun around and slapped Jimmie on the shoulder. She could feel the brick-like muscles in his upper arm. Her palm throbbed from the hit. "I don't want to hear that kind of talk, now. Go put some clothes on before you come to this table," she ordered.

Jimmie ignored her as he took his place at the table. "I'm hungry, Mama."

"Now Becky, we already been over this." Clifford warned. He leaned back in his chair and tossed the newspaper on the kitchen counter. "Jimmie Clifford's got football practice, and huntin', and he runs errands and different things for me."

"I got stuff to do, too," Becky argued.

"You gotdamn straight you do," Clifford began, raising his voice.

"Stop taking the Lord's name in vain in this house, and I mean it!" Evelyn hissed in that tone she used when she'd had enough. She poured a cup of coffee and hastily set it in front of Clifford.

Clifford looked up at his wife. He could see God's anger boiling in her face. He turned back to Becky and took a deep calming breath. "You need to be around here helping your mama and not out running the wheels off some car, wastin' gas and tires and raisin' my insurance payments. Now that's all I want to hear about it."

Clifford shot a quick look at Evelyn. He did not like being reprimanded in front of their children. There was silence as she brought a bowl of grits and the plate of eggs to the table. Another morning, another argument.

Evelyn stepped to the counter, slipped the Spam sandwiches into a plastic bag, and packed them in Clifford's lunchbox.

"You want a Twinkie in your lunch?" she asked, breaking the silence. "Yes," Clifford growled. "You ask me that ever' morning. Yes, I want a Twinkie. Yes, every gotdamn day I want a Twinkie.

"I guess it's just too much to ask for us to have one meal in this house without an argument." Evelyn said.

Becky pushed away from the table and started for her room. "Will y'all hush!" she cried. "This is the most dysfunctional family I've ever seen in my life." Her voice was still echoing when she disappeared down the hallway.

Clifford watched her go, then looked at Evelyn. "What the hell does that mean?" he asked.

Evelyn shrugged as she closed and snapped the lunchbox shut. "She's taking psychology this quarter. That's her new word."

Clifford thought for a moment. "Well, it better not be dirty." He huffed. "I ain't gonna have that kind of talk in this house from no sixteen-year-old girl, I'll tell you that much."

Clifford reached for the coffee cup, lifted it to his lips, then pulled it away. The mug was molded in the face of Jesus. He had placed his lips on the blunt crown of thorns.

"Shit," Clifford grumbled. He quickly put the cup down. "Now, Evelyn, I done told you I ain't drinking my coffee outta the head of Jesus."

10

Wesley and Jerry pulled the deer from the bed of the truck, leaving a thick crimson trail of warm blood across the tailgate and dew-covered grass. The deer was dead weight, and its wet fur slipped in their hands. They carried it to the rear of Wesley's mother and daddy's trailer, back where they burned the garbage in a fifty-gallon barrel under a large white oak, back near the empty clothesline that stretched between two T-shaped bars Wesley had welded for his mother at his friend Dover's garage.

Wesley had field-dressed the deer down by the old river bridge where he killed it. He had expertly slit the first layer of skin carefully into the wall of muscle that held the stomach and intestines. Then he had pulled vital organs from the animal.

All that had been left to do was to hang the deer upside down by its hind legs and let the blood drain from the meat, then skin it.

"Why do you reckon they call it *dressing* a deer?" Wesley asked. "I mean, what you're really doing is undressing 'em, ain't it? I mean, think about it. Why is it that you dress a deer, but you clean a fish? Heck, you just got the fish outta the water. He didn't need cleaning. And at Thanksgiving, you have turkey and dressing? I wonder why they call it that?" Wesley had raised his eyebrows and cocked his head toward Jerry. "Did you ever think of that? Who actually decides what you're gonna call it?"

"Where do you come up with this shit, Wesley?" Jerry asked.

"I just think about things a lot more than most people do," Wesley answered.

Jerry was bearing most of the deer's weight as Wesley climbed the ladder that leaned against the oak. He was hooking the deer's ankles on rusty nails driven into a stout branch when his mother, Blanche, opened the door of the trailer and stepped out onto the small metal stoop.

"Wesley, you better get in here and eat something. Breakfast is ready." Blanche ordered. She was a heavyset woman in her late sixties. She kept her long hair pulled tight and pinned in a bun on the back of her head.

"Morning, Mrs. Tubbs," Jerry called out.

"Morning, Jerry," Blanche sighed. "Silliest thing I nearly ever seen, going huntin' on a work day. Two grown men acting like a couple of ten-year-old boys. Come on in and eat, now," Blanche said again. She continued to complain as she stepped back inside. "Grown men ain't got the sense of a couple a young'uns."

"She's funny," Jerry laughed.

"I'll tell you what's the truth—she's about to drive me crazy." Wesley complained as he moved to the tailgate of his truck. "First chance I get, my young ass is going over to Nashville to that truck-driving school."

"Yeah, you told me," Jerry said.

Wesley began to untie his muddy hunting boots. "See you gotta have that class-five license before they'll let 'chu drive one of them big rigs. See you got 'chu class one, now, that's your cars and light trucks. Class two, now, that's your motorcycles. Class three is your buses, you know, like your Greyhounds. Class four is your—ah—" Wesley stuttered trying to remember, then brushed it aside. "Well it's your class-five that you need."

Jerry picked up a stick, then propped his foot on the back tire of the truck and started scraping the caked mud off his boot. "Wesley, you've told me this a hundred times." He shook his head as Wesley continued his spiel about truck driving. Jerry knew it by heart.

"Well, it's the damn truth." Wesley exclaimed. "Eighteen-wheelers is where the real money is. Big rigs. Damn gold mine. But you know what you need?"

"Class-five?" Jerry sarcastically answered.

"Hell, Jerry, they make you pee in a cup and everything."

Jerry laughed to himself as he grabbed his rifle and started up the hill toward his trailer. "You gonna drive this morning, Wesley?"

"Yeah. I'll pick y'all up in a little bit." Wesley said as he tiptoed in his sock feet through the wet grass. He dropped his muddy hunting boots by the trailer steps, opened the door, and disappeared inside.

11

He was seventy years old, but Freeman Tubbs was still feisty, still easy to anger over anything that violated his sensibilities of how life should be lived. And in the small, crowded trailer, as he waited for his wife Blanche to finish breakfast, he was angry. On the television, there was a news story about a squabble between a group of emotional flag-burners and an equally emotional group of patriots. He pounded the arm of his imitation leather recliner with his balled fist, making his forty-year-old Mongoloid daughter, Susie, look up from her coloring book.

"You're arrestin' the wrong people, damn it," Freeman bellowed at the television. "Derned idiots. Blanche, come here and look at this."

His wife, tired, old, silent, glanced at the brightly colored lights flickering from the television. She did not have her glasses on and couldn't make out a single image. "Uh-huh," she agreed. She shuffled to the table to help Susie drink her milk from a plastic cup with a lid covering it.

"You know this country's in a world of trouble when they arrest the people trying to defend the flag," Freeman complained. He coughed hard.

"Come on, honey, drink your milk," Blanche urged. Susie nodded and swallowed. The door opened and Wesley stepped inside . Susie's face billowed into a smile.

"You better set down and eat," Blanche said to her son. "You gonna be late for work again."

Wesley crossed to the sink, squirted some dishwashing liquid into his palm, and scrubbed the sticky blood of his kill off his hands. "No, I ain't," Wesley said. He wiped his hands on a dish towel then blew Susie a kiss as he crossed to the table. Susie broke into a smile as she reached out and caught the imaginary kiss in her hand as Wesley had taught her to do. She pressed her palm to her lips then sent a kiss back to Wesley. He caught it as he dropped into a chair.

"Damn it, I fought in World War II and Korea," Freeman railed. "Saw a lotta good men die for that flag, but now it's just okay to burn it up."

Blanche fixed Wesley a plate of biscuits, eggs, sorghum, and bacon and set it before him. He shoveled hungrily at the food.

"Well, if Jimmy Carter was still president, we wouldn't be in this mess," Blanche pointed out to Freeman.

"Jimmy Carter?" Freeman snorted. "Now there was a piece of work. Dumbest son of a bitch to ever shit behind a pair of wing tips."

Blanche rolled her head slightly and looked to the living room, where Freeman was pushing himself up and out of the recliner. "I don't know about that. He was the first president we had in a long time that wasn't a criminal," she said.

"Yep!" Freeman replied vigorously. "And it damn near ruined this country." He looked at Wesley as he drug into the kitchen. "You do any good?"

Wesley washed a mouthful of food down with a swallow of coffee. "I got one pretty good-sized one hanging out there. Ten-pointer. Saw two more big 'uns on the way out."

"Nobody's got any respect for the flag or nothing else anymore," Freeman said as he slid into a chair at the table. "This country's got the mule by the tail on a downhill slide. They oughta shoot the butts off of ever one of them flag-burnin' sons of bitches." He looked back to Wesley as he pulled a biscuit from the pan. "You wasn't huntin' down at that salt lick, were you?"

"Nope," Wesley said easily.

Freeman turned his attention to the television. "Just look at that. Illegal aliens, the ACLU, and the IRS is the three worst things that ever happened to this country." He glanced back to Wesley. "Jerry get anything?" He asked.

"Naw," Wesley drawled. "He has about the worst luck huntin' of anybody I nearly ever seen."

12

The lights were still out in Jerry Burnette's trailer when he entered and quietly closed the door. He unloaded his rifle and leaned it against the counter that separated the kitchen from the living room. Jerry poured himself a cup of coffee from the pot he had made before leaving. He was standing at the kitchen window looking out at the river, remembering the passion of the black girl he had held only an hour earlier, when a lamp snapped on in the living room behind him.

Jerry turned toward the light and saw his wife, Wanda, sit up on the old, worn sofa. She was wrapped in the quilt Jerry's mother had made them for their fifth wedding anniversary. He pulled another mug from the dish drainer beside the sink, filled it with hot coffee, and carried it to her.

"I wish you wouldn't sleep out here," he said softly, handing the hot mug to her.

"Jerry," she warned as she sipped the coffee. "I done told you I ain't ready yet. Why do you stay on me all the time about it?"

Jerry sat next to her on the sofa. He could feel the cushion sag where the springs had snapped. He brushed the long hair from her face and hooked it behind her ear. He had always thought Wanda's long brown hair was her best feature, and he especially loved it in the mornings before she brushed it. It had that sexy bedroom look like you see in *Playboy Magazine*. "Wanda, it's been a long time since the accident and I just wish—"

"Don't, Jerry. Don't even say it," She rolled from the sofa and untangled herself from the quilt. "I don't wanna hear it again right now." Wanda pulled the hair from behind her ear. She always hated it when Jerry did that with her hair. She took another sip from her mug, sat it on the table and moved down the hall and into the bathroom.

She was standing at the mirror wiping the sleep from her dark brown eyes when she noticed Jerry standing in the hall watching her.

"What time did you get in last night?" Jerry asked

She stared at him in the mirror for a long moment. Their eyes locked and held, then she turned and closed the door.

13

Elvis Presley was singing "Love Me Tender" from the records that Verdale had re-stacked on the record player. She was sitting at the kitchen table wearing her Piggly Wiggly smock, rubbing the calves of her legs and listening, her eyes closed against the ribbon of cigarette smoke that floated up from her lips. A glass of bourbon was on the table near her. She heard Nancy come into the living room; she opened her eyes and removed the cigarette from her lips. She looked around at Nancy, who was stretching her blouse tight across the ironing board. Nancy was almost ready for school, wearing a short skirt and bra as she licked her fingers and tested the heat of the iron. She shot a disgusted glance at her mother as she ran the iron over the wrinkled shirt.

"For your information, me and your Daddy never had a cross word between us until she started seducing him away from me, and you know that," Verdale scolded.

Nancy did not look at her mother. It was an old story, usually brought on by the combination of whiskey and Elvis.

"You're just like him," Verdale snorted a sarcastic laugh. "A smartass."

"Mama, I'm sure Daddy loved you—once," Nancy replied. "He just got tired of it, like I do. Like everybody who knows you does. I mean look at you, you're already drinking and it's—" She paused, looked at the Elvis clock that was sitting on the television. "It's six-thirty in the morning."

"You are just exactly like him." Verdale reassured her again. "You think your daddy was such a saint. He drinks a lot more than I do. And runs around—he was running around on me for years."

Nancy glared at her mother as she finished ironing her blouse and slipped it on. "You say that about Daddy every time you get mad at me," she said in an angry whisper. "I'll tell you one thing—you raise hell about Daddy committin' adultery, but you and Lloyd Pinkerton lay back there in your room and make the God-awfulest noise I ever heard. It's embarrassing, Mother! I know the neighbors hear you and see him come in and outta here, and he's married."

"That's different," Verdale answered quickly. "Your Daddy committed adultery first, which broke the biblical bond between us, and Lloyd's wife has cancer of the uterus and she can't—" She paused abruptly and pushed the glowing end of the short cigarette into the ashtray, then finished her glass of bourbon.

"Well, I'm very proud of the charitable work you're doing for our community," Nancy hissed as she crossed into the kitchen to put the ironing board into the broom closet.

A flash of anger flooded Verdale. She sprang from her chair and slapped Nancy hard across the cheek. Nancy stepped back and looked at her mother in shock as the tears began to well in her eyes. Verdale, surprised at herself, wanted to explain. "Now, see what you made me do," Verdale said.

Nancy grabbed her books and purse and ran from the trailer. After a moment, Verdale followed her as far as the trailer door.

"Nancy! Nancy, come back here!" she yelled angrily. "You know why your daddy left and it wadn't because of me. Nancy! You come here!" She took a deep painful breath as she watched Nancy race away. She realized that the neighbors had stopped to watch as they came out to get in their cars and go to work. "You can't do nothing with kids anymore," she said, forcing an awkward smile. Verdale looked back at Nancy disappearing around the corner of a trailer across the gravel road that curved down through the Captain's Point Trailer Park. She sighed and closed the door.

14

It was Wesley's habit to sit with his child-woman sister each morning before work and help her color cartoon pictures in her coloring book as he finished his coffee. Wesley believed—though he did not know it as fact—that his time with Susie was the happiest moment of her day. Sometimes, when he wondered about it, he accepted the fact that those moments were also the happiest time of his day. He loved his big sister. And he knew that she loved him, that he was the only familiar playmate she had.

"Good, Susie, good," Wesley would coo as she pulled the crayon across the page. "I like that, sweetie. You sure can color pretty."

And Susie would smile. Wesley's voice was like medicine to her.

It was that mood, that quiet, childlike joy of her two children, that Blanche broke when she dropped a copy of a girlie magazine on the table in front of Wesley.

"How you reckon that got under your mattress?" Blanche asked angrily.

Wesley could feel a flush of embarrassment cross his face. He glanced at his father, who had returned to the recliner in front of the television, then he turned the magazine over to hide the half-naked girl on the cover. If he was going to have an argument with his mother over this, it wouldn't help his cause to have a half-naked girl in a nurse's uniform staring up at him from the kitchen table.

"Mama, I'm thirty-three years old. I reckon I'm old enough to look at that magazine if I want to."

"Not in this house, you're not," Blanche replied as she cleared the last of the breakfast dishes from the table. "You're about to drive me crazy. Most boys time they're your age done married and got two or three young'uns. Don't have to look at filth like that," she added.

"Yeah, well, most boys time they're my age got a girlfriend to get married to," Wesley said. "I ain't even got a girlfriend, now how am I supposed to get married?"

Freeman coughed a cynical laugh. "Couldn't support a wife on what he makes if he had one."

"He's just too picky. Unless they look like movie stars, he won't have nothing to do with 'em," Blanche declared. She pushed the rubber stopper into the drain and began filling the sink with hot soapy water.

"Now Mama, that ain't so and you know it," Wesley argued.

"What about Norma Smothers, then? She's a cute girl," Blanche said.

"Norma Smothers?" Wesley shot his mother a look of astonishment. "Mama, Norma Smothers could haunt a two-story house from the front yard. That's how cute she is."

"See there?" Blanche shook her head. "Ain't nobody good enough for you."

"She ain't got but about six teeth in her whole head, and three of them are green," Wesley pointed out.

Freeman laughed, choked on his coffee, and coughed as he looked to Wesley and nodded vigorously.

"Well, it hurt her mother's feelings after I told her you'd take Norma out on a date and you wouldn't," Blanche reminded him.

Wesley peeled the paper from around the point of the red crayon and handed it to Susie. He watched as she dragged it across the page she was coloring, then lifted it and drew quick circles on the back of his *Hustler Magazine*.

"I'd ruther have gone out with her mother," Wesley countered. "At least she's got most of her teeth."

"Just too dadgum picky," Blanche replied in a whisper as she turned the water off and began to scrub the dishes. "If they don't look like movie stars—"

"What's that?" Wesley snapped.

"I said you're just too picky," Blanche grumbled.

"Mama, you remember I went out with Kay Wilson, don't you? And she sure as heck don't look like no movie star."

"Yeah, but she's married," Blanche said.

It was an old argument. "She was separated," Wesley reminded her, as he had done a hundred times before.

"Y'all hush," Freeman growled. "I can't never hear the TV in the morning for y'all carrying on. Now, just leave him alone about it, Blanche."

Blanche sulled up as she stepped to the cabinet and got a couple of extra-strength Excedrin headache pills. She pretended she couldn't get the childproof top off and without a word handed the bottle to Wesley, just to make sure he knew he had given her a headache.

Wesley pushed away from the table, removed the top from the bottle, and grabbed his coat from the back of the chair. "Mama, just as soon as I get that truck paid off, I'll move outta here and you won't have to worry so much about my love life. What little there is of it."

"Wesley, you don't have to act like that, now," Blanche said, frowning. "Nobody said nothing about you moving out."

"I wouldn't worry about it, Blanche," Freeman said. "Hell, he's got forty-eight more payments to make on that truck. He ain't going nowhere." He laughed, coughed, then turned back to the television.

"Shit," Wesley muttered under his breath. He grabbed his lunch sack from the table and left the trailer, slamming the door behind him.

Susie looked up from making circles on the back of the *Hustler Magazine*. She began to cry softly.

15

She was known in the Captain's Point Trailer Park as Fat Ethel. She never failed to remind anyone who cared to listen that she wasn't always fat. She didn't put on all this extra weight until after the birth of her first child, she would say. She just couldn't get her system lined back up. Her husband, Benny, could have been called the Thin Man. Benny was sun-dried skinny. When he stood next to his wife he looked ill, like he was from one of those famine-ravaged countries in Africa. Fat Ethel and Benny had four children, three more than they could afford.

Fat Ethel stood in the doorway of their trailer, wearing a cotton housecoat patterned with faded rosebuds. Her thin black hair was wrapped around soup-can-size curlers. She held a chubby baby on one hip. Another was clinging to her leg like a hungry vine. She was yelling at Benny. A cigarette hung from her bottom lip.

"I swear to God, Benny, I better not have to come looking for you again, and me with these babies," she said.

Benny nodded in fear as he climbed into his old Chevy Nova. He slipped the key into the ignition and listened as the motor coughed, died, then rattled to life again. What was left of the rusted muffler puffed a cloud of black smoke into the air behind the car. Benny looked back to his wife as he gunned the accelerator, shifted into reverse, and started to back out. He could see Fat Ethel's mouth moving. He knew she was shouting further instructions and warnings to him, and he was pleased that he couldn't hear them. He welcomed the rumbling of the untuned engine. He wished it could always be this quiet.

He did not see Nancy racing along the path that separated the trailers as he backed out, and if Nancy hadn't looked up in time to sidestep his car, he would have backed over her.

"Hey! Where did you learn how to drive? Wal-Mart?" Nancy scolded.

Benny caught a glimpse of Nancy in the side-view mirror as she jumped out of the way. He slammed on the brakes and rolled down his window. "Sorry, Nancy."

Nancy glared at him and walked rapidly up the gravel road toward the Sewell's trailer.

Benny took a deep sigh, rolled up the window, and looked back to his wife, who was shouting and pointing her hand at him. He could not hear her. Benny smiled to himself, shifted into drive, and headed to work.

Nancy heard Wesley's truck before she saw it.

"Hey, Nancy."

She looked up to see Wesley as he slowed his pickup beside her.

"Hey, Wesley," Nancy said weakly. She kept walking.

"You look awful pretty this morning," Wesley teased.

"Yeah, right." Nancy stumbled but caught herself. The gravel was hard to walk on in high-heeled shoes.

"You want a ride to Becky's house?" Wesley offered.

"No," Nancy frowned.

"You okay?" Wesley asked. "What's wrong?"

"I'm fine, Wesley. What do you want?"

"Nothing. Just wanted to say hey."

"Hey, Wesley," Nancy said sarcastically.

"Hey," Wesley laughed. "All right, I'll see ya."

Wesley winked at her and stepped on the gas. The truck leaped forward, spinning the back tires in the loose gravel. Nancy rolled her eyes in disgust.

"Jesus, Wesley, get a life," she mumbled.

16

Wesley was smiling eagerly, grinning like a teenager as he glanced in the rearview mirror of his truck at the image of Nancy Calloway growing smaller. He raced up the hill and slid to an abrupt stop in front of Jerry's trailer. He tapped on his horn twice. A country song about forbidden love played on the radio. Wesley tried to listen to the lyrics but he could only hear Nancy's voice: "Hey, Wesley." He rolled his head and smiled. "Damn, I bet that'd be something to get into."

Inside the trailer, Jerry drained the last of his coffee from his cup as he glanced out the window at Wesley's truck. The country music from the truck's radio drifted inside.

"Let's go," Wesley shouted as he waved to Jerry from his pick-up. He tapped the horn again.

Jerry grabbed his lunch and coat as he stepped to the table, where Wanda sat staring numbly into her coffee. He leaned to kiss her on the lips, but she turned away and he kissed her lightly on the forehead.

"I'll see ya tonight," he said softly. "I love you."

Wanda gave a half-nod and looked away.

"You gonna be here?" he asked.

"I don't know where I'll be, Jerry. Okay?" she snapped.

Jerry paused for a moment, then crossed the room and stepped outside. He saw Wesley standing beside his truck with the driver's-side door open. Wesley had spotted Sheila Pascal coming out of her trailer up on the hill next to the river road. She was carrying her garbage to the dumpster that sat just across from the long row of mailboxes on wooden posts. A sign on the dumpster read "Residents of Captain's Point Trailer Park. Only."

"I wish you'd look at that," Wesley said nodding toward Sheila. Jerry followed his gaze.

Sheila Pascal was beautiful. She was a country boy's dream in tight blue jeans, with a body that only a great artist could have sculpted. Wesley had caught her scent all the way down the hill between Jerry and Clifford's trailer. The garbage sack she was carrying split as she lifted it into the dumpster, and the trash fell at her feet. She threw up her hands and yelled something toward the sky. She bent to pick up the trash and stuff it into the split sack.

"Goddamn, if she ain't full grown I don't know what is," Wesley announced.

"Wesley, you got a bad case of oversexed and underfucked," Jerry laughed.

"It's the damn truth. Sad, ain't it?" Wesley lamented. "Where the hell is Clifford? We gonna be late again."

17

The leaving of her family for work and school was, to Evelyn Sewell, the last minute of the morning before the morning belonged again to her and God. It was always the most frantic, the one crowded with a blur of rushing bodies and babbling voices as her family jumped from the kitchen table and bolted into their day.

"Mama, I can't find my green skirt," Becky complained. She threw a "Bye, Daddy" over her shoulder as she rushed down the hall to her room.

"Yeah," Clifford said as Evelyn handed him his coat and lunchbox. Clifford opened the door and started to leave, but Evelyn stopped him.

"Wait just a minute, Cliff."

He stepped back inside. "They're waiting on me, Evelyn, what is it?" He watched her as she hurried to the kitchen counter and pulled the lid off the Jesus-head cookie jar.

"I need some money," she told him in a low voice.

Clifford sighed and reached for his wallet. "How much?"

Evelyn shushed him as she quickly counted the contents of the cookie jar, then looked toward the hallway and Becky's room. She did not want her daughter to hear.

"A hundred and twenty-six dollars," Evelyn demanded.

Clifford shot her a look, folded his wallet and stuffed it into his back pocket. "Well gotdamn, Evelyn, I ain't got that kinda money on me. What the hell you gonna do, run off to Mexico?"

"Hush! It's for Becky's class ring."

Clifford thought for a minute. "We got any under the mattress?"

"Yeah, but that's for first-of-the-month's bills," Evelyn reminded him.

He shook his head, then glanced toward the hallway. "Well, I reckon somebody'll just have to wait on one of them bills this month, won't they?"

Evelyn smiled. Clifford was a harsh man at times, but he had a tender heart. It was why she loved him. She stepped to him quickly, hugged him, and brushed a kiss across his cheek.

"You know something?" Evelyn asked.

"What? I got to go."

"You're not nearly as mean as you want everybody to think you are. I love you."

Clifford raised his eyebrows and looked toward the television, where the evangelist was promising to mail anyone who sent in a love gift of twenty-five dollars or more a vial of water from the Jordan River, which he had personally blessed.

"You know something?" he said to Evelyn.

"What?" She smiled up at him.

"If you'd stop sending our money to that lying son of a bitch on TV over there, we'd have enough for shit like this."

A tremor of anger waved through Evelyn. She stepped away from Clifford and back to the sink. "Just go to work," she huffed. "Go on now, get outta here before you make me mad."

"I'll see ya this evening," Clifford called back as he stepped through the door.

He inhaled the crisp morning air. It was Tennessee cool and Tennessee fresh. He could not understand why anyone would want to live anywhere else. He stepped to where Jerry and Wesley huddled at the front of the truck.

"What the hell y'all lookin' at?"

"A little piece of heaven," Wesley told him.

Clifford followed their stare up to Sheila Pascal as she moved back across the small lawn of her trailer to her car. She looked down to see Wesley, Jerry and Clifford watching her. She waved, and the men waved back enthusiastically.

"I swear, I'd nail her on the court house steps and give you thirty minutes to get my mother and daddy down there to watch," Wesley declared.

"That'd make 'em proud," Jerry said as the men loaded into the pickup.

"Hell, it might do her some good."

"She still after you to get married?" Clifford laughed.

"All she wants to talk about. Tried to get me to go out with Norma Smothers last week."

Clifford's face turned sour, as if he had tasted something bitter. "Norma Smothers? I used to have flashbacks of Norma Smothers when I was in Vietnam."

Wesley mashed on the accelerator and steered the truck up the gravel and dirt path toward the blacktopped river road. "Exactly," he said, waving to Nancy as she stepped from between two trailers.

"What happened to that last girl you was goin' out with?" Jerry asked.

"Kay Wilson?" Wesley said. "Went back to her husband. I tell you what's the truth—she could suck-start a Harley from across the street."

Clifford chuckled. "Shit, Wesley," he drawled, "Kay Wilson's been on more laps than a five-year-old napkin."

"That may be, but hell, I miss her," Wesley remembered as he pulled the truck onto the river road and headed north toward the factory.

"I heard dat," Jerry added.

18

"Only a few minutes longer, and me and God will have the morning to ourselves before I have to get off to work," Evelyn Sewell thought. She longed for the peaceful silence of the trailer when Clifford and Becky and Jimmie Clifford finally vacated it. Silence and coffee and a few minutes reading from her thumb-worn King James Version, where God and Jesus and everybody else spoke like God and Jesus used to speak—with a British accent. And then a quick scan of the Daily Devotionals, which Evelyn had received free of charge for a thirty-dollar love gift toward the television ministry's Ethiopian Leprosy, Widows' and Orphans' Fund.

Coffee and God. Evelyn needed coffee and God after enduring her family in the mornings. She needed coffee and God before heading to work at Juanita's Clip and Curl Beauty Salon. A few moments alone, with coffee and God. A few minutes that belonged only to them.

She was clearing the table when Nancy knocked at the trailer door and entered without an invitation.

"Morning, Mrs. Sewell," Nancy said as she plopped down on a bar stool at the Formica-topped counter that separated the tiny kitchen and dining area from the living room. "Becky, ready yet? Becky!" She yelled toward the hallway of the trailer. "Becky! You better hurry. We're gonna be—"

She did not finish the sentence. Becky came into the room from the hallway, carrying her blouse and a threaded needle.

"Hey, Nancy, I'm nearly ready," Becky said. Then: "Mama, will you sew this button back on for me?"

"Bring it here," Evelyn said wearily. She took the blouse and the threaded needle and sat at the table. "I don't know why in the world you wait til the last minute to do everything."

"Mama, it just came off. What am I, a button psychic? I don't know when they're gonna fall off."

"Good grief," Evelyn declared. "You always want to make something big outta nothing." Evelyn turned to Nancy. "How's Verdale doing this morning?"

"She's all right," Nancy answered solemnly. "About the same."

She crossed to the stove, picked up a biscuit from the biscuit plate, and bit into it. "You finished that report for Mr. Reynolds' class? she asked Becky.

"Of course," Becky said.

"Can I copy?

"Look kinda funny, wouldn't it? Best friends turning in the exact same report?" Becky said.

Nancy shrugged lazily. "I don't know. We're best friends, we probably think just alike."

Evelyn noticed Nancy reaching for another biscuit. "You want me to fix you something to eat, Nancy?"

"No m'am. I just stay hungry all the time lately," Nancy said as she chewed on the biscuit. "I must have a tapeworm or something."

"Gross!" Becky frowned. "We don't have time, anyway." Becky looked to the kitchen clock. We're gonna miss the bus if we don't hurry."

Jimmie thundered through the room from the back of the trailer. He grabbed his books from the chair, where he had dropped them the night before.

"You gonna be home for supper, son?" Evelyn asked.

"I got football practice," Jimmie said as he slammed the door behind him.

"Not much longer now," Evelyn thought. "Me and God and coffee." She bit the thread, pulled at the button, then handed Becky the blouse. Becky slipped it on.

"You get your ring money?" Becky asked Nancy.

"Naw," Nancy said casually. "Only rings I want are diamonds. I sure don't want nothing that's gonna remind me of school once I get out. If I get out," she laughed.

Outside, the engine of Jimmie's truck roared to life.

"Come on," Becky said grabbing her books and purse. "Let's see if Jimmie Clifford will give us a ride. Bye, Mama. Love you!"

"Bye, Mrs. Sewell."

"Bye." Evelyn watched them leave, a blur of bodies sprinting through the door. She heard the door close. The silence—the blessed silence—began to build in the trailer. On the television the evangelist was shouting "hallelujah" and crying as he told of Moses parting the Red Sea.

From his truck, Jimmie saw Becky and Nancy bolting from the door of the trailer. He knew what they wanted. He jerked the truck into gear and pushed hard on the accelerator.

"Jimmie Clifford, give us a ride!" Becky shouted.

"No way," Jimmie yelled back as the rear tires of the truck kicked up a cloud of dust and gravel as he sped away.

"Asshole," Nancy hissed.

The two girls started up the hill toward the row of mailboxes on wooden posts where the school bus picked up the trailer park kids.

"I gotta get me a car," Becky said desperately. "You're practically not a person without a car."

"Don't hold your breath," Nancy laughed when a car skidded to a stop beside them. It was Cecil Pinkerton, whose smooth face made him appear younger than his seventeen years.

"Hey Becky, y'all want a ride?" Cecil called over the loud music coming from his car radio.

Becky opened her mouth to answer, but Nancy's voice stopped her.

"No, Cecil," Nancy said firmly.

Cecil waved, gave a couple of quick hits on the horn, then pulled away.

"Why'd you do that?" Becky asked.

"You want to ride to school with Cecil Pinkerton?"

"He's a nice guy and It beats riding that bus."

"Cecil's a total spastic, and besides, I think he likes you," Nancy replied.

"Yeah, I know."

"Gross. He ask you out yet?"

"No. 'Hey Becky, y'all need a ride?' is the most he's ever said to me."

"I can't believe you broke up with Robert Simms," Nancy said. "He was cute."

"Nancy, I told you *he* broke up with *me*."

"Oh, like that asshole can do better." Nancy said then quickly realized her mistake. "I mean—you know what I mean."

"I wouldn't do it with him, so he said he'd find somebody who would. I told him to go ahead and see if I cared. And he did—Sharon Fetters," Becky explained.

Nancy stopped walking and looked at Becky with astonishment. "Sharon Fetters? That slut. You've got to be kidding me." They started walking again. "Becky, you're just gonna have to face the facts. Sooner or later, you're gonna have to do it. I mean, if you want to keep a boyfriend."

Becky took a deep sigh, considering Nancy's words as the school bus pulled to a stop and the trailer park kids began climbing aboard.

19

The visiting choir on the television ministry's *Sixty Minutes With the Savior* program was from the Early Morning Calvary Baptist Church, located twelve miles southwest of Dyersburg, Tennessee, off the old Holcomb Bridge Road. They were dressed in wine-colored choir robes rented from the ministry's wardrobe department, and their voices were lifted in shrill unison as they sang *How Firm A Foundation*.

The song found its way into the opened, receptive soul of Evelyn Sewell, who had read her Bible, studied her devotional, and had her second cup of coffee from the cup bearing the likeness of Jesus. "Oh, yes," she thought. "How firm a foundation." And that was what she needed in her life—a foundation, unshakable, a foundation that could not be destroyed by a disguised Satan, or by the drudgery of day-to-day life in the fragile egg-trailers nestled in a grove of Tennessee oaks beside the wide Tennessee River.

As long as God looked down every morning, as long as God knew and God cared, Evelyn could survive. She was sure of it.

Outside the sun had slipped over the ridge, untangling itself from the trees, and had begun to bathe the frost-tops of the trailers.

From God's eye, with the work-and-school crowd gone, Captain's Point Trailer Park looked deserted. The only thing God could hear was some man shouting about him from Evelyn Sewell's television set.

——————— BOOK TWO

the keys
to the kingdom

1

The Big Sandy Auto Accessories plant rose from the banks of the Tennessee River like a deformity, a malignant steel-and-concrete lump on a lovely arm of the valley that spread from the base of the mountains. It was large and ugly and dirty. It spit smoke into the air from its smokestacks and spilled waste into the river from its buried drain lines.

To its employees, the Big Sandy Auto Accessories plant was a daily visit into hell, a nine-hour, two-shift, monotonous torment that no television preacher could make bearable with his love gifts of Jesus coffee mugs, or Jesus salt-and-pepper shakers, or vials of water from the River Jordan.

A sign, burned into wood by a sign-maker from Nashville and hanging over the employee entrance, made a sad, caustic claim:

Through These Doors Pass the Happiest People in Tennessee

None of the employees ever looked at the sign. They knew the truth. To them, the sign should have read:

Give Your Heart To God; We've Got Your Ass

When Jerry Burnette began work at the plant, his father told him, "Son, it ain't much different'n share-croppin' used to be. You ain't gonna never pick a bale of cotton that's all yours."

Joe Burnette's observation was taken from almost forty years of work at the plant, a young veteran of the Second World War who had returned to Tennessee vowing to never again plow behind a mule. In the fifties, the plant had hummed with machinery, with the hissing, steaming noise of progress, the smell of steel and rubber. Everyone was young and strong and eager. Big Sandy Auto Accessories was a way out of the past, an opened door to the future, and those who left the farms for the punch-in, punch-out labor of the plant believed they had at last found a chance for change, a chance at a better life.

None of them knew that it was also a dead end.

"Like steppin' in quicksand," Joe Burnette warned Jerry. "You just drag along, you don't never get nowhere. But it's steady work, I reckon."

"Aw, Daddy, it ain't that bad," Jerry had argued. "Things'll get better soon as the economy picks back up. Ever'body says so.".

The getting-better rumor had been used by Richard Moss since he took over as president of Big Sandy Auto Accessories in 1982. Richard's grandfather Baily Moss had founded the company and his father Gerald had turned it into a giant of the industry, building and supplying rubber hoses, gaskets and molding to auto manufacturers and dealers throughout America.

"We're about to turn the corner," Richard Moss kept promising in his civic club speeches and in the monthly newsletter that employees threw into the trash without reading. "Things are looking up. Before long, we're going to start upgrading around here. Modernize. A complete retooling, for the benefit of our employees."

But nothing changed. Not the rumors, or even the promises.

And that was the speech that Jack Wimberley was making under the sign at the employee entrance where many of the workers would gather to finish off their morning cigarettes before clocking in. Standing close to Jack, nodding agreement, were Ed Stone, Ernestine Hammett, and Sammy Wilson.

"You think things are gonna change around here, you're crazy as hell," he bellowed. "How many times we gonna buy that old song before we get tired of being lied to and do something about it?"

Peggy Smith, whose husband owned the only barber shop in Big Sandy, and Harvey Williams, a large black man whose face was always twisted in a doubtful frown, weren't buying most of what Jack had to say.

"You boys gon' make things worse for the rest of us," Harvey said quietly.

"Hell, Harvey, we ain't had no pay increase in four years," Jack argued. "Four damn years I'm talkin' about here."

"We make as much as any plant around here, Jack," Peggy said.

Ernestine stepped close to Jack. She said, in a rough, deep voice, "Well, we don't get no sick pay. Consolidated does, and they get a Christmas bonus to boot."

"No forced overtime over there, neither," Jack added.

"That's right, and they get three weeks paid vacation a year." Ed Stone announced. "What'd we get? Two. Ain't I right?"

"You know why, Harvey?" Jack asked.

"The union," Ed said emphatically.

"Damn straight. Plus, we're working with this faulty, outdated equipment," Jack cried.

"Somebody's gonna get killed, you mark my word," Ed added.

"Well, why don't y'all go work over there at Consolidated if you're that crazy about it," Peggy snapped.

Ernestine leaned toward Peggy. "I would if they was hiring," she hissed.

"Well, they ain't, Ernestine, and neither is anybody else. You oughta be glad you got a job," Peggy countered. "They're hard to come by."

Harvey nodded thoughtfully. He shifted his lunchpail from his right to his left hand. "I think Mr. Moss has been pretty good to us."

"Shit, Harvey, stop and think about what you're sayin'," urged Ed.

Harvey nodded again. He looked evenly at Ed. "I have," he said. "What I think is you're just repeatin' what that union organizer told you to say."

Ed's face flushed with sudden anger. He looked away from Harvey and saw Clifford and Jerry and Wesley approaching. "Hey, Clifford, come here a minute. See if you can talk some sense into ol' Harvey here."

"Don't start on me again this morning about that damn union," Clifford said. "Besides, Harvey's been to college. He don't need me tellin' him nothin'. But now you, Ed, you didn't even finish high school. You might better listen to him." He walked past the group and into the plant.

The workers laughed as the first bell sounded.

"What do you mean by that?" Ed said quizzically as he drew deeply on his cigarette then dropped it to the pavement and twisted the toe of his boot on it. He quickly followed the group inside and fell in line at the time clock. "Hey Clifford, whatdaya mean by that?"

Inside the plant, Clifford listened to the mumbling of daily greetings. He inhaled deeply. The odor of work—of machinery, of oils, of human perspiration—filled his lungs. He remembered when the odors made his body tense with eagerness. He had been born into the hard-work, feel-good ethic of the American farmer, and that was the ethic he had taken into the plant as a young man. A dollar paid for a dollar's effort. Pride. Honor.

Clifford no longer felt eager. The system that worked with silent arrogance in the sweetly scented corporate offices upstairs had broken him years ago. The system took, but the sytem did not give. The only break you could hope for was that the system would spot you among the masses and crook its finger and beckon to you. If you were among the lucky, you might be pulled out of line and given a small blessing by the system. Clifford hated the system, but he had waited for so long and was now so close. A promotion. It was more than just getting away from the constant roar and heat and wrestling of the radial front press. It was a pat on the back by one of the chosen. To be singled out in front of your peers for a job well done. A moment in the sun. Something that rarely happened in Clifford's life.

Clifford and Jerry and Wesley had just clocked in when Jerry's father, Joe Burnette, trudged across the floor of the plant toward them.

"How's it goin', Joe?" Clifford asked.

"Keepin' it pointing toward the ground, Clifford. You?"

"'Bout the same, "Clifford replied. "See you boys later." He left, walking slowly, trying to bring a pause to the few minutes he had left before work began.

"How is Mama doin' this mornin'?" Jerry asked his father.

"She got up with a sick headache like she does ever' mornin'."

"I'll take her to get her radiation treatments next week," Jerry said.

"She'd like that," Joe told him. "Appreciate it, son."

Jerry nodded. They began to walk toward their work stations.

"I tell you what I'm gonna do, Joe? Did I tell you about goin' over to Nashville, that truck-driving school and trainin' on them big rigs?" Wesley said pleasantly.

"Uh-huh," Joe mumbled. "Believe you did, Wesley. Every time I seen you for the last two years."

"You know you got your class four, and that's for your dump trucks. Them's the twenty-four thousand pounders—"

"Damn, Wesley, will you shut up about that truck-driving school?" Jerry said.

"I ain't just talkin'. I'm gonna do it," Wesley vowed.

"Then, go do it," Jerry said.

"By God, I will," Wesley enthused. "You wait and see. Cause big rigs is where the damn money is."

2

The school bus was crowded and noisy, and Nancy and Becky hated everything about it. The stops. The crowding. The pushing. The wobbling motion as it crept from place to place. The squeaking of the brakes. The slapping of the mechanical stop-arm as it reached out from the side of the bus to warn traffic.

"We should've gone with Cecil," Nancy complained.

"Don't start that again. It was you who told him no," Becky said.

They were sitting on the rear seat. Wilma Tate and Judy Oliver sat three rows in front of them, whispering and giggling as they turned to look at Nancy.

"Hey, Nancy, guess what I heard?" Wilma said.

"What, Wilma?"

"Steve Holly told me he saw you and Bobby Richards parkin' under the river bridge."

"So?" Nancy said.

"He said a bunch of 'em were hidin' and watchin' y'all doin' it," Wilma said smugly.

Judy laughed sharply. She covered her mouth with her hands.

"At least I can get somebody to do it with me," Nancy said easily. "Which puts me one up on you."

A chorus of oohs and aahs rose from the students around Wilma.

"Bobby Richards is goin' steady with Marcy Ruffin, and you know that," Wilma snapped.

Nancy smiled. She lifted her hand and carefully, slowly, showed Wilma her middle finger.

"She's such a slut," Wilma mumbled.

Becky leaned forward, over the seat. "Shut up, Wilma," she hissed. "You're so stupid." She leaned back and looked at Nancy. She could see Nancy staring out of the window, fighting tears. "I hate ridin' this stupid bus," Becky said irritably. "I gotta get a car."

3

Jerry Burnette had learned quickly that his father's warning about the Big Sandy Auto Accessories plant was true. The work was repetitive and numbing. It killed from the inside out, from the soul to the skin. Six months after he had accepted his job, Jerry wanted to leave; he could not. There were no other jobs in the area, at least none that were as certain. He had swallowed his pride and continued to work. He needed the money, and after the death of his son he had needed to be busy.

Yet there was another reason that Jerry had stayed at the plant. It was his father. There was something in him, some instinct, some power he did not understand, that made him want to be close to Joe Burnette. In the plant, he constantly watched for his father like an alert sentry.

And it was that instinct, that power, that made Jerry look up at mid-morning and see his father struggling with a large cart, stacked high with cartons of radiator hoses. He turned off his stamping machine and went to Joe.

"You all right?" Jerry shouted over the hammering noise of the plant. He took the cart from his father and began to push.

Joe nodded. He leaned weakly against the cart and walked with Jerry to the loading dock, then pulled his handkerchief from his pocket and began to wipe the perspiration from his pale face.

"Thanks, son," he said. "Lost my grip there for a minute."

"Yeah, well, you got it too loaded down," Jerry told him.

"Saves trips," his father replied.

"Ain't worth it," Jerry said. "They need more people loadin'."

Joe nodded again and again wiped his face. He said, "Your mama wanted me to tell you and Wanda to come eat dinner with us on Sunday."

"I'll ask," Jerry said. "You know Wanda. Depends on what mood she's in."

"Ray's home," Joe said simply.

Jerry's head jerked toward his father. His face widened in surprise.

"They come in last night," Joe explained. "Gonna stay with us for a little while."

"Don't loan him no more money, Daddy," Jerry warned.

Joe looked away. He ran his fingers across his mouth. "I think it'd mean a lot to your mama if you come by the house and at least act like you'n Ray had made up," he said. "She don't like to think her boys is fightin'."

4

Louise Burnette was sixty years old, a frail, thin woman with a pale, washed-out face. People who knew her clucked their tongues and whispered among themselves, "Well you know she's sickly. Always was. Keeps Joe worried half to death. Jerry, too. Jerry's always over there checkin' on her."

Yet, as frail as her body seemed, Louise Burnette's spirit was robust and her tongue sharp.

She sat patiently in the Clip 'n Curl Beauty Shop as Evelyn Sewell trimmed at the splitting ends of her greying hair. Across from Louise and Evelyn, sitting in the waiting area, Donna Burnette watched her two children with a bored expression. Donna wanted to be anywhere on God's earth except the Clip 'n Curl Beauty Shop, but Ray had ordered her to take Louise to get her hair fixed. When Ray asked you to do something you did it, or there'd be a fuss.

"I tell you what's the truth, Evelyn," Louise complained in a loud voice. "Wanda has just treated Jerry awful ever since little Clayton died."

"Uh-huh," Evelyn mumbled. She fingered Louise's hair and snipped at it with her scissors.

"We tried our best to talk Jerry out of marryin' her, but he wouldn't listen. Just gon' do as he pleased." Louise continued.

"Now, wadn't Wanda married to your other son Ray before she married Jerry?" Evelyn said.

"Yeah, and she was nothin' but a pure tramp then. Treated Ray like dirt." Loiuse answered emphatically. She lifted her hand from beneath the plastic hair bib that Evelyn had looped around her neck and pulled at a dangling lock of hair. "Get that one, honey."

Evelyn flashed the scissors over her hair, cutting it away.

"That's better," Louise announced. "I've heard different ones say Wanda's out slippin' around on Jerry right now, and it wouldn't surprise me one little bit."

Evelyn sighed. Such gossip always saddened her. "I'm sorry to hear about that, Mrs. Burnette. Me 'n' Clifford both just think the world of Jerry, bless his heart."

Louise nodded gravely. "He's the sweetest boy you nearly ever seen, Evelyn. Now Ray, he was always gettin' into somethin'. You knew he served time in the pen for passin' them bad checks, didn't you?"

"Yes ma'am," Evelyn said softly. "I hated to hear about that."

"Like to killed his daddy," Louise said. "But Jerry, now he's just as good as gold. I don't know what me 'n' Joe would've done since I've been sick if it hadn't been for Jerry."

"How long have Ray and Donna been married?" Evelyn asked. She glanced at Donna, who was thumbing through a magazine.

"Little over four years now," Louise replied. "He met her when he was workin' up in Detroit. She's a sweet girl—" She lowered her voice: "She's dumb as a stick, but I don't guess it matters. Her 'n' Ray seem to get along all right. As long as she does what he tells her. You know she used to dance nekkid in a honky-tonk up there in Detroit, but Ray says she's cut that out since they got married."

Evelyn stepped back from Louise and inspected her work. "Well, their little baby's as cute as as a button," she said absently. She reached forward and patted down a wave on the top of Louise's head. "Oh, my, Mrs. Burnette, I wish't you'd look. You are *so* pretty."

Louise glanced at herself in the mirror. A scowl blossomed in her face. "I just look awful, Evelyn, and you know it."

"Now, don't say that, Mrs. Burnette. You look pretty as can be."

Louise touched her mouth with her fingertips and turned her mirror-face to admire the sheen that Evelyn had sprayed into her hair. "My hair's got thin as ribbon anymore, Evelyn. Hardly keeps my head warm."

Evelyn and Donna helped Louise out of the shop and to the car as Juanita, the owner of the Clip and Curl, held the door.

"Now you be sure and give our love to Joe, Louise," Evelyn reminded.

"If I can remember. Got so's I can't remember nothing since I started taking them treatments."

5

The lunch room of Big Sandy High School was divided by an invisible wall that was as real and as immovable as brick; on one side of the wall were the Chosen, and on the other side was everybody else.

Those who lived in Captain's Point Trailer Park were not among the Chosen.

There were no rules that divided the Big Sandy students, no one standing at the end of the serving counter checking pedigree and sending one student to one part of the lunchroom and another student to an opposite table. It was what Becky Sewell called "just one of them things you can't explain." Though she did not know it, "just one of them things you can't explain" was history and inheritance, the finely tuned distinctions of name and address, of job description, of the year and model of a car parked in a driveway, of where you shopped for clothes and groceries. "Just one of them things you can't explain" was place—as in lunchroom place—and if you knew your place, you went there.

Becky's place, and Nancy's place, was among the Everybody Elses.

They sat nibbling at their lunches, casting glances mixed with yearning and hatred across the lunchroom to the tables where the Chosen were sitting—flawlessly beautiful Susan Taylor and her flawlessly handsome boyfriend, Scott Mitchell, the senior class president; Bobby Richards with his tough sexuality and his public girlfriend Marcy Ruffin with her large breasts, the largest at Big Sandy High School. The others. All Chosen.

"You hear about Marcy?" Nancy said in a low voice.

Becky looked at her quizzically. "What?" she said.

"About Marcy's boob job?"

"What boob job?" Becky said. "They're already the biggest things in the world. I don't know how she stands up straight."

"She's gonna have 'em reduced," Nancy replied. "That's what I heard. Ain't it funny how the preacher's kid gets the best equipment? Somebody that's never gonna get full use of 'em."

Becky grinned. "Like Mama says," she whispered, "the Lord works in mysterious ways."

Both girls laughed quickly, gleefully.

"You ever wondered what it'd be like to be a cheerleader?" Becky asked casually.

"I know what it's like," Nancy answered. "It's stupid."

"I don't mean just be a cheerleader, but, you know, be real popular, and stuff like that?"

"You'd have to hang out with bimbos like Susan Taylor and Marcy Ruffin."

Becky bit into her fish stick and chewed slowly. She was watching Susan whisper playfully in Scott's ear. If they were bimbos, Becky thought, it didn't seem to be bothering them. She saw Scott smile and blush.

"I don't know," Becky said after a moment. "They seem nice enough to me."

Nancy looked at her in disbelief. "They're idiots."

Becky pushed away her plate. She looked at Nancy and asked, "Were you and Bobby really parkin' down at the bridge?"

"Yeah, but nobody was watching," Nancy said.

"How come y'all never eat together, or hang out at school or anything?" Becky asked.

"Good Lord, Becky. You can't spend twenty-four hours a day together. I mean, after we get married, we'll be spendin' all our time together."

"Married?" Becky nearly choked on her food.

"He brought it up to me," Nancy confided.

"He's dating Marcy Ruffin, Nancy," Becky argued. "Ever'body knows that. They been goin' together for two years."

Nancy shrugged. She toyed with a curl in her hair, twirling it with a finger. "Well," she said, "he told me he's dumpin' her just as soon as football season's over. And I understand that, 'cause we got a chance of going all the way to state this year."

Becky looked at Nancy, puzzled by her reasoning. "You mean he can't break up with Marcy and play football at the same time?" Becky asked.

"Becky," Nancy huffed, "he needs to stay focused. You don't know anything about sports, do you?"

Nancy rose, grabbed her tray, and started across the cafeteria toward the window where students deposited their empty trays. Becky followed.

As they neared the Chosen table where Scott and Susan and Bobby and Marcy were sitting, Becky warned Nancy, "Don't say nothin'."

The warning was too late.

"Hey, Bobby," Nancy said cheerfully.

Bobby glanced at her and nodded. Marcy slid her arm through Bobby's as she glared at Nancy.

"Bitch," Nancy hissed in a whisper as they passed.

"Why'd you do that?" Becky asked as she dumped the uneaten portion of her lunch into a large trash can, then slid her tray through the empties window.

"She makes me sick," Nancy snapped. "Oh, I need to borrow your English homework for next period."

Becky did not answer. She noticed that Scott was staring at her. His eyes scanned her body, then held on her face. He smiled. Becky quickly looked away. She could feel her face coating in a blush.

"Becky. Homework. English," Nancy said.

"Huh?" Becky said. "Oh, yeah. All right. But I gotta have it back by sixth period. Promise?"

"Okay," grumbled Nancy. "You're worse than my mother."

The bell rang, echoing down the long corridor that led from the cafeteria to the main building of the school. As Nancy and Becky stepped through the double doors, Becky took one last glance toward the table where Scott was sitting. "God, he's good-looking," she thought.

6

Ruby Jenkins could see her reflection in the front window of the Piggly Wiggly as she stood at the check-out counter. Ruby was fifty-two, a plain-faced woman with a plain, square figure, but she was dressed in her dark blue church outfit, with a fluffed-lace collar that hugged a sagging jowl underneath her chin. To Ruby, the outfit made her look sophisticated. "Stylishly striking," she would have described herself, if she had to say it with her hand on the Bible.

She turned her head back from the window to Verdale Calloway, who stood at the cash register punching in prices. Verdale looked tired and harassed. In fact, she was still hung over.

"Price check on two," Verdale said into a small microphone that dangled from a metal stem above the cash register.

"How you been doin', Verdale?" asked Ruby.

"Just takin' it one day at a time since Robert left," Verdale answered wearily. She keyed the microphone again. "Price check on two."

"How long's Robert been gone, now?" Ruby said.

Verdale wagged her head. "Be five years, this September," she replied. There was a heavy, serious tone in her voice. She keyed the microphone again. "Price check," she barked.

From across the store, sitting in his windowed office, Lloyd Pinkerton watched Verdale. A thoughtful frown rested on his forehead.

"You sure are dressed up today, Ruby," Verdale noticed.

"We've been to the funeral home this morning to see Fred Atwater," explained Ruby.

"Did Fred die?"

"Uh-huh. Friday. Got up from the supper table and fell dead with a heart attack," Ruby answered pitifully.

Verdale looked around. "Price check on two," she called into the microphone. The sound of her voice echoed throughout the store. "Wadn't he the president of Commercial Bank?" she asked Ruby.

"Yeah," Ruby said. "He was a good man. Deacon in the church.

A good man. But now, I got to tell you, Verdale, that Commercial Bank ain't much 'count."

"Really?" Verdale replied. "I ain't never had no trouble with 'em."

Ruby lifted her face defiantly. She pulled at the fluffed-lace collar at her chin. "Well, Charlie and me wrote several checks on that bank, and they sent ever' last one of 'um back marked *'insufficient funds'*. They don't keep enough money down there for nothing."

Verdale crooked her face to look at Ruby. Ruby, she decided, was dumb as a stick.

"Just a minute, Ruby," Verdale said. "Looks like I got to check this myself."

Lloyd Pinkerton watched Verdale leave the cash register and disappear into one of the food aisles. He sprang from his chair, left his office, and hurried down the opposite aisle. He looked around, but saw no one. Then he crept around the head of the aisle, slipped up behind Verdale, embraced her from the back, and kissed her on the neck. Verdale pushed away from him.

"Lloyd, stop it before somebody sees us," she whispered.

"I thought I might come over tonight," Lloyd said easily.

"I don't know if that's a good idea. What about your wife?" Verdale replied.

"I don't think she'd want to come." Lloyd laughed.

Verdale frowned, then a smile brushed across her lips.

"Well, think about it," Lloyd urged. He leaned quickly and playfully kissed her on the neck. She dropped the mayonnaise jar she held.

"Okay, Lloyd, okay, but just for a little while. Now go on, leave me alone," Verdale said. She checked the price on another jar of mayonnaise and headed back to her station.

Lloyd smiled triumphantly. He yelled, "Clean up on aisle five," then watched her go.

7

The Dew Drop Inn was like a halfway house for the workers of the Big Sandy Auto Accessories plant, a resting place where the drudgery of work was left at the pool tables, the pinball machines, and the bar.

While the Big Sandy Auto Accessories plant took the reality of toil from its workers, the Dew Drop Inn countered with an illusion of spirit. It was like a see-saw—reality and illusion rocking in an up-and-down motion, never quite finding a balance.

The air of the Dew Drop Inn was thick with cigarette smoke that swirled eerily against the multicolored glow of neon beer signs. The sounds were loud laughter and argument, country music from the juke box, and the sharp clacking of ball against ball from the pool tables. The sounds were like harmony from an ancient music. The sounds were comforting.

Clifford was at the bar, sitting with Jack and Ed, Joe and Ernestine, and Peggy and Sammy Wilson. Nearby, Wesley and Benny were shooting pool. Janice was behind the bar serving drinks. Her ebony face glistened in the neon light. Her eyes flashed over the crowd, looking for Jerry, but Jerry was not there. Janice was the only black in the Dew Drop. She was only the second black to have ever been inside the building, the other being Toby Johnson, her grandfather. He had worked as a clean-up man at the bar for thirty-two years before failing health forced him to retire. He had always hated the thought of the government keeping him up.

It was still early, but Wesley was already high from the three beers he had quickly chug-a-lugged. "Hey, I'm a cheap date, and what's the use of drinking if you don't get drunk?" Wesley had often answered those who claimed he couldn't hold his liquor. He was talking in an excited voice about his favorite sport, wrestling.

"He by-God got him in the Manchurian death grip, but Skull Darby ain't no damn fool," Wesley proclaimed as he watched Benny line up a shot. "Shit, pulled a reverse Ayatollah flip and gave him a Romanian Devil poke in the eye. Ever'body that knows anything knows that stuff's illegal as shit. If I'd of been refereeing, I'd of disqualified that big sumbitch."

Sammy shook his head from his stool. He said, "God'a'mighty,

Wesley, when you gonna wake up and smell the coffee? Ever'body knows wrestling's fake. They just actin'.''

Wesley shot a dangerous look toward Sammy. "Fake?" he said. "You watch wrestlin' last night, Sammy?"

"Hell, no," Sammy replied arrogantly. "I don't watch that shit."

"Well, there you go," Wesley declared. "Last night, the Human Mountain hit Super Stud Number Two over the head with a god-damn chair. Knocked his ass out of the ring. Damned near killed him. Now, you can't fake somethin' like that." Wesley smiled and nodded at the others leaning against the bar.

Sammy turned back to the bar, picked up his beer, and swallowed. He muttered to Joe, "Stupid son of a bitch."

"Why don't you mind your own business, Sammy, and let them boys shoot pool?" advised Clifford.

"Yeah, what I say," Jack said. "Shit. Let it go." He leaned toward Clifford. "Caught the game the other night," he added. "Jimmie Clifford played his ass off."

Clifford rolled his shoulders with pride. He said, "He does fairly well."

"Fairly well?" Ed exclaimed. "This is the best damn football team we've had here in forty years."

Jack nodded agreement and motioned to Janice for another beer. "You mark my words, Clifford, that boy's gonna wind up playin' college ball somewheres."

Clifford laughed. "Shit. He'll be lucky to graduate high school."

"Won't make no difference the way colleges are today," Joe said. "If he can play football, they'll take him if he can't read or write a word. And they'll pay him for it."

Clifford swallowed from his beer and dipped his hand into the popcorn basket. He said, "If he goes to college, they'll have to pay it, 'cause I sure as hell can't."

Ed drew from his cigarette and crushed it out in the ashtray. "You see, Clifford, that's what I been talkin' about. We ain't had a pay increase in four years, but college tuition and groceries and ever' damn thing else keeps goin' up. That's why I'm always talkin' about the union. We gotta have it. Shit."

"Ed, why don't you just shut up about that union stuff," Peggy begged. "I come in here to get drunk, not talk about work." She shook her head at Ernestine. "I bet he's a lot of fun at home."

Ernestine huffed a laugh and drained her beer. "Well, he ain't wrong about what he's sayin'. We don't get our ass in gear, we all gonna be in trouble. Big trouble."

"C'mon, Ernestine, I don't wanna hear it," Peggy said. "I just damn well don't wanna hear anymore about that stupid union."

Ernestine shrugged. She leaned back and listened to the woeful strains of an electric steel guitar. The music vibrated inside her, rubbing against her soul. She felt tired.

8

At night, the cars of the teenagers of Big Sandy High School circled the Dairy Queen like moths gliding around a street light. The Dairy Queen was the milkshake version of the Dew Drop Inn, a gathering place where teenagers practiced for the ritual of adulthood, and for Becky Sewell and Nancy Calloway, it was a place to see and to be seen.

They were sitting in a window booth, slow-sipping soft drinks from straws, munching on ketchup-covered french fries, and watching the circling cars as though something was about to happen, some unexpected moment that would pull their faces close to the window and amaze them.

The unexpected was Bobby Richards and Scott Mitchell walking across the parking lot.

"There's Bobby and Scott," Nancy said excitedly. She waved through the window.

Bobby waved, smiled, and said something to Scott; then they turned and walked toward the window where Becky and Nancy sat just inside. At the window, Bobby quickly unbuckled his belt, whipped his pants down, and pressed his bare ass against the window. He quickly pulled his pants up.

Nancy laughed uncontrollably. She tapped on the glass. "Hey, we're trying to eat in here."

"Good grief," Becky sighed.

They watched as Bobby and Scott continued into the restaurant and ambled toward them.

"Hey," Nancy said cheerfully.

"What's happening?" Bobby replied. He slipped in beside Nancy and leaned to nibble on her neck.

"Quit it!" Nancy said playfully. She looked up at Scott. "Hi."

"How's it going?" Scott mumbled.

"Becky, you know Scott Mitchell, don'chu?" Bobby asked Becky.

She nodded and smiled shyly. "Yeah," Becky said. "I mean, I voted for you for class president."

"Really? Thanks. You're Jimmie Clifford's sister?"

Becky nodded.

"So, what are y'all doin' tonight ?" Bobby asked.

"Nothin'. Hangin' out. Eatin'," Nancy told him. "What's happenin' with you?"

"Nothin'. Just hangin' out," Bobby said. "How about a little dessert?" He kissed Nancy on the neck again and slipped his hand over her leg.

Nancy pushed him away, laughing. "You're drunk," she said.

"So?" Bobby replied. He kissed her again. His hand stroked along her leg.

"Stop it," Nancy giggled. "I'm about to pee in my pants."

"I can't help it," Bobby whispered. "You just look so good." He pulled her to him and kissed her hard. She took the kiss eagerly.

Becky could feel the heat of embarrassment flowing from her neck. She glanced up at Scott, smiled, then quickly looked out the window.

"Wait a minute." Nancy objected in a low voice. "This ain't exactly the place for it."

"All right. Let's get out of here then," Bobby pleaded.

"No, I can't—" She nodded and looked at Becky,

"Scott'll take you home, Becky." Bobby offered. "Won't you?"

"No problem," Scott said.

Becky looked up at Scott. She moved back in her seat. She wanted to leave, to run. "No, that's okay," she said. "Nancy!" She pleaded, begging with her eyes.

"Hey, I don't mind," Scott assured her.

"Great, let's get outta here." Bobby said as he pulled Nancy out of the booth and toward the door.

A cold shiver shot through Becky as she watched Nancy and Bobby heading across the parking lot toward Bobby's truck. Suddenly Nancy stopped, looked back to Becky, then pulled away from Bobby and ran back inside. Becky sighed with relief. Nancy approached the booth, then reached down and grabbed her purse from under the table. "Forgot my pocketbook." She winked to Becky and whispered, "Good luck," then raced out the door and climbed into Bobby's waiting truck.

Becky looked up at Scott and smiled shyly, "You don't have to drive me." She cleared her throat and swallowed hard. "I could just walk. It's not very far. It's just—not far."

Scott smiled and shook his head, "No problem, I'll give you a ride."

Becky smiled and nodded. She popped a French fry into her mouth as she looked out the window to see the taillights of Bobby's truck disappearing down the road. "Oh, ah, great . . . that's just great," she mumbled.

9

For a week, each night had been the same—Wesley and Jerry and Clifford in the sideyard of Clifford's trailer, gathered at the opened hood of Clifford's car as Jerry and Clifford watched Wesley pull apart the motor and piece it back together. There was magic in Wesley's hands. "Borned to it," was Clifford's admiring evaluation of Wesley's skills as a mechanic. "Sumbitch can listen to an engine and tell you what's wrong with it."

A work light plugged to the end of a long orange extension cord running from Clifford's trailer was hanging over the motor, casting a glow from beneath the yawning lip of the hood. Wesley worked; Jerry and Clifford watched, sipping beer from long-neck bottles. Clifford filled his bottom lip with a pinch of chewing tobacco. The air was thick and humid along the Tennessee River.

"Clifford," Wesley said without looking up from his work, "You fought in Vietnam. What do you think about these sons-a-bitches burning the American flag?"

Clifford spit expertly across the ground. "Well, I'll tell you, Wesley," he drawled, "we fought that war so people in this country would have the right to burn the flag if they wanted to. It's the damn First Amendment, freedom of expression."

Wesley looked up from the motor, surprised.

"'Course, if I catch any of 'em doin' it, I'm gonna exercise my freedom of expression and kick the livin' shit out of 'em," Clifford added.

Wesley laughed. He stood away form the car and rolled his shoulders, tight from leaning over. He took a long, hard swallow of beer. "Well, you need any help, you give me a holler. We'll straighten some people's asses out."

The light beams of a car swept over the three men and pulled to a stop at Sheila's trailer just up the hill near the blacktop river road. The men watched as Sheila Pascal got out of the car and went into her trailer.

"There she is, right on time," Wesley motioned with his beer bottle. "Wonder where she goes ever night?"

Inside her trailer, behind the flimsy curtains of the small windows, Sheila began to undress. Watching her was like watching a strip-tease artist in silhouette.

The three men began a slow move away from the car, toward Sheila's trailer.

"You hear anything about that promotion yet, Clifford?" Jerry whispered as he stared at Sheila's window.

Sheila pulled off her coat and tossed it on a chair.

"Naw," Clifford answered woodenly. "I'm supposed to find out somethin' next week."

The boys edged closer as Sheila moved past another window.

"Hell, Clifford, you got the job. You got seniority," Wesley muttered.

"There was a pause. Sheila slipped her blouse off her shoulders.

"I tell you what," Clifford said, "I'll be happy to get out from under them damn machines."

A car passed and the men ducked into the shadow of a large water oak, then emerged again, slowly.

"What you gonna do with all that extra money, Clifford?" asked Wesley in a low voice.

"What extra money is that?" Clifford replied.

"Shift foreman. That's a damn good raise," Jerry added.

Sheila unzipped her skirt and let it drop to the floor, then she skinned out of her half-slip.

"Jesus," Wesley said softly. "Come on, I got to get a better look at that."

The men checked both ways, making sure the coast was clear, then quickly tiptoed across the gravel road and up the hill toward Sheila's trailer.

"All that extra money ain't all that much," Clifford whispered.

Sheila unsnapped her bra and her breasts ballooned free.

Sheila ran her fingers through her hair. Her breasts lifted with the motion.

"That raise'll just about get me even," Clifford continued from somewhere in his subconscious. His conscious mind was on Shelia Pascal.

The men, slowly moving as one, eased closer.

"Goddamn. Now that's what a woman's body is supposed to look like." Wesley said.

The men stalked closer toward Sheila's trailer, toward that back bedroom window, their eyes fixed on the shadowy figure behind the sheer curtains.

Suddenly a voice—a loud, demanding call—came from behind them, out of Clifford's trailer. It was Evelyn. "Clifford! Clifford!"

"Oh, shit," Wesley hissed. He dropped his cigarette and began sprinting down around the back path behind the trailers. Jerry and Clifford followed him, trying to run downhill without slipping on the dew wet grass.

"Clifford! Clifford! You out here?" Evelyn's voice was louder, more demanding.

The path the men were taking was familiar but dark, and as they rounded a corner Wesley crashed into a row of garbage cans. Jerry, close behind,went down hard, falling over Wesley.

"Hell! Shit! Damn!" Wesley hissed, his shins aching from the blow to the iron garbage-can holder that Wesley had welded for his neighbor at his friend Dover's garage.

Clifford passed his downed co-conspirators at a dead run. He did not slow down as he turned to look back, then changed directions to cut across Mavis Campbell's small patch of yard. He did not remember or see the clothesline that caught him in the throat, sending him down with a thud, flat on his back.

"Clifford! Clifford!" Evelyn's voice echoed throughout the park.

When the three men walked around the corner of Clifford's trailer in a casual stroll, Evelyn was standing in the front yard, her hands on her hips.

"Yeah?" Clifford said. "You callin' me?"

"What are y'all doin' out here?" demanded Evelyn.

"Nothin'," Clifford replied arrogantly, rubbing his throat. "We been workin' on the car. Why? What're you doin'? Writing a book?"

Evelyn's eyes scanned the men. She could see the film of perspiration on their foreheads and the look of guilt in their eyes. Like little boys caught with their hands in the cookie jar, they stood shoulder to shoulder, eyes toward the ground.

"You got a phone call," Evelyn said, as she turned to go back inside.

"Who is it?" Clifford asked.

"I don't know," Evelyn snapped. "Ed Stone, I think."

Evelyn disappeared back inside her trailer and slammed the door behind her.

Clifford looked to Wesley and Jerry, nodded his head a couple of times, rolled his eyes and blew a deep sigh up the hill toward Shelia's trailer. "I'll see you boys tomorrow."

"Yeah! Yeah. We'll see ya," Wesley and Jerry said as they stumbled toward home.

10

Becky sat close to the door on the passenger's side of Scott's car, leaning against it. She tried to look ahead into the night as Scott drove slowly along the narrow river road, but her eyes blinked constantly at the distance separating them. It was a safe but uncomfortable distance. If anyone saw them, she believed, it would be obvious that Scott was merely driving her home—a friend giving a friend a lift, nothing more. She was not like Nancy. Such a ride for Nancy would have meant teasing, laughter, perhaps a play for Scott. She was not like Nancy. Sometimes she wished that she was.

Jimmie Clifford's a good football player. Probably be All-State this year," Scott said easily, breaking the silence.

"Yeah," Becky replied. "He's good."

Scott nodded. The silence began to build again.

"Aren't you datin' Robert Simms?" Scott asked.

"Not anymore," Becky told him. "We broke up."

"Really? His loss."

A smile broke across Becky's lips. That was nice. She could feel the humming of the car's motor vibrating in her shoulders.

"You like Miss Alexander?" Becky spoke up.

"What?"

"Miss Alexander. Algebra."

"Oh," Scott said. "Ah, yeah. She's okay. I mean if you gotta take algebra, she's as good as anybody, I guess."

Becky twisted in her seat toward Scott. She was growing more comfortable. It was easier to talk about algebra than boyriends.

"Yeah, I hate it," Becky admitted. "I mean, when is anybody ever gonna use algebra in real life?"

"Never," Scott said. "Who do you have?"

"Miss Alexander," Becky answered, a little disappointed. "I'm in that class too. We have math together."

"Really?" Scott said. "Well, I'm usually asleep in that class."

Scott turned onto the gravel road of Captain's Point Trailer Park, down past the dumpster and the long row of mailboxes on wooden posts.

"Well—uh, I sit in the back—" Becky paused, smiled then pointed, "I live just right down there on the left."

"Yeah, I know." Scott laughed. He pulled his car to a stop in front of the Sewell trailer. "I figured you and Jimmie Clifford lived in the same trailer."

"Oh yeah," she smiled shyly. "Well, thanks for the ride."

"No problem." Scott leaned toward her suddenly and kissed her gently on the lips.

Becky opened her mouth to speak, but did not. She pulled on the handle of the car door and stepped out. She watched as Scott drove away.

11

It was her duty, Evelyn Sewell believed, to make certain everyone and everything in her trailer home was safe and at peace before she closed her eyes and prayed for the sleep she desperately needed. It was a memory she carried from her own childhood—being in bed, eyes closed, pretending to sleep, listening to the quiet, deliberate nightly tour of her mother. Being certain. Knowing. It was the mother's instinct, Evelyn had decided, and the mother's privilege. The mother protected, nurtured. The mother was a giver.

Evelyn's tour always began in the kitchen, then traveled down the hallway to the bathroom, where she took her pills, washing them down with a palmful of water. From the bathroom she checked the bedrooms, turning off the lights that only she seemed to know how to operate.

She paused at Jimmie's bedroom, but did not open the door. There was no light to turn off, and she did not want to know whether her son was in bed asleep or out somewhere. She worried when he stayed out, but she could no longer control him. Jimmie did as he pleased—with his father's blessing.

She opened the door to Becky's room. The light blazed, but Becky was curled against her pillow. Her sketch pad and charcoal lay on the floor by her bed. On it was the portrait of a teenage boy Evelyn did not recognize. She turned off the light, closed the door, and dragged down the hall to her own bedroom. Clifford was snoring gently. She turned off the light and eased into bed beside him. From outside, she could hear the muffled, mournful cry of an Elvis Presley song floating across the park from Verdale's trailer. She closed her eyes and began to pray silently: "Dear God, help my friend, Verdale—"

The window to Becky's room slowly begin to rise, and suddenly Nancy was hanging on the window sill, half in and half out of the trailer.

"Becky," whispered Nancy. "Becky?" She reached down to the bed below the window and tugged at Becky's leg.

Becky rolled over, then sat up. She rubbed the sleep from her eyes. "What? What're you doin'?" she asked softly.

"You asleep?" Nancy asked.

"What?"

"Wake up," Nancy said. She pulled herself through the window and into the room.

"Shhhh," Becky whispered. "You're gonna wake Mama up."

Nancy squatted on the edge of the bed, smiling. "So what happened? Tell me about it?"

"What're you talkin' about?" Becky yawned.

"What am I talkin' about?—Scott. Tonight, with Scott. What happened?"

"You woke me up to ask me that?"

"Yeah."

"Nothin' happened," Becky said, frowning at Nancy's implication.

"Nothin'? He didn't put the move on you or nothin'?"

"He just brought me home," Becky answered.

"Ah," Nancy smiled knowingly. "Oh, he's smooth. Very good move," she said.

"What?" Becky asked.

"Nothin'. I'll see you tomorrow," Nancy replied. She slipped from the bed and climbed back out the window as quickly as she had entered. Becky watched her, shook her head, and sighed. She fell back into the pillow and stared up at the ceiling for a moment. She touched her lips with her fingers, tasting the memory of the kiss from Scott.

". . . and for my babies, help them to follow the good and righteous path. And for my husband, Clifford . . . " Evelyn continued in her closed-eyed prayer. "Help him get that promotion, Lord, if it be Thy will." She paused, opening her eyes. She could hear the soft, sweet voice of Elvis crooning *Love Me Tender.*

12

It was lunchtime, and the break room was crowded and divided—blacks on one side, whites on the other. The room was filled with a droning of voices.

Lunch break at the Big Sandy Auto Accessories plant was forty-five minutes. With alternating schedules, beginning at eleven o'clock, three lunch shifts lasted until one-fifteen. The lunch breaks were taken in the breakroom, which seated a hundred and fifty-five people. Soft-drink and snack machines lined one wall. Five large trash drums, lined with heavy black plastic bags, were stationed at the doorways and near the service machines.

"Look at that crazy sumbitch," mumbled Wesley, as he watched Ed Stone tack a "Union Yes" sign to the bulletin board. He turned his head and watched Jack Wimberly persuade a co-worker to sign the union petition. He shook his head. "Damn!"

"Well, you better grab your ass and hang on," Clifford said. "Here comes Ed."

Ed moved casually among the crowd, waving, speaking, patting his co-workers on the back. He looked like a politician working for votes.

"If there were any babies in here he'd be kissing 'em." Joe Burnette observed.

"Let me get you boys signed up here," Ed said cheerfully, as he approached the table where Wesley and Clifford and Joe and Jerry and Benny were sitting.

"Man, get that thing away from me," Clifford said irritably.

"You gonna get ever' last one of us fired," Joe grumbled.

Ed laughed. He looked around. "That's what management wants you to think," he said. "Shit, they ain't gonna fire you."

"Old man Moss said if we bring a union in here, he'll shut the plant down tighter 'n a drum," Benny said. "And I for one think he'll do it."

"They can't do that," Ed argued. "Won't do it. Can't afford to." He sat at the table. "Don't y'all want more money, for God's sake? Better benefits? Better workin' conditions?"

Wesley coughed a laugh. "Naw, Ed. We like workin' for low

pay and less benefits. Shit, that's the only reason I work here. It's fun."

"If you think this union's gonna get us all that, you're crazy as hell," Clifford said to Ed. "You got your elevator stuck between floors."

Ed shook his head. He leaned toward Clifford. "I know they will," he said emphatically. "Look, signin' this petition don't mean we gotta vote the union in. It just means we got the right to vote on it if we want to."

Clifford pushed his lunchpail away. He glared at Ed. "Ed, why you keep after me about this all the time?" he demanded.

"Ever'body likes you, Clifford," Ed said in a quiet voice. "They'll listen to you. If your name's on here, some of 'em will feel better about signin' it."

Wesley reached into his shirt pocket, pulled a cigarette from its pack, and tapped it on the table. He said, "Clifford's in line for that shift foreman's job, Ed. You think he wants to take a chance on losin' it just to put his name on a piece of paper that ain't gonna do him no good anyhow?"

Ed turned his gaze to Wesley. He pushed the paper across the table. "Well, what about you, then Wesley? You ain't in line for no foreman's job."

"Naw," Wesley said, "but I'd like to keep the one I got. Besides, first chance I get, I'm gonna go over to Nashville to that truck-drivin' school and make some real money. See you got to have a class-five license—"

Ed sighed in desperation. He threw up his hand to stop Wesley. "Don't start that crap again, Wesley. You ain't going nowhere." He turned his attention back to the others. "Two years ago, we had a chance to get a union in here and we pissed it away. You tell me how things have changed in two years. If anything, we're worse off."

Wesley smiled and lit his cigarette. He sucked smoke into his lungs and let it roll from his lips toward Ed. Ed stood and made a sour face. "Yeah, I get'chu now. Y'all don't want to help make things better around here, but you'll damn sure want your share of the benifits once the union comes in." He turned and stomped away from the table, shaking his head.

"Ed's got the red ass, don't he?" Jerry said quietly.

"I'm about a C-hair away from slappin' the shit outta him," Wesley mumbled.

"Wouldn't do no good," advised Clifford. "That boy don't know the difference between horseshit and chocolate candy."

Benny and Joe laughed.

"Well, we're about to find out how he stands up to the pressure," Joe said slowly. He nodded toward the door.

The room quietened to a hush as Richard Moss stepped through the door into the breakroom. He was followed by Artie Phillips, who held a clipboard containing a shipping manifest. He nodded to a couple of workers sitting close to the door, then crossed the room in a bold stride and pushed coins into one of the soft-drink machines. The sound of the drink can rattling through the machine pinged through the room. Richard took the can and opened it. The spew of the carbonated drink was like the hiss of a cat.

"You wanta sign this, Mr. Moss?" Artie said in a quiver.

Richard glanced at the manifest, took the pen offered by Artie, and swiped his signature across it. Artie turned and hurried away.

"Enjoyin' your lunch?" Richard said to no one in particular.

A few voices muttered, "Yes, sir."

Richard's eyes swept over the bulletin board and stopped on the union sign. He stepped to the board and ripped it down. Ed and Jack slid the petitions they were carrying out of sight.

"I don't know who put this up here," Richard said in a high voice, "and I don't want to know. I don't care. But if you want to talk union, you do it on your own time, and you do it somewhere else."

His eyes swept the room again. He meant business. When he left, the sounds of his footsteps clicked from the walls. The breakroom sat in stunned silence. All wanted to speak, none had the courage.

"Well, shit," Wesley whispered. "Look at ol' Ed over there, white as a sheet. Stupid son of a bitch."

"Shit stinks bad enough without stirring it up," Clifford huffed.

They gonna keep on till ever'one of us loses our job," Joe said wearily.

Ed caught Clifford's gaze. Clifford cocked an eyebrow and shook his head in disgust.

13

Becky wondered if too much of her mother's blood pumped through her. She did not like the crush, the moving wave of people who shoved at her in the hallway of Big Sandy High School. Sometimes, she only wanted peace and quiet and the blessed sense of being alone. But being alone in Big Sandy High School was impossible—especially when classes changed. The hallways were canals of rushing flesh.

She knew it was Nancy who tugged at her elbow even before she turned. Nancy was her best friend. Best friends knew one another better than they knew their parents, or their sisters and brothers, or even the people they dated.

"What?" Becky said.

"You do your math homework?" Nancy asked.

Becky stopped in the hallway, against the wall. She rolled her eyes and began to thumb through her notebook.

"What're you gonna do when you get to finals?" she said irritably. "I don't think they're gonna let me take the test for you."

"I don't know," Nancy said blithely. "I'll think of somethin'. Guess what?"

"What?"

"You're not gonna believe this."

"What?"

"You're gonna love it."

"Nancy! What?"

"Well, if you're gonna be that way—"

"I'm not bein' any way. I just don't wanna be late for class, that's all."

"Okay. You'll never guess who wants to go out with you."

"Who?"

"Scott Mitchell," Nancy said eagerly.

Becky's face furrowed into a question.

"Yeah. It's the truth," Nancy added quickly. "Bobby just told me. Said he thought you were cute. Wants to get together."

"Why would he want to go out with me?" Becky asked.

"I don't know. He wants to. You're cute," Nancy answered.

"But, he's goin' steady with Susan Taylor," Becky reminded her.

"Yeah, well," Nancy said flippantly. "Bobby says they're havin' a lot of problems. Anyway, what difference does it make?" Nancy stepped back. She studied Becky's reaction to what she believed was earth-shattering news, then shook her head and threw up both hands in an expression of disbelief. "The most popular, best-lookin' guy in this school wants to go out with you and you're actin' like—I don't know what you're actin' like, but you're crazy. You're goin'!"

Becky began to move slowly down the hallway. "I don't feel right about it," she said softly.

"Forget it," Nancy said cheerfully, grabbing the homework. "You're goin'. I'll give this back to you later."

"But—"

It was too late for Becky to argue. She watched as Nancy disappeared into the flood of bodies changing classes. She smiled.

14

When Nancy appeared at her window, after the lights of the Sewell trailer had been turned off and Evelyn Sewell was praying her closed-eyed, silent prayer to God, Becky was sitting in the dark on the side of her bed, nervously waiting. Nancy's face appeared at the window like a smiling close-up in a television program.

"Let's go," Nancy whispered.

Becky tiptoed to her door, eased it open, and looked down the hall to her parents' room. There was no light coming from beneath their closed door. She quietly slipped out of her small bedroom window.

They did not speak until they were on the narrow gravel road that circled the trailer park.

"I don't know why we gotta meet 'em like this," Becky said.

"Would your folks let you go out this late on a school night?" asked Nancy.

"No."

"Okay, then."

"They would on a weekend," Becky countered.

"It ain't a weekend, Becky," Nancy said. "I can't believe you sometimes."

They walked quickly, quietly on the cut-off through the woods, passing over Beaver Dam Creek and walking the railroad tracks toward a gorge where the Tennessee River snaked its way around Hogback Ridge, then down across the clay pits where Big Sandy Gravel Company mined clay for kitty litter. When they emerged from the windbreak of trees bordering the clay pits on the west, they were in the parking lot of the Dairy Queen.

The parking lot was crowded with cars, and the sound of music floated harshly from Cecil Pinkerton's truck.

"There they are," Nancy said eagerly.

Bobby and Scott were near Cecil's truck with a group of boys from Big Sandy High School. Jimmie was sitting in the truck on the passenger side.

"Oh, no," Becky muttered. "There's my brother."

"So what?" Nancy said.

The two girls moved across the parking lot to the truck.

"Hey, Becky," called Cecil. He was surprised to see her here this late.

Becky smiled and nodded. She looked at Jimmie. He swallowed from a can of beer he was holding.

"Hey, Jimmie Clifford," Becky said timidly.

Jimmie did not reply. He burped and crushed the empty can in his huge fist.

"C'mon, let's get outta here," Bobby said. He took Nancy's hand and began to pull her toward Scott's car. Scott waited for Becky.

"Becky? You goin' with us or not?" Nancy asked.

Becky glanced once at Jimmie and followed Scott to the car. She got in the front seat and slid next to the door.

As they pulled out of the parking lot and onto the main road, Becky looked back to see Jimmie and Cecil watching. This was something she had definitely not anticipated.

"Forget it, Becky," Nancy said from the back seat. "Jimmie Clifford ain't gonna say nothin'. Will he?"

The ridge rose high above the wide bed of water flowing gently below it. Even in the worst of storms, when the river turned to rage, the water did not reach the ridge. A canopy of trees—water oaks and poplar and beech—covered the land. It was rumored that a regiment of Union soldiers had camped the winter there in their march through the South, and that artifacts of their stay could be found with metal detectors.

To Scott Mitchell, the ridge was the most beautiful place in the valley.

"One of these days, I'm gonna buy this property and build a house up here," he said thoughtfully. "Gonna sit out on my porch every night, drink a beer, and listen to the river."

Scott's car was parked under an oak, pointed toward the river. A full moon shimmered across the water below them. Becky was still sitting next to the door, leaning against it. She was watching the rolling water. In the back seat, Bobby and Nancy were locked in passion, softly muttering.

"If kids wanta come up here and park, drink a beer, nobody can hassle 'em, 'cause it'll be on my property," Scott continued.

From the back seat, Nancy whispered an excited, "Oh, God."

Scott glanced at Becky and smiled uncomfortably.

"Hear that?" he said as he pointed. "That's a barge signalin' over by the point."

Becky listened as the barge's foghorn called its distant, painful cry.

"Oh, yeah," she said quietly. She smiled and motioned with her head toward the backseat. "I thought it was them," she added.

Scott stifled a laugh. He shook his head, then put his beer on the dashboard of the car. He slipped next to Becky and put his arm around her. He could feel her body tensing.

"Oh, shit," Nancy muttered. "That's it—oh, oh, oh, yes!"

Scott smiled again. Becky ducked her head to stop the laugh trembling inside her throat.

"You gonna go to college?" asked Becky after a moment.

"Sure," Scott answered. "I'm gettin' a lot of letters from schools that want me to play football. But, I don't know. My dad wants me to go to Vanderbilt. That's where he went, but I don't wanta play football there."

"What do you wanna do besides play football? I mean, like a job or something—"

Scott tilted his head. "I'll probably study law, like my old man. Come back here, work for him, make a lot of money, build a house up here."

Scott nodded agreement with himself. He turned his head to Becky, then leaned and kissed her gently on the lips. He held the kiss for a moment, knowing she was frightened. Then he pulled away and smiled at her.

"Art," Becky whispered.

"Huh?"

"Art," Becky said again. "I'm an artist. I wanta go to art school and—study—"

From the backseat, Nancy inhaled quickly in a short cry.

Becky's face swiveled quickly to the backseat, then back to Scott.

"Art?" Scott asked.

"Yeah." She swallowed hard.

"Susan Taylor says you're really good."

"We—we have art together, me 'n Susan." Becky paused. She looked away, down toward the river. "Aren't y'all goin' together?" she asked. "You and Susan?"

"Well, kind of," confessed Scott. "I mean, there's some problems."

"I think she thinks y'all are goin' together," Becky said.

"That's one of the problems," Scott replied.

The breathing from the backseat was loud and rapid. There was a rocking movement in the car.

Scott leaned to her again and kissed her. She could feel a

heartrush building in her chest. His lips were warm and soft. The tip of his tongue touched her mouth, and she opened her lips slightly. Then she could feel his hand skimming her breasts, and she knew her nipples were becoming erect. She felt his fingers fumbling with the buttons on her blouse, and she pushed his hand away. Scott's mouth pressed harder against her, his tongue parting her lips, touching her tongue, filling her mouth with heat.

His hand dropped to her skirt, slipped beneath it. She could feel his hand on her bare leg, stroking it, moving to her panty line.

"No," she whispered. She pushed Scott's hand away, grabbed the door handle and slid quickly from the seat. Scott fell forward. The interior light of the car snapped on.

"Hey," Bobby snapped from the back seat.

Becky looked quickly into the car. She could see Bobby's bare ass in the air, and Nancy's legs wrapped around him. Scott pulled himself up, got out of the car and closed the door.

"I'm —I'm sorry," Becky said. "I really need to get back. I've got a test tomorrow and I need to wash my hair and ever'thing. I'll just see you later—sometime."

"You wash your hair at twelve-thirty at night?" Scott asked.

"Becky, what are you doin'?" Nancy asked from the car.

"I really need to get home, Nance," Becky replied. "I'll just see you in the mornin'."

Becky hurried away.

"Wait a damn minute," Nancy called. She struggled to push Bobby away from her.

"What're you doin'?" Bobby said. "I'm not through yet."

"If you didn't drink so much, it wouldn't take so long," Nancy snapped. She opened the door to the car, got out and started after Becky.

"You gotta be kiddin'," Bobby cried. "This is bullshit. Nancy?"

"Hey, I'll give y'all a ride home," Scott said to Nancy and Becky.

"That's okay. I like to walk," Becky called back. "Bye."

Scott and Bobby stood beside the car, watching Nancy as she struggled to pull on her panties. Hopping on one foot, she followed Becky down the path that led to the riverbank.

"I'll call you," Nancy called back to Bobby.

The boys watched the girls disappear into the woods.

"I thought you said she'd do it," Scott said irritably.

"That's what Nancy said. Maybe she's on the rag," Bobby answered.

"This is bullshit, man," Scott grumbled. "I could've popped Susan tonight instead of this."

The boys climbed into the car and pulled away.

The path beside the riverbank was easy to follow under the ribbon of light from the full moon, but it did not matter to Becky and Nancy. They could have followed the path blindfolded. The river and the ridge had been favorite playgrounds for them since childhood.

"Thanks a lot," Nancy grumbled as she caught up with Becky.

"Nancy, he had his hands—he was, well, you know," Becky said as she pushed past the low branches that bordered the path.

"Why are we leavin' then? What do you think we came out here for?" Nancy said.

"Not that," Becky paused, looked away. She could hear the river gurgling and, in the distance, the foghorn of a barge. "I thought we'd like make out and stuff, but—"

"Make out and stuff?" Nancy mocked. "You were makin' out and he was tryin' to do the stuff. Look, Becky, this is just part of bein' a woman." Nancy paused, gathering her thoughts. "You remember when you first got your period, and that meant you were, like, growin' up? You were becomin' a woman. Well, now, that you're a woman, doin' it, is like—becomin' an adult."

Becky shot a puzzled look to Nancy "You think havin' sex means you're an adult?"

"Well, sure—that and gettin' your driver's license," Nancy answered. "You're not like savin' yourself 'til marriage or nothing, are you? I mean, because your mother—"

Becky shook her head. "No," she said. "I don't know. I guess I'm just scared."

Nancy smiled sympathetically. "I was, too, the first time," she admitted softly. "That's normal. But it's like divin' off the high dive. Once you do it, you're not afraid anymore, and it's fun. You'll see. Besides," Nancy continued as she passed Becky along the narrow path that angled down toward Eagle Creek, "you're never gonna be able to date boys like Scott Mitchell unless you *do it*, with 'em. How do you think Susan Taylor landed him?"

"Yeah, I guess," Becky said as she considered Nancy's advice.

The two girls walked across a fallen log, then hopped from rocks to sandbar at the point where the creek widened and spilled into the river.

"Let me put it to you this way Becky," Nancy said as she reached out a hand and helped her friend take the last jump across the rushing water to the safety of the bank." What do you have to lose? I mean try it, if you don't like it you don't have to do it again."

The girls pulled themselves up the steep embankment by grabbing onto the low branches of the dogwood trees that lined the deep revine.

"But trust me," Nancy said. "You'll like it."

They reached the old gravel road where the mussel divers parked their dump trucks, then started for the blacktop river road that led toward home.

15

The plant's machinery hummed around them like the idling of an old car as the workers gathered at the large bay doors of the loading dock, smoking cigarettes and drinking soft drinks on their fifteen-minute morning break. The workers of Big Sandy Auto Accessories continued their almost neverending quarrel about the union.

It was a quarrel that simmered like heated water, with curls of small bubbles threatening to boil into scalding steam.

"I know this damn much," Jack said. "We're the backbone of this company, but we got no say-so about nothin' that goes on around here."

Ernestine nodded vigorously in agreement. "A union'll give us some say-so," she declared.

Harvey cracked the knuckles of his large black hands and shook his head wearily. "A union can't guarantee you nothin'," he argued patiently. "They have to go to management with a problem the same as you do."

"Yeah, well, if Moss won't listen to the union," countered Ed, "we'll just strike then."

"That'd teach 'em, wouldn't it?" Harvey replied. "Who you think's gonna pay us if we go on strike?"

Ed pulled hard on his cigarette and spit the smoke into the air. "The union pays you out of a strike fund, Harvey. Jesus, ever'body that knows anything knows that. Ain't that right, Clifford?"

Clifford shrugged. He pinched an empty Pepsi Cola can into a neat fold.

"Hell, Clifford, you know that's right," Ed continued.

"Yeah, you right," Clifford answered, "but ever'body that knows anything also knows them union checks ain't but about a third of what you're makin' now. Can you live on that? I sure as hell can't."

"All the union wants is our dues money and what do you get for it? A bunch of promises about what-all they gonna do for you," Harvey added. "That's what it's all about."

Benny coughed a loud warning. "Y'all better hush, or we're all gonna be out of a job and it won't matter if we get a union or not." He motioned with his head toward the door.

Inside the plant, Richard Moss slowed his stride. He was holding a clipboard in his hand. Standing beside him like a servant was David Auchmuty, a quality control supervisor. Richard paused and looked toward the loading dock. His eyes glanced at the time clock and swept back at the workers. He nodded once and walked away.

"Richard Moss sits up there in that office and takes away our benefits, and hires and fires and does as he damn well pleases," complained Jack. "And that just ain't right."

"Union'll put a stop to that right quick," added Ed.

"Y'all seem to think this union is some kinda magic cure for all our problems," Peggy said. "It ain't."

Ed lit another cigarette from the burning tip of the butt he held between his fingers. He thumb-smashed the butt against the concrete wall and looked at Peggy. "Let me ask you somethin'," he said. "How many times you gone to management with some kinda problem and had it solved the way it ought to be?"

Peggy wagged her head. "Old song you singin', Ed."

"May be old, but it's a damn good tune," Ed said.

The sharp ringing of the bell split the air, and the workers began to shuffle back inside.

"The point is this," Jack added. "With a union in here, one person's problems become everybody's problems. We stand together."

"Hell, I got enough problems of my own," Clifford muttered. "I don't need nobody else's."

"Come on, Clifford, help up us out here," Ed pleaded.

Clifford shook his head. "I hate to salt your puddin', Ed, but it don't look to me like we got it all that bad."

"Well, tell that to Johnny Parker," Ed argued. "He got laid off, and he's got five kids to feed."

Clifford ducked his head. He had liked Johnny Parker. Johnny Parker had been a damn good worker, a damn good man.

"He got laid off for wavin' that union petition in front of everybody's face, Ed," Harvey said softly. "If you ain't careful, you'll be in the unemployment line with him, and you got three kids."

Ed inhaled slowly. His eyes blinked in resignation. He turned and walked away toward his work station.

"I can't believe they laid off Johnny Parker," Clifford said. "He was the hardest worker in this plant. I can't believe they did it."

16

The carburetor was on the kitchen table before Jerry, spread out on folded newspaper sheets like a child's puzzle. He had worked with it for three hours almost subconsciously, his hands touching, polishing, fitting, adjusting. It was a job that he could have done in a few minutes, but he needed to be busy, to keep his hands moving. When he was working, the restlessness that skimmed across his chest and gurgled in his throat was not as bothersome.

It was Saturday, in the first hour of night. On Friday, he had gone to the Big Sandy football game and watched Big Sandy roll like an army over Bruceton High School. He had pounded Jimmie Clifford Sewell on the back and had a beer with Clifford and Wesley as they waited by Clifford's truck for the crowd to leave the stadium.

"Jimmie Clifford's one helluva football player," he had proclaimed to Clifford.

"He's a mean little sumbitch out there, ain't he?" Clifford had said proudly.

"Ain't nothin' little about him," he had replied to Clifford. "He's been able to whip my ass since he was thirteen."

The men laughed and talked and remembered the football games they had played wearing the Black and Gold of the Big Sandy Wildcats.

When he had returned home that night, Wanda was not there. He had heard her slip into the trailer after midnight.

They had not spoken on Saturday morning. After lunch, Jerry had gone to the auto junkyard to search for parts he did not need. In the afternoon, it was his turn to mow the grass and weeds from between the graves in the cemetery behind the church. Members who had kin buried there took turns cutting the grass. He spent extra time clipping and cleaning the gravesite of his son.

His hands touched the parts of the carburetor. Lifted them. Dipped them in an empty tin coffee can of gasoline. Put them down. They were shining from the rubbing of his polishing rag.

He looked up when he heard Wanda's voice.

"I'm goin' out," she said bluntly.

She was dressed in tight-fitting jeans and a red blouse that billowed open at her breasts.

"Couldn't you stay home once in a while?" Jerry said. "You go out somewhere ever' night."

Wanda did not reply. She picked up her pocketbook from the kitchen table.

"We're supposed to go over to Mama and Daddy's house for dinner tomorrow," Jerry told her.

"I don't know," Wanda said. "Maybe."

He knew that would be her answer. He took a deep breath, then mumbled, "Ray's home."

He saw the twitch of surprise in her face, the almost-blink of her eyes. She paused for a moment, then shrugged and left.

Jerry watched out the kitchen window as Wanda's car pulled away. He folded the rag and began to scrub a small spot of grease from his knuckle. From Verdale's trailer, he could hear the voice of Elvis.

Whenever she went to the Dew Drop Inn, Wanda Burnette knew she was daring fate. She knew she would drink too much and tease some man into pawing at her, and she knew the story of what she had done would find its way back to Jerry. Jerry was well-known at the Dew Drop, and well-liked.

There were nights when Wanda did not care, nights when a wildness raged in her and it was a wildness to put on parade.

And it was that wildness that filled the Inn like a sweet perfume, clinging to the clothing and the skin of the men who watched her shooting pool with Garry Gray and Hoyt Beasley.

"Damn," Benny whistled. He was standing at a nearby pool table, grinding chalk into the tip of the cue.

"You gonna shoot pool, or you gonna look at Wanda Burnette's butt?" demanded Wesley.

"Both." Benny laughed. "That's a damn good-lookin' woman."

"Yeah, she looks all right, but she's a full bubble off plumb, I'll tell you that," Wesley replied. He turned his beer up and swallowed hard. "Just like her daddy. Wouldn't work a lick. Drank hisself to death. Mother wadn't nothin' but a whore."

Benny turned back to look at Wanda. "Still, I wouldn't mind rubbin' uglies with her ever' night. That damn Jerry is one lucky sumbitch."

Wesley laughed. "Shit. He ain't gettin' any more of that than you are."

"What do you mean?" asked Benny. He leaned over the table and lined up his shot.

"Just between me 'n' you," whispered Wesley, "he ain't had any of that in two years. Not since she was in that car wreck. You know she killed their kid, don't you?"

Benny snapped off the shot. It missed and careened over the table. He stepped back, shaking his head. "Yeah," he said at last. "I heard she was drunk."

Wesley circled the table, close to Benny. "Oh, goddamn!" he exclaimed in a covered voice. "Drunk? Commode huggin'. She was at some bar down there in Buchanan. Had the kid with her. She started back out the lake highway and slammed head-on into a pickup. Killed their little boy. Damned near killed her. Ever since then, she can't bring herself to give ol' Jerry any."

"That's a damn shame," Benny said. "It's a waste."

Wesley tossed a glance over his shoulder to Wanda. She was bending over the table and he could see her breasts pushing at her blouse. "Don't get me wrong, now," he said. "It ain't slowed her down none. She'll fuck at the drop of a hat."

Benny shot a look to Wanda. "Hell, I wish I'd worn my hat."

Benny retrieved the cue ball under the next table. "What does Jerry have to say about all this?"

"I don't reckon he knows," Wesley answered.

"Well, shit," Benny replied. "You're his friend. Why don't you tell him?"

Wesley shrugged. He took sight of the cue ball over the rim of the table. He said, "Hell, it ain't none of my goddamn business."

——————— BOOK THREE

no good deed
goes unpunished

1

Sunday was God's day, and being God's day, it was also Evelyn Sewell's day.

On Sunday, Evelyn was a warrior in the Lord's army, and her specific task was as difficult as Moses' run-ins with Pharoah. Maybe more difficult. All Moses had to do was ride herd on a few hundred thousand Israelites; Evelyn had to get Clifford and Becky and Jimmie Clifford out of bed, fed, scrubbed, dressed, and in the car on time for church services at Big Sandy Pentecostal, First Covenant Assembly of God.

A normal person leading a normal life would have surrendered to the opposition without a fight. Evelyn was not a normal person on Sunday morning.

"Jimmie Clifford, I want you to wear socks this mornin'," Evelyn shouted from the living room. She was standing at the folded-out ironing board, pressing a pair of gray pants for Clifford. Becky was sitting on the sofa, polishing her toenails. She cringed at her mother's voice.

"Mama, do you have to be so loud?" Becky said.

"Don't take that tone with me," Evelyn snapped. "Around here, I do. Now you get busy, or we'll be late."

"Evelyn, will you just shut the hell up?" Clifford said, walking into the living room. He was wearing boxer shorts and white socks, and a faded white shirt with a tie dangling from it.

"Sometimes I think that's what I got to do to get anybody movin' around here," Evelyn mumbled. She turned her head toward Becky. "I mean it, young lady. You get busy. Clear them breakfast dishes and finish getting dressed." She turned her face to Clifford. "And you," she commanded, "you tie your tie."

"Evelyn, how 'm I supposed to tie my damn tie without my pants on?" Clifford said in exasperation.

Evelyn stared at her husband in disbelief. "Good grief," she sighed.

"You ever try to tie a tie without your pants on?" demanded Clifford. "No, you didn't. Cause you can't do it."

Becky laughed cynically and rolled from the sofa. "I love this family," she said. "I love it." She strolled past her father into the hallway, to the bathroom. The door was closed. She pounded on it with her opened palm. "Jimmie Clifford, get out of the bathroom," she shouted. Then, back toward the living room: "Mama, I can't get Jimmie Clifford out of the bathroom."

"Jimmie Clifford, hurry up," Evelyn called.

The bathroom door opened and Jimmie stepped out, wearing only boxer shorts.

"I don't think it's ready for round two yet," warned Jimmie. He paused, watched Becky step inside, then he called to his mother, "Mama, I don't feel like goin' to church this mornin'. I'm sick."

"You're going," Evelyn replied from the living room.

The bathroom door opened quickly and Becky stepped out, gagging.

"I warned you," Jimmie said, laughing.

"I'd listen to him if I was you, Mama," Becky cried. "He's definitely sick. Somethin' crawled up his butt and died."

"Becky, I don't want to hear that kinda talk! Jimmie Clifford, get ready!" The sound of Evelyn's voice was like the bellow of a madwoman. "Cut it out! Right now!"

In the living room, Clifford slipped his legs into his pants. He could still feel the heat of the iron in the cloth. "Evelyn," he said, "will you shut up?"

Evelyn did not shut up. She shouted and threatened and overwhelmed her family. In fifteen minutes, they were dressed and in the car, solemnly riding toward Big Sandy Pentecostal, First Covenant Assembly of God.

"I think all of this is just damn dumb," grumbled Clifford.

"What, Clifford?" Evelyn countered. "It's dumb that I want our family to go to church? That I want to try and raise these kids right? Is that dumb to you?"

Clifford shook his head and sniffed. He said, deliberately, "Goin' to church is the problem, Evelyn. Ever' Sunday we get up late. Rush around to eat. You run around actin' like a damn drill sergeant. Before we get out of the house, we're fightin' and fussin' and at each other's throats. We'd be a hell of a lot better off if we'd just stayed in bed and got some peace and quiet."

"Yeah, that's what I think," Jimmie mumbled.

"I think Daddy's right. Definitely," agreed Becky.

Evelyn lifted her head and looked out of the car window. A sadness churned in her. Her family did not understand about the Lord and the Lord's day. But she did. She lifted her eyes skyward. In the clouds, she could make out the image of the Last Supper. God was sending her a message about suffering, she thought. She closed her eyes.

Inside the church, the small congregation sang lustily: *"There is power, power, wonder-working power, in the blood of the lamb . . ."*

Evelyn could feel her throat quivering with the joy of the song and the words. It did not matter that Clifford and Jimmie stood silent beside her. The power of the blood had invaded her, making her body tingle with gladness, with hope, with certainty. The power of the blood was greater than all the power in the universe, and it was in Evelyn, pumping like a great, roaring engine. Power in the blood of the lamb. Yes. Evelyn's eyes filled with happy, God-filled tears.

When the song was over, they sat. Clifford stared at his wife and shook his head. The only time he had ever seen her as spirited was the first year of their marriage, when they had made love three times a day.

Brother John Ruffin, the minister of Big Sandy Pentecostal, First Covenant Assembly of God, moved to the pulpit. He was tall and heavy. His hair was slicked back with hair oil that gave him the appearance of having a glued-on halo. He smiled. A row of perfectly even, perfectly white teeth flashed to his congregation.

"Amen!" Brother Ruffin bellowed.

"Amen!"

"Now, before we're dismissed, just a few words," Brother Ruffin said in a glad, loud voice. "First, I'd like to welcome Sister Louise Burnette back with us. Louise, as many of you know, has been in Baptist Hospital in Memphis for the past few weeks receiving radiation treatment for her stomach cancer. She asks that we remember her in our prayers, along with the other sick and shut-ins in our membership.

Brother Ruffin leaned dramatically over the pulpit. "And lastly," he said, "let us remember our Big Sandy Wildcats football team this week, as they try to end their season with a perfect ten and zero record this comin' Friday night against the Henry County Patriots. May the Lord bless our boys. Go out there and win one for the Lord and for Big Sandy. Amen!"

"Amen!"

Evelyn smiled a proud smile, then turned to her son Jimmie, who was nodding in sleep.

2

Wesley had stalked the moment as carefully as he would have stalked a deer. To Wesley, there was a curious similarity to hunting deer and hunting women. It was a matter of knowing habits, of practicing patience, of being at the right place at the right time.

Wesley did not know why Nancy Calloway intrigued him, as young as she was, but she did. He had thought of her on Saturday night, had dreamed of her, and when he awoke on Sunday morning, he had had an urge to see her. Seeing her would be easy, he reasoned. And it was. Wesley was at the right place—kneeling beside the front wheel of his mother's jacked-up car—when Verdale and Nancy drove into the small yard of their trailer. They had been grocery shopping, as they did every Sunday morning at Piggly Wiggly. Wesley took one last pull from his cigarette and flipped it aside. Then he stood and ambled over to Verdale's car.

"Why don't'chu let me give you a hand with that?" Wesley said easily.

"Thank you, Wesley," Verdale replied. "Ever' hand counts. How's your mama and 'nem?"

"Fine," Wesley said. He lifted two bags of groceries from the trunk of the car and turned to Nancy. "You sure look pretty today, Nancy. I mean, your hair and ever'thing."

Nancy glanced at him, but did not speak or smile. She reached for a bag.

"So, what you been doin', Wesley?" asked Verdale.

"Nothin'," Wesley answered. "Puttin' some brakes on Mama's old car. Workin' all the time. You know how it is."

"Workin' hard or hardly workin'?" Verdale laughed. She walked into the trailer, followed by Nancy and Wesley.

"Just set them things anywhere, Wesley," Verdale said inside the trailer.

Wesley put the bags on the kitchen table.

"Be back in a little while," Nancy muttered. She opened the door.

"Where you goin'?" Verdale asked.

"Becky's."

"Nancy, I told you I needed you to give me a permanent this afternoon," protested Verdale.

Nancy sighed and leaned against the door jamb.

"Why you reckon they call it a permanent?" Wesley asked.

Nancy turned to stare at Wesley.

He stepped toward the door and stopped. "I mean, if it was permanent, you wouldn't have to get it done but once, would you? It oughta be called a temporary or—somethin' like that."

Verdale's face pinched into a quesion mark. She looked at Nancy. Nancy shook her head and laughed in disbelief.

"What?" Wesley asked.

3

J oe Burnette was sitting in his easy chair, reading the Sunday newspaper. The chair was old, and threadbare at the headrest and arms, but it was comfortable, the way it took his body and held it. The chair had been a Christmas present from Louise, purchased from the eight hundred dollar inheritance she had received at the death of her father. Louise had always called the inheritance "the little extra," and even after it had long been spent, she would speak wishfully of buying something with "that little extra," if she just had some of it left.

It was twelve-thirty. Across the room, in the dining area of the living-dining room, Donna Burnette, wearing a skin tight spandex jumpsuit, was arranging place settings at the table. Her two children, Rachel and Carter, were circling around the table, squealing happily and ducking swipes from each other in a game that only they understood.

"Rachel, Carter, y'all settle down now," Donna warned. "Y'all make me drop some of these dishes and I'm gonna wear you out."

Joe looked up from his newspaper. He liked the sound of children, the way their voices filled the house. He remembered the sounds of his own children, of Ray and Jerry and their friends. When they had moved away, the house had been eerily silent and lonely.

The two children danced toward him, laughing.

"And leave your Papa Joe alone," warned Donna. "Let him read his paper in peace."

"Aw, they all right, Donna," Joe said pleasantly. "They just playin'."

"They're just about to drive me out of my mind," complained Donna. "Lord, I don't know where they get all that energy."

"It's called bein' young," Joe said. "It's all they need."

"I guess," Donna replied. She looked through the living room window. "Car just pulled up," she added. "Must be them."

Joe leaned forward in his chair and looked through the window. He pushed himself up and stood. "Yeah," he said. "It is." He moved to the front door and opened it and watched Jerry and

Wanda removing covered food dishes from the back seat of the car. "Y'all need any help?" he called.

"Naw, Daddy, we got it," Jerry answered from the driveway.

Joe held open the door as Wanda and Jerry entered.

"Y'all come on in here," Joe said. "I sure am glad to see you, Wanda. I don't know when I seen you last."

"It ain't been that long," Wanda said. She wrapped an arm around Joe and hugged him.

Joe followed Jerry and Wanda into the kitchen. Donna was pouring tea into glasses of ice, while Louise sliced the cornbread into wedges.

"Hello," Donna said, faking a smile.

"Hi," Wanda replied. She smiled at Louise. "How are you, Mama Louise?"

"Oh 'bout the same, Wanda," Louise said. She looked curiously at Wanda. "You lost some weight, ain't 'chu?" she asked.

Wanda nodded. "A little," she said. "I needed it."

"Why don't y'all let me have them coats?" Joe said.

Jerry pulled off his coat and handed it to his father, then stepped to his mother and hugged her. "How's my gal?"

Louise blushed happily. "Now, you stop that," she sputtered. "Y'all go on in and sit down. Dinner's just about ready to be set on the table. Donna, set another plate out there for Wanda."

Donna glanced at Wanda. The smile fluttered and failed.

"This'll be the first time in I don't know long we've had the whole family together," Louise said. "It just seems like—oh, I don't know. It's been a long time."

"Come on, let's get out of their way," Joe said. "Give me your coat, Wanda."

Jerry and Wanda followed Joe from the kitchen back into the living room. Joe disapeared into the front bedroom and tossed the coats on the bed, then returned.

"Gettin' cold out," Joe said. "Y'all sit down, but watch out there. Them kids is always leavin' things in chairs."

"That's all right, Daddy," Jerry said. He turned to Wanda. She was staring at the mantel shelf above the fireplace. "Wanda?" he said.

Wanda did not reply, and her eyes did not move from the mantel shelf.

On the shelf were two family portraits—Ray and Donna and their children, and Jerry and Wanda and their dead son, Clayton.

"Oh, shit," whispered Jerry.

"What is it?" Louise asked. She was standing at the dining room table.

"Mama—" Jerry began.

Joe stepped over to the mantel shelf. He lifted the picture and held it.

"Oh," Louise muttered sadly. "I'm sorry. I forgot all about that. I'm sorry. Here, Joe, let me have that." She crossed to Joe, took the picture, and walked away toward the back bedrooms.

"It's—it's all right, Mama," Jerry called after her. "Don't worry about it."

Louise returned immediately.

"I've just had so much on me here lately," she said.

"Louise, it's all right," Joe said softly.

"Wanda's been doin' a lot better about it lately," Jerry said. He embraced Wanda gently. "Ain't that right, baby?"

Wanda nodded. Her eyes turned back to the empty spot on the mantel shelf.

The rushing water of a toilet echoed from the back of the house. "Mama, you ain't got no more toilet paper in the back bathroom."

"All right," Louise called. "Come to the table."

Footsteps clacked down the hallway from the bedrooms, and Ray entered. He was dressed in gray slacks and a blue pullover shirt with a rolled turtleneck. His hair glistened from hair cream. He stopped when he saw Jerry.

"Jerry!" Ray exclaimed gladly. "How's it goin', hoss?"

Wanda pulled instinctively from Jerry.

"Ray," Jerry said. He extended his hand and Ray crossed quickly and took it, squeezing vigorously.

Ray turned to Wanda. "Wanda," he said. "How you doing?" He stepped to her and they embraced, politely, awkwardly.

Wanda nodded. She did not speak.

A pause, heavy and awkward, filled the room.

"Come on in here and sit down, dinner's on the table," Joe said.

"Let's eat before ever'thing gets cold," Louise added.

"Sure," Ray said. His eyes held on Wanda.

It was, as Joe knew it would be, a meal eaten under an umbrella of tension, of strained civility. His sons could not be more different. Jerry was steady and reliable; Ray was a fast-talkin' dreamer with the soul of a con artist. They were not alike, but they were his sons. He wanted only to survive the meal in peace. He wanted Louise to believe that her sons had mended their life-long feud.

The talk at the table was of Big Sandy Auto Accessories.

"Well, I'll tell you this much—I'd rather make six dollars an hour with a job than ten an hour without one," Jerry reasoned.

"If Moss lets a union in that plant, he's got six more that's gonna want the same thing," Joe added. "He's gonna make an example out of us. You watch and see."

Jerry nodded in agreement as he scooped another helping of black-eyed peas onto his plate. He glanced at Wanda. Her eyes wandered from Ray to her plate, then back to Ray. Ray was watching her. Ray's eyes jerked back to his food when he noticed Jerry looking at him. "Ever'time I come home y'all are talkin' about the same thing," Ray said. "I don't know why y'all don't just quit that place and find somewhere else to work."

Jerry's face flushed red. "What do you know about workin', Ray? You ain't never worked."

Ray smiled. It was an old argument. "There's two kinds of workers, Hoss. Them that work for somebody else, and them that work for themselves."

Rachel and Carter swirled about the table, laughing the giddy laughter of children.

"Hey, y'all settle down," Ray said harshly. He turned his face back to Jerry. "You ain't never gonna get ahead workin' for the man. Franchise is where it's at."

"Franchise?" Jerry questioned with a smirk in his voice.

Ray nodded. "You know. Like Dairy Queen, Jiffy Lube, One Hour Martinizing. That sort of thing. You buy into the company and they supply you with ever'thing, but you're the boss. What you say, goes."

Carter ducked a grab from Rachel and curled himself into Wanda's lap. She caught him and pulled him close to her and held him. Jerry watched her sadly.

"We know what a franchise is, Ray," Jerry said evenly.

"Well, I come across a deal of the century. Doughnuts. You can get in for practically nothing," Ray announced. "Make a killin' on it." He looked across the table to Wanda. "Carter, get down off her and hush. Donna, get him down."

Donna looked at Wanda with a puzzled expression. Wanda shook her head slightly. She held on to Carter.

"Like I was tellin' you, Daddy, my partner—Frank—knows this guy up in Detroit—"

"Doughnuts?" Jerry said.

"Yeah, doughnuts," Ray replied. "You havin' trouble hearin'?"

"No, I can hear fine," Jerry said. "I'm havin' trouble believin' what I'm hearin'. You don't know the first thing about doughnuts, except how to eat 'em."

Rachel shoved her hand through Wanda's arm and jabbed at Carter. He cried in a giggle. Ray turned to Donna and glared at her, then turned back to Jerry.

"I told you, *they* get you up and runnin'. They do the trainin', ever'thing," Ray said irritably. He slapped the table with his hand. "Hey," he snapped. He pushed from the table and caught Rachel as she ran past him, then moved to Wanda and pulled Carter from her grasp. "I said to leave Wanda alone and quiet down, and I meant it. Y'all are gonna go to the bedroom 'til you can learn to mind."

"They ain't hurtin' nothin', Ray," Joe said softly.

"Here, let 'em sit in my lap," Louise begged.

Ray released Rachel and Carter and watched as they sprinted to the protection of their grandmother. He sat again at the table.

"Gotta teach 'em," Ray mumbled. "When you tell 'em to do somethin', they better do it. It'll just get worse when they get older."

Jerry smiled and shook his head. Words—"look who's talking"—filled his mouth, but he did not say them.

"They weren't botherin' me, Ray," Wanda said. "They were just playin'."

"Look, Wanda, if you had kids, you'd understand what I'm talkin' about," Ray replied authoritatively.

There was a pause, a chilled stillness.

"I did, Ray," Wanda said quietly. "I know what you're talkin' about." She stood and walked away from the table, through the kitchen door to the outside.

"I didn't mean that," Ray mumbled. "Wanda—"

Jerry glared at his brother. He stood and followed Wanda outside.

"I didn't mean anythin' by it," Ray said to the others. "Nothin'."

"Ever since we lost little Clayton, she's been like this," Louise whispered. "You can't mention his name that she don't go all to pieces."

Ray sipped from his tea. He shook his head. "She always was strange."

"When she got out of the hospital, she went and threw ever'thing out of his little room, bless his heart," Louise said. "You can't so much as mention his little name around her that she don't go all to pieces."

"I can't believe Jerry puts up with that," Ray added.

"Y'all go ahead and eat," Joe said firmly. The tone of his voice was a message: quit talkin' about it.

"If I hadn't left that picture out," Louise sighed.

"Louise," Joe said.

"All right," Louise replied.

The kitchen door opened again, and Wanda returned to the dining room.

"I'm sorry," Wanda said. She leaned and kissed Louise on the cheek.

"You're not leavin', are you?" asked Louise.

"I need to get on home," she said. "I got some things I need to do. Thank you for dinner. It was real good."

"Honey, you hardly touched your plate," Louise protested. "Sit down here and finish eatin'."

"I better go home," Wanda said. "I've got to go by the nursing home and see Aunt Rena this afternoon." She looked once at Ray, then turned, walked into the bedroom, grabbed her coat from the pile on the bed, and left through the front door.

"If I just hadn't forgot to take that picture down," Louise whispered again.

"Mama, that ain't the problem here," Ray advised. "And you know it."

Jerry did not return to the table. He stood on the back porch and smoked. What had happened did not surprise him. He knew Ray. Ray's presence was like a dark, dangerous cloud.

The door opened and Ray stepped outside. He tapped a cigarette from a package and lit it.

"Sorry about that thing with Wanda in there," Ray said casually. "I wadn't thinkin'."

"She'll be all right," Jerry told him.

"She always was touchy. Go off at the least little thing," Ray added.

"She's all right, Ray. You don't worry about it."

Ray nodded and laughed easily. "Okay, you're right, she's your problem now." Ray motioned with his head to two junk cars that Joe had hauled to the backyard. "Still got them old pieces of junk," he said. "I asked him the other day if he was still thinkin' about fixin' 'em up."

"You know he's too old to do that," Jerry said.

"Yeah," Ray replied. "You remember when we ran that old Buick into that woman's house? Mama and Daddy like to have killed me for havin' you in the car with me."

"How long you gonna be here, Ray?" Jerry asked in a blunt voice.

Ray looked at Jerry. He drew slowly from his cigarette. He

said, "'Til I can get back on my feet. I'm workin' on this deal up in Detroit—"

"I know," Jerry said. "I heard. A week? Two?"

"I don't know, Jerry. What difference does it make to you how long I stay?"

"You hittin' Daddy up for money again?" Jerry asked.

Ray laughed cynically. "You know what your problem is, Jerry? You're jealous. You never had the guts to do anythin' big. You're a follower. Even when we was little, you'd tag along on my damn coattail. The second somethin' happened, you'd come runnin' home to Mama. Hell, you even married my ex-wife. You're gonna wind up just like Daddy. Spend your whole life workin' in a damn factory, livin' hand-to-mouth, gettin' old young. I'm not. I'm independent, and that just about kills you."

Jerry flipped his cigarette over the porch railing into the grass. He looked away for a long moment, then he said, "It don't kill me, Ray. You don't wanna work for a livin', that's your business. But if runnin' home, spongin' off Mama and Daddy ever'-time you go broke is what you call bein' independent, then you're right—I don't wanna be independent." He glanced up at Ray. "But I can tell you this, I don't want you upsettin' Mama, either. She's sick, and she don't need it."

Ray turned to open the door. He looked back angrily at Jerry. "You don't worry about it, Jerry," he hissed. "She was my mama before she was yours—asshole." He opened the door and stalked back into the house.

4

Of all her classes at Big Sandy High, Becky loved art more than any of the others. She had always loved art. She was relaxed with a drawing pencil or a brush in her hand. The lines and strokes of the pencils and brushes grew into images that often surprised Becky. It was as though her hand, her fingers, were persuaded by something she did not understand, something more complicated and accomplished than her life or her experiences. In art class, Becky was someone special, someone that other students admired and respected. Being special was too rare to dismiss.

The assignment had been simple: paint anything, any scene; imagine it, then paint it.

Arthur Hunt was the art instructor. Art for art, the students teased. He was an easy, gentle man, well-liked by his students.

"Nancy, what are you painting?" Art Hunt asked, standing beside Nancy's easel.

"The funeral home," Nancy answered almost defensively. She threw a languid look at him. "You said we could paint anythin' we wanted to."

"Yep, I did," Art Hunt replied. "Interesting." He took a deep breath and blew it out as he moved through the maze of easels to where Becky worked. The scene Becky painted was of a football game.

"Is that Jimmie Clifford?" Art Hunt asked.

Becky smiled and nodded. "Uh-huh."

"That's very good work, Becky. Excellent."

Becky blushed. She knew that other students near her had stopped their work to listen and to watch.

"You really should give some thought to a career in illustration," Art Hunt said.

"Really?" Becky replied. "I think I'd like to do that."

Behind her, Susan Taylor, the head cheerleader, stepped away from her own easel to study Becky's painting.

"I have some literature on several good art schools," Art Hunt continued. "Stop by my office after class and I'll get it for you."

"Thanks," Becky said quietly.

Art Hunt nodded and strolled away, watching other students work.

"Gosh, that's really good, Becky," Susan said. "I wish I could paint like that."

"Thanks," Becky said. "You could. I mean, with practice you could. Let me see what you're doing."

Becky stepped away from her own easel and moved to Susan's. The canvas was covered in paint smears.

"It's—it's good," Becky said hesitantly. "It's—it's very, ah—very—"

Becky looked at Susan. A smile was building in Susan's face, and the two began to laugh.

"What is it?" Becky asked.

"It's supposed to be a self-portrait," Susan told her.

"I'm sorry," Becky laughed, "I thought it was a bowl of fruit."

They laughed harder, in rolling, silly giggles.

Nancy passed the easel. She said, "I thought it was a pig."

Susan's face snapped up. Her laughter stopped, her smile faded. She opened her mouth to speak to Nancy, but she did not. She turned instead to Becky.

"What do you have sixth period?" she asked.

"Mrs. Lowry. English Lit," Becky answered.

"Oh," Susan said brightly. "If I can get you a pass, will you help us do the signs for the game? It's just the Pep Club and your brother plays ball and ever'thing, and you're really good." Her voice was high-pitched, rapid, excited.

Becky fought the smile of pleasure. She looked at Nancy. Nancy rolled her eyes and looked away.

"Sure," Becky said. "Yeah, that'd be great."

"Okay," Susan told her. "I'll get you outta Lowry's class. It'll be fun."

Becky smiled. She looked again at Susan's painting and swallowed a short giggle. Then she moved back to her own easel, where Nancy was standing pretending not to be listening.

"You've got a test in Old Lady Lowry's class sixth period, Miss Popularity. You know that?" Nancy whispered.

"I can make it up," Becky said. She glanced at Nancy's painting. "The funeral home?"

"I like it all right," Nancy said huffily. "I think it's pretty."

5

Clifford knew the call to Richard Moss's office would come at an unexpected moment. There would be nothing formal about it. No memorandums, no prearranged time for an appointment. It would be a tap on the shoulder, a wag of the head. Clifford did not care. He had worked for years waiting for the call that would change his life.

He heard Richard Moss' voice over the hard clattering of the radial front press: "Clifford!" He turned to see Richard Moss nod his head in a follow-me motion. He nodded and followed. His co-workers glanced at him knowingly as he passed them. Wesley winked and jerked a thumbs-up signal in the air, like an eager hitchhiker.

Clifford stood obediently just inside the doorway of Richard's office.

"Have a seat," Richard said, as he settled behind his desk.

"Thanks," Clifford mumbled. He sat in a straight-back chair. Richard picked up a folder from his desk and thumbed through it. He said, "You've been working here a long time now."

"Since your daddy took over from your granddaddy," Clifford said. "I was about the fifth man your daddy hired when he started runnin' things.

Richard pinched the bridge of his nose with his fingers. He nodded thoughtfuly. "You've done a damn good job for us," he told Clifford. "Ain't nobody can run that radial front press like you can."

"Well, I appreciate that, Mr. Moss," Clifford said. "I been doin' it long enough to know how it works."

"Richard," Richard Moss said. "Call me Richard."

Clifford could feel a flush of pride. He nodded.

"If I had ten more people like you, Clifford, we'd make production every week," Richard said. "I mean that."

Clifford swallowed. He could feel his heart racing. He bit back a smile of pleasure. He said, "Well, ah, Richard, I've enjoyed workin' here, and I'll tell you one thing, I'm gonna do an even better job as shift foreman. You can count on that."

"Uh-huh," Richard mumbled, nodding. He stared at Clifford. "That's what I wanted to talk to you about," he said evenly. "There's a little problem that's come up."

6

When she pushed open the door to the gymnasium, Becky believed that she was about to step into a new and different world. And it was. At the far end of the gym, she could see the cheerleaders for Big Sandy High frolicking like small children around long rolls of paper that had been stretched across the floor. One strip, standing against the wall, was the goalpost banner. On it, crudely painted, were the words: "Claw 'em, Wildcats!" The face of a wildcat was in one corner. It did not look like a wildcat. It looked like the smashed face of a flower. Becky wondered if Susan had painted it.

She crossed the gym slowly, trying to be casual, but feeling the trembling of uncertainty.

"Hi," called Susan as Becky approached the cheerleaders. Then, to the others, "Y'all know Becky Sewell."

There were a few hellos. Becky smiled acknowledgement. Most of the girls had not spoken to her since elementary school.

"I asked Becky to give us some help with the posters and stuff," Susan said lightly. "You should see her paint. She's fabulous."

"Isn't Jimmie Clifford your brother?" asked one of the girls.

"Yeah," Becky answered. She added, "Unfortunately."

"Really?" another cheerleader said. "I think he's cute. Is he datin' anybody?"

Becky smiled. She said, "We're talkin' about my brother here. Right? Jimmie Clifford Sewell?"

"Yeah, he's a hunk," the girl replied.

"He's a hunk all right," Becky said. "A hunk of what I don't know, but he's definitely a hunk."

The girl wiggled a fake smile, then turned away. Becky could see two other girls rolling their eyes.

"Anyway," Susan said, "here's the plan." She moved to the sheets of unrolled paper and pointed to them. "We need to have these signs finished by fifth period tomorrow for the pep rally, and then these have to be finished by Friday to take to the game."

"Wow," Becky said, "that's a lot of work."

Susan smiled at her. "You can do it," she said. "I've got faith in you."

Becky's eyes widened in surprise. She watched as the girls began to gather their books.

"This is really great of you to help us out like this," one of the girls said.

"Sure is," another added.

"Now, here's a list of all the signs, and on the back here are some rough sketches of the posters and ever'thing," Susan said. She handed Becky the clipboard of instructions and reached for her books. "Oh," she added, "I've already done a lot of work on the Wildcat goal post sign, so if you wanna just finish that up."

"Where are you goin'?" asked Becky.

"To class," Susan said cheerfully. "I've got a test. Hey, thanks a lot. I'll see you tomorrow."

Susan turned and rushed away, followed by the rest of the cheerleaders of Big Sandy High. Their shrill, giggling voices filled the gymnasium.

Becky stood for a moment, watching, listening to the echo of the voices, then she turned a sheet on the clipboard and looked at it. She shrugged as she reached for a paintbrush.

7

Clifford sat at the bar of the Dew Drop Inn, staring at the can of beer that Janice had just placed before him. The cold sweat on the silver can made it glisten. Clifford reached with his finger and drew a line across it. In the background, Kenny Rogers was singing *The Gambler* from the jukebox. Jerry and Wesley were shooting pool at the table near the corner of the bar.

> *You got to know when to hold 'em*
> *Know when to fold 'em*
> *Know when to walk away*
> *Know when to run*

"I should've walked away from that damn plant years ago. Worked my ass off for that son of a bitch and this is the thanks I get," Clifford mumbled, listening to the song

"Get you some popcorn?" asked Janice.

Clifford shook his head. "Twenty-two gotdamn years and for what? So they could just kick dirt in my face," he said.

"Yeah, I hated to hear that, Clifford," Ed said. "You deserved that job."

"If we had a union, that kinda shit wouldn't 'a happened," Jack said. "Union wouldn't allow such as that."

Clifford lifted his head and looked at Jack.

"I can't believe they give Harvey Williams that promotion ahead of you, Clifford," said Ernestine in a rough, angry voice. "It ain't right, and I don't give a damn what they say."

"Shit, Harvey ain't been there but five damn years, either," added Jack. He sucked the last sip of liquid from his beer bottle and swallowed hard.

"He got that damn promotion 'cause of one thing, and one thing only. He's the right color," Clifford growled.

The sound of ball against ball cracked in the air over the pool table. "Got it," Jerry said enthusiastically. He leaned back from the table and moved close to Clifford at the bar. "I always thought Harvey was a pretty sharp 'ol boy," he said in jest.

"That sumbitch couldn't put three pieces of shit together to make a pile," Clifford snapped. He gulped from his beer.

"Union'll come in and straighten that kinda shit out, right quick," Ed said.

Jerry laughed. "You don't know but one song, do you, Ed?"

Ed turned away, shaking his head slowly.

"Hell, I'm not so sure Ed ain't right," Clifford said slowly.

"Harvey's got some college and that probably worked in his favor," Wesley said.

"Hell, Wesley, he went to Tennessee State. Damn nigger college," Clifford grumbled. "And our asses paid for it, I guaran-damn-tee you."

Jerry saw Janice's face turn quickly toward Clifford, then away again. He could see a quiver in her lips.

"Hey, Clifford, c'mon," Jerry said. He nodded toward Janice.

"Ah, hell, Janice knows I ain't talkin' about her," Clifford said. He looked at Janice. "Don't'chu? Hell, I wouldn't hurt her feelin's for the world."

Janice forced a small smile. She nodded, then turned and walked away.

"I can't believe they hired her in here," Ed said softly. "Gotta watch ever'thing you say anymore."

"That's something I ain't never been able to figure out," Jack said. "How they can have black colleges and black beauty pageants and black ever'thing else, and you try to have anything for the white people and they'll pitch a damn fit?"

"What do you care if they got a beauty pageant or not, Jack? Hell, you ain't even got a TV set," Jerry said.

Ed sat up on his stool and looked irritably at Jerry. He said, "What the hell's wrong with you, Jerry? Why you defendin' 'em with ever' word outta your mouth?"

Jerry chalked the end of his cue, watching the blue powder covering his fingertips, then turned to Ed. He could see Janice behind Ed's face. "I ain't defendin' nobody," he replied easily. "But I can tell you this Ed, people can't help what color they are when they come into this world."

"Naw, but they can damn sure help how they act once they get here," Jack retorted.

"God-o-mighty, Jack," Jerry said, "that's sharp. Yes, it is." He could feel his hand tighten on his cue stick.

"All I know is that some people shouldn't get promoted ahead of somebody else just because of what color they are," Ed complained. "That's all I'm sayin'."

Clifford nodded vigorously. "Exactly," he declared, lighting a cigarette. He blew the smoke over his beer can. "Twenty-five gotdamn years I work my butt to the bone, and for what? So they can kick dirt in my gotdamn face."

Jerry stepped toward the bar, toward Ed. "Harvey Williams didn't give himself that promotion," he said in a hard voice. "What's he supposed to do? Say, 'No thanks, I don't want that extra money. Give it to somebody that's white.' That what he supposed to do?"

There was a pause. The sound of Wesley's shot jumped from the pool table.

"Aw, forget it," Jerry mumbled.

"Goddamnit," grumbled Wesley, tossing three dollars on the pool table. "Why don't y'all go talk politics somewhere else? Can't shoot no pool with all this shit goin' on."

"You just don't like losin'," Jerry said.

"Rack 'em," Wesley snapped.

"Naw," Jerry replied in a drawl. "I think it's time I got out of here." He strolled to the bar and handed the money from the game with Wesley to Janice. "Give these boys and girls a bottle of that cheap wine, Janice," he said. "The stuff you supposed to cry in when you drink it."

"You leaving?" Janice said quietly, keeping her eyes away from his face.

"Yeah," Jerry said. He put his arm heavily on Clifford's shoulder. "I think I'm raining on ever'body's parade around here."

"Ah, shit, Jerry," Clifford muttered. "You know better'n that."

Jerry shrugged. He turned to go, then stopped. At the door, a huge woman filled the door frame like an eclipse of the sun. She was holding two small children in the crooks of her elbows. "Jesus," Jerry whispered. "It's Fat Ethel." His eyes swept the room. He saw Benny, Fat Ethel's husband, ducking under a table.

"I see you, Benny," Fat Ethel boomed.

Every voice in the Dew Drop Inn fell quiet. Every eye turned to Fat Ethel. The only sound was Dolly Parton's voice from the jukebox.

> *I I I will always love you u u u*
> *I I I will always love you . . .*

Fat Ethel stormed forward, toward the table where Benny was sitting low in his chair.

"I'm gonna run your sorry ass off," Fat Ethel screamed. "You got plenty of money for cigarettes and beer, but you can't buy these kids a pair of jeans when they almost naked, damn you."

Benny stood bravely. His face began to quiver in anger. "You can kiss my brown round," he hissed.

A chorus of laughter rolled across the Inn.

"I'm gon' kiss it with a two-by-four, you don't get out of here right this minute and help me take care of these young'uns," Fat Ethel roared.

Benny glared at Fat Ethel. Then he fingered three dollars from his pocket and slapped it on the table and rushed pass Fat Ethel through the front door. Fat Ethel turned to follow, yelling: "You better wait up for me. You leave me, I'll skin your head when I catch up to you."

The door to the Inn closed behind her. There was a pause from the onlookers, then a snicker that began in the back of the room and rolled into hard laughter by the time it hit the bar.

Jerry turned to Janice. "You open that wine yet?"

Janice shook her head. Her eyes flashed to Jerry's face. She could see anger and pride shining in his eyes. It was a look that made her want him. She swallowed hard and handed the money to him.

"Then let 'em buy their own drinks," Jerry said, forcing his voice to be cheerful. He pushed the money across the table to Ernestine. "Next time you see Fat Ethel, give that money to her. Tell her to buy them kids some clothes with it."

Ernestine nodded. She folded the ten-dollar bill and stuck it in her pocket.

"Aw, hell, tell her to buy 'em socks, too," Clifford mumbled. He tossed a five across the bar.

It was a gesture that commanded giving. Ernestine collected sixty-two dollars. She said to Janice, "You'd think these old hard-asses wouldn't be such soft touches, would you?"

"Y'all good to do this," Janice said softly. She glanced at Jerry, giving herself to him with her eyes—a promise—and then walked away.

"Hey, Ed, you reckon the union can do anything to help ol' Benny out?" asked Wesley in a teasing voice.

"Go on and make fun out of it," Ed said, "but anybody don't vote for the union don't care about what's best for them, or their families." He turned to Clifford. "You got two kids, Clifford. That shop foreman's job you just lost sure would've come in handy, wouldn't it? Hell, I feel for you, buddy." He waved to Janice. "Janice, give ol' Cliff here a shot of his favorite." He leaned closer to Clifford. "I'll tell you this much, if we vote that union in, I bet you wind up shop steward anyhow. You got seniority. Every'body likes you. Shit, I'd vote for you right now." He looked at the people surrounding him. "Wouldn't y'all vote ol' Clifford in as shop steward if the union comes in?" he asked in a loud voice.

"Hell, yeah," Wesley said. "In a New York minute."

"Yeah," someone else said enthusiastically.

Other voices agreed.

Clifford picked up the drink Janice placed before him. He sipped from it. His eyes were narrowed in thought. "Shop steward?" he said.

"Damn straight," Ed exclaimed.

Clifford nodded confidently. "Hell, yeah, I oughta be shop steward. Shit, I got seniority up to my ass and eyeballs."

"D straight," Ed said again. He could sense the tumbling of the wall of resistance in Clifford. "I guaran-damn-tee you, you got my vote." He pounded Clifford on the back. "Janice, hand me the whole bottle. Put it on my tab. Hell, this is worth drinkin' to."

Jerry laughed quietly. He slid onto a stool near the front door and lit a cigarette. Wesley took the stool next to him.

"We're watching history in the makin'," Wesley whispered.

"We're watching a man get his ass kissed in public," Jerry sighed quietly.

Wesley turned on his stool. Sheila Pascal came through the door with another woman and crossed the room to a table.

"Shit," Wesley said. He shook his head and nudged Jerry. "You talk about ass-kissing in public, gimme a chance and I'm gonna' be first in line."

Jerry glanced toward Sheila. "Yeah," he muttered. "Who's the girl with her?"

"Got me," Wesley said. "But she can put her pumps under my bed any time she wants to."

Ed's arm shoved between Jerry and Wesley. His hand held the bottle of bourbon.

"Here, boys, y'all want a touch of this?"

"Hell, why not?" Wesley said.

Ed poured two fingers in the glasses that Janice pushed across the bar.

"I just hate to see anybody get treated the way they treated Clifford," Ed said sadly.

"Like a damned dog." Jack said.

Ed poured more bourbon into Clifford's glass.

"Someday we gotta stand up and be counted," Jack said.

"Yeah, we do," Clifford agreed in a strong voice. "And right now's as good a time as any." He looked at Ed. "Hell, Ed, give me that petition. I'll sign that sumbitch. They think they can treat me like shit and get away with it, they got another thing comin'."

A radiant smile crossed Ed's face. He pulled a sheet of paper from his shirt and unfolded it and pushed it in front of Clifford.

"Right there it is," he said. "Put your John Henry on the dotted line." He handed Clifford a ball point pen and watched eagerly as Clifford pressed his signature into the paper.

"You got any more of these petitions?" asked Clifford.

"All you want."

"Good," Clifford said. "I'll get some people signed up and we'll get this damn union going."

A scattering of applause surrounded Clifford.

"Now you cooking with gas," enthused Jack.

"We on the road," said Ernestine.

Clifford smiled happily. The bourbon had flooded into his face and eyes. He bellowed, "Damn right. We'll teach them ungrateful bastards they better be careful who they fuck with." He raised his glass. "To the union!" he shouted.

The chorus answered: "To the union!"

8

Nancy stood in the middle of the surging students who spilled in a torrent from the front door of Big Sandy High School. She turned in circles, like a buoy anchored to swirling waters, her head bobbing up and down as she rose and fell on tiptoes.

She could not see Becky.

A boy wearing a Big Sandy letter jacket bumped her with his shoulder, then caught her as she began to fall away.

"Jesus, Nancy, you gon' get run over if you don't get out of the way," he said. "You all right?"

"Yeah," Nancy replied irritably. "Have you seen Jimmie Clifford Sewell's sister ."

"She was in the gym, painting signs," the boy told her.

"Oh?" Nancy said. "Still there?"

"Last time I saw her," the boy repeated. "See you." He hurried off.

Nancy glanced at her watch. In a few minutes the bus would be gone. She began to move against the torrent of bodies pushing against her.

When she shoved open the heavy doors leading into the gym, Nancy saw Becky kneeling over a long roll of paper, carefully edging the large, red letters of "Wildcats" in black paint.

"Hey, you'd better hurry or we're gonna miss the bus," Nancy called from the door.

Becky looked up, then back at the banner. She said, "You go ahead. I've still got a lot of work to do."

Nancy crossed the gym floor. "How much?" she asked.

"A lot. I'll call Mama to come get me."

Nancy looked at the banner. "That looks great," she said. "Best we've ever had." She looked around the empty gym. "Where's your new best friends?"

Becky blushed. She pulled the brush against the letter S. "They had to go—go do something," she answered quietly.

"Bitches," Nancy mumbled.

"Nancy—"

"Shut up, Becky," Nancy snapped. She dropped her books and picked up a brush. "I didn't expect to find them here."

"To tell you the truth, I'm kinda glad," Becky said. "They can't paint very good." She looked at the brush in Nancy's hand. "What're you doing?" she asked.

"What's it look like I'm doing?" Nancy said. "I'm gonna help you."

"No offense," Becky replied, "but you can't paint, either,"

Nancy laughed cynically. "No, I can't," she admitted. "But I'm here, and not off doing *something*. And I can stay in the lines, and in case you haven't noticed, you need help. Now, where do I start, or do you want me to guess?"

"No. Oh, Lord, no," Becky said. "Here, you can work on some of these. I've already got the outlines drawn on."

"I feel like I'm in kindergarten again," Nancy sighed. She took the can of paint that Becky offered. A smile—familiar, warm, good—passed between them.

9

The good feeling of putting his name on a petition calling for the right to vote for a union at the Big Sandy Auto Accessories plant had mixed with the bourbon Clifford had poured into himself in an act of celebration, and the good feeling had turned to anger and bitterness. He had been blind, he kept thinking as he drove to the Captain's Point Trailer Park. Blind and stupid. A gotdamn fool to believe his loyalty and his years of sevice would pay off. He had never liked Ed very much, but Ed had been right: Richard Moss was a taker, a spoiled son born to power and abuse. To hell with him, Clifford thought. Fuck him and the Cadillac he arrived in every morning. The union would make the son of a bitch squirm. The union would pucker his rich ass.

He pulled to an abrupt halt in front of his trailer and sat in his truck, staring at the trailer he had purchased in 1972. He had long quit thinking of building a home somewhere, but he had never thrown away the plans that he had clipped from a magazine after he returned from Vietnam. He had been a dreamer in those days. A trailer would be all right for a couple of years—just until he could get his feet on the ground and start them running in the right direction. But he wanted a house. Nothing big. Nothing fancy. Just a house. A nice one. Painted white. The picture of the house that he had clipped from the magazine had looked like a house made of cake frosting, it was so white.

Clifford opened the door to the truck and stepped out. He remembered the shoebox that he kept in the back of a closet with his tools. The plans for his cake-white house were in the box, and he could feel an urge—a flutter—to pull them out and look at them.

"Fuck'em," Clifford muttered. "Fuck Moss. Fuck all of 'em."

He stomped across the yard, opened the front door to his trailer and stepped inside. He stood, his eyes sweeping the room. It was cheap and cluttered. Across the room, the television was blinking in white flashes as a preacher in a hairdo that was swirled to look like a halo cried like a mourner about Jesus paying the price for the sins of all mankind. He shook his head, went to the kitchen, and took a beer from the refrigerator. He popped the ringed top and drank in a deep, long swallow. From down the hall-way, he heard the flushing of the toilet.

"Evelyn, you here?" Clifford called. "Evelyn!"

"Back here," Evelyn answered. He could hear her walking up the hall. "So, you finally decided to come home," she said as she entered the living room.

"You ever wonder what this place might look like if it was ever cleaned up?" Clifford replied bitterly.

"Don't start with me tonight, Clifford," Evelyn said. "I got cramps."

Clifford hacked a mean, short laugh. "What? Again? You're the only woman on this planet that's got cramps three hundred and sixty-five days a year," he said. "What are you? A field-tester for Kotex?"

Evelyn did not reply. She sighed painfully and slumped on the sofa.

"I oughta sell ever'thing we got and buy stock in Maxi Pads. I'd make a fucking fortune," Clifford growled. He put down his beer and picked up the mail from the kitchen counter. His fingers fumbled through the envelopes. Bills, bargains, sales, coupons ad-dressed to Occupant. A thank-you, God-bless-you-for-your-contribution note from a preacher in Memphis—addressed to Mrs. Clifford Sewell.

He threw the envelopes on the counter. "Where's the kids?" he asked.

"Out somewhere, Clifford. I don't know," Evelyn answered wearily.

"What's for supper?"

"Good grief, Clifford, I told you I didn't feel good," Evelyn said. "Can't you go pick up a bucket of chicken or something?"

Clifford sloshed the beer in the can and shook his head. "If I came home and this place was cleaned up and supper was on the table, I think I'd have a gotdamn stroke."

"Hush that talk. I don't want to hear it." Evelyn told him.

"You don't ever want to hear about nothing unless one of them damn preachers says it," Clifford snapped. He took a step toward the hall, then stopped. A package was on the coffee table, with the paper torn from it. He reached for it. "What's this?" he asked.

A wave of terror swept over Evelyn's face.

"What?" she asked.

"This!"

"It looks like a Bible, Clifford."

"I know it's a Bible, gotdamn it. Where'd it come from?"

"What do you mean?"

"I mean just exactly what I said," Clifford hissed. "Where'd you get it? Did you order it?"

"Yes, Clifford." Her voice was meek, resigned.

"What'd I tell you about ordering shit from that TV preacher? How much?"

"How much what?"

"Gotdamn it, you know what I mean," Clifford yelled. "How much did it cost? How much of my hard-earned money did you send that lying bastard this time?"

"Clifford, hush. It's for a good cause."

"Well, I'll tell you one gotdamn thing. It's going back."

"Would you stop taking the Lord's name in vain in this house?"

"I make the payments on this gotdamn trailer, and I'll say any gotdamn thing I want to in my own gotdamn house."

Evelyn sat quietly, watching her husband. She knew she could not stop his rage. It would have to blow over. She saw him tearing at the package, clawing through it, looking for the bill. She closed her eyes when he pulled it from the package.

"One hundred dollars!" Clifford exploded. "Gotdamnit! Are you out of your mind? Who the hell you think I am, Rockefeller?"

"Clifford, they needed the money—"

"So do we, gotdamnit!"

"—or they were gonna take the show off the air."

Clifford laughed in disbelief. He began to pace the room, waving his hands in the air like a man trying to keep his balance. "I tell you what," he said. "I'll take that sumbitch off the air my own self." He stopped his pacing and inhaled deeply. "If I catch you ordering another gotdamned thing—and I mean anything—I'll take and throw that TV out the window, and you damn well better believe I will."

Clifford was breathing in deep, hard, labored gulps. A silence as thick as heat filled the room. He could feel tears cupping in his eyes.

Evelyn said, very softly, "You didn't get the promotion, did you?"

10

If he could not hide from the truth, he could learn to bear it. For Clifford, bearing it in his own house—even if that house was a 14-by-60-foot trailer—before his own family was as close to comfort as he would get, short of death and the end of worry.

He had not answered Evelyn's question about the promotion. There was no need; she knew. She had stood, had moved to him, embraced him, and then she had gone into the kitchen and picked up her pocketbook, and without a word, she had walked out of the trailer.

She had returned forty minutes later, at the skimming darkness of night, with Jimmie and Becky and a huge bucket of Kentucky Fried Chicken, with apple turnovers for dessert.

"All right," Evelyn had said, "we are going to sit down right here and eat us the best chicken in America, bar none, and I don't care what all them other places claim. Besides, Colonel Sanders was the spitting image of my granddaddy, and my granddaddy could cook chicken that'd melt in your mouth."

"Mama, we got to hear that story again?" Jimmie had complained.

"No son, we don't," Evelyn had answered, "but we do have to thank God that we've been blessed with Colonel Sanders and with your granddaddy Pruitt. You got genes from one and chicken legs from the other."

They had laughed obligatorily and thanked God and were eating in silence from the grease-stained bucket when Becky spoke: "I'm sorry about the promotion, Daddy."

Clifford chewed on his chicken. He bobbed acknowledgement with his head. "Yeah," he muttered.

"I thought you were gonna get it," Jimmie said.

"No reason to talk about something we can't help, Jimmie Clifford," Evelyn suggested gently.

Clifford swallowed his chicken and drank from his tea. "I thought I was gonna get it too, but the government made 'em hire a nigger," he said.

Evelyn's face jerked up. She looked at Becky and Jimmie Clifford. She turned to Clifford. "Clifford, don't," she said in a tone of voice that her family rarely heard.

Clifford dropped his head, took another bite of chicken, then wiped his fingers on the Kentucky Fried Chicken napkin and pushed away from the table.

When she saw him beside the river, under an oak, Evelyn thought Clifford looked like an old man, used and tired and beaten by the odds of fortune. He was smoking, staring at the water rolling over the bed of the Tennessee River. She walked softly to him and stood close, but away. She knew there were moments he did not like being crowded.

"I'm sorry, honey," Evelyn said quietly. "It's just that things are gonna be different for the kids than they were for us. The world's changing."

Clifford dropped his cigarette and crushed it with the toe of his shoe. He said, "Yeah, I know. You're right. Ever'thing's changing." He paused, then continued. "Funny thing is, while ever'thing else is moving full speed ahead, we're slipping further and further behind."

Evelyn reached with her hand and touched his arm and squeezed it.

"We're doing fine, Cliff."

"Sure," Clifford said. "We're doing fine." A tired laugh caught in his throat. "When we got married, I was gonna build you a house out there on that property across from your mama and daddy's place. You remember that? Have us a garden. Plenty of room for the kids to play. You wanted a swing on the front porch so we could watch the boats go by. You remember?"

"I remember," Evelyn said. "But that don't matter now, Clifford. Now that Mama and Daddy's gone, I wouldn't want to live way out there, anyhow."

"And here we are, just twenty-two short years later, and we're still living in a house with wheels on it," Clifford said. He shook his head. "We're in a rut, Evelyn. I've done ever'thing I know to get out of it, and nothing seems to work. I don't know what else to do." He shook his head again and lifted his face and inhaled the clean night air. Then he began to walk down the bank of the river, away from the trailer park.

Evelyn wanted to speak to him, to follow him, but she knew he wanted to be alone. She stood, watching, aching for the hurt she knew her husband was feeling.

Across the Captain's Point Trailer Park, the voice of Elvis Presley flowed like a benediction of the evening from Verdale's opened window. A child cried. A dog barked. And on the river, in the woods, a mockingbird sang madly.

11

They had never talked about it, but Jerry had always been able to read the messages in Janice's eyes, and at the Dew Drop Inn, as she served him his last beer, her eyes had said, "I want to see you tonight."

It was an old message, often given but almost always ignored, though Jerry knew she would be waiting for him in the dark hayloft of the barn on the abandoned Harley Reed farm.

She never asked why he did not answer the begging of her eyes on those nights that she waited. She understood. She knew that she loved Jerry Burnette, but that Jerry Burnette could not afford to love her; he could only afford to be tender, and for his tenderness, she willingly gave him her body. It was, to Janice, an exchange of gifts worth giving, and having.

"I want to see you tonight," her eyes had said, and when he read the voice of her eyes—as soft as a whisper—Jerry had known immediately that he would go to her.

The mockingbird was near the barn. Its voice was like a happy drunk singing at the moon in remembered imitations of tunes heard from roadside jukeboxes. Jerry paused and listened and smiled. He knew that the mockingbird was giddy with life, that high on a limb in one of the giant oaks, it was flitting about in little dance steps, preening, thrusting its chest of feathers to the cloudless sky.

He stepped inside the barn. The smell of old wood and hay and the lingering ribbons of a crushed cigarette filled his senses. Jerry climbed the old plank ladder that led up into the loft.

"Janice?" Jerry said quietly.

He saw her step from the shadows near the open bay doors of the loft, saw her silhouette in the backlight of the full moon. She was nude. In silhouette, her hard, rising breasts moved evenly with her breathing.

"I'm glad you came," she said.

Jerry did not answer. He moved to her and held her. He could feel her sliding her body against him. A slow, teasing, motion. The motion of a languid dance. Her body was like a warm hand covering him, stroking him gently.

"I've missed you Jerry. It's been too long," she whispered.

She pulled her chest away from him and began to unbutton his shirt, letting the tips of her fingers play over his throat, his nipples, along the ribs. Then her hands slipped to his pants. She unbuckled his belt and thumbed open the buttons.

"Jesus," he mumbled. His hands rubbed her back. He lowered his face and nuzzled against her breasts. He could feel the nipple on his tongue.

His hand dropped to the curled dark hair covering her pubic mound. He could feel the moisture seeping from her.

"Yes," she said. "God, Jerry, yes. I want you."

He scooped her into his arms and carried her to the blanket that he knew was unfolded across the hay and placed her gently on the blanket.

"Kiss me," she begged.

He kissed her.

"Take me," she said.

He took her.

12

"Mama?"

"What?"

"Becky just called. She said she wanted to come over."

"So, let her come."

"Do me a favor? Just don't drink while she's here. All right?"

Verdale waved her hand in the air, flicking ashes from her cigarette. She watched as Nancy picked up the empty glass on the coffee table in front of the sofa and carried it into the kitchen. "You'd think she was the queen of England or something," Verdale said.

Nancy returned with a clean ashtray and put it on the arm of the sofa. She glanced at the television. Verdale was watching *Wheel of Fortune*.

"She's my best friend, Mama," Nancy said. "She wanted to come over."

"What for? She don't never come over here," Verdale replied.

"That's 'cause I'm almost always over there," Nancy told her.

"Well, don't y'all go messing up back there," Verdale warned. "I'm tired of picking up after you."

"We're just gonna talk, Mama," Nancy said. She wanted to laugh. Her mother had not spent ten minutes cleaning the trailer in five years. On television, Vanna White turned two side-by-side T's in the category of Thing.

"Shutter," Verdale screamed. "Damn, that's easy."

"So, what's wrong?" Nancy asked. "Susan call and tell you she wants you to do a mural on her bedroom wall?"

"Don't start that, Nancy," Becky said. "I was just helping 'em out."

"Yeah, sure," Nancy muttered.

They were in Nancy's bedroom, with the door closed against the sound of clattering from the spinning wheel on television. Both were stretched across the bed.

"All right. So what's the problem?" Nancy asked.

"It's no problem or anything, really," Becky told her. "I just needed to get out of the house for a while. It's a nightmare over there."

"And you came over here?" Nancy said. "God, somebody must've died."

Becky smiled. "Not that bad, but nearly." she answered. "Daddy was supposed to get a promotion at the plant, and somebody else got it, and he's totally bummed out about it, and he thinks everybody else is supposed to feel as bad as he does. Mama's making us walk around like we're in the library or something."

"Oh," Nancy said. She sounded disappointed.

"You don't know what it's like when Daddy gets mad," Becky explained.

"No, I don't guess I do," Nancy replied. She glanced at her dresser, at the only picture she had of her own father.

"Ah—that was the wrong thing to say, Nancy. I'm sorry," Becky told her.

Nancy rolled on the bed and sat up. "Forget it," she said, lightly. "Hey, if I show you something, will you promise not to laugh or tell anybody?"

"Sure."

"It's a secret. Promise?"

"Nancy, I'm your best friend. With best friends it's automatically understood that you don't tell secrets on each other. What is it?"

Nancy stood and turned her back and slipped out of her jeans. "I don't think I want to know a secret you have to pull off your pants to show me," Becky said.

Nancy turned back and pointed to the inside of her thigh just below her panty line.

"What is it?" Becky asked. She gazed at an oblong splotch discoloring Nancy's thigh.

"What'd you mean, what is it?" Nancy said. "It's a tattoo. What do you think it is?"

Becky rolled off the bed for a closer look at the tattoo. "Oh—what's it supposed to be?"

Nancy lifted her leg. "You kidding? It's a football. See what it says: 'Go Wildcats.'" She pointed. "And there it says 'Bobby.' And that's his number: 69."

Becky snickered. She looked up at Nancy. "What did Bobby say about it?"

Nancy dropped her leg and stepped back into her her jeans. "He loved it," she said. "But it was sore and had this gross scab on it for a long time, and I wouldn't do it until it healed up and that pissed him off."

"He's so understanding," Becky said cynically.

"Swear to God you won't tell," Nancy urged. "If Mama finds out, I'll be grounded for life."

"It's gonna be a little hard to hide next summer with a bikini on, don't you think?" Becky said.

"I'll think of something by then," Nancy assured her. She flopped on the bed beside Becky.

Then after a moment, "Does it hurt much?" Becky asked.

"Naw, not any more."

"Not the tattoo," Becky said. "You know, I mean . . . doing it?"

Nancy giggled. She pulled the pillow under her shoulder and leaned on her elbow and looked at Becky. "The first time," she said quietly. "I told you that. But then after that, it's not bad. It's fun. You'll see. I mean, you're not planning on being a virgin forever, are you? Jesus, Becky, you're nearly seventeen years old."

Becky rolled her head to look at the ceiling. After a long pause she said, "Yeah, that's true."

13

Richard Moss had always been aware of the slight, almost imperceptible vibration—a vibration that hummed more than moved—in his office. Even as a child, visiting his father, he knew it was there. As a child, he had believed it was a special soothing voice, one that numbed him into pleasant, peaceful thoughts. He had never said it, but the magic of his father's office had more to do with his decision to work for, and become president of, Big Sandy Auto Accessories than anything.

Richard understood that the vibration, and the magic, were nothing but the constant, unheard droning of the plant's machinery, and yet it was still comforting, especially when his father rose up from retirement and stormed back to the plant bellowing demands.

His father was back, seated behind the desk that Richard had inherited, but always relinquished as the obedient child.

"This, by God, better be stopped before it gets out of hand!" Gerald Moss roared. "I'll be goddamned if the union will ever set foot in here, and by God, I mean it."

Richard stood at the window, looking out over the plant. He could see trucks moving to and from the loading docks, and on the docks he could see the workers of Big Sandy Auto Accessories laboring to meet the day's projected schedule. Even from this distance he recognized Joe Burnette and made a mental note to transfer Joe to a less demanding job. Joe was too old for such work, he thought.

"Do you understand me, Richard?" his father snapped.

"Yes sir," Richard said, turning away from the window, "but we can't prevent them from distributing petitions. We do that, we'll have the federal goverment on us."

"I don't give a damn what the government thinks," Gerald Moss growled. "It's my goddamned business, not theirs. They don't make my payroll, I do."

Richard looked at his father. He heard the words echoing: "My business . . . my payroll." He wondered why he could not challenge his father, why he couldn't respond: "It's not *your* business any longer, or *your* payroll. It's mine now."

"Yes sir," Richard said.

Gerald Moss tapped the head of a pencil on the desk. His face was furrowed in anger. "You could've stopped this at the git-go," he said, "if you'd had the guts."

"What does that mean?" Richard asked. He knew his voice was trembling.

"It means, goddamnit, that you let 'em get by with too much," his father said. "You fire their ass when they start rocking the boat, and you'll see the water calm down."

"Christ, Daddy, we're talking about people here," Richard protested. "Some of 'em have been around a long time."

"Somebody always gets hurt in a fight," Gerald Moss said evenly. "It's you or them. You better, by God, remember that."

There was a pause. Richard could feel the vibration of the office in his legs. He waited for it to sing through his body, but it did not. The vibration that only he seemed to know about was frozen in the tight muscles of his calves.

"Yes sir," he said again.

14

In the Big Sandy Auto Accessories plant, where the vibrations and the loud humming were so constant they were no longer recognized by the workers, Wesley and Benny moved through a maze of machinery, carrying their lunchboxes. Sheila Pascal moved in front of them, the firm muscles of her ass twitching beneath her skintight jeans. She passed Clifford, who was waiting for Wesley and Benny. Clifford nodded and smiled at Shelia.

"Son of a bitch!" Wesley exclaimed to Clifford, nodding his head toward Sheila.

"Yeah, she's a work of art, ain't she," Clifford mumbled, falling in step with Wesley and Benny.

"Give me five minutes with that woman—"

"She'd kill ya," Benny interupted.

"Maybe, but it'd take the undertaker three weeks just to wipe the smile off my face," Wesley declared.

Clifford laughed. He said, "You like her that much, I don't know why you just don't ask her out."

"Shit," Wesley replied. "Good-looking girl like that? Shit. She wouldn't go out with me."

"I don't know," Clifford suggested. "She might. I don't never see her with any men over at her place."

Wesley nodded agreement. He tilted his head in thought, then he said, "Naw. I can't take getting turned down by somebody that I'm gonna have to see ever'day. Work with. You know what I mean?"

Benny snickered. "Yeah, you're chicken shit, that's what it is."

"Kiss my ass," Wesley said. He shifted his lunchbox from his left to his right hand, then touched Clifford on the arm and nodded across the warehouse to Joe, who was pushing a cart of boxes toward the loading dock.

"Ol' Joe looks about wore out, don't he?"

"Yeah," Clifford said.

"Keeps Jerry worried all the time," Benny added.

On the dock, Jerry hurried over, took the cart, and rolled it to-

ward the open end of an eighteen-wheel truck. Joe leaned against
the wall of the dock, breathing slowly. He wiped the perspiration
from his face.

"You all right?" Jerry asked.

Joe nodded. "Son, you gonna get in trouble helping me do my
job."

"The hell I am," Jerry said.

"Hate to think I'm getting too old for whatever they say to do,
but I guess I am."

Jerry wiped his face with his hand and rolled his shoulders to
ease the fatigue. He and Joe moved down the long concrete loading dock, past the large open bay doors, and into the plant. Jerry
said, after a moment, "Hey, I'm sorry about dinner the other day. I
guess you know me 'n' Wanda ain't getting along too good here
lately."

"I heard something about it," Joe replied.

"I don't know what we're gonna do," Jerry confessed.

Joe looked at his son. He knew his son was asking for advice,
or understanding, or both.

"I always thought a lot of Wanda, even when she was married
to Ray," Joe said. "I thought she did all she could. I've seen her be
just as sweet as anybody can be."

Jerry looked back, toward the truck. He watched the two men
shoving cartons inside. Then he looked back at his father.

"Daddy," he said softly, "I think you was the only one I know
who didn't ask me why I was marrying Wanda."

Joe smiled. "You're a full-grown man," he said. "I figured you
knew what you was doing. Wouldn't of done no good for me to try
and talk you out of it, would it?"

"No sir, I reckon not."

"Do you love her?"

Jerry tilted his head toward his father, then looked up across
the large open space of the factory. He had never heard Joe ask a
question like that. He answered, "Yes sir, I do. I thought at first I
just felt sorry for her—I mean, the way Ray beat up on her. But
after we got married, I realized that I'd loved her all along. I just
didn't know what it felt like."

"Uh-huh," Joe mumbled.

"After the accident, ever'thing just come apart," Jerry continued. "I knew it'd take some time, but I thought by now she'd be
getting over it. I don't know what we're gonna do."

A whistle from inside the plant blew a sharp blast.

"Nobody said it was gonna be easy, son. You just got to do

whatever you can to help her. Until maybe there'll come a time when you can't do no more."

"How do you know when that time is, Daddy?"

"Nobody can tell you that," Joe answered. "You'll just know."

They were inside the plant. The noise of the machinery enveloped them. The floor beneath their feet trembled steadily.

15

It had been a long day for Clifford Sewell. The news of his signing the petition to vote on a union had swept through Big Sandy
Auto Accessories like a flash fire, and he had spent the day dodging questions and back-slaps and suspicious stares. He did not go
to the Dew Drop Inn after work. He made one stop—at the Get-It-
And-Go convenience store to buy a newspaper and a twelve-pack
of Old Milwaukee—and then he went home. At home, in his recliner, with the sports pages before him, he knew he would have
peace.

His peace was shattered in fifteen minutes.

"How do you like this one, Mama?" Becky said.

Evelyn slipped the hot bowl of black-eyed peas on the table
and looked at the painting Becky was holding.

"That's really good, honey," Evelyn said. She looked over at
Clifford. "We've got a real artist here, Clifford," she added.

"Uh-huh," Clifford mumbled.

"Come on to the table," Evelyn said. "Supper's just about
ready."

He folded the pages of his paper and dropped it on the floor beside his chair, then pulled himself up.

"You really like it, Mama?" Becky asked eagerly.

"I really do," Evelyn answered. She turned back to the kitch-
en, picked up the plate of cornbread, and carried it to the table as
Clifford sat at his customary place.

"I had fun doing it," Becky said. She pulled another painting
from the large envelope she was holding. "I did this one for you,
Daddy." She handed him a painting of a flock of ducks rising out
of cattails growing at the edge of a pond. "I know you like duck
hunting and ever'thing," Becky continued.

Clifford glanced first at the painting and then to his daughter.
"Uh-huh," he said. "That's real good."

"Becky's art teacher—what's his name again, honey?" Evelyn
said.

"Mr. Hunt."

"That's right. Mr. Hunt. Anyhow, he said he thought Becky
really had some talent," Evelyn said to Clifford.

"That's good," Clifford replied. He reached for the peas.

"Clifford, wait till we say the blessing," Evelyn said gently.

Clifford put the plate back on the table, then picked it up again and stared at it. On the plate was a picture of Jesus hanging on the cross.

"Evelyn, what the hell is this?" demanded Clifford.

"Mr. Hunt even gave me some pamphlets for some art schools," Becky said brightly, pulling the pamplets from the envelope.

Clifford was not listening. He picked up the silverware. The image of Jesus on the cross was molded into each handle.

"Evelyn," Clifford repeated, "what the hell is this?"

Becky moved to his side. "Daddy, I want to show you these pamplets," she cooed.

"Clifford, Becky's talking to you," Evelyn said.

Clifford looked up at Becky, then to Evelyn. "I know she's talking to me," he hissed. "I can hear her. What I want to know is why there's a picture of dead Jesus on my plate."

Evelyn smiled sweetly, but she could feel her lips quivering. She did not want an argument. "It's just a plate, Clifford. Why have you got to make a big deal out of ever' little thing?"

Becky dropped into her chair at the table. She begged, "Don't y'all start again."

Clifford ignored her. He leaned across the table, pointing a fork. "It is a big deal, Evelyn. It is to me. I don't want to eat my mashed potatoes off a plate with a dead man's face on it, and I don't care if it's Jesus or John Kennedy or Jesse James. Why's that so hard for you to understand?"

Evelyn sniffed. She unfolded her paper napkin and smoothed it in her lap. She said, "Well, Clifford, it's supposed to remind us of the many blessings we receive each day because our precious Savior died for our sins."

Clifford's face colored in a building anger. "We got Jesus on ever'thing in this house," he growled. I don't need Jesus under my food to remind me how good I got it," he said.

"Daddy, I want to show you this. There's a really good school over in Nashville," Becky chattered as she unfolded the pamphlet. "And one down in Memphis. Of course, I'd need a car to get around and ever'thing."

Clifford twisted his chair and waved the fork toward Becky. "How many times have we been over this?" he asked. "What the hell do you think you gonna be able to do with art, anyhow? What kinda job is that?"

Becky lifted her face in defiance. "There's lot of things you can do if you're a good artist," she said. "Like illustrate children's books, or commercial art. Stuff like that."

"That's nice," Evelyn said gently.

Clifford twisted back to his wife. "Nice?" he sputtered. The veins in his neck were bulging. "Why don't we get *her* to paint Jesus on ever'thing we own and save me some money?"

Evelyn's body stiffened in indignation. She said, "Good grief, Clifford, can you be serious for once? Becky's trying to talk to you about something that's important to her."

Clifford glared at his wife. The fork trembled in his hand. He fixed her with a threatening stare. "I ain't through with you," he said. "You—"

Becky's voice interrupted him: "There's lots of things you can do with art, Daddy, and that's what I really want to do. But I need to go to school so I can get better at it."

Clifford leaned back in his chair and shook his head. He looked at the fork he was holding and dropped it on the table. He disliked the conversation with Becky about college about as much as he disliked the way Big Sandy Auto Accessories had treated him.

"Let me tell you about college," he said in a low voice. "It don't mean shit no more."

"Not art college, Daddy. Art school," Becky corrected.

"Art school, college. Hell, it's the same damn thing," Clifford argued. "Used to be, a college education was worth something, but anymore it's just a waste of money. People go to college nowadays, get out, and can't get a damn job nowhere. I can't tell you how many people we got working over at the plant that's been to college, and they ain't making a bit more money that I am."

Becky shoved her paintings back into the envelope. "I don't want to work in a factory, Daddy," she said.

"Can we say the blessing now?" Evelyn asked brightly.

"Just a damn minute," snapped Clifford. He turned back to Becky "What's wrong with working in a factory?" he demanded. "It's kept your young ass clothed and fed."

"Clifford." Evelyn's voice was an old warning.

"Look," Clifford said in a quieter, reasoning tone, "a young girl that goes to college today is just wasting time and money. You'll hook up with some little ol' boy, get married, start having babies, and all that college and my money'll be wasted." He looked at Evelyn. "Tell her," he commanded.

Evelyn did not respond. She glared at her husband.

Becky swiped at her eyes with her fingers, feeling for the tears that were almost there. "I—I don't know how to say it," she mumbled, "but when I paint or draw something and ever'body makes a big deal over it I get this real good feeling, like what I did was important, and I think—"

The door to the trailer opened suddenly. Jimmie stepped inside and dropped his books. His hair was pulled back in a ponytail.

"What's happening?" he asked cheerfully. He crossed to the table, sat, and reached for the mashed potatoes with one hand and the cornbread with the other.

"Jimmie Clifford," Evelyn said. "We—"

She did not finish the sentence. Clifford's hand shot up like an ax, its palm opened.

"What in the hell is that?" demanded Clifford.

"What?" Jimmie asked.

"You've got a gotdamned ponytail," Clifford growled. He looked at Evelyn, waving his hand. "He's got a gotdamned ponytail, Evelyn."

"So?" Jimmie said.

The veins again began to bulge in Clifford's neck. "So? So? So I want it stopped, and I mean now," he ordered.

"Goddamn, Daddy," Jimmie said.

"Don't you take the Lord's name in vain at this table," snapped Evelyn.

Jimmie did not look at his mother. He said, "Ever'body's wearing them. It's no big deal."

"I don't give a shit if ever'body's painting their ass green and howling at the moon, as long as you're putting your feet under my table you ain't gonna wear no gotdamn ponytail."

"Clifford, hush," Evelyn said.

Jimmie rolled his eyes toward the ceiling, reached behind his head, pulled at the rubberband knotting his hair, and shook his hair free. He scooped three pieces of cornbread from the plate, stood, and stalked out.

"Jimmie Clifford, you come back here and sit down and eat," called Evelyn. Then, to Clifford: "Good grief, go in there and apologize to him right now and make him come out here and eat."

Clifford threw up his hands in disgust. He rose, kicking his chair backward, and crossed the room to the front door.

"Daddy, I wanted to show you these pamphlets," Becky begged.

Clifford opened the door, paused, looked back at the table. "Evelyn, I'm gonna go get a beer and a ham sandwich, and when I get back, I want this shit straightened out, and I want our old dishes back on the table, gotdamnit."

Becky's voice was now a whine: "Daddy, I was trying to talk to you."

Clifford glared at his daughter. He swallowed hard against the rush of anger, then he stepped through the door and slammed it behind him. The echo of the door careened through the trailer, leaving a wake of silence that was like a long, depressing sigh.

"Honey," Evelyn said after a moment, "I think what you're talking about sounds real good, and I think if you really want to do it, the Lord will provide a way." She touched her fingers over the plate of Jesus hanging from the cross. A smile rippled across her lips. "Let me tell you something about your daddy," she continued. "See, he's real proud, takes after your granddaddy, and what he can't bring himself to tell you is that it don't look like we're gonna be able to afford to send you to college. You know he would if he could, 'cause there ain't nothing in this world he cares about more'n you kids."

Becky nodded once. She said, in a whisper, "I understand. It's still more than a year away. I'm just a junior. You never know how things might change."

Evelyn stood and moved to her daughter. She kissed Becky gently on the forehead.

"I like your dishes, Mama," Becky said.

16

It had been a false summer day in autumn—hot, muggy, thick, with the fumes of the Big Sandy Auto Accessories plant suspended in the humidity. It was as though the air currents of autumn had swirled on a faraway bank of clouds and drifted back from east to west, bringing with them sheets of sun from some burning spot in the Atlantic. In the trailers of Captain's Point Trailer Park, the heat cuddled and its invisible glue bubbled in a thin perspiration on the bodies of those who stayed inside.

Outside, near the river, a slice of cool night air slid under the low limbs of oaks and gum and beech trees, and that was where Becky and Nancy walked, talking in quiet, conspiratorial voices, until they found Jimmie sitting alone against the dark side of an oak, facing the river. Jimmie was drinking one of his father's beers that he had slipped from the refrigerator.

"What're you doing out here, Jimmie Clifford?" asked Becky.

"What's it look like?" Jimmie answered. He sipped from the beer.

"You mad about Daddy throwing a fit over your ponytail?"

"It's my damn hair. I'll wear it any way I want to," Jimmie sniffed. He crushed the empty can with his fist.

"I like it, Jimmie Clifford," Nancy said. She sat in the grass near him.

"Yeah, me, too," Becky said, sitting. "It looks a lot better'n Eddie Carter's."

Jimmie rubbed his shoulders against a tree, like a goat scratching a fence.

"Parents just don't know what it's like," Nancy sighed. Her voice was as languid as the weather.

"Yeah," Becky muttered. "By the way, Jimmie Clifford, thanks for not saying anything to Mama and Daddy about the other night."

Jimmie tilted his head and thought for a moment.

"You know, the Dairy Queen," Becky reminded him.

"Oh, yeah. You owe me," he said. "You can clean up my room."

"No way," Becky said.

"That's blackmail, Jimmie Clifford," Nancy added.

"Don't matter to me what you call it," Jimmie replied easily. "Wonder how long you'd be grounded when I tell Daddy—"

"I'll do it," Becky said.

"If I was you, I'd watch who I go out with," advised Jimmie.

"Who I go out with is none of your business," snapped Becky.

"Is if I have to go tell Mama and Daddy," Jimmie said teasingly.

"God, Jimmie Clifford, you can really be an ass at times. You know that?" Nancy grumbled.

Jimmie laughed. "Yeah," he said proudly. "I can be, can't I?"

"Who you think she oughta be going with?" Nancy asked.

Jimmie leaned his head against the tree. "Cecil Pinkerton wants to go out with you, but he's afraid to ask."

"Yeah, I know," mumbled Becky.

"Why don't you go out with him then?" asked Jimmie.

Nancy spit the word: "Gross!"

Jimmie turned his head to her. "What's wrong with you? Cecil's all right."

"Yeah, if you like geeks," Nancy answered.

Jimmie's look turned cold, a mean hard stare that drove into Nancy, making her lean away from him involuntarily. He said, evenly, "Nancy, you ever heard how people talk about you?"

"Jimmie Clifford, shut up," Becky said angrily.

"It's—it's all right," Nancy stammered. "I know what he means." She looked away toward the river. A can floated by on the current, spinning lazily. Then she looked back at Jimmie. "I don't mean he's a real geek, Jimmie Clifford, but he's kinda—I don't know how to explain it. Geeky-like, I guess," she said.

"Ain't nothing wrong with him. He's a nice guy," Jimmie told her.

"That's what I mean," Nancy countered. "Cecil's too nice. He, like gives you the creeps, he's so nice. That's all I meant."

"Yeah," agreed Becky.

Jimmie nodded thoughtfully. He said, "I get it. Y'all don't like nobody unless they treat you like shit."

"That's not true," Nancy said.

"Good grief, Jimmie Clifford," Becky sighed. "You don't have a clue."

Jimmie laughed and stood and stretched. He looked down at the girls. "Y'all are just fucked up," he drawled. He shook his head and started away. "Oh, you can start on my room anytime."

17

By morning autumn had returned, and the first strike of air on the faces of those who stepped outside their trailers at the Captain's Point Trailer Park was a cool slap. Fog billowed over the Tennessee River like a fallen ribbon of grey-white clouds.

To Nancy, the morning air was clean enough to taste. She stood outside the closed door of the trailer, lifted her face, and inhaled slowly, feeling the air in her throat and lungs. The dead, cigarette-and-bourbon smell of the trailer had made her queasy during the night and the queasiness had lingered in her mouth, but the morning air washed it away.

Behind her in the trailer, she could hear the first Elvis Presley record begin playing, and she knew her mother was standing beside the record player, watching the record turn, her dull, heavy eyes filling with the moisture of some remembered moment that ate away at her like a slow-nibbling cancer.

Nancy shook her head and walked briskly away from the trailer.

An old truck passed as she crossed the road, heading for Becky's trailer, and a weak horn sounded. Nancy looked up to see Benny waving from the rolled-down window. She liked Benny and Fat Ethel, even if they were always fighting. She smiled and waved back.

At the Sewell trailer, Nancy knocked lightly once, then opened the door and stepped inside. She saw Evelyn at the table, clearing away the breakfast dishes. The television set was on and a choir was singing *Whispering Hope* while the preacher swayed, his bowed head nodding and his deep, urgent voice mumbling, "Amen, Amen, Amen . . . "

"Morning," Nancy said.

"Hello, Nancy," Evelyn replied. "How's your mama this morning?"

"'Bout the same," Nancy told her. She moved to the table, picked up a biscuit, and sat nibbling.

Evelyn watched her and wondered sadly if she ever had breakfast.

"Well, you tell her I said hello," Evelyn said.

"Yes ma'am," Nancy replied.

Evelyn stepped to the hallway. She cried, "Jimmie Clifford, you better hurry up."

From his room, Jimmie answered, "I'm coming." The trailer shook as he rushed down the hallway, tucking his shirttail into his pants. He glanced at Nancy, grabbed his books from the table, and rushed through the door.

"You got lunch money?" Evelyn yelled after him.

"Yes, ma'am," Jimmie answered from outside.

Nancy stood and moved toward the door. She called: "Becky, we're gonna miss the bus."

Evelyn picked up the gravy bowl from the table. She said, "She's gone already, Nancy. She got a ride to school this morning."

Nancy's brow furrowed in a question that Evelyn understood.

"Susan Taylor and some of them other girls picked her up," Evelyn explained. "They were going to paint some signs for the football game, I think."

"Oh," Nancy muttered. She smiled and walked out of the trailer.

Outside, Jimmie was backing his truck off the grass and onto the gravel drive.

"You wouldn't want to give me a ride, would you, Jimmie Clifford?" Nancy called.

"No, I wouldn't," Jimmie answered. He jerked the gear and snapped his foot off the clutch. The truck bolted forward, spinning in the loose gravel.

Nancy bit her lip to stop the anger and hurt. She could feel the queasiness of the night filling her mouth. She muttered, "Fuck you, Jimmie Clifford." She turned and started walking rapidly toward the school bus, but it was already pulling away. She stopped and threw her books on the ground. "Shit," she said angrily.

She picked up her books and wiped the morning dew from them, then turned toward her trailer. Suddenly, a car skidded to a stop near her. She stepped instinctively aside and looked up. It was Cecil.

"Hey, Nancy," Cecil called cheerfully. "Need a ride?"

Nancy drew in a tired breath. She nodded, opened the door to the car and slid inside.

"Great morning, ain't it?" Cecil said.

Nancy frowned as she looked to the smiling, pimply-faced Cecil. "Well, this is going to be a shitty day," Nancy thought.

Nancy was still angry as she shoved and side-stepped her way through the crowded hallway leading to the lockers. The jabbering of voices, of high-pitched, bird-sharp laughter, rang in her ears. The mix of sweet, inexpensive cologne from girls mimicking other girls and of harsh after-shave lotion from boys barely old enough to shave floated in the air, and Nancy could feel the nausea licking at her tongue. She stopped at a water fountain and drank.

She saw Becky at her locker, standing before it reading from a notebook.

"Where were you this morning?" Nancy asked bitterly. "I missed the bus, waiting on you."

Becky looked at her quizzically. She said, "I called last night and told your mother I wasn't riding the bus this morning. She didn't tell you?"

Nancy forced a disbelieving laugh. "Mama? Of course not," she said. She paused and glanced at the notebook Becky was holding. "Did you do your math homework?" she asked.

Becky shook her head wearily. "Yeah," she answered, "but I've got to have it back by third period. Promise?"

Nancy reached for the notebook and Becky pulled it back.

"Promise?" Becky said.

"Yeah, yeah, I promise," Nancy mumbled.

As Becky handed Nancy the notebook, her face rose and her eyes glanced past Nancy. She smiled. "Don't look now," she whispered, "but you've got company."

Nancy turned to see Bobby lumbering down the hall toward them.

"God, he's gorgeous," Nancy sighed. Then, to Bobby as he passed: "Hi, baby."

In the moving crowd up ahead, Marcy Ruffin stopped and waited for Bobby to reach her. She was smiling, happily watching him. Becky and Nancy looked on in stunned silence while Bobby strolled past as if Nancy didn't exist.

"I thought you said he was breaking up with her." Becky questioned.

Nancy shrugged and opened her locker. "He is," she said. "He just don't want to hurt her. That's the kind of person he is. He wants to let her down easy."

Becky and Nancy turned to see Bobby embrace Marcy and kiss her tenderly.

"If he lets her down any easier, they'll be engaged by fifth period," Becky said.

Nancy slammed the locker door and walked away, her eyes rimming with tears.

"Nancy?"

Nancy did not turn. She said, in a loud voice, "Third period. I promise I'll have it back by third period."

Becky swallowed a deep sigh as she watched Nancy hurry away, nudging through the crowded hallway.

BOOK FOUR

that old David and Goliath thing

1

Evelyn Sewell did not know if it was her awesome battle with cramps, or if God had indeed selected her to become His eyes while He rested for a few days, but when she awoke on that Monday morning Evelyn could sense a curious, inspired power: everything happening around her, she knew. It was as though she could close her eyes and think of someone, or something, and the vision of that person, or that thing, invaded her, and for long, pure moments she watched them, or it, and she understood.

Evelyn knew that Verdale cried that morning, cried with sick, terrible tears, cried for a husband long gone. She knew that Verdale opened her scrapbook and looked at the fading Polaroid photographs of Graceland.

Evelyn knew that the captain of the river barge drifting past the Captain's Point Trailer Park was breathing hard against a pain deep in his chest. She could see him lift his arm and pull on the cord that threw the warning blast across the valley. She paused. She heard the blast, and the echo of the blast, and her body jerked involuntarily. "God's proof," she thought.

Evelyn knew that Becky was lying in bed with her annual open, looking at the picture of a boy, thinking of the boy. A name snapped in her mind: Scott. "The boy's name is Scott," Evelyn thought.

She knew that Freeman and Blanche were already at their kitchen table, shelling peas, and that nearby, Susie was holding a red crayon, her confused mind trying to decide where to color on the blank page in front of her.

She knew that Fat Ethel was hanging baby diapers on the clothes line behind her trailer.

Evelyn stood at the sink in her trailer and looked out of the window and knew all these things that were happening around her. Her eyes misted with joy. She sucked in a sudden breath. "So this is what God sees," she thought.

And then she remembered a band of gypsies that had traveled by wagon along the Tennessee River, and the gypsy woman who could see into the future by staring at a pool of stilled water. Those who believed in the gypsy woman whispered that she had

". . . the Gift," saying the words with reverence. Evelyn wondered if " . . . the Gift" had been placed on her by God, an ordination that could be considered payment for her loyalty, her unswerving belief in what the preachers from the television promised with their shouting and their dancing demonstrations of jubilation.

"Thank you, God," Evelyn whispered.

That morning, while rubbing a creme rinse into Sarah Timberlake's thinning, orange-tinted hair, Evelyn had an image of Clifford. He was standing with a group of workers outside the break room at the Big Sandy Auto Accessories plant, the union petition in his hand, and he was arguing with them. She paused, her fingers stopping at the crown of Sarah's hair. She closed her eyes, and she could see and hear Clifford.

"You ain't doing nothing but signing a piece of paper, for God's sake," Clifford was saying forcefully. "It don't do nothing but give us the right to take a vote. Hell, ain't this America? Ain't we supposed to have that right?"

One of the workers shook his head. He said, "I don't know, Clifford. I hear tell they'd lay you off if they even *think* you're in favor of getting a union in here."

"That's a bunch of crap," Clifford snapped. "They can't do that. They start them rumors just to scare us off."

Evelyn's head twitched. She could see Richard Moss walking past, glaring at Clifford. And she cold see the workers duck their heads and disperse, leaving Clifford standing alone. She shook her head in worry.

"Evelyn, you all right?" Sarah asked.

"Huh?" Evelyn said.

"You're gouging my scalp," Sarah complained.

"I'm sorry," Evelyn said. "My mind just flew away for a minute."

"Well, don't let it take my hair with it," Sarah said.

Evelyn's powers of perception, of her God-appointed ability to slip out of her body and fly, free-will, anywhere her curiosity would take her, lasted for three days. It left her drained of energy and with a headache that drove her to stay in bed on Thursday, and when she awoke late Thursday afternoon, she was glad the powers had deserted her. Doing God's work was too great a task, and what she had seen was too discouraging:

Verdale and Lloyd Pinkerton making awkward love in Verdale's trailer.

Jimmie Clifford stretched across his bed, touching himself into an erection.

Becky, standing before her mirror, examining the size and shape of her breasts.

Ray Burnette driving slowly through the trailer park, his fingers drumming over the top of the steering wheel as he listened to the blaring of country music from a Memphis radio station.

Wesley watching from his truck as Nancy crossed the road to her trailer, a smile growing in his face like a flower.

A woman named Arlene Pitts teasing Clifford at the plant, grabbing at his ass as he passed her with the petition in his hand. The laughter of Arlene as she prissed away, her sagging body jiggling under the too-tight blouse she wore.

Wanda in a parked car with a hard-faced man that Evelyn did not know. The man was pawing at Wanda's breasts.

All these things Evelyn had seen, or thought she had seen. When she awoke, with her headache at ease, she made a cup of hot tea and honey and sat at the kitchen table and wondered: Did it happen? Did I have the Gift? Or was it just my imagination? Maybe it was the sour blood of her period, the power of cramps rather than the power of God. Everything she had seen in her flyaway moments she had either seen from the windows of her trailer or she had thought about in secret.

She thought she might ask the preacher about it.

No, she decided. The preacher would make an issue of it. If it was the work of God, she would know it. If it was only her imagination, she would have to accept that she was either too tired to think straight or she was losing her mind.

She got up from the table and went to the television and turned it on. An overweight woman was testifying to a beaming evangelist about being cured of warts that were about to drive her crazy.

That night, in bed with Clifford, Evelyn whispered, "You think Jimmie Clifford plays with himself?"

Clifford rolled to stare at her. "God-a-mighty, Evelyn, what's wrong with you? Of course he plays with hisself. He's got a tally-wacker that makes blisters on his knees. You think he just pees out of it?"

"You don't have to be nasty about it," Evelyn sniffed.

"I ain't being nasty, I'm being truthful," Clifford replied. "What made you ask such a question anyhow?"

"Nothing."

"Nothing, my ass."

There was a moment of silence.

"You seen Arlene Pitts lately?" asked Evelyn.

Clifford pulled up to one elbow. "All right," he said, "what's going on?"

"I'm just talking to you," protested Evelyn.

"Evelyn," Clifford said patiently, "you ask me about Jimmie Clifford playing with hisself and then you ask me about Arlene Pitts, who is about as big a bitch as God ever put on earth, and you tell me it's just talking. What's going on? Is Jimmie Clifford diddling Arlene Pitts? Is that what you're trying to tell me?"

"Good Lord, Clifford, how could you think such a thing?"

"By putting one and one together," Clifford answered.

"I was just thinking about Arlene," Evelyn said. She added, quickly, "I saw her cousin today and she just come to mind. That's all."

Clifford dropped back to his pillow. "All right," he mumbled. "Yeah, I see Arlene Pitts. Ever'day."

"Has she signed the petition?" Evelyn asked.

"No," Clifford answered bitterly. "The bitch."

"How's that going?" Evelyn asked.

"Slow."

"What's people scared of?"

"They're scared of losing their jobs."

"Can they?" Evelyn asked.

"Hell no," Clifford snorted. "Old man Moss ain't about to kick nobody out of a job. He'd have hell to pay and he knows it."

"Reba Fuller was in the shop a couple of days ago. She said she'd bet Moss closes down the plant if the union's voted in."

"Reba Fuller don't know her ass—and it's the biggest one I know—from her elbow," muttered Clifford.

"She was just listening to what Hobart was saying," Evelyn suggested.

"Hobart Fuller's too damn lazy to know what's going on over there. They should of fired his ass ten years ago," Clifford said.

"Well, goodnight, Clifford."

"Yeah."

Clifford rolled on his side, away from his wife. He pulled the covers up over his shoulders and wiggled his head into the pillow. Outside, he could hear a lone car driving through the park, its tires crunching over the loose gravel.

"Clifford?"

"What, Evelyn. Gotdamn, I got to get some sleep."

"You believe in visions?" asked Evelyn.

Clifford sighed. He did not turn back. "Evelyn," he said slowly, quietly, "if you start talking to me about Jesus, I swear I'm gonna kick you off the bed."

"I don't mean that," Evelyn replied. "I mean, you ever thought you knew what was going on, someplace where you wadn't, and it really was going on, just like you thought it wa~?"

Clifford wagged his head in the pillow. It was the most confused question he had heard in ten years.

"Have you?" Evelyn asked, pressing.

"Yeah, once," admitted Clifford. "When we was in 'Nam. I had this feeling that some of them creepy little shits was hiding up on a hill when we was on patrol one night."

"What'd you do?" Evelyn asked.

"I blew the fucking hill away, Evelyn," Clifford said.

Evelyn sat up. She had never heard Clifford talk about the war so openly. "You killed them?" she said in an anxious voice.

"That's what we was there for," Clifford answered simply.

2

On Friday night the Big Sandy Wildcats kicked ass, beating Bruceton 38–3. Jimmie Cifford Sewell made seventeen tackles, broke the leg of the Bruceton fullback, and was cheered lustily when he emerged from the locker room holding the game ball in the air like a trophy.

Becky ran up to Jimmie and hugged him, then stepped aside and smiled at Scott, who had a bandage on his chin covering a grass burn suffered when he was buried by his own teammates in the end zone after running sixty yards for the game's first touchdown.

"Hey there, Jimmie Clifford's sister," Scott said, teasingly. "You see the game?"

"You were great," Becky sighed.

Scott winked at her. Becky blushed and stepped back. Her heart pounded in her chest, and her hand covered it involuntarily.

At his car, waiting for Becky and Evelyn, Clifford stood with Jerry and Joe Burnette, smoking a cigarette and talking in low tones about the campaign to get signatures on the petition.

"It ain't going like it ought to," admitted Clifford. "Too many people still taking a wait-and-see attitude."

"What I been hearing," Joe said.

"A lot of people just don't believe in unions, Cliff," Jerry said. "I guess I'm one of 'em. We friends, and you know that, but I can't bring myself to sign something I don't believe. I know Daddy's signed, but I just can't."

Clifford nodded seriously. "I can appreciate that, Jerry, and to tell you the truth, not having your name might be hurting the drive."

"How's that?" Jerry asked.

"Lots of the young people over there look up to you," Clifford told him. "You know how it is—monkey see, monkey do. And you young monkeys could make the difference."

Jerry rolled his shoulders, fished a cigarette from his shirt, and lit it. He said after a minute, "Well, I'll try to get word out that I don't want nobody to back off because of me."

Clifford could see Evelyn and Becky crossing the parking lot from the locker room. Nancy was with them.

"How about the two of you coming over to the Dew Drop Inn tomorrow?" suggested Clifford. "There'll be a pretty good crowd over there to watch the Tennessee game. Hope to get some of 'em on the dotted line while they're feeling good."

Jerry drew from his cigarette and spit the smoke into the night air. It was a pale blue against the lights. He said, "Well, me 'n' Daddy was planning on some bird-hunting tomorrow. But if Daddy wants to go over—"

It was a lie, but it was also an out for Joe. He coughed. "Well, we done made the plans. I guess we'll skip it tomorrow, Clifford. Unless it rains and turns off nasty."

"We'll be there if you change your mind," Clifford said.

Joe and Jerry began to move away from the car. They waved at Evelyn and Becky and Nancy.

"Tell Jimmie Clifford he played a helluva game," Jerry said over his shoulder.

They walked a few steps, too far to be heard in whisper.

"Appreciate that, son," Joe said.

Jerry laughed easily. "Tell you the truth, I was planning on going out. You want to go?"

"Yeah, I'd like that," Joe answered.

Jerry chuckled again. "Clifford oughta get Jimmie Clifford over there to bust a few noggins. That'd put some names down."

"He gets worked up, don't he?" Joe said.

3

Bender Cawthorn had been Jerry Burnette's closest friend from
the fifth grade until the car crash that crushed Bender's chest
against the front seat of an ancient Plymouth, killing him in-
stantly. Bender was twenty-two when he died, a man with laughter bubbling up from his soul, a dreamer with dreams of far-away
places and adventures that only people in the movies seemed to
understand and live.

At the funeral home, Jerry had stood aside and watched as
Bender's mother, Erma, placed a photograph of Bender and Jerry
in the coffin. The photograph was of Bender and Jerry holding the
limp form of a wild turkey that Bender had killed on a hunt with
Jerry.

Erma Cawthorn had said to Jerry, "He loved that picture
more'n anything he had. I had to put it in with him."

Since that time, Jerry had never hunted without remembering Bender, his mind tricking him with Bender's absurd, ram-
bling stories and with the yodeling cry of victory—a tragic mimic
of Tarzan's ape cry—whenever Bender bagged a bird, or rabbit, or
deer.

In the autumn, with rich spills of color drizzling down the
earth-dying leaves of trees, with the clean, autumn smell of wood-
earth, with the clear, homing cry of birds rising on their wings to
follow the wind currents drifting south, Jerry loved the pretense
of hunting. He did not go into the woods to kill—not any longer.
He went into the woods in search of what he had most loved: innocence. It was a religious act, no different than approaching the al-
tar of a church for the symbolic wafers and wine of Christ's body.
In the woods, as he searched for Bender and innocence, Jerry
Burnette always found bits of himself, like a scattered puzzle.

He was standing beside his father in the field of harvested
wheat, with the stubby rows of brown stalk. Both men cradled
their shotguns loosely in their arms, watching the dogs leap and
yelp, sniffing the air eagerly. One of the dogs—Belle—came to
point like posing for a portrait, and Joe Burnette leveled his gun
slowly and began to move forward. Jerry followed, keeping the
barrel of his gun pointed toward the ground. A few feet later, they

heard a rustling of feathers. Belle barked and a covey of quail rose in a net of wings from the ground.

"There they go," Joe shouted. He lifted his gun and fired without sighting. Jerry threw his gun quickly to his shoulder and pulled the trigger twice. His aim was thirty feet over the quail.

"Missed," Jerry said.

"Yeah, me too" Joe said.

"Well, that's the way it goes some days," Jerry suggested.

"That's the truth," agreed Joe.

Both men breached their double-barrels and reloaded. Both were privately pleased that the other had not killed anything. Nothing was as remarkable as a covey of quail on wing. Nothing.

"You ready to go in?" asked Joe.

"I guess," Jerry said. "I got some work I need to do around the trailer. Wrap the water pipes."

"Thought you'd done that already," Joe replied.

"Couple of years ago," Jerry told him. "Needs to be replaced."

"Yeah, you can't be too careful," Joe said. "Bust some of them pipes and you got more trouble than a man wants."

"Uh-huh," Jerry mumbled.

They whistled the dogs to them and began to cross the field. The sun balanced on a shelf of clouds holding over the valley.

"Daddy," Jerry said as they walked, "I know it's none of my business, but I hope to God Ray's not being a burden on you and Mama."

"We're handling things all right," Joe replied.

"I just hate seeing him take advantage of you and Mama," Jerry continued.

Joe nodded thoughtfully. He shifted his gun to his left arm. He said, "Well, son, you can't take advantage of somebody unless they let you." He paused, stopped, waited for one of the dogs. He added, "We realized a long time ago you were gonna be all right. You never gave me or your mama, either one, a minute's worth of worry, but with Ray it's different." He paused again. The dog nuzzled against his leg, and Joe patted it on the head. "I guess it's just natural that a parent'll favor the weaker child." He looked at Jerry. "You know what I'm saying?"

Jerry glanced, across the field. He could see a red fox creeping against the tree line.

"Do you, son?" Joe asked again.

"Yeah," he said. Jerry rocked his body, then looked at his father. "But it's kinda funny. I never thought of Ray as weak."

4

Clifford was tired and irritated.

On Saturday at the Dew Drop Inn, he had spent more than forty dollars buying beer to bribe potential signees for his union petitions and he had consumed more than a gallon himself—playing the political game, being one of the boys.

He had lost another twenty dollars on the game when Alabama beat Tennessee.

He had lost three games of pool—on purpose.

He had broken up a fight between Azel Capes and Lonnie Hightower.

And he had had to change a flat tire on his truck when he left the bar.

On Saturday night, he had not slept well because of stomach gas and a cigarette headache.

On Sunday morning, he had awakened to Evelyn's shouting about church, and when he had staggered into the bathroom to wash the sleep from his eyes and brush his teeth, he had found a new toothbrush in the holder—a toothbrush that had a handle formed like Jesus with out-stretched hands.

His cry of anguish was heard three trailers down: "Evelyn! Gotdamnit!"

He had suffered through a sermon that went ten minutes too long and made Evelyn weep with joy for some mysterious reason, and now he was standing beside his car waiting for Evelyn to confer with the preacher and a few deacons about God-only-knew-what, and he was talking with Grady Lester about the union.

"I'm telling you, Grady," Clifford said with an exasperated edge to his voice, "they can't fire you for signing a piece of paper. Don't know how many times you got to hear that before you believe it."

Grady pawed at the ground with the tip of his scuffed Sunday shoe. He crossed his arms. His face screwed up in serious thought. "You sure about this, Clifford?"

"I wouldn't ask you to sign it if I didn't believe in it a hundred percent," Clifford said. He was holding the petition and a pen. "Don't you want to make more money, get more benefits?"

"Well, hell, yes," Grady said, as though the question was simply to stupid too believe.

Clifford thrust the petition toward him. "Well, then, sign the damn thing."

Grady stepped back slightly. He kept his arms crossed. He stared at the petition.

Clifford leaned toward him. He whispered, "Grady, you know what I seen you doing over at the Dew Drop yesterday?"

Grady's face paled.

"I seen you running your hand up that old Bailey girl's dress, playing some grab-ass," Clifford continued in a low growl. "Supposing I got the spirit right here and now and started confessing the sins I know to ever'body in the churchyard. How you reckon May and the kids are gonna take what I'd have to say about that?"

"Jesus, Clifford, that's blackmail," Grady said, his voice quivering.

"Damn right it is," Clifford snapped. "But somebody's got to do something to get you off-center." He pushed the petition in Grady's hand. "Sign it before the Lord starts my tongue to wagging."

Grady took the petition, spread it across the hood of Clifford's car, and signed it.

"Appreciate that, Grady," Clifford said pleasantly. He took the petition and slipped it inside his pocket. Grady nervously lit a cigarette. "Good sermon, wadn't it?" Clifford added.

"Yeah, I guess," Grady mumbled.

"Yes sir, that old boy can flat-out preach," Clifford said, smiling as he moved on to get the next unsuspecting sinner to sign his petition.

5

The Big Sandy Wildcats had finished the football season undefeated and the euphoria of that accomplishment blazed across the
valley like an out-of-control fire. Rolls of crepe paper, twisted in
the school colors, hung from door fronts like skinny curtains.
Posters declaring the victory over Bruceton were taped to windows. Rolling signs in front of service stations and barber shops
blared the words: *Congratulations, Wildcats!* or *Hey! Hey! All the
Way!*

All the way meant the state championship, and at Big Sandy
High School there could be no doubt that the Wildcats were going
to do exactly that: *Hey! Hey! All the way!*

On Monday, Tom Phillips, the principal of Big Sandy High,
proclaimed a schoolwide pep rally for the Wildcats during sixth
period. He made the announcement himself, enthusiastically declaring, "The spirit's in the air, and it's going to take us to victory!" A cheer could be heard throughout the school, and there were
those who swore they heard Tom Phillips scream, "Hot damn!" as
he clicked off the intercom.

In the overcrowded gymnasium at sixth period, the Wildcat
band played the Wildcat fight song and the Big Sandy students
sang lustily and cheered. A chant started, with the rhythmic
pounding of feet on the floor and on slabbed seats: "All the way!
All the way! All the way!" Tom Phillips wiggled his way to the microphone. He tapped it and the tapping echoed. He said, "Testing,
testing, testing," and someone, a boy from deep in the stands,
yelled, "Hot damn!" A peal of laughter rolled over the crowd, and
Tom Phillips blushed.

"All right, all right," Tom cried into the microphone. "Let's
calm down a minute." The students began to quieten. Then Tom
said, "We're here to thank this year's Big Sandy Wildcat football
team and their coaches for the wonderful job they've done in going
through the season undefeated."

A chorus of shouts rose from the students. Tom smiled and
raised his hands again. The students quieted.

"We also owe a big thanks to our Homecoming Queen, Sue
Taylor, for the wonderful job she and the cheerleaders have done

this season, especially with the great Pep Club signs that keep us reminded of how great out team really is," Tom continued. "Susan, Susan. Where are you?"

Again the cheers erupted. High in the stands, Nancy leaned to Becky and said, "You did those signs. Jesus, I can't believe she just takes credit for that. The bitch."

Becky shrugged and smiled. She was too caught up in the frenzy to care about Susan Taylor. "Oh, I don't care," she said lightly.

"I do," Nancy replied bitterly.

Susan moved through the circle of cheerleaders like a golden haired goddess, holding pompons high over her head. At the microphone, she paused, then leaned forward, her full, gleaming lips almost kissing the rounded mesh covering. She said, seductively, "Hi."

Boys began to whistle and cry out in loud, exaggerated moans. Susan blushed appropriately, stepped back, smiled, soaked in the adoration, then stepped to the microphone again.

"Thank you, Mr. Phillips," Susan said, her voice growing in energy. "If it hadn't been for the support of the teachers, and all, we wouldn't be here today." She smiled, looked toward the door leading into the dressing rooms, then turned back to the microphone. "But the people we're really here for are the players, so, without any further ado, won't all of you join us now as we bring out the next Tennessee high school football champions—our Big Sandy Wildcats!" She shouted the last words.

The dressing room doors opened, and the cheerleaders rushed toward the doors, forming a corridor of jumping, leaping, yelping bodies. The players, led by Scott and Jimmie, poured into the gym and trotted to the middle of the floor. They were all wearing their game jerseys.

The sound of cheering was like a rock concert gone mad. It filled the gymnasium, echoes bombing against echoes. Someone started the chant and the foot-pounding: "All the way, all the way, all the way." The team stood smiling, waving.

It lasted five minutes, until Susan approached the microphone again and, with her pompons, begged for silence. It took another two minutes before anyone followed her instruction.

"All right, now," Susan said at last. "Let's see if we can't get a few words out of our team captains, Scott Mitchell and Jimmie Clifford Sewell." She began to clap and the crowd erupted again.

Scott and Jimmie moved to the microphone, poking at each other. Finally, Jimmie stepped forward. He cleared his throat, laughed, then said, "All right, we want ever'body to come out on

Friday night and watch us kick Knoxville's ass, and then party!"
He threw his fist into the air and shouted, "Hot damn!"

The chorus of students answered, "Hot damn!"

Tom Phillips stepped forward and caught Jimmie by the arm
and pulled him away from the microphone. Tom's face was red
with embarassment. Jimmie rolled his shoulders and smiled at
Scott.

Scott eased to the microphone. He inhaled and held his head
high, his handsome, quarterback-commanding face shining as
though covered by a spotlight. He said, in a controlled, comfortable voice, "On behalf of the team and the coaching staff, we want
to thank you all for the support and school spirit you've given us
all year. We couldn't have done it without you, believe me. Now,
let's go beat Knoxville."

In the stands, crushed with the weight of the sound around
her, Becky gazed longingly at Scott, a pleased smile curling in her
lip. She thought: "God, he's beautiful."

The mood of the pep rally left the gymnasium with the depart-
ing students and rushed along the corridors of Big Sandy High
School, spilling into classrooms with the exhilaration of uncon-
trollable happiness. None of the teachers bothered with class-
work; they knew it would be impossible to go from Jimmie Clifford
Sewell and Scott Mitchell to Shakespeare or algebra or the Battle
of Bull Run. The teachers let the escaping steam of giddiness sub-
side with high fives and loud bragging. When the classes ended,
the teachers simply stepped back and let the students run free.
There was nothing else that could have been done.

At their lockers, with the herd storming around them, Nancy
and Becky put away the books they had been carrying and took
out others. They were talking about the excitement when Scott
passed, followed by a wave of younger, giggling girls.

"Hey, Scott," Nancy called.

Scott turned, smiled. He said, "How's it going?"

"Great," Nancy said.

"Fine," Becky said. She could feel heat in her face.

Scott smiled again and moved down the corridor, the girls
trailing him, still giggling.

"God, he's good-looking," Nancy whispered. "I can't believe
you, Becky. I'd jump at the chance to screw Scott Mitchell if I
could, and you—" She paused. "Ah, I mean—if I wasn't in love
with Bobby, and if Scott wasn't interested in you. You know what
I mean."

They closed their lockers and began to walk down the corridor, staying close to the wall.

"Don't get me wrong," Nancy said. "Back there. What I said."

"You don't have to apologize," Becky told her. "I know what you mean." She stopped, looked at Nancy, smiled. She said, "I'm gonna do it."

"What?" Nancy said. "You are?"

"Yeah. If he still wants to."

"Trust me, he still wants to," Nancy said quickly. "Guys always want to."

"I've been thinking about it a lot lately," Becky confided. "I really like Scott. I don't know, but, well, maybe it's time to jump off the high dive."

Nancy's face beamed. "All right," she said. "That's great. Really great." She turned to walk away. "I've got to tell Bobby." She turned back to Becky. "You're gonna do it? Really? That's great. I'll be right back."

She was gone before Becky could speak.

6

It was late and the slivered moon, a backward comma hanging in the westward sky, was dull and weak, almost lost in the black velvet coat of night.

Standing outside the Dew Drop Inn smoking a last cigarette with Benny, Jerry Burnette commented on the night.

"Black as the inside of a owl's ass," Benny noted.

"Too dark for stars," Jerry said.

"Yeah, you're right," Benny agreed, looking up. "Ain't never seen it this dark but once or twice."

Jerry played his truck radio on his way back to the trailer park, wondering if there would be some news about the starless night—some curious, heavenly thing that happened once every three hundred years, but could be explained by scientists as easily as reading directions for boiling water. Maybe something to do with UFOs.

He smiled at the thought of UFOs. He knew it was the child in him—the child still wanting to play *Star Trek*—but he wanted to see one of the UFOs that the *National Enquirer* and other newspapers were always writing about. Once he had thought of driving to Montana, where several sightings had been reported, sightings verified by citizens who were neither drunk nor crazy: the preacher, the policeman, the high school principal. There had been a photograph of a singed spot in a cow pasture. The spot was as round as a ball, and nothing would grow in the bleached-out soil.

He turned off the highway and into the park and eased the truck down the narrow road that snaked through the trailers. "Better keep it to a crawl," he thought. Dark as it is, somebody could jump out and not be seen until it was too late. He saw Benny's truck stopping in front of his trailer, saw Fat Ethel at the door. He smiled. Benny was about to catch hell.

There was no one else on the road or in any of the yards, and he parked near his trailer, beside Wanda's car, and got out and went inside.

The inside of the trailer was as dark as the night and Jerry flipped on a light and walked toward the kitchen. He opened the refrigerator, took out a beer, and fingered open the top. He paused, turned his head. He thought he heard voices.

"Wanda?" he called.

There was a moment of silence, then the voices floated through the trailer again. He put down the beer and looked around. He saw the clothes that Wanda had been wearing scattered about the living room.

"Wanda? You here?"

He began to move cautiously down the hallway to the bedroom. At the bedroom door he heard a scraping sound, and he opened the door quickly and snapped on the light. Wanda sat up in bed, dragging the sheet to cover her nude body. Jerry glanced up to see the backside of a man rolling out of the window. He turned back to Wanda.

"Jerry—"

Jerry turned and ran down the hallway and out of the trailer. He could hear Wanda's voice: "Jerry, don't! Wait!"

He jumped off the small stoop leading to the front door of the trailer and began to run, turning the corner of the trailer. He saw a man several yards in front of him, carrying a shirt and his shoes, running hard down the hill, behind Wesley's parents' trailer and across Verdale's yard.

"Goddamnit," Jerry bellowed. He lowered his head and sprinted for the man, catching him from the back with a diving tackle. The man rolled over, dropping his shoes and shirt, then bounced to his feet and swung a heavy fist toward Jerry.

"You son of a bitch," Jerry growled. He grabbed the man and pulled him into the night. The man looked up.

"Jesus," Jerry whispered.

It was Ray.

Ray stepped back, laughing and holding his hands up. He said, "What's the matter, little brother? You're not surprised, are you?"

Jerry shook his head in disbelief. His right fist was still cocked.

"You've been wanting some of me for a long time, ain't you?" Ray continued. "Well, come on, take your best shot."

Jerry lowered his fist. He was still staring at Ray.

"You afraid I'll whip your ass again, ain't you?" teased Ray.

Jerry stepped back. He looked back up the hill toward his trailer. He could see Wanda standing close to the front door wrapped in a sheet.

"That's what I thought," Ray said. A short laugh fell from his lips. He dropped his hands. "Hell, I don't blame you. We shouldn't let that little slut come between family."

Ray's eyes saw the blur of Jerry's fist, but he did not have time to raise his hands or drop the smile from his lips. The blow caught him flush and hard on the left cheek, snapping his head and sending him to the ground. He rolled once and was back on his feet. He lowered his shoulder and drove into Jerry's chest, driving him into the dog pen behind the trailer. The dogs jumped and began barking furiously.

"Stop it!" Wanda shouted. She ran to where the men were fighting. "Stop it! Jerry! Ray!"

Around them, in the nearby trailers, lights began to pop on and doors opened and people began gathering—Verdale and Nancy, Clifford and Jimmie and Becky and Evelyn, Benny and Fat Ethel, and Wesley, dressed in boxer shorts and boots.

"Clifford, stop them," urged Evelyn. "They're gonna hurt each other."

"Shit, Evelyn, I ain't messing in somebody's else's business," Clifford snapped. He smiled.

"Jimmie Clifford, do something," Becky begged.

Jimmie leaned against the railing of the stoop. "Aw, it won't last long," he said easily.

The fight between the brothers continued, but it was more exhausting than punishing. They wrestled and punched and rolled across the ground. Finally, Jerry kicked Ray in the chest, sending him hard against the trailer. He fell to one knee and struggled to catch his breath. Jerry stood over him, dazed, breathing hard.

"You had to come back, didn't you, Ray?" Jerry said in a labored voice. "You've got such a shitty life that you can't stand it if anybody else is the least bit happy."

Ray sucked air into his lungs. Blood dripped from his nose. He wiped at it with his hand and looked up at Jerry. He said, "Happy? Your wife's fucking ever'body in town but you. Does that make you happy?"

A sudden, new energy surged in Jerry. He charged Ray, hitting him hard on the temple. Ray grabbed him and rolled and threw an elbow into Jerry's stomach.

Wanda rushed to them, trying to grab Jerry. "Stop it!" she shouted. "Leave him alone, Jerry!"

Ray tumbled backward, caught the fence around the dog pen, and pulled himself up. Jerry was still on the ground, gasping.

"Let me tell you one thing, little brother," Ray hissed weakly. "She's a good piece of ass. I've got to admit that about her."

A pained cry rose in Jerry's chest. He pushed off the ground and drove into Ray, catching him by the arms and flinging him. Ray hit the ground with a thud and rolled twice. He was at the edge of the small creek that ran through a deep ditch overgrown with weeds and cattails at the back of the park. He tried to stand, but couldn't. He staggered once and fell backward down the bank and into the creek.

"Damn you, Jerry!" Wanda screamed. She ran to Ray and knelt beside him, trying to help him up.

Jerry turned away and shook his head. Tears were bubbling in his eyes.

"You all right, Wanda?" Clifford asked. "I think it's time ever'body went to bed." He gestured with his head and Jimmie and Becky and Evelyn went back into the trailer. He looked once at Benny and Fat Ethel, and they too turned and walked away. He saw the door to Verdale's trailer closing quietly. Wesley smiled, sniffed the air, and walked off, his boots hitting the gravel with an easy crushing sound. Clifford looked at Wanda. He said, "Y'all ought to get inside now." Then he went into his trailer.

Wanda tried to touch Ray's face. She whispered. "I still love you, Ray. I always have."

Ray pushed her hand away. He shook his head. "You know, Wanda, you're just plain stupid," he said. "I think that's what I hated most about you. Did you think just because you gave me a little, I was gonna take you back?" He pulled himself up, crossed the lawn, and picked up his shirt and shoes. He smiled at Jerry. "You know, little brother, you always did have a helluva right." He rubbed his chin and walked off.

Jerry stood for a moment, watching his brother leave, then he turned to Wanda. She was standing at the creek, the wet, muddy sheet clinging to her body.

"Jerry—"

He whirled and walked back to the trailer and went inside. In the bedroom, he opened the closets and began throwing Wanda's clothes into a pile on the bed. He jerked drawers out of the dresser and spilled the contents on the pile. He swept his arm over shelves of makeup and medicines and tossed them onto the bed. Then he gathered the bedspread, dragged it through the trailer to the door, and threw it into the yard as Wanda stood watching.

"Jerry—," She was crying.

He slammed the door and locked it.

From Verdale's trailer, the voice of Elvis Presley floated through an opened window. He was singing *Are You Lonesome Tonight?*

7

It was, Evelyn protested, too much a fuss for a simple birthday "which I'd like to forget about in the first place."

Her face was part frown, part smile. She sat at the table, as instructed by Becky, and listened to the ceaseless talk. The talk came from those crowded into the trailer—Verdale, Nancy, Blanche, Freeman, Wesley (carefully watching Susie), Fat Ethel, Benny, Jimmie, and Clifford.

"All right, Mama." Becky announced, clapping her hands for attention. "Close your eyes." She disappeared into the kitchen.

"Oh, Lord, honey—"

"Do it, for Christ's sake," Clifford said impatiently.

Evelyn closed her eyes. The frown furrowed. The smile deepened.

"C'mon," Jimmie said to Becky. "Bring it out."

Becky and Nancy appeared from the kitchen, holding a cake covered in burning candles.

"Okay, Mama, you can open them now." Becky said.

Evelyn opened her eyes and looked at the cake. The frown faded from her forehead.

"Happpppy birthday to you . . . "

The song rang in the trailer in lusty, off-key voices. Susie's face beamed.

Becky placed the cake on the table before her mother. The orange tips of the candle flames flickered in Evelyn's eyes.

"Damn," Clifford exclaimed. "How many candles on that thing? I've seen smaller forest fires."

"Hush, Clifford," Evelyn said. "I'm younger'n you are."

"Yeah, but I'm prettier," Clifford teased.

Evelyn looked admiringly at the cake. It was four layers high, covered in a swirled white frosting. "Did you make this cake, honey?" she asked Becky.

"Nancy baked it and I decorated it." Becky said. She added, "And Jimmie Clifford cranked the ice cream freezer."

"Y'all beat all I've ever seen," sighed Evelyn, happily. "Thank you, girls. Thank you, Jimmie Clifford."

"Well, hell, we gonna frame it, or we gonna eat it?" Clifford said enthusiastically.

"Make a wish, Mama," Becky urged.

Evelyn closed her eyes, thought for a moment, then opened them and blew across the candles. The candle flames fluttered and died.

"I hope you get what you wished for, Mama," Becky said.

"I've already got more than most people ever get, honey," Evelyn replied softly.

They ate the cake and ice cream in noisy chatter, and then the dishes were taken away and the gifts brought to the table and put before Evelyn.

It's the only thing worth having a birthday for," Verdale said. "Getting presents. Here's ours' Evelyn." She handed Evelyn a wrapped box and watched gleefully as Evelyn carefully tore away the paper. Inside the box was a pair of panties and a bra.

"Oh, I wish you'd look," Evelyn cooed. "I needed these. Thank y'all so much. Nancy, honey, thank you."

Verdale and Nancy smiled acknowledgement.

She opened a box from Jimmie—a housecoat. She stood and slipped around her shoulders, praising Jimmie's selection. "Oh, thank you, Jimmie Clifford. You're so thoughtful, honey."

"What is it?" Jimmie asked.

"Jimmie Clifford!" Becky said in exasperation. "I told you what it was."

"No, you didn't," Jimmie said. "You just told me you'd got it."

"Don't fuss now," Evelyn said lightly. Then, to Becky: "Honey, all men are the same way. They can't buy and they can't remember what somebody else bought for 'em."

Blanche and Freeman gave placemats with a picture of Niagara Falls on them. Blanche explained that she had bought them on a trip she took with the ladies' Bible class.

Fat Ethel and Benny gave a green flower vase with artificial jonquils stuck in it.

And then Becky handed her mother a present that was large and flat. She said, "Open mine next, Mama."

Evelyn took the present and began unwrapping it.

"It's a picture," Evelyn said. "Oh, honey, did you paint me a picture?" She looked up at Verdale as she pulled away the paper. "Last year, she painted me the prettiest picture of Mama and Daddy's old place. I just loved—"

She pulled the painting from its paper. Her eyes widened in surprise.

"What is it, Evelyn?" Fat Ethel asked.

Evelyn held the painting up, tentatively. It was a portrait of Evelyn and Jesus, standing side-by-side. Jesus had his arm around Evelyn's shoulders. His crown of thorns slightly tilted to one side.

A gasp—almost too low to be heard—escaped from Blanche. Clifford broke into a laugh, followed by Jimmie.

"Way to go, Becky," Jimmie said.

"What?" Becky asked.

"My Lord," Blanche whispered, "that's the most sacrilegious thing I ever saw."

Wesley's head jerked in surprise. He said, "Mama!"

Becky's puzzled face scanned the room, looking for support. Clifford and Jimmie were still laughing.

"You don't like it?" Becky asked painfully.

Jimmie laughed harder.

"I love it, honey," Evelyn began. "It's just—well, I love it. Thank you." She stood and hugged Becky. "Clifford, will you and Jimmie Clifford just hush? I'm gonna hang it in the living room where ever'body can see it."

Becky smiled triumphantly.

"The hell you are," Clifford said.

"I guess we'll see where it goes," Evelyn countered.

A pause filled the room. Benny hacked a cough. Everyone was looking at Becky.

"Ah, Daddy, didn't you get Mama a birthday present?" asked Becky.

"Yeah, Clifford," Verdale said.

Clifford leaned back in his chair. He said, "Don't worry about it. I got it handled. I'm gonna take your mama out tonight for a little surprise."

8

They had begun planning it as they baked the cake for Evelyn's birthday party—selecting their dress and their makeup—and as soon as the cars began to leave the trailer park, as soon as they knew they were alone, they changed their clothes and sat before Nancy's mirror and applied the makeup, coating the lipstick heavily, drawing dark arches in their eyebrows, painting their eyelashes.

When they finished, they stood before the mirror and admired themselves. Their look was Hollywood white trash.

"We look like whores," Becky whispered.

"We look like we're going to get some attention," Nancy said. "Come on, we got to go."

They left the trailer and slipped among the dark shadows of trees until they reached the highway.

"I never hitchhiked before," Becky said nervously.

"Nothing to it," Nancy assured her. "Just stick out your thumb. I guarantee you somebody'll screech to a halt when they get a look at us."

"We could get raped," Becky protested.

"There you go again," Nancy sighed. "Letting your imagination run away. You said you was goin' to do it, and I'm just showing you how it's done."

"I guess," Becky murmured. Then: "Nancy, if you love Bobby so much, why do you do it with other boys?

Nancy fluffed her hair with her fingers. She watched an eighteen-wheeler approach, but turned away from the road. She said, after a moment, "I don't know. Different reasons. Depends on who it is, I guess. I mean, like, I was doing it with David Atkins before Bobby."

"Yeah, and you still do it with David."

Nancy twisted her mouth in thought. "Just sometimes," she said. "He's cute and he says he loves me and I like him and stuff. Anyway, we were going steady."

"You do it with ever'body you go steady with?" Becky asked.

"Well, no. Well, yeah, I guess I do. I mean, why go steady if there's nothing different about it? Doing it is, you know, special. It's like signifying the way you feel about the guy."

"What about Mark Warmack?" questioned Becky. "You always said you hated him, and you did it with him."

"Yeah, but, God, he's so good-looking, Becky. Anyway, we didn't actually do it. I was on my period, so I just gave him a blow job. That's different."

"Oh," Becky said quizzically. "What about Stevie Hart?"

A car approached. Nancy's thumb flew up. She saw the brake lights flash once, twice, then hold. The car stopped and the back-up flashed on.

"Well?" Becky said.

"What?"

"Stevie Hart."

"Look, Becky, you don't have to be in love to do it. I mean it's just as much fun one way as the other. But it's just that if you are in love and going steady, it's better—kinda. Okay?"

"Yeah. Okay."

Nancy started walking toward the car. She turned back. "Remember, act twenty-one."

The man in the car was in his mid-thirties. He wore a pin-striped business suit and a yellow power tie. He said, through the window, "You girls need a lift?"

"Sure do," Nancy said. She opened the door and slid into the front seat. Becky opened the back door and got in .

"Where to?" the man said cheerfully. His eyes were on Nancy's breasts.

"Up the road," Nancy told him. "I'll show you where to drop us."

"You got it, sweetheart."

The car lurched forward.

9

Clifford paid for the tray of food and drinks and took it out of the snack bar and crossed the parking lot, walking among the rows of cars parked on the slightly raised tiers of the Big Sandy Drive-In. He felt good. It was a cool, dark night. A double-feature in the annual Big Sandy Elvis Presley Festival was playing. He had a pint of Jack Daniels under the seat of his truck. Evelyn was beside him, nicely dressed, wearing a cologne that smelled like roses. The only thing he did not understand was why Evelyn was in a dark, irritated mood.

He got into the truck and placed the food tray between them.

"Got you a hot dog and a Diet Coke and some popcorn," he said, cheerfully.

Evelyn rolled her head away from his look. She crossed her arms.

"What?" Clifford said. "What the hell's the matter with you now?"

Evelyn leveled her eyes on him. She said, "Well, Clifford, if you don't know, I ain't about to tell you."

"Jesus," Clifford muttered. He pulled the Jack Daniels from beneath the seat and poured a generous slug into his Coke. Then he adjusted the speaker and turned down the volume. A preview of coming attractions was showing. "Guess who I saw parked back there?" he said.

"I wouldn't know," Evelyn sniffed.

"Wesley and Norma Smothers," Clifford told her. "Guess he gave in to his mama's whimpering about dating Norma." He laughed and picked up a hotdog and bit into it. He said, chewing, "Poor bastard. He was right about that one. That's the ugliest white woman in Tennessee." He laughed again.

"She can't help it." Evelyn said.

Clifford wagged his head. "Guess she can't," he agreed. "Know where Verdale is tonight?"

"It's none of my business, Clifford."

"Well, I know it ain't, but she's parked back yonder on the back row."

Evelyn's eyes glanced at the side view mirror.

"Yeah, she's sitting back there all by her lonesome." Clifford continued. "Well, almost." He smiled at Evelyn. "Just by coincidence, ol' Lloyd Pinkerton's sitting in his car right next to her."

Evelyn frowned. She thought: "Verdale ought to know better, being in public like this."

"Give you ten to one that before ol' Elvis swings his first hip, Verdale's over there with him and they'll be tied up like two dogs in heat."

"Clifford!"

He chewed on his hotdog and drank from his drink and looked at some half-dressed woman planting a wet kiss on some good-looking actor in a scene from an upcoming feature. "Lucky sumbitch," he thought. Beside him, Evelyn squirmed restlessly in her seat.

"What's the matter with you?" he asked.

She was silent for a moment, then she answered. "I just thought we might get to go out to Sizzler or Big Boy since it was my birthday. I never get to go anywhere nice."

Clifford looked at her with disgust. "Good God, Evelyn, I took you to Sizzler a couple of weeks ago."

She glared at him hatefully. She said, "It's been at least four months since we went out anywhere to eat. I just thought since it was my birthday, we might get to go out somewhere nice, not some drive-in movie. That's all. I guess it's just too much to ask."

"Yeah, well, we're here," Clifford grumbled, "and, by God, I plan to watch the movies. You can set there all night and pout if you want to. Gotdamnit, Evelyn, you are the hardest woman in Tennessee to please."

He turned the switch on the volume. The overture to *Tickle Me* began to play.

10

The man was puzzled when Nancy told him to stop in front of the Big Sandy Drive-In and let them out.

"Y'all can't get in without a car," he said. Then he smiled. "Want me to take you?" he offered. "Hell, I got a cooler full of beer in the trunk."

"That's all right," Nancy said, opening the door and stepping out. Becky was already standing outside.

"How much?" the man said.

"What?" Nancy asked.

"How much you girls charging?"

"Fuck off," Nancy snapped. She slammed the car door and stalked away, with Becky following. "Asshole," she muttered. She looked back as the car was pulling away. "Can you imagine doing it with a man old enough to be your daddy?"

Becky was surprised to learn that Nancy knew exactly how to get into the drive-in without paying. There was a path smoothed down by use, leading to a rip in the hogwire fence. They ducked under the fence and followed the path through a windbreak of trees and emerged at the back of the drive-in.

"Well, here goes ever'thing," Nancy announced. She looked around, saw a car parked on the back row. "There they are," she said.

Becky saw the car. Bobby and Scott and two other boys—Lyle White and Heyward Wells—were standing at the car, drinking beer. Their boyish laughter drifted across the drive-in lot.

As they approached, the boys turned to them. Becky could see the expression of surprise on Scott's face, followed by a smile.

"Y'all didn't drink all that beer, did you?" Nancy said.

"Why, hell, no," Bobby responded. He opened his arms and Nancy walked into his embrace. He kissed her passionately and rubbed his hands over her ass. "You look good enough to eat," he said.

"Promises, promises," Nancy said teasingly.

"Hey, guys, we gotta cut," Lyle said. A knowing grin was plastered on his face. He signaled to Heyward and the two walked away, laughing.

"Looks like that just leaves us," Scott said.

"Lucky us," Bobby replied. He ran his hands over Nancy's breasts and kissed her again.

"Where's our beer?" Nancy asked.

Bobby reached into a cooler and pulled out two beers and opened them, handing one to Nancy and one to Becky.

"You look—ah, different," Scott said to Becky. "I mean, you look great."

Becky ducked her head and smiled. She sipped from the beer. The taste was bitter and it burned on her tongue.

"Smoke?" Bobby asked. He tapped cigarettes from his pack and offered one to Nancy.

"Sure," Nancy said. She took the cigarette and waited for Bobby to light it.

"Becky?" Bobby said.

Becky hesitated, then accepted. She held the cigarette awkwardly in her mouth, trying to remember how her father and brother looked when they smoked. Scott lit it and she drew hard, choking on the sudden, harsh rush of the smoke.

"Smoke much?" Scott asked. There was teasing in his voice.

"I've been trying to quit," Becky replied. She dropped the cigarette on the ground and stepped on it.

No one at the Big Sandy Drive-In watched the movie with great interest. Everyone there had seen every movie Elvis Presley had made at least a half-dozen times, but still they filled the lot each year during Hoyt Frazier's Elvis Presley Festival. Hoyt owned the drive-in. He thought Elvis Presley was the greatest actor who ever lived, including Richard Burton and Clark Gable. His Elvis Festival was something eagerly anticipated, something talked about in the cafes and fast-food restaurants at morning coffee time. It also made a lot of money for Hoyt.

"You know something," Clifford complained bitterly, sipping from his Jack Daniels-and-Coke mixture, "this movie ain't worth a pinch of owl shit. Ol' Elvis has done better. I like that one with Ann Margaret where she wears them skimpy little Vegas outfits, where you can see her titties."

"I wish you'd clean up your language," Evelyn told him. Her tone was cool.

Clifford looked at his wife and smiled. "God," he thought, "she's on her high horse tonight." He leaned down and reached under the seat.

"Don't you think you've had enough of that stuff?" Evelyn said.

"Now, who said I was reaching for a drink?" Clifford replied. He sat up, holding a small, wrapped package. He handed it to Evelyn.

"What's this?"

"It's your birthday present," Clifford said. "What's it look like? Hell, I shouldn't even give it to you, after the way you been acting."

Evelyn's face brightened. She slipped off the ribbon and tore away the wrapping with her fingers. She opened the box slowly and stared in disbelief at a ring.

"Oh, Clifford," she cooed, "it's beautiful."

"Yeah," Clifford said smugly, "it's the kid's birthstones. Red for Becky and purple for Jimmie Clifford."

Evelyn slipped the ring on her finger and held her hand up to the flickering light from the screen. She said, "Oh, honey, I just love it, and I love you."

"Happy birthday," Clifford said.

Evelyn slipped quickly across the seat and kissed Clifford tenderly on the mouth.

"Feel like shit now, don't you?" Clifford said.

Two rows back, Norma Smothers pushed her body close to Wesley, resting her hand on his knee. Wesley could smell the gardenia odor of her perfume and the sweet clay odor of the makeup that she had caked over her face in an attempt to hide her ugliness. A surge of horror struck him: "Jesus, what if somebody sees me?"

"Norma, I'm trying to watch the movie here, okay?" Wesley said in a huff. He pushed her away.

Lloyd had not returned to his car after going to the restroom on a pretense of having to pee. He had slipped into Verdale's car, and now the window was fogged with the steam of their breathing. She was stroking his thigh, her thumb touching, as though by accident, his erection.

"Honey, you got to stop that, or we got to get out of here and go back to your place," begged Lloyd.

"Can't you hold it?" Verdale teased.

"Lord, no," Lloyd whispered. "Not much longer."

"Well, you better, or you gonna be a mess," Verdale said. Her thumb touched him again.

Lloyd threw his head back against the seat and moaned.

On the back row, in Scott's car, Bobby and Nancy were kissing passionately in the backseat, trying to balance cups of tequila they held in their hands. In the front seat, Scott sat close to Becky, cuddling her. He kissed her gently, his mouth slightly open, his tongue flitting across the flesh of her lips. She held her breath and tasted the kiss.

"You kiss real good," Scott whispered in her ear.

"Really?" Becky said.

"Yeah, I mean it."

He kissed her again. She closed her eyes. His tongue was like fire on her lips. She could feel it prying her mouth open, feel it burning on the tender inner skin, feel its torch-flame on the tip of her own tongue. She wanted to swallow the heat.

"Yeah," Scott said again, "you really know how to kiss."

His hand swept across her breasts. She could feel her nipples growing at the touch. A weakness shot through her abdomen and drove into her knees. She thought she would faint.

"It's all right," Scott whispered. "Just relax."

He began to unbutton her blouse, spreading it with his fingers. Then he ran his hand to her back and snapped open the bra. She could feel it fall free from her breasts. She leaned back against the seat. From behind her, she could hear Nancy moaning and whispering, "I love you." She glanced into the rearview mirror and saw that Nancy was nude from the waist down and that Bobby had rolled on top of her and was shoving himself into her.

"God, you're incredible," Scott sighed. His mouth swept over her breasts. She could feel his tongue flicking at a nipple, and then the pull of sucking. Her body seemed to be blazing from the inside.

"Yes," Nancy cried softly from the backseat. "Yes, yes." The car began to rock, like a rapid heartbeat.

"Don't worry about them," Scott said. "They're back there; we're up here."

His hand touched her knee and began to slide slowly up her thigh, beneath the short skirt she was wearing. Her body arched and she could feel Scott's fingers reaching the top of her panties. He pulled at them, rolled them down, and with one sweep of his hand, yanked them off her feet. His hand moved back up, his fingers stroking her legs, until he touched the fine, curled hair between her legs.

"Scott. Scott, wait a minute," Becky begged in a whisper.

His hand began to massage her.

"Scott—"

"Relax baby," he said. "It's gonna be okay."

A lump of fear lodged in her throat. Her body tensed as he rolled himself over her, unzipping and opening his pants.

"It's allright," he whispered.

He was working rapidly, his hands moving expertly at the buttons of her skirt. It was down and off her body before she could protest. He searched for penetration, plunging at her as she squirmed to push him away.

"No, Scott, really. Please. Don't," she said.

"It's okay," he said again. "I love you."

Becky pulled her hands to his shoulders and pushed hard. She said, forcefully, "Scott, stop! Please. No! I'm sorry. I just can't."

Scott shoved himself harder against her, wiggling his body between her legs. His erection jabbed painfully against her abdomen.

"No!" she cried. Her hand flew away from his shoulder and she slapped him viciously across his neck. He pulled back instinctively and Becky rolled up. She grabbed her panties from the floorboard of the car and opened the door and tumbled out. Outside the car, she slipped her legs into her panties and crossed her chest with her arms.

Scott leaned out of the door, glaring at her. He said, "Are you gonna pull this shit again? What'd you come out here for?"

"I thought—I—I just can't do this right now. It's not you, it's—"

Scott pulled the door closed, forcing Becky backward. He locked the door.

"Scott, open the door, please." Becky said, glancing around. She could see faces in the windows of the few cars parked around them.

"No," Scott said angrily.

"Scott, let me in," she begged.

"You're just a prick-tease," he snapped.

The lights from a car parked near them, at an angle, flicked on, silhouetting Becky. A wolf howl rolled from the window. Becky ducked. Her heart was racing.

"Let me in!" she shouted.

"No," Scott said from the opened window. "Car rules—put out or get out. Nothing I can do about the rules."

Becky's face appeared over the edge of the window. "Then give me my clothes," she said.

The wolf howls continued. A horn from another car sounded. Becky leaned into the window and started grabbing for her clothes. Scott pulled them away, ducking her swinging hands. He was laughing.

From his sideview mirror, several rows in front, Clifford could see the form of a shapely woman in panties fighting with someone in the car. He laughed and nudged Evelyn. "Wonder what the hell's going on back there?" he said. He stuck his head out of the window and joined the chorus of howls that were rolling over the drive inn lot.

In the car, Nancy was struggling to push Bobby away. Her face bobbed over the front seat as Becky raced around the car in panic.

"You son of a bitch, give her clothes back to her," Nancy hissed.

"What's going on?" Bobby said, his voice a slur.

"The bitch copped out on me," Scott said.

Bobby pulled Nancy back and turned her to face him. "What's going on?" he demanded. "I thought you said she wanted to do it."

"I thought she did," Nancy shot back. She leaned out of the window and said to Becky, "I thought you said you wanted to do it."

Becky's voice was shrill and panicked. Flashlights aimed from car windows danced over her body. She tried to press against the car.

"I thought you wanted to do it," Nancy said again.

"I can't," Becky cried. "I'm sorry. I just can't. Give me my clothes, please."

"You might as well get back in here and do it," Scott said, smiling arrogantly. "I'm gonna tell everybody at school that we did it anyway."

"Give her her clothes," Nancy demanded. She was pulling her own clothes back on.

"Shut up," Scott snapped. "You're the one who said she'd fuck."

The car horns were now blowing in celebration. The beams from flashlights struck the car like bullets. In his truck, Wesley yelped and pushed Norma out of the way for a better view. He did not know the panty-clad girl crouched against the dark metal of the door, but she had a body that was remarkable. Clifford had turned and was watching from the back window of the truck. He said to Evelyn, "You remember when we used to come out here and fool around like that?"

"No, Clifford, I don't," Evelyn said. "We never did that."

"Bullshit," Clifford drawled. The smile was deep in his face.

Nancy leaned forward and grabbed Becky's bra from Scott's hand and threw it out the window. She hissed, "Maybe she de-

cided not to do it with an asshole like you." She turned to Bobby
and dared him with a look. "Let me out," she growled.

"Bitch," Scott said.

"Let me out," Nancy repeated.

Bobby picked up the tequila bottle and took a sip. His eyes
covered Nancy with a warning. "You ain't going nowhere," he
said. Then, to Scott: "Give her her clothes, man. We're attracting
attention."

From outside, Becky begged, "Open the door, please." She was
crying.

"Let her in, Scott," Nancy said angrily. She grabbed Bobby by
his shirt. "You better do something, or I'm never gonna let you
touch me again."

From his truck, his neck twisted for a clear look, Clifford
mumbled, "Bunch of damn kids. Probably drunk."

"It's disgusting," Evelyn said.

"Aw, hell, Evelyn, they're just young."

"I don't care how old they are, it's disgusting," Evelyn replied.
"So are you, staring at 'em."

Clifford ignored the remark. "I wish you'd look at the body on
that girl," he said. "Now, that's a set of tits."

"Clifford, hush!" Evelyn commanded. She turned to look at the
car. "That's all you men have on your mind—naked women,
and—" Her voice froze. She turned her shoulders for a better
view. She gasped, "Clifford, that looks like—"

She did not have to tell him. Clifford knew. Suddenly, clearly,
he knew.

"Son of a bitch," Clifford whispered. He opened the truck door
and got out. In two steps, he realized Evelyn was beside him.

At the car, Becky's hand shot through the rolled-down window
and she grabbed her shirt and yanked it out. Scott reached for the
skirt, but Nancy caught him from behind and pulled his head
back. She looked up and saw Clifford and Evelyn rushing toward
them through the row of cars.

"Oh, shit," Nancy hissed, "that's Becky's old man and her
mother." She stuck her head out of the window. "Becky, your parents."

Scott whirled in the seat and pulled on the car lights and
snapped them on high beam. The light struck Clifford and Evelyn
in the eyes, blinding them. He saw them pause and throw their
arms up over their faces, then he dumped Becky's blouse out of
the window and threw the speaker to the ground. He tried to start
the car, but it stalled.

"Run, Becky, run," Nancy called. She saw Becky gather her

clothes and start to run for the windbreak of trees, her face covered with her blouse. Car horns were playing catcalls. The beams from flashlights followed her, panning over her body, until she disappeared into the trees.

At the car, Nancy struggled to pull on her skirt as Clifford and Evelyn approached. Bobby sat back in the shadows. He could feel the tequila rolling in his stomach. In the front seat, Scott nervously tried to start the car.

Clifford leaned in through the window. His eyes were cold on Scott. "What's going on back here?" he said in a low, hard voice. "You got car trouble?"

"Uh—" Scott muttered.

From the backseat, Bobby rolled to the window. He mumbled, "Oh, God, I'm gonna be sick." He thrust his head out of the window and began to throw up as Verdale and Lloyd arrived at the car.

"I think I'm gonna be sick too," Nancy said as she slumped back in the seat. She could feel Verdale's cold stare as she covered her breasts with her shirt.

11

Becky stood in the shadows of the road, watching the cars speed by on the highway. She was breathing hard, still crying. Her dress was wrinkled and caked in dirt. One of the heels on the pair of high heels that Nancy had loaned her was broken. She held the heel in her hand, rolling it nervously.

She did not have to wait long. She stepped back, deeper into the shadows, as her father's truck moved slowly down the highway. She could see his face peering out the side window, searching the road. She stood for another few minutes after the truck had disappeared, then she stepped out to the highway and waited for the far-off beams of the car to come near. She raised her hand reluctantly, pointing her thumb toward the Captain's Point Trailer Park.

It was an older couple who stopped for her. She told them that her car had stalled on a side road and she was trying to get home to have her father drive back and check the car. They smiled and nodded and looked at her suspiciously, but they did not ask why she was holding the broken heel, rubbing it.

She insisted that they drop her off at the entrance to the trailer park, thanking them in a small girl's voice. As they drove away, the man shook his head sadly. "Poor white trash," he said. "I feel sorry for them." His wife agreed, "Me, too. Seems like they can't ever get a break away from how they grew up. You wait and see. That little girl'll wind up living in a trailer, just like her mama, having a dozen crying kids pulling at her."

Becky lingered at the window, in the dark cup of the trees, where no one could see her, and waited until the lights in her trailer clicked off, and then she slipped across the yard and opened the door quietly and slipped inside. As she closed the door, the light snapped on, and she turned to face her parents.

Clifford was sitting in his recliner. Evelyn was by the light switch. She moved to the sofa and sat. They stared silently at Becky.

"I—I didn't do anything," Becky began, stammering. "I mean—nothing happened."

Clifford inhaled slowly, controlling himself. His eyes did not move from Becky. He said, "I'm gonna tell you something, young lady. What I saw out there tonight hurt your mama so much. I'm damned disappointed in you."

Becky blinked to clear the tears that were welling in her eyes. "Daddy, don't," she whimpered. "I'm sorry. I really didn't do anything."

A car screeched to a halt outside the trailer, and a car door slammed. The sound of voices drifted inside. Clifford pulled from his chair and went to the window and looked out.

"Who is it?" Evelyn said.

"Jimmie Clifford and some of the boys," Clifford mumbled. He looked back at Becky. "We give you ever'thing we can," he continued. "Your mama does without so you can have things, and this is how you thank her."

The door opened and Jimmie stumbled in. The smell of beer floated from him. His eyes were glazed. "What the hell's ever'body doing up?" he asked.

Clifford's voice was firm: "Go to bed."

"That's right where I'm headed," Jimmie replied, a crooked smile crossing his face. He winked at Becky, then ambled off, humming tunelessly.

Clifford sat again in the recliner. He drummed his fingers on the armrest. Finally, he said, "I want your ass home right after school, young lady. I expect you to help your mama around here and you can just forget art school and ever'thing else. I don't even want to see you painting or drawing or nothing." He paused, let the words drive into Becky. "Now, go to bed," he ordered.

Becky chewed on her lower lip. She started down the hall, then stopped and looked back. "Can I say something?" she asked.

"No. Go to bed."

"Clifford," Evelyn said softly. She nodded to Becky. "What is it?"

The tears were streaming down Becky's face. She sobbed as she talked: "I just want to tell you that I'm sorry. It was wrong, and I won't do something like that again. I know I let you down, Daddy, but I want to know why Jimmie Clifford can stay out all night and come in drunk and wreck the car and you don't say a word to him. No matter what he does, it's all right, but if I make any kind of mistake at all, you're disappointed in me."

Clifford leaned forward in his recliner. The muscles in his face rolled under the chewed words. "That's different," he insisted. "Jimmie Clifford's a boy, and you're a girl. There's a difference, as I'm sure you're aware after tonight."

"Clifford, hush," Evelyn warned. "I think you're the one that ought to go to bed."

Clifford shot an angry look at Evelyn. He stood. "All right, I will," he said. "Can't say nothing in my own gotdamned house without being chewed out." He stalked away, but paused when he passed Becky. He added, "We'll finish this in the morning, young lady." He disappeared down the dark hallway.

Becky stood, the tears rolling from her face. She lifted her head to her mother. Evelyn opened her arms.

"Come here, honey," Evelyn whispered.

Becky rushed to the sofa and fell into Evelyn's arms. The sobs spilled from her.

"I'm—I'm sorry, mama," Becky cried softlly. "I'm sorry I messed up your birthday, but I didn't do anything. I thought about it, but I didn't do it. I thought if I did it, he'd like me, but I just couldn't."

Evelyn stroked her daughter's hair. She said, "I think you made the right decision, honey. That shows me you're growing up."

"Why can't boys just like you, and be friends?" Becky wondered bitterly. "Why do they always want something? Why am I so stupid?"

"You're not stupid, honey. I think you're very smart," Evelyn said.

Becky pulled away and wiped her eyes with her hands. She said, "Right. I'm a genius. What would Scott Mitchell want with me when he's got the prettiest, most popular girl in school? I'm so sure he's going to drop her for me." She paused, inhaled, then added, "But I really thought he liked me."

Down the hallway, in the shadows, Clifford and Jimmie stood, listening. They could hear Becky's painful weeping and Evelyn's comforting voice. Clifford bowed his head, swallowed, and slipped noiselessly into his bedroom. Jimmie's face narrowed with anger.

12

Jimmie had entered the locker room in a brooding, angry mood, wearing a mean and dangerous look, causing one of the coaches to mutter, "Sumbitch. Ol' Jimmie Clifford looks like he's about ready to chew nails."

One of the other coaches had agreed. "We keep him this way until Friday night and we gonna put that trophy up in the case."

On the field, he had been a maniac, playing with the first-team defense against the second-team offense. Finally, he had been taken out of the lineup by the coaches.

"Damn, Jimmie Clifford," one of the coaches had complained, "you gonna kill one of your own teammates. We got to have ever'body healthy."

Jimmie shrugged. He did not give a damn what the coaches said. He stood watching the practice, and then, without permission from the coaches, he trotted onto the field and joined the second-team defensive unit, practicing against the first-team offense.

"What the hell's Jimmie Clifford doing?" one of the coaches asked.

"What he wants to, it looks like," another coach replied.

"Well, get him off the field," the first coach ordered.

"Coach, you ever hear about the eight-hundred-pound gorilla?" the second coach replied.

"Yeah," the first coach muttered. He stared at Jimmie under his pulled-down cap and tapped subconsciously on his whistle.

On the field, Jimmie pushed players around and moved to the middle linebacker's position, close behind the line of scrimmage. He danced on his muscled legs as the offensive team folded from the huddle to the ball.

Scott looked up, saw Jimmie. An expression of fear and surprise flickered across his face. He thought: "Oh, shit." He turned and called an audible. He was not about to run the option that had been directed in the huddle. If Jimmie Clifford was going to tackle somebody, it would be somebody else.

It did not matter. At the snap of the ball, Jimmie exploded forward, bulling his way through bodies. He saw Scott thrust the ball into the arms of Willie Evans and saw Willie dodge left. He didn't care. He caught Marty Upshaw, the blocking back, and tossed him aside like a toy, and then he rose up in the air in a powerful leap and came down across Scott like a falling rocket. He could hear Scott cry out in pain. He rolled up, turned Scott by the face mask, and threw a single punch into his stomach. Scott gasped and tried to find his breath. Whistles were blaring in the air.

"What the hell's going on?" one of the coaches yelled from across the field.

Jimmie leaned close to Scott's face. He said, "If I ever see you near my sister again, I'll tear your fucking head off and shit down your throat." He slapped Scott's helmet hard against the ground then stood and walked away, pushing through the gathering coaches and players.

From the ground, Scott whispered, "Coach, Coach—"

The coach kneeled beside Scott. He said, "Son, I'd damn well stay away from his sister, if I was you." He stood, then blew his whistle and yelled, "All right, let's hustle up. We got a lot to do."

13

"If Jesus was to come back this week and wind up in Big Sandy, he'd have to wait till after the football game for anybody to give him the time of day."

Someone said that Edie Hart, a waitress at the Big Sandy Cafe, was the first to make the declaration about Jesus, though there was an argument that it was in fact Edie's husband, Harold, who uttered the words. It did not matter. There was more than a little truth in the observation, and by Wednesday morning everyone in Big Sandy had either heard or said it.

No one could remember anything as anxiously awaited as the state championship football game between the Big Sandy Wildcats and the South Central Mountaineers out of Knoxville.

It was more than a game; it was a classic confrontation. The Mill Village vs. the Corporate Suits. Us vs. Them. And everywhere in Big Sandy there was some reminder of the importance of playing, and of winning.

But it was not the banners and the signs and the cars with purple-and-gold crepe-paper streamers fluttering from radio antennas that fueled the blaze of expectation; it was the talk.

Everyone knew what had to be done to win.

And everyone freely offered an opinion, regardless of how ridiculous it was.

Freddy Spencer, who had played for Big Sandy High in the late forties, declared that the Wildcats ought to put in the single-wing attack. "Hell, ain't nobody on earth would expect that," Freddy said proudly.

Rosemary Chandler believed the Wildcats should go on a diet of tea and honey, and that the players should suck on oranges filled with confectionery sugar at halftime. "Instant energy," Rosemary advised.

Arthur Daly seriously schemed collecting money from Big Sandy merchants to hire a busload of whores from Chattanooga.

Norm Mason asked him why. "Hell, the way I hear it, our boys are getting all the pussy they can handle," Norm said.

"Well, you damn fool," Arthur replied indignantly, "them girls won't be for our boys. They'll be for the South Central team. They get wore out the night before, our boys would knock what's left of their pricks up in their watch pockets."

Even at Wednesday night prayer meeting, the Big Sandy Wildcats were high on the list of prayerful consideration.

"My friends," said Brother Ruffin, "before we part this night, all of us going our separate ways, let's remember Louise Burnette in our prayers. Like most ever'body here knows, Louise had to go back into the hospital this week and was transferred to Baptist Hospital in Memphis. Am I right about that, Sister Sewell?"

Brother Ruffin looked at Evelyn, who was seated with a dozing Clifford. She jabbed Clifford in the ribs and nodded gravely, looking for confirmation from those sitting around her. A few heads wagged, equally grave.

"Well, I know she'd appreciate any calls or visits," Brother Ruffin continued. "Now, if there's nothing else, let us pray."

Brother Ruffin picked up a tattered, well-used Bible from the podium and raised it above his head.

"Dear Heavenly Father," he intoned, "we come humbly before thee, asking thy blessings on our families and friends. Guard, guide, and direct us in thy service. We ask thy blessing, Lord, on Louise and her family as she fights this terrible and valiant battle against cancer. Also, dear Heavenly Father, we ask thy special blessing on our Big Sandy High School Wildcats, who will be playing for the State Division Three-A football championship this Friday night, up in Nashville at Vanderbilt Stadium. Protect these young men, Lord, as they battle an undefeated and untied team. We want you to look down on all of them—them boys from South Central as well as our boys from Big Sandy. But, Lord, if you could—this time—look down on our boys with just a little more favor. Not much. Just a point or two. And if it be thy will, as much as it's our will, merciful Heavenly Father, bring our boys home safe and victorious, giving our community its first state championship since nineteen forty-nine.

"Amen!"

The congregation shouted in response: "Amen!"

14

The caravan was led by the newest Bluebird school bus in the Big Sandy school system, followed by a line of cars that stretched for miles, like a writhing, speeding snake, along Interstate 40. The caravan was gaudy, a purple-and-gold carnival that had people in other cars gawking curiously at the Big Sandy cars and trucks, headlights burning, horns blowing, as they sped past them on the expressway. Fletcher Carmichael's Ford had a crudely painted hand with the middle finger extended on both doors. Beneath the hand were the words, "Take This, South Central."

Even Clifford thought the caravan was a joke.

"Know what I feel like?" he said, as they left Big Sandy. "I feel like I'm in the middle of a New Orleans funeral going down Bourbon Street."

"Yeah," Becky said. "Talk about country going to town. Now I know where that came from."

They had ridden in silence for fifty miles, listening to a talk show out of Nashville, before Becky spoke again. She said, "You think Jimmie Clifford is scared?"

Her mother was sitting beside her in the front seat. Verdale and Nancy were in the back seat with a picnic basket of food and a cooler of Coke and beer.

"I think it's fair to say he's scared, honey," Evelyn answered.

Clifford laughed. "I bet you couldn't drive a ten-penny nail up his ass with a sledgehammer," he said.

"Clifford!" exclaimed Evelyn.

In the back seat, Nancy giggled. Clifford glanced at her in the rearview mirror and winked.

In the team bus, three cars in front of Clifford's car, Jimmie had his head cushioned against the seat by his letterman's jacket. He was asleep and snoring. Around him, his teammates stared solemnly out of the windows, the look of uncertainty clouding their faces.

The Big Sandy caravan pulled into the parking lot at Vanderbilt Stadium and within minutes, individual picnics were beginning at the back of each car and truck. The smell of hamburgers and hot dogs and ribs cooking over small, portable charcoal grills swept across the lot, and the sound of loud, nervous chatter and loud, nervous laughter rang out. Clifford and Evelyn and Verdale sat in the folding lawn chairs Clifford had crammed into the car, eating cold fried chicken and potato salad and slaw. Evelyn drank a Coke, Clifford and Verdale cans of Budweiser. Becky and Nancy wandered among the cars, visiting with classmates, nibbling from dishes offered them by exuberant Wildcat fans.

"By God, Evelyn," grumbled Clifford, "I told you we could of brought the grill."

"Honey, it's too big to put in the car," Evelyn said. "You could put a cow on that grill we got."

"Well, we could of bought us one of the hi-baa-key things," Clifford argued. "I told you I seen 'em on sale at Wal-Mart."

"We're fine," Evelyn told him. "Verdale, you want some more chicken?"

When they entered the stadium, the nerves of the people of the Big Sandy caravan were raw. They were like addicts high on drugs or too much caffeine. They shouted, blew cheap party horns, rang cow bells. Some of them had painted half their faces with gold paint, half with purple paint, some with capital W's painted on their foreheads.

Inside the stadium, their celebration was stilled.

"Sumbitch," mumbled Arthur Daly, "this place is big, ain't it?"

"I thought you'd been here," Freddy Spencer said.

"Have," Arthur answered, "but, Jesus, that was a long time ago, and I ain't never been here when they was so much at stake."

"I guaran-damn-tee you them South Central boys has been in a place this big," Freddy suggested. "Bet you a dollar to a dough-nut that coach of theirs had 'em working out over at the U of Ten-nessee just to get an edge."

"South Central has played here six of the last seven years, you idiot," Arthur declared. "They're state champs! We ought to of hired them whores."

"Maybe we still can," Freddy mused.

"Well, shit, Freddy, they ain't no time for that now," Arthur countered. "The game's about to start."

"I wadn't talking about no whores for them," Freddy replied. "I was thinking about me 'n' you."

The only person from Big Sandy who thought of bringing a ra-

dio to listen to the play-by-play was Harley Lovejoy, who owned a
radio and television repair shop, and it was more by accident than
plan that Clifford, Evelyn, Verdale, Becky, and Nancy were sitting near him.

"Oh, this is an added plus," cooed Evelyn, when she heard
about the radio. "Clifford, don't you think this is an added plus?"

"What the hell's an added plus?" Clifford mumbled. He cut his
eyes to Wesley and Jerry, who were sitting behind them. Clifford
did not like Harley Lovejoy. He believed that Harley was, in his
private life, a queer, because Harley was not married, was never
seen with a woman, and made frequent weekend trips to Knoxville or Atlanta.

"I can play it real low so everybody can hear the pregame,"
Harvey explained, "but when it starts, I'll have to plug it in my
ear. That way, it won't disturb anybody." He smiled. "Ballpark et-
iquette," he added.

"That's all right," Evelyn said.

"But whatever happens during the game, I'll let you know,"
Harley promised Evelyn.

"Well, shit, Harley, we can see what's happening," Clifford
said.

Harley blushed. "Well, I guess that's right," he admitted in
that soft voice that made Clifford uncomfortable. He placed the
radio on the side of the folded blanket he was sitting on and
turned up the volume. Clifford always wondered if Harley sat on a
folded blanket because his ass was sore.

". . . and, again, this is John Ward from Vanderbilt Stadium,"
the voice from the radio said in a deep melodious tone, "here with
the former great from the Tennessee Volunteers, none other than
Richmond Flowers, Jr., Richmond, we've got quite a game brewing here."

"That's right, John," Richmond Flowers, Jr., said. "The Triple-
A state championship between the powerful South Central Moun-
taineers of Knoxville and the surprising Big Sandy Wildcats from
Big Sandy, Tennessee."

"So, what do we know about these two teams, Richmond?"
asked John in his serious radio voice.

"Well," Richmond began, "State Champs South Central come
in with a record of eleven wins and no losses, and most impressive
is the fact that they haven't even been scored on in the last seven
games."

"That certainly is impressive," agreed John. "Many experts
believe the Mountaineers may be the best high school team in

America, but they'll have their hands full tonight against the
Wildcats, who also have a perfect eleven-and-zero record."

Evelyn oohed and applauded. Nancy and Becky exchanged
smiles. Wesley let out a loud "Kick ass, Wildcats" and Verdale
poured Jack Daniels in her Coca Cola.

At the Dew Drop Inn in Big Sandy, Ed Stone pulled the plug
on the jukebox and rushed back to his seat at the bar. The sound
of John Ward's voice boomed from a radio sitting on a counter beside a row of cheap liquor bottles.

"Turn it up, Janice," ordered Ed.

Janice turned up the volume. The voices in the Inn began to
fade.

"What Big Sandy has to be aware of is how well the Mountaineers protect their quarterback, Jason Etheridge," John was
saying. "He's only been sacked four times the entire season, while
throwing for twenty-two touchdowns. This boy's got quite an arm,
Richmond, and he's got a great corps of receivers, especially in
Robert King."

"Bullshit," somebody said from a table. "Sounds like a couple
of fags to me." Laughter rose and died quickly.

"No doubt about it, John," said Richmond, "but I doubt if
they've seen any defensive player this year with the speed and the
sheer power of Big Sandy's Jimmie Clifford Sewell. He's a blue-
chip prospect—maybe the most talented player on the field. If the
Mountaineers keep him away from Jason Etheridge, they'll win
this game. If they don't, the Wildcats might have a chance, partic-
ularly with Scott Mitchell running the team. He's not the passer
that Etheridge is, but he's a deceptive runner and can hit the
short routes."

"Well, let's take a break and then we'll be back for the kickoff,"
announced John Ward. "This is your Tennessee Volunteer Net-
work."

A cheer erupted in the Dew Drop Inn.

"Kick their ass, Wildcats, kick their ass . . . "

A pounding began on the tables and floor.

"Kick their ass, Wildcats, kick their ass . . . "

15

The stands of Vanderbilt Stadium were filling. On the field, the Big Sandy band was marching in the formation of a giant W. The larger, more polished South Central band waited in the end zone for their turn.

"What's that W for?" a heavy, red-bearded man standing in the aisle near Clifford asked. "I thought we was playing some little town called Big Sandy."

Clifford could feel his muscles tense. Evelyn touched his arm firmly.

"That's for Wildcats," Harley Lovejoy said. "W for Wildcats."

The man laughed. He said, "Well, I guess they couldn't do a BS, could they? BS stands for a lot of things other than Big Sandy, don't it?"

Clifford's body began to rise. Evelyn's nails dug into his arm. He sat and glared at the man.

"Why don't you just go on and find your seat?" suggested Verdale. "I didn't ride all the way up here to watch Clifford—" she gestured toward Clifford "—whip somebody's ass."

The man smiled confidently.

"We just got him out of jail for cutting up on some smartass," Verdale added. "I'd sure hate to see 'em haul him back in for what he's gonna do to your scrawny butt."

The smile dropped from the man's face. He turned and walked away quickly.

"Mama, you see that sign on the goalpost, the one with the Wildcats' name on it?" Nancy asked.

Verdale nodded as she gulped down her Jack Daniels and Coca Cola.

"Becky painted that sign," Nancy said. "She painted most of the signs we got."

Verdale's mouth opened in astonishment. She said, "I swannee, Becky, you really have a talent for painting."

"Thank you, Mrs. Calloway," Becky said shyly.

"That's really good work," agreed Harley Lovejoy softly.

"Yeah," Jerry said. "Real nice, Becky."

"Sure is," Wesley added. "You ever think about painting signs on them Big Rig Trailers? You could make a goddamn fortune."

"Wesley, do you have to cuss?" Evelyn called over her shoulder.

"I'm sorry," Wesley shrugged. "Sorry, Nancy," he added.

"I don't care if you cuss, Wesley. I don't care what you do," Nancy said as she frowned at Becky.

"You oughta be real proud of her, Evelyn," Verdale said. "She's so good at something like painting. I just wish Nancy had a talent for something like that, or anything."

There was a pause. On the field, the drum major for the South Central Mountaineers blew his whistle, and the band began playing. Becky looked at Nancy, who had turned away to hide the hurt in her face. Evelyn touched Becky on the hand. She said, "Well, Verdale, I think Nancy is talented. I never saw a better birthday cake than the one she made for me."

"It was nice," conceded Verdale. "You know what I mean."

"Yeah, Mama, ever'body knows," Nancy mumbled.

Wesley, who was sitting behind Nancy, reached forward and touched her on her shoulder, massaging her neck gently. Nancy said nothing.

In the Dew Drop Inn, Ed Stone was taking bets that Big Sandy would pass on the first play.

"I heard a couple of the coaches talking about it over at the cafe," Ed said.

"Well, shit, Ed, that ain't much of a bet if you got inside information," Benny told him.

"All right, I'll give you two to one on what kinda pass it's gonna be," Ed bargained.

"You probably already know that," Benny said.

Ed shook his head. "Didn't hear nothing about it," he vowed. "But I'm saying it's gonna be a banana route."

"What the fuck's that?" Bill Atkinson said.

Ed stared at Bill with contempt. He said, "You must've not played any football."

"Hell, Ed, we was on the same team," Bill replied, "but damned if I remember any such thing as a banana route."

"It's where you slice into the middle and peel off to the outside," Ed explained.

"Shit, Ed," mumbled Benny. He picked up his beer and sipped from it.

From the radio, there was a roar. In the background, the public address announcer shouted, "And here come the Big Sandy Wildcats . . ."

A cheer exploded in the Inn.

Evelyn watched excitedly as Jimmie Clifford and Scott led the Wildcats through the end-zone sign that Becky had painted. She said, in a loud, distressed voice, "Honey, they tore up your sign."

"It's all right, Mama, they're supposed to," Becky said.

The announcer boomed, "And from Knoxville, the South! Central! Mountaineers!"

The Mountaineers roared through their own end-zone sign, ripping it into confetti. The Mountaineer fans screamed their praise, drowning out the smaller Big Sandy contingent.

From the field, Becky could hear her voice: "Becky, Becky Sewell . . ." She looked down to see Susan, holding a megaphone, waving to her. "Come down here," Susan shouted.

Becky stood, hesitated. She looked at Nancy. She said, "I'll be right back."

"Sure. Okay," Nancy said. She turned her face. She could still feel Wesley's hand on her shoulder, rubbing against her neck muscle.

Becky slipped over the railing and onto the field as the announcer said, "Ladies and gentlemen, please rise as the combined bands of South Central and Big Sandy high schools join in playing our National Anthem, under the direction of Curly Wakefield, the band director of Big Sandy High School."

In the Dew Drop Inn, everyone stood, awkwardly, during the playing of the National Anthem. On the last note, Benny shouted, "Bring it home, boys." He sat and grabbed his beer and leaned toward the radio. His eyes swept the faces around him. Everyone leaned toward the radio, necks cocked to favor their best ear.

"Two to one, Ed," Benny said, as the alcohol clouded his judgment.

"You got it. First play, a pass. Banana route," Ed said.

Big Sandy lost the toss and South Central elected to receive. "Well, Richmond, we're about to get started," John Ward said from the radio. "Any predictions?"

"It's hard to say, John," Richmond responded. "On paper, it looks like South Central by as much as fourteen to twenty-one points, but you don't play these kind of games on paper. This group of kids from Big Sandy are keyed up—and you know they've got a lot of pride going for them."

Ed was stunned. He shouted, "Twenty-one points? God-o-mighty, Richmond must not of done his homework. Ain't no-body—not even the goddamn Dallas Cowboys—gonna beat the Wildcats by twenty-one points."

"And heeeerrreee's the kickoff . . ." John Ward sang.

There was a roar, muffling the radio broadcast.

"What the fuck happened?" Bill Atkinson yelled from a back table.

"Jimmie Clifford just knocked the living shit out of some ol' boy from South Central," Benny yelled back.

"How many yards did he get?"

"About twenty," Ed answered. "Ball's on the thirty."

On the field, with the roar of the crowd pouring down on both teams, the Mountaineers broke from the huddle, jogged confidently to the line of scrimmage, and made their first mistake of the game.

"Which one of you assholes is Sewell?" growled the center, a huge, muscled boy with the dark, mean face of a street fighter.

Jimmie stood up from his middle linebacker's crouch. "I am," he said, evenly.

"I hear your mama sucks dicks," the boy said with a sneer.

"Oh, shit," Franklin Cross said. Franklin was the Wildcats' outside linebacker. He made a move for Jimmie, but Jimmie waved him away with his hand.

"My mama," Jimmie said across the line, "is one of the greatest women on earth. Now you better tell ever'body goodnight, 'cause you about to play the only down you gonna play in this game."

The center laughed arrogantly. He leaned over the ball. From behind, Jason Etheridge began calling signals. The ball snapped up, slapping into Jason's hands. Both lines bulled into one another, and over the slap of bodies colliding, Jimmie screamed a savage cry. He took two running steps, dipped his body and thrust down with strength he did not know he possessed. His shoulder caught the center across the right side of his knee, and he could hear the joint separate, like a snapping stick. The center's cry of pain rose over the field.

"Incomplete pass," John Ward shouted into the microphone "and it looks like we've got somebody hurt, Richmond."

"Let's see," John Ward said. "The man on the ground is South Central's Wade Ottinger, the key to the Mountaineers' offensive line."

"A devastating hit by Jimmie Clifford Sewell," Richmond announced.

The cheers in the Dew Drop Inn became bellowing.

"Kick 'em in the ass, kick 'em in the ass . . . "

"Way to go, Jimmie Clifford . . . "

"We're number one . . . "

On the field, the stunned Mountaineers gathered around Wade Ottinger. He writhed on the ground, tears welling and spilling from his eyes. Jimmie stood nearby, glaring down at him.

"All right, all right," the referee ordered, "move out of the way. Let the doctor get in here."

Jimmie walked away. He could feel someone at his shoulder and he stopped and turned. It was Jason Etheridge.

"Hey, man, sorry about what Wade said," Jason mumbled. "He didn't mean nothing by it."

"Then he should of kept his fucking mouth shut," Jimmie said calmly as he walked back to the Big Sandy huddle.

"What happened, honey?" Evelyn asked Clifford.

"Jimmie Clifford just laid that big boy out," Clifford said proudly. "They must have pissed him off."

"Well, I hope he don't get hurt," Evelyn replied.

"I don't think you got to worry about Jimmie Clifford, Evelyn," Clifford assured her.

16

Clifford was right. The game became a classic standoff, two armies fighting in the trenches, pushing forward, falling back—forward, back, forward, back. Both teams missed field goals in the first half. In the third quarter, Big Sandy recovered a fumble caused by Jimmie's quarterback rush. Three plays later, Scott threw an interception.

Forward, back, forward, back.

In the pressbox, John Ward's voice became hoarse and Richmond Flowers, Jr., shook his head in awe of Jimmie Clifford Sewell.

"He's the best linebacker I've ever seen at the high school level," Richmond enthused. "I know it may sound like an overstatement, but he could start for a number of colleges right now, and I mean the big ones."

In the Dew Drop Inn, the beer and bourbon flowed. The shouting was like the roar of an engine.

On the sidelines, Jimmie watched the offense struggle. He held his helmet tucked under the crook of his elbow. A stream of perspiration flowed from his neck and hair. Blood trickled down the bridge of his nose and slipped off his lips.

"With just fifteen seconds left to go in the game," John Ward rasped, "the Wildcats have the ball on their own twenty-four yard line. That's seventy-six yards to go with no time outs remaining. They've only got one choice—the bomb—and the way the Mountaineer secondary's been playing tonight, the chances of that working are—plainly put—slim and none."

"But this is high school football," interrupted John, "and you and I have seen too many games, Richmond, not to know that anything can happen."

"That's true," Richmond agreed.

"Still, if it ends in a tie, that would be almost as good as a win for Big Sandy, since they came in as the prohibitive underdog,"

John observed. "Anyway, the teams are huddling again. Fifteen ticks left on the clock and . . ."

Jimmie dropped to one knee. He could feel the muscles in his body crying for rest. He mumbled, "Come on Scott, goddamnit. For the first time in your life be as good as you think you are."

He watched the snap of the ball, saw Scott turn and back-pedal, saw him look downfield, saw his arm go back. Then he saw the blitzing Mountaineer tackle diving through the air, saw him barrel into Scott, saw the ball tumble from Scott's hand, saw the linebacker roll once and cover it, saw the referee jabbing his arm toward the Big Sandy end zone.

Jimmie spat blood from his lips, stood, pulled his helmet on, and trotted onto the field. He glanced up at the clock. There were four seconds left. There was no score.

John Ward's mouth was firing words: "What a break for the Mountaineers. With four ticks left on the game clock, South Central has the ball on the Big Sandy twelve-yard line—a chip shot for Mike Bostick. And, hanging in the balance, is the sixth state championship in eight years for the Mountaineers.

Evelyn was standing beside Clifford, pulling at his arm. Nancy was holding onto Wesley, her eyes closed.

"Looks like we ran out of gas," Wesley yelled to Clifford.

"I ain't heard the fat lady start singing yet," Clifford yelled back.

In the Dew Drop Inn, a tired silence fell like a blanket.

"Well, we give 'em a hell of a fight, anyway, goddamnit," Benny whispered.

"Yeah," Ed said sadly. "We give 'em a fight."

"And here comes the South Central field-goal unit," John Ward proclaimed. "Mike Bostick may have missed one field goal tonight, and it was from forty-eight yards out, but he's one of the premiere place-kickers in the country. In fact, I believe he has already said he'll attend Notre Dame next year."

"You're right, John," Richmond Flowers, Jr., added. "He's missed only three field goals all season, and he's twelve for twelve from this distance this year."

In the Wildcats' huddle, Jimmie's voice was an angry hiss: "All right, goddamnit, we ain't gonna quit. Let's push 'em back. Don't quit! We ain't gonna let these assholes from Knoxville leave here thinking they played a buncha pussies, are we?"

A roar of "No" bellowed up from the tired young faces. Jimmie called the defensive formation—the Wildcats clapped their hands in unison, then split off to take their positions. As they came to the line they could hear the chant from the Wildcat faithful in the stands: "Block that kick, block that kick, block that kick . . ."

Jimmie would remember seeing nothing but the kicker moving forward. He would admit to Clifford later, in his room at their trailer, that he did not know if he hit anybody or not. His father would laugh and say, "Well, son, you damn sure did. Knocked the left guard right back into the holder."

Jimmie would remember that he jumped and that he felt the sting of the ball in the palm of his left hand, and that he saw the ball spinning, like a slow-motion scene in a movie, upfield.

"Oh, my God! Oh, my God!" John Ward screamed to the anxious crowd at the Dew Drop Inn and anyone else listening. "It's blocked! It's blocked! I don't believe it! Jimmie Clifford Sewell! Now, he's got it and he's racing down the sidelines. Oh, my God! Oh, my God! What a play! He's at the forty! The thirty-five! The thirty!—"

"I don't think they're going to catch him John," shouted Richmond Flowers, Jr.

"—the twenty. He's going all the way!" John Ward yelled. "Touchdown! Touchdown! Touchdown! The game's over! Big Sandy wins the Triple-A state championship! Jimmie Clifford Sewell has recovered the blocked field goal attempt and raced seventy-six yards for the score. Unbelievable! Simply unbelievable!"

Ed would tell Clifford on Monday that the crowd at the Dew Drop Inn "didn't know whether to shit or go blind. That's what it was like. And I guaran-damn-tee you we almost died on the spot when ol' Furman yelled out that drinks were on the house." Clifford was impressed. Furman Mason, who owned the Inn, had never given away a drink to anyone, including his own family.

In the stands, Evelyn was leaping for joy like a teenager. She grabbed Clifford who lifted her and danced and kissed her hard on the mouth. "Lord," Evelyn screamed at Verdale, "we oughta win the state championship more often."

Wesley screamed, "Kick ass and take names," then hugged Nancy.

Nancy looked for Becky on the sidelines.

Verdale howled. She grabbed Jerry and squeezed him.

Becky sprinted down the field toward the players with the cheerleaders.

"Why don't you go on down there?" Wesley said to Nancy.

"It's all right," Nancy told him. "I'll just stay up here," She watched Becky disappear into the crowd that engulfed the players.

On the field, Jimmie Clifford Sewell was hoisted onto the shoulders of his cheering teammates. His body burned with pain as he thrust the football into the crisp night air.

BOOK FIVE

that dog
won't hunt

1

In the weeks following the state championship game, Jimmie's heroics began to build into the kind of legend that would last forever in a small town. College recruiters from throughout the country swarmed over Big Sandy, smiling and glad-handing, drifting in and out of business establishments to make their leave-behind impressions, sniffing like hunting dogs for the one soft spot, the one enticement that would cause Jimmie to scribble his signature across a letter of intent.

Jimmie would not see any of them. When they called, he would say only, "Talk to Coach," and hang up. When they talked to the coach—priming him with bottles of whiskey and wine and dinners of steak and lobster—they learned only that Jimmie Clifford Sewell would not be an easy plum to pluck.

"Might as well get this out of the way up front," the coach said to each recruiter, "you ain't gonna get nowhere with that boy by talking about girls and parties. Shit, Jimmie Clifford probably gets more pussy than a breeding bull working off a sign-up sheet. The only thing that boy would do in a fraternity house is clean it out when somebody pissed him off by trying to make him wear one of their little hats. And let me give you one other piece of advice: you boys don't want to show up at Jimmie Clifford's unannounced. That whole family's trailer-park proud, if you know what I mean. You go fucking around down there and you gonna know what it's like to wake up a hungry bear with your dick dipped in honey."

The signs of congratulations and the purple-and-gold streamers that lingered in Big Sandy for two weeks following the game were gradually removed and replaced by Christmas decorations, and the cold, short days seemed to spin faster and faster toward the end of the year.

After he calmed from the euphoria of his son's dramatics against South Central High School—euphoria that was rewound like a watch each place he went—Clifford began to concentrate again on getting reluctant workers at the Big Sandy Auto Accessories plant to sign his petitions for a union vote.

"If this goes through, I oughta give Jimmie Clifford a bonus," Clifford confessed to Evelyn. "Hell, I got people talking to me that ain't said a word since I got involved with the union."

"Don't you think that's taking advantage of Jimmie Clifford's accomplishments?" asked Evelyn.

"Ain't my fault ever'body wants to talk about him," reasoned Clifford.

"You not forcing them, are you, Clifford?" Evelyn wanted to know.

"Naw," Clifford said. "Seems fair to me. I tell 'em what Jimmie Clifford had to say about the game, and they put their name on a piece of paper to hear it."

"But Jimmie Clifford don't talk about the game," Evelyn protested.

Clifford smiled. "Well, gotdamn, Evelyn, they don't know that, now do they? And he is my son, my own flesh 'n' blood. If he was to talk, don't you think I'd know what he'd have to say? The big stupid SOB. First person in our family to do something worth talking about and you can't get a word out of him with a crowbar and a stick of dynamite."

2

Two days before Christmas, Jerry whispered to Janice as he paid his bill at the Dew Drop Inn. "Tonight," he said. Janice nodded and walked away.

It was cold in the barn on Harley Reed's deserted farm. Jerry lay close to Janice in his insulated sleeping bag, her smooth skin warming him, the scent of their musk and the faint sweetness of a weak cologne that she wore filling his breathing. Their love-making had been tender and easy in the hugging confines of the sleeping bag, and when they finished, she had turned her back to nuzzle against him and he had wrapped his arms around her, touching her breasts with his hands.

"You cold?" Jerry asked.

Janice shook her head.

"You sure?"

"Not with you." she said. "I'm never cold with you."

"I can't stay long," he told her. "I got to go to my Mama's house and see how she's doing."

"It's all right," she said. "I understand."

He did not speak for a few moments, then he said, "You know about Wanda, I guess."

"I heard," she answered. She added, after a pause, "You better off."

"I guess," he said. His voice was empty.

"She's always in the Inn with some man, Jerry."

He did not answer and she was sorry she had spoken of Wanda and the other men.

"I shouldn't of said that," she whispered.

"It's all right. I know about it."

"It's none of my business," she said.

"I guess it's more of yours than it is most people," he replied.

"I got no rights, Jerry. I know that," she told him. "I'll just take what I can get, but I want you to know something."

He did not ask what. He did not want to hear what he knew she was about to say.

"You're the only man I ever felt this way about. And I wish I didn't have that feeling for you. I wish to God I'd never seen you. Sometimes I can't think of nothing else but when I'll see you again."

His body tensed. His hands rubbed over her shoulders. He could feel her quivering.

"Funny thing," he said, "I guess I know what you mean."

"No, you don't, Jerry. You think you do, but you don't. When people find out about us, they gonna laugh and talk about you getting a good piece of ass. That's what they'll say—'good piece of black ass.' But they'll treat me like a whore, something easy to play around with. They'll look at my baby, at my Sudie, and say she's got your eyes, or she walks like you, or something."

Her quivering had become a jerking, and he held tightly to her shoulders until she began to relax.

"I'm sorry," she said softly.

"I don't want you to be," he said. "I don't guess I think about them things like I ought too."

Janice moved her head and kissed the fingers of his hand. "I got to go too," she said.

They dressed quickly in the cold air, and as he stood holding her, Jerry said, "Close your eyes."

"Why?"

"Just do it."

She closed her eyes and he reached into his coat pocket and pulled out a necklace with a heart on it.

"All right, you can look."

She gasped when she saw the necklace. "Jerry—"

"Merry Christmas," he said. "I wanted to give it to you when we were alone. C'mon, let me put it on you."

She turned and he draped the necklace around her throat and snapped it. She stood, holding it, balancing it on one finger, looking down at it.

"It ain't much," he said. "But I like it. When I saw it I thought of you."

"I got nothing for you," she replied softly.

"I don't want nothing," he said. "Just being here with you is more than enough."

She nodded and turned to him. Her dark eyes were shining. She said, "I was thinking about it the other day, when I was shopping for Sudie."

"What'd you get her?" Jerry asked.

"Nothing, yet. She wants a tricycle, but I can't find one that won't cost more'n I can spend."

"She'll be fine." Jerry said.

"Jerry—"

"What?"

"I need—well—you know—" She paused. "Nothing." She pulled at the necklace. "I love this. Thank you." She leaned forward and kissed him, then turned and walked away.

3

On Christmas Eve, the choirs of the Big Sandy churches congregated at the town square, under the statue of a Confederate soldier clutching a battle flag, and sang Christmas songs in the chilled night air. A large, bundled crowd listened. On the last song—*Silent Night*—the crowd lit small, white candles and sang along.

"I wish we could do that ever' week," Evelyn said as she walked back to the car with Clifford and Becky and Nancy.

"Uh-huh," Clifford mumbled.

"It was nice," Becky said. "I might paint a picture about it."

"I liked it, too," Nancy said. "Wish Mama was here."

Evelyn stopped and looked across the square. "Oh, my," she whispered sadly. "There's Jerry and Joe helping Louise back to the car. I swear she's going downhill so fast."

"Yeah," agreed Clifford. "It's hard on Joe. I guess it's got him about worried to death."

"Jerry's a good boy," Evelyn said. "Always helping out. Not like Ray. That boy's worthless. I hear tell he got another loan out of Joe before him and his wife and kids went back to Detroit."

"Yeah. What Jerry said," Clifford acknowledged. "Looks like that fight they had over Wanda pretty much tore it up for them ever getting along."

A sprinkling of snow began to swirl in the night air.

"Well, here it comes," Evelyn said. "It's felt like snow all day."

"On Christmas Eve, too," Becky enthused. "Daddy, can we drive by the Dairy Queen and get some hot chocolate?"

"I guess."

"Hot chocolate?" Nancy said. She made a face.

"What's the matter? You like hot chocolate," Becky said.

"Not much anymore. All that chocolate makes me sick. I'll get a Coke," Nancy answered.

4

The snow floated from the cupped darkness of the night, and the Big Sandy valley became frosted in a crystal white. Inside Joe and Louise Burnette's house, Louise sat in a rocking chair near the Christmas tree, its blinking lights dancing across the snow through the window. She gazed peacefully at the tree and the snow outside and remembered other Christmas Eve nights, when Ray and Jerry were children. Good memories, she thought. She could hear the voice of her sons as children. Shrill, giddy, expectant. Her memory-eye saw them in bed together, lying close, sleeping the restless sleep of excitement.

Louise looked across the room. Joe was sitting near the fire, reading a magazine. A food tray was beside his chair. Her eyes moved to Jerry. He was kneeling in front of the fireplace, arranging a fresh log over the licking flames.

Jerry turned, saw her watching him. He said, "You need anything, Mama?"

Joe looked up from his magazine.

"Mama?"

Louise shook her head.

Jerry pushed the screen back in front of the fireplace and crossed to his mother. He frowned at the bowl of soup on the food tray.

"Here, Mama, you better eat your supper before it gets cold." He dipped a tablespoon into the soup and held it for his mother to sip from it. She swallowed hard, painfully, and shook her head to refuse the rest. He said, playfully, "You mean to tell me you don't like my cooking?" He offered her the spoon. She shook her head.

"Hard for her to swallow sometimes, son," Joe said from his chair.

Jerry nodded. "Mama, I know it may hurt a little bit, but you need something to keep your strength up," he said gently.

Louise shook her head once again. She looked away, at the tree. The blinking lights shivered in the mirror of her eyes.

"Okay," Jerry said, "I'll keep it on the stove in case you get hungry."

He stood and picked up the bowl. Louise lifted her frail hand

and touched his arm. A faint, sad smile skimmed her lips. She said, "Son, I hate to die on your account more'n anything, because I know how much I mean to you. I know how it's gonna hurt you."

Jerry looked at his father. Joe's face was turned from him, toward the fireplace.

"Mama, don't say that. You're gonna be fine," Jerry said. He leaned over and kissed her on the forehead. Louise patted him on the arm and nodded, then she moved her eyes back to the tree. Jerry turned and walked away, tears trickling down his cheeks.

5

There were only two people in the Dew Drop Inn—Furman Mason and Wanda. Furman was behind the bar, wiping it with a cloth. Wanda was sitting at a stool, fingering the empty glass in front of her.

"Let me have another one, Furman," Wanda said.

"Nope. You had enough, Wanda," Furman answered. "It's Christmas Eve and I'm going home before I get snowed in here."

"Don't you think you oughta give me a go-cup for a Christmas present?"

"Wanda, you had enough and you know it," Furman answered bluntly. "Wherever it is you making home these days, that's where you oughta be. Now, go on. Weather's getting bad outside."

Wanda picked up her pocket book and slid from the stool. She threw an angry look at Furman. "Merry Christmas to you, too," she said bitterly.

"Yeah, Wanda. Merry Christmas." Furman shook his head wearily.

6

After he left his parents' home, Jerry drove to Toby Johnson's shack. He knocked on the door, and Janice opened it.

"Jerry? What're you doing here?" she asked. She glanced back over her shoulder. The room was filled with aging friends of her grandparents. They were staring at Jerry with blank, patient faces.

"Can I see you a minute?" he said.

Janice stepped outside and closed the door. She hugged her arms to her body. "It's cold out here," she said, her breath clouding the air.

"Just take a minute," Jerry promised. He went to his car and opened the trunk and lifted a tricycle from it. "Put this out for Sudie in the morning," he said. He put the tricycle on the porch.

"Jerry—"

"Don't say nothing. I was thinking about—about her," Jerry said. "Something I wanted to do."

Janice did not reply. She stood staring at Jerry.

"Merry Christmas," he said.

Janice nodded. "You too," she whispered. She watched him get in his car and drive away, and something—some surprising fear—stabbed at her. She believed she would never see him again.

7

Nancy sat alone at the kitchen table, tying a red bow on a box wrapped in the colored comic section of a newspaper. Behind her, in the living room, the lights that draped over a small, thin Christmas tree blinked monotonously, and the low tones of Elvis Presley singing *Blue Christmas* hummed from the speakers of the record player. The record had been playing constantly since she returned home from the evening with the Sewells. She had not turned it off, even after she had discovered her mother asleep on the sofa, a glass of bourbon spilled across her housecoat. She knew Verdale had been listening to the record and crying. Streaks of black mascara had dried on her puffed cheeks. Nancy had let the record play, believing that even in sleep, Verdale heard it, and that it was like a lullaby to her.

She finished wrapping the present for her mother—a scarf with bars of music from Elvis' *Love Me Tender* running along the border—and put the present aside. She picked up the butt of a cigarette that Verdale had crushed out in a filled ashtray and lit it. The harsh, bitter smoke filled her mouth and made her queasy. She gagged and crushed the cigarette out.

. . . I'll be so blue thinking about you . . . Elvis sang.

She got up and took the present and placed it under the tree, then she went to her mother and shook her.

"Mama, c'mon, let's go to bed," Nancy said softly.

Verdale's glazed eyes opened slightly and she mumbled something that Nancy did not understand, but she did not resist. She let Nancy's arms lift her and guide her down the hallway to her bedroom. She could feel Nancy peeling the nightgown from her.

"Good night, Mama," Nancy whispered.

Verdale muttered a wordless word and rolled over into the pillow.

Nancy went back to the living room and turned off the record player and unplugged the Christmas tree. She turned out the living room lights and stood at the window looking out. A car passed slowly outside, its tires making a soft, crunching sound over the snow and gravel.

8

Wanda did not know why she had decided to return to Captain's Point Trailer Park. She had been driving and her hands had turned the steering wheel at the entrance, and she obeyed her hands. At her trailer—at Jerry's trailer—she slowed to a stop. The lights were still on inside. She could see the red and green strobes of the Christmas tree and she remembered the trees she had decorated with Jerry, remembered the laughter, remembered the warm, comfortable moments of sitting on the sofa, drinking coffee with cognac, watching the red and green strobes flickering across the walls. Wanda rested her head on the steering wheel for a long moment, then sighed and eased her car on through the park and back up to the blacktopped river road. She glanced in the rearview mirror as the lights went out in Jerry's trailer. She was not sure where she would spend Christmas night, or with whom.

9

The gathered light of the cold Christmas morning was beginning to spin over the banked rim of the horizon, rolling like a thrown ball toward Tennessee, toward the snow-covered Big Sandy valley.

Verdale blinked and lay back into the pillow and listened again. Again, she heard the sound, and she knew it clearly: the retching, the awful retching. A flash-memory of the sour bile filling her mouth made her lick her lips. She inhaled quickly, swallowing the memory.

It was the sound that awoke Verdale. The sound was familiar but old, something from her youth, a remembered thing that had been put away in her mind's collection of bruising experiences.

She rolled on the pillow and looked at the illuminated digital clock on the nightstand. The clock read 5:37. She could see the dull shaft of light coming from the bathroom.

She slipped out of her bed and went to the bathroom door. Inside, Nancy was on her knees before the commode, her body jerking in small convulsions as she vomited. Verdale stood watching for a moment. Her hand slipped involuntarily to her hip, as though reaching for a pocket. She realized what she had done and pulled her hand back. Her hand, her body, wanted a cigarette, but there was no pocket on the thin cotton nightdress that she wore.

She stepped into the bathroom, pulled a bath cloth from a rack and turned on the cold water and let it soak the cloth. She squeezed the cloth and moved to Nancy and placed it on the back of her neck. Nancy nodded gratefully.

"How far along are you?" Verdale asked gently.

Nancy began to sob. She answered, "I—I don't know, Mama."

"Here," Verdale told her. "Lean your head back. Let me wash your face."

Nancy tilted her head back. The cold bath cloth felt good on her face. "Thank you, Mama," she whispered. "Don't guess this is what you wanted for Christmas, is it?"

"Hush," Verdale said.

10

Christmas slid into January like time on ice—quickly, off-balance, in a long, echoing cry of excitement.

And then it was over, and the new year began as new years always begin—grim, sober with resolutions, certain that this year would be different, perhaps even better.

To Clifford, it meant getting the union voted in at Big Sandy Auto Accessories. He had spent his holidays knocking on doors, pleading. Many doors were closed without the signatures he thought he would get, but he did not despair. Each rejection made him more determined, increased his energy. He became daringly public with his criticism of the plant that had provided him a living since he returned from Vietnam.

At night, in his trailer, the fatigue would fall on him, and he would sit, sipping his beer, and read again and again the list of names that were not on the petition.

And Evelyn would ask the same question, as she did on that late Friday night, the second week of January, when Clifford opened the door and stepped inside:

"How'd it go tonight?"

Clifford shook his head. He glanced at the television set across the room. A telethon for God was playing, and a preacher who looked no older than eighteen was prancing across a stage, spouting, "Give, give, give."

He crossed to the kitchen and got a beer and returned to his recliner.

"Clifford, did you hear me?" asked Evelyn.

"We got a few more," he answered. "It's like pulling teeth for some of these people. Old man Moss has 'em scared to death." He sipped from his beer, then continued. "We don't lack much having seventy-five percent signed up, though. We get there, we'll call a meeting with management, and they'll give us what we want or else." He stretched in his chair and looked at the television set. The young preacher was now on his knees, begging like Blind Charlie on the courthouse square. "Is this crap on twenty-four hours a day?" he asked.

"Don't start on me tonight," Evelyn warned. "I just hope you're doing the right thing, Clifford."

Clifford sighed. He was tired of Evelyn's badgering about the union. He said, "There comes a time, Evelyn, when you gotta stand up to people or they'll just keep treating you like shit."

"That sounds like something that union organizer from Nashville would say," she told him.

Clifford rocked agreement, settling into his chair. "It is," he said, "and he was right. You don't worry about it. I know what the hell I'm doing." He paused. "I think I'll get Jimmie Clifford to ride around with me tomorrow."

"You won't do any such thing," Evelyn warned.

Clifford unlaced his shoes and pulled them from his feet. His eyes were on the television set.

"God needs this money. Oh, yes, He needs it . . ." the preacher was crying.

"Ain't that a crock of shit," Clifford said. "God needs money? What's God gonna do with money. What that little turd means is that *he* needs money." He waved his hand toward Evelyn. "Look at that suit. I guaran-damn-tee you, he didn't get that suit at Wal-Mart."

"Shhhhhh," Evelyn said. She was watching the preacher pull himself wearily to one knee, his wrists locked together in front of him, his face twisted in emotional pain.

"I'm this close to turning that damn thing off," Clifford said.

Evelyn turned her face to him and glared. She said in a firm voice, "They're trying to raise enough money to buy a satellite, Clifford. Now, hush."

Clifford blinked in surprise. "A satellite?" he said. "What in God's name does God need a satellite for?"

"Good grief, Clifford. Just hush and let me watch my program."

"If God needs a satellite, or money, or anything else, He could take care of it by hisself," Clifford argued. "He sure don't need some little fart in a thousand-dollar suit handling his finances for him."

"Anything that has anything to do with religion, you're against," Evelyn said bitterly.

Clifford sat forward in his chair. He studied his wife's face for a moment, then said, "Let me get this straight. God knows ever'-thing, right?"

"Clifford, just shut up."

"No, now wait a minute. He can see ever'thing and hear ever'-thing, right?"

"Yes, Clifford, yes! He's omnifi—omni—He's ever'where."

"Then, what's he need with a satellite? He's already ever'-where."

Evelyn's voice was a voice of exasperation: "He wants us to reach out to people in third-world countries."

"Third-world countries?" Clifford said.

"Yes. Third-world countries, like Ethiopia and—ah—places like that."

"People in Ethiopia ain't even got TV sets, Evelyn," Clifford said. "What good's a satellite gonna do 'em?"

"Oh, good Lord, just go to bed and leave me alone," Evelyn snapped. "I'm sick 'n' tired of hearing you run down the Lord's helpers all the time."

Clifford pulled up from his chair, picked up his shoes, and started for his bedroom. He paused near the television and watched as the word GOD began whirling and turned into a giant, shining satellite. He shook his head.

"God wants to help people in Ethiopia, but he didn't lift a finger to help me get that promotion down at the plant. I guess that means God likes Harvey Williams better'n he likes me. That's about it, ain't it, Evelyn?"

He dragged out of the room, chuckling cynically.

Nancy and Verdale had made an agreement not to tell anyone of Nancy's pregnancy until they had decided what to do.

"If I keep the baby I'd want to stay in school as long as I can, before I start showing," Nancy had said in the early hours of Christmas, lying in bed with her mother.

"Well, honey, that's what you oughta do." Verdale had replied. "We'll just keep this between us for right now."

Nancy examined herself in the mirror of her mother's dresser, watching for signs of the rounding belly. Yet, though she had gained a few pounds of weight, she could not tell that she was pregnant. Each morning as she left for school, she was grateful.

She was feeling surprisingly energetic when she stepped into the English classroom at Big Sandy High School, looking for Becky. The room was empty except for the teacher.

"Mrs. Farmer," Nancy said, "have you seen Becky?"

"I imagine she's gone to lunch with everyone else," the teacher answered.

"Oh," Nancy said. "I thought we were going to meet here. Thanks." She started to leave, but was stopped by the teacher's voice.

"Nancy, I'm still waiting for your book report," the teacher said.

"Yes, ma'am," Nancy replied.

The lunchroom was chaotic with the confused rushing in and rushing out of class changes and the chattering voices released from the silence of classrooms. In a far corner, at a table that was reserved by claim and habit for the elite of the student body, Becky was sitting with Susan Taylor, feeling both giddy and uncomfortable. She had never been invited to the table, and now she was there, beckoned to the inner circle by Susan's waving arm.

"You know, Becky, you really should think about going out for cheerleader next year," Marcy said.

"Really?" Becky said tentatively.

"Sure," Marcy enthused. "You'd make it. No problem. Don't you think so, Susan?"

Susan smiled her always radiant smile. "Absolutely," she said to Becky. "You'd be perfect. I'll put in a good word for you with the committee. You'll get in. No problem."

"Okay," Becky said happily. "Hey, that'd be fun. Thanks."

In the serving line, standing next to Cecil Pinkerton, Nancy swept the lunchroom with her eyes, wondering if Becky had skipped lunch and gone to the library, as she often did.

"Who you looking for?" Cecil asked.

"Becky," Nancy told him.

Cecil stretched his neck and scanned the room. He said, "She's over yonder, with Susan Taylor and them."

Nancy waited for Cecil and walked with him across the room toward the table where she and Becky always sat.

Marcy's eyes followed Nancy across the lunchroom. She leaned toward Susan and giggled. "Look at Nancy Calloway," she whispered. "Look what she's wearing. Where does she shop?"

Becky turned to see Nancy and Cecil.

"She makes me sick," Marcy said. "Last night, I was over at Bobby's house and she calls, wanting to know if he wanted to study for their history test together."

"She did?" Susan said. "You're kidding."

"I was there," Marcy replied.

Susan's lip curled in disgust. "She's such a slut," she said.

Becky's face flushed with anger. She opened her mouth to speak, but said nothing. Around her, voices were agreeing with Susan.

"*Slut* . . . "

"*Slut* . . . "

"*Slut* . . . "

Nancy dropped her lunch tray on the table and sat. Cecil ambled away.

"See you," Cecil said.

"Cecil."

Cecil turned. "Yeah?"

"Sit down."

Cecil grinned foolishly. He looked around and then back to Nancy. He said, "You want me to sit with you?"

"Just sit down, Cecil," Nancy ordered.

Cecil sat across from Nancy. He noticed her jaw muscles were taut. Her lips pursed as she stared across the crowded lunchroom. Cecil followed her gaze—she was watching Becky sitting at the *popular* table. Becky was laughing as one of the football players stole her milk, then gulped it down in one swallow. "She seems to fit in with that group," Cecil thought.

"Why's Becky sitting over there with them?" He asked Nancy as she turned back. He saw a single tear escape from Nancy's eye.

12

There were four days in January when the winter brown of the Big Sandy valley was coated white from snowstorms that whipped down from Indiana and Kentucky, riding the curved arrows of wind currents that weathercasters on television pointed to while trying to describe the mystery of nature.

On those days, the residents of Captain's Point Trailer Park shivered behind the thin walls of their trailers and believed they would freeze. It was not the weather that made them colder than usual; it was the sensation of being cold.

They sat close to furnaces fed by propane gas and wished desperately for the boiling sun of summer. "I don't care if it gets up to a hundred and ten in the shade this year, I ain't gonna complain," they muttered.

With each snowfall, Clifford became more restless. He had found his magazine plans for the home that he had wanted to build hidden away in his shoebox, and he would take them and sit in his recliner and study them.

"I'm gonna build this gotdamn house," he said to Evelyn, "if it's the last thing I do.

"That'd be nice," Evelyn agreed during each snowfall. She would look at the plans with Clifford and remember the home of her parents. "I like the fence going around it," she said.

"Wonder what color white that house is?" Clifford mused.

"Good grief, Clifford, it's white, that's what color it is."

"They's all kinds of white, Evelyn. Shell white, off-white, white-white—all kinds of white."

"Well, that looks like white-white to me," Evelyn judged.

"Could be shell white," Clifford suggested. "That's just a little bit duller than white-white. It's like a hen egg—the white ones. That's where they get the name."

"It's pretty," Evelyn said. Kind of puts me in mind of the snow before anybody walks or drives on it."

"Then we'll paint it yellow," Clifford said. "Maybe that'll put you in the mind of some sun and warm this place up."

In February, there were two snowfalls.

In early March, there was one snowfall.

And then the earth seemed to puff and rise beneath the hard, cold winter topsoil, like bread dough with yeast folded into it.

"Be spring before long," the people of the Big Sandy valley said to one another, tapping the earth with their shoes.

"Won't be long, that's for sure."

13

From their childhood, Nancy and Becky had played games of dress-up, mimicking the women of Hollywood they found in the pages of Verdale's magazines. To Verdale, the games had been natural, and she had never scolded them for the spilled face powder and the swipes of lipstick left in tell-tale traces on her dresser. To Verdale playing dress-up was one of the crucial rituals of becoming a woman.

"To get the part, you got to look the part," Verdale had taught.

She had never explained what the part was, and Nancy and Becky had never asked. It was implicit in Verdale's enthusiasm that the part was important—perhaps the most important thing the girls would ever experience.

The ritual had followed them into their teens, but it was no longer a game. It was a part of their friendship, a ceremony to confirm that, among all people, they were special to one another.

Nancy was sitting at the kitchen table, her foot propped on a chair in front of her, with wads of cotton separating her toes. She was carefully painting her toenails. Becky stood behind her, her hair in rollers. She was rolling Nancy's hair. Rock music played from the radio in the living room.

"Do you still like me?" Nancy asked lightly.

"What kind of question is that?" Becky said. "Of course, I like you. You're my best friend. I love ya."

Nancy lifted her foot to examine her toenails. She said, "Well, we don't spend that much time together anymore. You're always off with Susan Taylor and that bunch."

Becky turned the roller with her fingers and slipped a bobbie pin in it. "They're just friends," she said after a moment. "A person can have more than one friend, you know." She paused, brushed out another strand of hair. "You're being silly," she added.

Nancy dipped her head in a shrug. Holding up her foot she said, "you think?"

"Where's that dark red polish you had?" Becky replied. "That'd look really good."

"On my dresser," Nancy answered. She started to rise. "I'll get it."

"No, I'll do it," Becky told her. "Your nails are wet."

Becky pulled the strand of hair and pressed it against one of the rollers, then she went into Nancy's bedroom and turned on the light. She stepped back in surprise. She could not remember seeing Nancy's room as messy. She frowned quizzically, then moved to the desk and began to search for the polish.

"It's behind the makeup mirror," Nancy called from the kitchen.

Becky picked up the bottle, looked at it. She called back, "I found it." She turned to leave, but stopped and looked back at the dresser. She picked up three pamphlets and glanced at them. They were all on abortion.

"You find it?" Nancy called.

"Yeah," Becky answered. She walked back into the kitchen, holding the bottle of polish and the pamphlets. "What're you doing with these?" she asked.

"What?"

"These," Becky said, shoving the pamphlets toward Nancy.

"Oh," Nancy replied. She hesitated, then said, "Ah . . . I was thinking about doing my science project on abortion."

"You're kidding?" Becky said.

Nancy took the pamphlets and the nail polish. "No. What's wrong with that?"

"Well, nothing," Becky said, returning to Nancy's hair, "but give me a break. I mean, you did your social studies paper on Wrestlemania."

"I like wrestling," Nancy answered. She opened the nail polish and pulled the applicator out. "What do you think about it?" she asked.

"I don't know," Becky said. "It might be too dark."

"I'm not talking about the nail polish," Nancy replied. "I mean, what do you think about abortion?"

"It's all right with me," Becky told her. "At least you're doing your homework for a change. I'm doing mine on the use of illustration in advertising."

"No," insisted Nancy, "I mean, what do you think about *abortion*?" You know. Do you think it's like—ah, wrong, or—or, anything?"

Becky slipped another bobby pin into another curl. "I don't know," she said after a moment. "I never thought about it. Mama says it's killing babies, and it's a sin, but you know Mama. She thinks ever'thing's a sin." She paused, brushed out another palm-

ful of hair. "I remember once when my cousin Sylvia got pregnant," she continued. "And she always called the baby . . ."

"The fetus," Nancy said expertly. "It's called a fetus before it's
born."

"Yeah, the fetus. Anyway, she always called it her 'unwanted
pregnancy,' and stuff like that. So she got an abortion. But then,
later, after she got married—"

"Is Sylvia the one that married that man that got killed when
the ditch caved in on him?" asked Nancy. "That construction
worker?"

"Uh-huh," Becky said. "And she got pregnant again, but this
time, she always called this one her 'baby,' and she took good care
of it and made a big fuss over it all the time. What I always wondered was, what's the difference between the baby that she kept
and the baby that was the 'unwanted pregnancy?' I mean, what's
the difference? The baby can't help it."

Nancy pulled her hands back from her toes, listening.

"Maybe Mama's right," Becky said. "What if it *is* killing
babies?" She shook her head at the thought. "That'd be too weird.
I hope I don't ever have to think about doing something like that."

Nancy thought for a moment then said, very quietly, "Yeah.
Me neither."

14

The late afternoon air was unseasonably warm, a prelude to spring, a kiss blown from a promising summer, and Nancy walked alone beside the river, watching small tornadoes of water swirl against the bank. The breeze—not brisk, not gentle—blew through the curls of her dark, brushed-out hair.

Becky had left to work on her science project, urging Nancy to do the same—"while it's on your mind," she had said. Nancy had replied, "Sure. I think I will."

She crossed the road, returning to her trailer. A half-block away, Benny and Fat Ethel's children were playing in the yard, squealing, laughing. A dog jumped around them, barking, grabbing at a tennis ball they were throwing. She stopped and watched them for a few moments, wondering what it would be like to see her own child playing on a false-spring day.

She heard Wesley's voice—"Hey, Nancy!"—and she turned to see him sitting at the edge of his truck, sipping a beer. He had grease on his hands and face. He dug through an old tool chest until he found the wrench he was looking for.

"Hey, Wes," she said. She walked toward him. "What're you doing?" she asked.

Wesley rubbed his face across his shoulder, smearing his shirt with grease. "Replacing the seal around the crankshaft," he answered. He dropped down and slipped back under the truck.

Nancy bent over. "Got an oil leak?" she asked.

"Uh-huh," Wesley answered from underneath the truck. "Shit. You know what a three-sixteenths open-end wrench looks like?"

"Just a minute." She squatted and began moving tools around in his tool box, then pulled out a wrench and shoved it under the truck.

"Yeah, good," Wesley said. He took the wrench. From under the truck, he could see Nancy's legs. He whistled softly to himself.

"That the right one?" she asked.

"Just a second," Wesley answered. He tried the wrench. "Nope," he called. "Shit. Hand me a quarter-inch." He waited a moment. Nancy's hand shoved another wrench at him.

"Try the half-inch," she said. "Hey, can I have a sip of this beer?"

"Yeah," Wesley said. He tried the wrench. It worked. "Well, I'll be damned," he muttered. Then, to Nancy, "This damn truck ain't a year old and it's already falling apart."

"You're leaking transmission fluid, too," Nancy said.

"I know it, but I ain't got the money to get it fixed yet," Wesley replied.

"You'll burn out the clutch if you ain't careful."

"How come you know so much about cars?" Wesley asked. He could see Nancy's legs spread slightly as she sat on the toolbox.

"I used to help my Daddy before he left," Nancy said simply.

Wesley pulled out from under the truck and sat, his arms draped over his knees, looking at Nancy.

"Most girls don't know shit about trucks or cars, or stuff like that," he said.

Nancy handed Wesley the beer. He swallowed from it and handed it back.

"I always liked it," Nancy said. She dangled the beer in her hand, then looked away to Benny and Fat Ethel's trailer. The dog was running in circles, holding the tennis ball in its mouth and dodging the laughing children.

15

There was a mood that lingered from the false-spring day—a restlessness, an aura as thick as heavy smoke—and it trailed into Big Sandy High School and fell over the student body like a poison gas. It was a day that something would happen, though no one knew it.

It happened after first period, in the madness of changing classes.

Becky was joined by Susan and Marcy and two other cheerleaders as she walked down the corridor toward her locker.

"Oh, God," Susan moaned dramatically, "there's Nancy Calloway." She looked at Becky. "You hear about her?"

"Hear what?" Becky asked.

"She got knocked up," Susan said in a loud voice waiting to be heard.

A confused smile crossed Becky's face. She said, "No way."

One of the cheerleaders giggled, covering her mouth with her hand.

"Oh, yes," Susan said. "Definitely pregnant. My daddy works at the free clinic on weekends, and I heard him tell my mother that the Calloway girl was about three months pregnant."

"Oh, my God," said another. "I wonder who the father is."

Marcy laughed. "Are you kidding?" she said. "I doubt she even knows."

Becky stared, unbelieving, at Nancy.

"The little tramp," Susan said in an arrogant voice, "she's just white trash. She'll screw anything that don't move out of the way."

Becky turned and glared at Susan. "What?" she demanded.

"I said Nancy Calloway, will screw anything that won't move—"

She did not finish the sentence. Becky's hand flew from her side in rage and slapped Susan hard in the face.

"Don't you ever say something like that again," Becy hissed.

Susan stepped back, seething. She touched her face with her hand. "Bitch," she snapped. And then her hand swept from her face and caught Becky on the neck.

"Fight!" someone yelled.

Becky dropped her books and sprang across the space separating her from Susan. She caught Susan by the hair and pulled and they both fell to the floor, screaming and slapping furiously. Becky lifted her elbow and pushed against Susan, then rolled on top of her, pinning her arms.

"You think just because you live in a nice house, or your family's got lots of money, that makes you better'n ever'body else. Well, it don't," Becky cried. She lifted her hand and hit Susan again.

"Stop it, Becky," Marcy yelled. "Quit it!" She looked at one of the other cheerleaders. "Go get Mr. Phillips."

The cheerleader rushed away, wedging herself through the gathering crowd.

"Somebody stop it," Marcy begged. She saw Scott moving through the crowd. "Scott, help."

"Jesus," Scott muttered. He reached for Becky and tried to pull her away. "Goddamnit, Becky, let go," he ordered.

Jimmie was laughing at a joke that Bobby had been telling when he rounded the corner of the corridor and saw the crowd and heard the cheering. Craig Alford and Pete Douglas passed him laughing.

"What's going on?" Jimmie asked.

"Well, you ought to go down and take a look, Jimmie Clifford," Pete told him. "Becky and Susan's in a cat fight."

"Ah, fuck," Jimmie muttered. He began to race down the corridor.

Jimmie heard Scott's voice before he saw him: "Becky, goddammit, let go."

Someone in the crowd said, "It's Jimmie Clifford," and the crowd parted. Jimmie took two steps and caught Scott by the arm and yanked him away and then he threw a forearm into Scott's chest, driving him back into the crowd.

"Wait a minute," Scott gasped. "I was just—"

"I warned you, dickhead," Jimmie growled.

Scott ducked and dove toward Jimmie, throwing a fist. The blow caught Jimmie on the chin. Jimmie did not move. He said, as though aggravated, "Ah, shit." And then he caught Scott by the shirt and lifted him up until Scott was over his head, looking down at Jimmie.

"I—I—" Scott stammered.

"Shut up, asshole," Jimmie ordered.

The sound of adult voices careened down the hall and Jimmie

turned, still holding Scott, to see Tom Phillips and the head football coach, Darrell Ross, approaching in a rush.

"What's going on here?" Tom Phillips demanded angrily. He reached for Becky and pulled her away from Susan. "That's enough of this, and I mean it."

"Put Scott down, Jimmie Clifford," the coach said firmly. "Do it. Right now."

Jimmie began to lower Scott.

"My daddy'll sue you for this," Scott sputtered, looking at Jimmie. "He'll sue you and your family and this whole damn school." He dared Jimmie with his eyes, and then he said, "Asshole."

Jimmie's arms went rigid, lifting Scott effortlessly. He said, "Well, shit, in that case." He bridged with his knees, pulled Scott toward him, and tossed him into the trophy case. The glass exploded and trophies spilled out on the floor.

"Jesus, Jimmie Clifford," the coach bellowed.

Jimmie turned to Becky.

"You all right?" he said.

"Yeah, I'm all right," Becky answered.

Jimmie raised his hand and Becky leapt to slap it.

16

It was the kind of meeting that Evelyn had prayed would never happen, because she knew what it would be like—awkward, tense, bitter, with hard, hateful glaring thrown across the room like invisible warheads. She knew also that she would struggle to remain calm and, most important, dignified. But she knew that she must control her emotions, especially with Clifford and Jimmie Clifford sitting near her. The slightest hint of anger would be a signal that would send them into rage. The thought of her husband and her son—her *men*— defending her and Becky made Evelyn smile slightly as she watched Tom Phillips shaking his head wearily over the burdensome decision facing him as principal of Big Sandy High School. Tom also knew that he could not offend Evelyn or her family; Tom knew that Clifford and Jimmie Clifford were proud men.

Evelyn's eyes turned to Mary Taylor and Bob Taylor sitting with Susan, then to Karen and Dave Mitchell sitting with Scott. They were uncomfortable, embarrassed, righteous.

Tom Phillips's voice was low, and official. He was looking at Jimmie. He said, "You do know that Scott could have been hurt very badly, Jimmie Clifford."

Jimmie nodded once. A wrinkle, like the beginning of a smile, twitched in his lips.

"Luckily, nobody was injured this time," Tom continued. He sighed, leaned back in the leather chair that was pushed up to the large desk, and said, "When this type of problem occurs, I've found it's necessary for a principal to take the kind of action that leaves an impression, and it's always been my policy to suspend those involved." He paused, looked at Scott and Susan and Jimmie and Becky. "That's for the first offense. If the problem persists, it's expulsion."

The gasp was from Mary Taylor. She said, indignantly, "You don't mean you're going to suspend Susan and Scott also?"

"I'm suspending all students involved for one week," Tom replied firmly.

Susan trembled in her chair. She looked at her mother, then back to Tom. "A week?" she said. "You can't suspend me, Mr. Phillips. Not this week. I'll miss the contest." She sat forward, almost standing. "What about the Fairest of the Fair contest, Mr. Phillips I'm gonna win." Her voice was a plea.

"Yes," her mother agreed.

"I don't think that's been decided yet," Tom said.

"I mean, I *think* I might win," Susan corrected. "It's just not fair."

"She's right, Tom," Mary Taylor added. "As I understand it, these other children were responsible for the fighting." She cut her eyes to Becky and Jimmie.

"And as I understand it, there were some pretty harsh words said about another student that started this whole thing," Tom replied.

Susan stood, wringing her hands. There were tears in her eyes. "I worked hard for this, Mr. Phillips," she whined. "They did it. We didn't do anything. All I said was that Nancy Calloway was a slut and ever'body knows that she is."

"That's enough, Susan," Bob Taylor said firmly, his embarrassment showing.

"But . . . " Susan began.

"Enough," her father repeated. His voice was a warning.

"Excuse me," Becky said quietly, "but can I say something?"

"Yes, Becky," Tom replied.

"I did start it," Becky said. "I hit her first."

Evelyn smiled. Her daughter had character. Her daughter was honest.

Tom looked at Becky for a long moment. He began to nod thoughtfully. "I see," he said. "Well, maybe because the beauty contest is this week, I can make an exception in this case."

A haughty, triumphant smile broke across Mary Taylor's face. She reached to pat Susan's hand.

"No, I don't think that will be necessary," Bob Taylor said evenly.

"What?" The response was a chorus from Mary and Susan.

Bob ignored the question. "Suspension might do us some good, if you know what I mean."

"I think I do," Tom said. "Yes, I think I do."

Susan began to cry. She turned angrily to her father. "Thanks a lot, Dad," she hissed. She whirled and stormed out of the office.

"I'm sorry," Bob said. "She's a little upset."

"So am I," Mary snapped. Her eyes coldly roamed the faces in the room. "I hope you people are satisfied. See what you've done and for what? Because this little piece of white trash can't fit in with the decent children of the school." Her eyes had settled on Becky.

Bob Taylor's face flushed red with anger. "Mary!" he exclaimed.

"I think that's uncalled for, Mrs. Taylor," Tom warned.

And then Evelyn was standing in front of Mary. She was breathing heavily, trying to control the temper that flared in her. "Let me tell you something, Mary Taylor. If I ever hear you call anybody in my family that again, I'll snatch you bald-headed."

"Uh, Evelyn—?" Clifford muttered. He was fighting a smile. Jimmie covered his mouth with his hand. A small snicker escaped through his fingers.

"Hush up," Evelyn shot back.

"You see what I mean?" Mary replied arrogantly.

Evelyn turned back to her. "What's the matter with you?" she demanded. "What gives you the right to insult my children like that? Even back when we were in school, you walked around with your nose up in the air. Wouldn't have anything to do with anybody unless they could do something for you."

"You were always jealous of the rest of us," Mary sniffed.

Evelyn's face burned. "Yeah, I *was*," she admitted. "You were all the things I wanted to be." She turned to look at Becky. "But I'll tell you one thing. Right now, I wouldn't trade places with you for ever'thing you've got or ever will have." She looked at Clifford and Jimmie. "Let's go," she commanded. Then she turned to Tom. "We'll take our punishment, Tom, and I can promise you that nothing like this will happen again."

The Sewell family stood. "I'm sorry, Mr. Phillips," Becky muttered.

Evelyn glared at Jimmie.

"Yeah," Jimmie said casually. "Sorry."

The Sewell family walked out of the room.

In the hallway, Evelyn and Becky walked swiftly toward the front door, followed by Clifford and Jimmie. They passed the broken trophy case.

"Jimmie Clifford, I'm disappointed in you, son," Evelyn said. "You could have hurt Scott real bad, throwing him into that glass case."

Behind her, Clifford glanced at the case and then at his son. They both smiled and Clifford raised his hand for a high five. Evelyn was not looking, but she heard the slap of the hands and she knew what was happening.

"I don't know what you're so happy about, Clifford," she said. "We've got to pay for it."

Clifford stopped. He turned to look at the trophy case. "Shit," he mumbled. He reached up and popped Jimmie on the head.

17

Her mother was talking about Estelle Lister's divorce in a droning of words that Becky only half-heard, and from the living room the high-pitched threats of an evangelist's sing-song about the Second Coming cried from the television. Her mother's voice and the evangelist's voice crowded the trailer, their words flying wildly about, colliding. Becky was not sure which voice she was responding to when she nodded and mumbled, "Uh-huh, uh-huh." It did not appear to matter. Neither her mother nor the evangelist seemed to notice her replies.

Becky's attention was outside the trailer, from the kitchen window where she filled tea glasses with ice: Nancy hanging clothes on a line that stretched between the two trees.

"Anyhow, I get so tired of that beauty-shop gossip, I got to where I can't stand listening to it anymore," Evelyn said.

"Uh-huh."

Evelyn crossed the kitchen to Becky.

"You hearing anything I'm saying, Becky?"

Becky turned to her mother. "Oh . . . yeah, I'm listening." She glanced back through the window.

"What's going on out there?" Evelyn asked. She stepped beside Becky and looked.

"Nancy's just hanging up the wash," Becky said.

Evelyn's brow furrowed. She said, "Did you and Nancy have a falling-out?"

"I don't know," Becky answered. "I didn't."

Evelyn nodded gravely. "Sometimes," she said, "people act one way on the outside and something else is really bothering them on the inside. You know what I mean?"

"You mean like when Daddy yells at us but he's really mad at you?"

"Well, yes, that's sorta what I mean," Evelyn said.

"I think I'll go talk to her," Becky said.

"Well, go on," Evelyn suggested. "I'll finish up in here."

Becky crossed to the door, then turned back to her mother. She said, "You knew about Nancy, didn't you, Mama?"

Evelyn nodded sadly.

There was a pause, like a distance between two places, and then Becky said in a quiet voice, "You don't have to worry about me, Mama."

"I'm not, honey," Evelyn told her.

"You know something," Becky said. "I think I'm gonna wait. Maybe even 'til I get married."

A flutter of pride raced through Evelyn. "I think that's a pretty good idea," she said.

"Be back in a minute."

"That's all right. I'll call you when supper's on the table."

"Hey," Becky said as she approached Nancy.

"Hey," Nancy answered. She snapped a wet towel in the air and whipped it over the clothesline. She did not look at Becky.

"How you doing?" Becky asked.

"I'm all right," Nancy said.

Nancy pulled a sheet from the basket and began to drape it over the line.

"Here, let me help you with that," Becky said. She caught one end of the sheet, walked it away from Nancy, and folded it over the line. The late afternoon wind billowed against the sheet, lifting it. Becky could smell the detergent.

"You see that storm coming up?" Becky asked.

Nancy glanced toward the rim of the mountains. A head of dark, swirling clouds rolled over the trees. Lightning flicked in the mouth of the clouds like the striking of a snake's tongue.

"Looks like it might rain," Becky added.

"Yep," Nancy said.

"Then why are you hanging out clothes if you think it might rain?"

"Cause I want to," Nancy said. She pinned a green blouse to the line.

"How come you didn't tell me you were pregnant?" Becky said after a moment.

Nancy turned to her, surprised by the bluntness of the question.

"I didn't figure it was any of your business," she answered.

"None of my business? Are you kidding? I thought we were best friends."

"So did I," Nancy said coolly. She pulled a pair of jeans from the basket and moved down the line. Becky followed.

"We are," Becky exclaimed angrily. "What's the matter with you?"

Nancy threw the jeans over the line. A rumble of thunder could be heard from the mountains. She said, bitterly, "There's nothing wrong with me, Miss Popularity. I ain't the one that's been ignoring her so-called best friend."

"Is that what's been bothering you?" Becky said. "That I was hanging around with Susan Taylor and the rest of them?" She paused, waited for an answer. But there was no answer. Only a cold, hard look from Nancy. "Yeah, that's it," she continued. "Look, if you weren't screwing their boyfriends, they might be a little more interested in being friends with you."

Nancy's head snapped toward Becky. She opened her mouth to speak, but did not. She grabbed the half-filled clothes basket and started toward her trailer.

"Wait," Becky said, following after Nancy. "Look, I'm sorry. I shouldn't have said that, but they're just friends, Nancy. Or were. That doesn't change us any."

Nancy stopped and turned. "I needed you, but you just dumped me." She turned again for her trailer.

"Nancy, damn it, stop," Becky said. She grabbed the clothes basket. "Are you just plain out crazy?" She released the basket and Nancy fell backward. "I can't believe you," Becky cried. "You're my best friend. You've always been my best friend."

Nancy shook her head. She could feel the tears bubbling behind her eyes, could feel them stinging, then slipping down her cheeks. She grabbed her knees and hugged them, pressing her face against her legs. She could not stop the sobbing. Becky moved to her and knelt and touched her on her hands.

"I—I wanted to tell you," Nancy stammered. "But I was embarrassed. I don't care what those bimbos at school think of me, but I love you and I don't want you to think bad of me."

Becky slipped her arms around Nancy and embraced her. She could feel the dampness of the tears against her shoulder.

"It's okay," Becky whispered. "Shhhhh. It's all right." She moved her own head against Nancy's face. "You know something? You're right. I haven't been a very good friend. I'm sorry."

Nancy's voice was small and pained: "No. It's not you. I should've known better."

"Do you know who—whose it is?" Becky asked quietly.

"Bobby—I think."

"Does he know?"

"Yeah. He said I was crazy and to leave him alone."

Becky swallowed hard. She nodded. The wind whipped through her hair. She could feel the first stinging drops of rain from the boiling black cloud that now thundered over them.

"Who needs him?" Nancy mumbled. "I don't."

"Yeah. I know. You don't."

The rain began, a sudden, powerful pouring—hard, thick drops of rain. The two girls held to each other, crying.

BOOK SIX

fish or
cut bait

1

For Clifford, getting signatures on his union petitions had become a crusade, and yet he felt queasy about the begging.

He stood beside his car drinking a beer with Jerry while Wesley leaned under the hood like a body being swallowed by the opened jaws of a shark. It was night, and the work light hanging from the hood of the car made Wesley appear grotesquely large.

"Damn nice night," Jerry said. "I thought it'd keep raining, after that shower we had last night."

"Yeah," Clifford replied. "Me, too. That was a helluva storm."

Jerry laughed easily. He said, "someday we gonna get a tornado come through here and it's gonna make this place look like a bunch of tin cans that's been stepped on."

"Be our luck," Clifford offered as he shifted from one foot to the other. He looked at Jerry. "You know, Jerry, I sure would like to get you signed up on our petition. We don't like much having all the signatures we need to go to management."

Wesley leaned back from the car. He was holding something in his hand and his hand was covered with grease.

"Well, I'll tell you this, Clifford, you gonna need a ring job on this heap." He held up the part he had removed from the car. "Look at that. Damn bearing done burnt out."

Clifford shook his head and sighed. "Shit. How much that'll cost me?"

"More'n you want it to," Wesley said. "I'd say—" He paused. A car rolled past. "There she is, boys."

The car pulled up the hill and stopped in front of Sheila Paschal's trailer. The doors opened and Shelia and another woman—sexy like Shelia—got out and went inside.

"Shit," Clifford whispered. "I must be drunk. I'm seeing double."

"Yeah," Wesley said. "One for the money, two for the show." He put the part on the fender of the car and wiped his hands on a towel hanging from his coveralls. "If I do it, Clifford, it ain't gonna cost you nothing but parts and a case of beer," he mumbled.

"You got it," Clifford said. He was watching Shelia's trailer.

"Uh-huh," whispered Wesley.

The lights in Shelia's trailer began to pop on, and the men could see silhouettes of the two women moving from window to window.

"I'm scared of this union mess," Jerry said absently.

"Uh-huh," Wesley said again. He began to climb slowly up hill toward Shelia's trailer, followed by Jerry and Clifford.

"Yeah, I'm scared stiff," Jerry repeated.

"Uh-huh," mumbled Wesley. He moved near the bedroom window of the trailer, looking around cautiously.

"What you scared of, Jerry?" Clifford asked. He turned to look at his own trailer. There was no sign of Evelyn.

"Uh-huh," answered Wesley. He reached suddenly and caught Clifford's arm and squeezed it and began nodding vigorously toward the bedroom window.

Inside, the silhouettes of Shelia and the other woman began undressing.

"Same thing could happen to you, Jerry, that happened to me," Clifford whispered, his eyes fixed on the window. "They'll just steal your damn job right out from under you."

The three men moved in unison closer to the window, like burglars.

"If you carry that car over to Owell's, he'll charge you about four hundred dollars," Wesley said in a voice so low it was barely audible

The silhouettes moved away from the window, deeper into the room.

"Shit," muttered Clifford.

"Up here," Wesley instructed. He stepped on the platform holding the propane gas tank and then pulled himself up on the tank. Clifford and Jerry followed.

"Jesus," Wesley said. "Get a look at that."

The three men strained to see through the window. Shelia and the woman were nude, their firm, sculptured bodies flashing signals of sex in the dim lights.

Wesley moaned. "Oh, shit," he sighed. And then his head jerked up and his eyes widened. "Oh, shit," he said again, but with surprise.

Inside, Shelia and the woman embraced and kissed—tenderly, then passionately, stoking one another toward the bed. And then they fell from sight.

The three men looked at one another in amazement.

"I can't believe that," Clifford said. "You see that shit?"

"How would you like to take your shoes off and run barefooted through some of that?" Jerry said.

"Sumbitch, she likes girls," Clifford mumbled. "Sumbitch . . ."

"That ain't no girl," corrected Jerry. "That's a full-grown woman."

"I mean she's a lesbian," Clifford said.

"Then I must be one, too," Wesley whispered, "'cause they ain't doing nothing I wouldn't do." He inched forward on the propane tank, trying for a better look. The tank began to rock on its standards.

"Damn, Wesley, be careful," Clifford warned.

It was too late. The tank tilted and one of the standards buckled and the tank began to move.

"Gotdamn!" Clifford exclaimed. He jumped from the tank and rolled in the grass. He could hear a loud crash against trash cans and he turned to see Wesley trying to free himself. He twisted the other way and looked at the tank. Jerry was still on top of it like a logger, trying to steady its trembling. The tank seemed to balance on air, held by the thin metal tubing that carried the gas into the house, then the tubing broke and the tank toppled, throwing Jerry over Clifford's head.

"Sheeeeet!" Wesley cried.

The three men jumped to their feet and watched the tank rolling across the lawn and down the hill, gas spewing from the tubing.

"Oh, shit. Oh, no," Clifford mumbled.

He watched the tank gather speed, cross the gravel road and leap a small mound of grass before it slammed viciously into his car. He heard the popping of sparks as the work light hanging from the hood shattered. An arc of electricity spit over the motor, igniting the gas escaping from the tubing.

The sound of the explosion was like a bomb, echoing over the Big Sandy valley. A bright, curling flame billowed over the tank and car.

"God-o-mighty," Wesley cried.

Lights popped on in trailers, doors opened, people filled the yards.

"Clifford!"

The voice belonged to Evelyn. It was a hard, demanding, punishing voice.

"Oh, shit . . ." Clifford whispered again. "I'm up to my ass in alligators now, boys."

2

The runaway propane tank in the Captain's Point Trailer Park
was a laughable legend by noon the following day.

Wesley had taken responsibility for the accident.

"We was chasing a skunk that ran under Sheila's trailer," he
had lied to Evelyn, and to everyone else who had gathered to
watch Clifford's car wrinkle into a waste of metal under the gas-
fed heat of the flame. "I sorta nudged it with my shoulder, and the
damn thing just started rolling."

"Yeah," Clifford had agreed.

"Yeah," Jerry had added.

"Biggest damn skunk I ever saw," Wesley had said.

The story had been so absurd, it was half-believed—until the
following day, when Wesley began to brag about seeing Shelia
making love to another woman.

"You so full of shit it's leaking outta your eyeballs, Wesley,"
Sammy said.

Sammy was sitting in the break room with Wesley and Jerry
and Clifford and Benny and Ed, eating lunch.

"I ain't shitting nobody," declared Wesley. "Clifford?"

Clifford's mood was sour. He had had a night of hell-catching.
"Shut up, Wesley," he growled.

Wesley turned back to Sammy. "I ain't lying. I saw it with my
own two twenty-twenties. She was on that girl like a cheap suit. It
was great."

"Damn lucky that thing didn't burn down the whole damn
park," Benny said.

"Well, I ain't—" Wesley began again. He looked up, paused.
"Shhh," he whispered. "Here she comes."

The men looked up. Shelia was crossing the breakroom, approaching them. She stopped at their table.

"Clifford," Shelia said.

Clifford swallowed hard. "Yeah?" he said quietly.

Shelia smiled at him for a long moment. She looked at the other men sitting at the table. The other men turned their eyes away.

"I think I'm gonna sign that petition," she said.

"What—?"

"The union petition," Shelia said. "I want to sign."

Clifford's face brightened. "You do? Okay. Good. That's—that's good.

Clifford opened his lunchbox and pulled a petition from it and slipped it across the table to sign. Her work blouse billowed open at the top, exposing her full, round breasts.

Wesley coughed.

Jerry lit a cigarette.

Benny blushed and looked away.

Sammy crushed an empty Coca-Cola can.

"All right," Clifford said enthusiastically when she pushed the paper back to him and handed him the pen. "Thanks, Shelia. There's gonna be a meeting with management here shortly. I'll let you know."

Shelia nodded and turned to walk away. The men inhaled, held their breath.

"I wish I had a swing like that on my back porch," Wesley whispered, as he followed Shelia's tight jeans with his eyes.

Shelia stopped and turned back. She said in a loud voice, "Oh, and Clifford, if my propane tank ain't replaced pretty quick, I'm gonna call the law on you and your buddies." She paused, smiled. "I think you know what I mean," she added. She twisted on her heel and wiggled out of the room.

"Shit," Wesley sighed in awe. He looked at Clifford. Clifford's face was burning.

A snicker began across the room, was joined by a cackle, and then the room filled with laughter.

3

Clifford sat in his truck outside the Elks' Club, away from the entrance to the auditorium, and smoked a cigarette. He watched the cars and pickup trucks pull in and park, watched the workers of the Big Sandy Auto Accessories plant lingering before entering the auditorium. He could hear the sounds of their voices, but not the words. The voices were eager, too loud, uncomfortable. It was like the chatter of soldiers in Vietnam, before wading into fields of fighting—fields that would become smeared with the blood of the dead and dying.

Clifford knew that what was about to happen would also be a war, with words used as bullets and hand grenades and razor-sharp knives. He knew the enemy would hide in the camouflage of statistics and charts and threats, and that their trickery would be as dangerous as an assault on a trapped patrol.

He looked at his watch. It was five minutes until seven. He saw Wesley drive up, park on the lawn near the door, leap from his truck, and rush inside. "Time to go in," he thought. "I've worked for this for weeks, and now it's time. Got to go inside. Get it over with." He could hear Evelyn's warning: "Y'all push Gerald Moss too hard and he'll shut the place down." He also heard his argument: "Well, hell, Evelyn, he can't kill us, can he? I mean, we still gonna be breathing the next day, ain't we? Gotdamnit, Evelyn, I'm tired of living this way. I'm gonna have me a real house before I die."

He got out of the truck and crossed the parking lot.

"Don't matter what happens, it was worth it," he thought.

"Gotdamnit, you can't let yourself be walked on every born day. You can only eat so much crap before you get a bad taste in your mouth."

He paused at the door of the auditorium. It was strange, but he remembered suddenly—out of nowhere—the morning that Delano Francis of Selma, Alabama, was killed in Vietnam, cut in half by a machine gun that seemed to be buried in the side of a hill. Delano had always talked himself into believing he would not die in Vietnam. *"Yeah, boy, yeah, you gonna come back. Hell, yeah, boy, you ain't seen New York City yet and them fucking Yankees ain't seen you." And then Delano would try to psyche up his fellow soldiers: "Come on, boys, let's go get it over with. Shit, it ain't nothing but another day at the plow. Let's go! Let's go! Let's go!"*

Clifford spat the cigarette from his mouth and stepped on it. He saw Delano's blood spraying the air. He saw the hill the machine gun fire had come from exploding in a volcano of dirt when he swung the grenade launcher to it and pulled the trigger.

"Let's go," Clifford mumbled. He stepped inside the auditorium.

Sitting at the head table were Richard and Gerald Moss and two attorneys who would only whisper to them. The only person representing the workers at the table was Jack Wimberly.

Richard Moss opened the meeting with a short, mild speech about his family's concern over the possibility of a union vote. "We want to know—and I mean, we *sincerely* want to know—what problems you have," he said.

"Yeah, I bet you do," a voice mumbled from the audience, and it was as though the voice struck a blow that caused Richard to step back and sit.

"We've got a lot of problems," Jack said calmly. He looked at the audience. "Who wants to speak first?"

Benny raised his hand.

"Benny," Jack said.

"What bothers me most of all is hearing about other plants around here and what they doing for their workers," Benny said forcefully.

"Yeah," someone added.

Richard leaned forward at the desk. He glanced at his father and then turned back to Benny. "I'm not sure I know what you mean," he said tentatively.

A man named Felton Davis stood, surprising everyone. Felton Davis seldom spoke, even in greetings.

"What he means is this," Felton thundered: "What about Consolidated Press over at Murray, and Caltrex over in Dover? They give their people at the very least a cost-of-living raise ever' year."

A chorus of voices agreed.

"Not to mention extra benefits and no forced overtime," Felton continued.

Ernestine shot up from her seat. She shouted, "My sister-in-law works over at Buchanan Assembly and they get three extra days a year vacation more'n we do."

Richard cleared his throat. "The businesses that you've mentioned have very little in common with our factory here," he said. "We manufacture an entirely different product line."

"Well, hell, work's work, ain't it?" Benny said angrily. "Don't matter what comes out the end of the line, it's what goes on on the line that matters."

The auditorium exploded in applause.

Benny was on his feet, looking around the room. He called, "Clifford? Clifford? Ain't that what you said? Where you at, Clifford?"

Clifford stood. "Back here," he said in a loud voice. Faces turned to him. He knew he was on the spot because he had pushed so hard for the signatures. He looked at Richard Moss. "We're not asking for nothing extra. We'd like to do as well as the others in this area are doing is all."

Richard nodded thoughtfully and shuffled papers that were spread out in front of him. He said, "I believe you need to check your figures again, Clifford. Our employee benefits package is on par with every plant in this area." He turned a paper over and appeared to read from it, then he looked at Clifford. "Economics dictate that, in order for us to stay in business and show a profit, we have to hold down certain costs—and, yes, as hard as that is for some of you to believe, we are in business to make a profit. When we cease to make a profit, this company—and your jobs—will cease to exist."

"We been hearing that for years," Felton said.

Again, a chorus of voices restlessly agreed.

"Well—" Richard began.

The room fell silent as Gerald Moss pulled himself from his chair and shook away the hand of an attorney attempting to get his attention.

"I've known many of you for a number of years now," Gerald said in an assured voice. "You helped me build this company. I consider you friends. As a friend, I'm asking you to give up this idea of a union here. As the owner of this company, I'm *telling* you that if you vote a union in, I'll close the plant down. Then where will you work? What will you do? I'd advise you to weigh your decision very carefully, because those of you who know me know I mean what I say, and unlike what you've been told, I do care about you."

Jack leaned back in his chair and glared at Gerald Moss. He said, "If you care so much about us, what about these latest cutbacks you're asking for?"

"Jack, those are necessary cuts," Richard said quickly. "We know that it'll put a strain on you. It'll be a difficult time for all of us, but we see light at the end of the tunnel. We hope the burden will just be temporary."

Felton was again on his feet. His voice trembled with anger: "Why should we be penalized because you screwed up the business? We have no say in what goes on around here, yet we're the ones that have to suffer when you make a mistake."

Ernestine added emphatically, "Well, I ain't giving up nothing. I'll tell you that much right now."

Again, applause rang out in the auditorium.

Gerald Moss nodded arrogantly and waited for the applause to end. "I'm afraid, Ernestine, if this union comes here you'll be giving up everything," he said evenly.

Jack spread his hands on the table. He looked into the audience and then back to Gerald Moss. "Well, I think that we are all in agreement that the workers here should have the right to decide for themselves whether or not they want a union," he said. "Seventy-eight percent of the employees have signed these petitions, recommending that the union question be put to a vote. Under the law we have that right, and that's what we're gonna do."

Gerald Moss did not speak. He turned and walked off the stage and through the audience and out of the auditorium, followed by Richard and the two stern-faced attorneys. The door closed behind them with a sharp bang.

No one spoke. No one knew what to say.

4

After the meeting, on the drive back to Captain's Point Trailer Park, Clifford had again sensed the image of Delano Francis walking to his death, muttering psyche-up speeches to himself like one of the demented preachers that Evelyn watched on television. He heard again the sudden spitting of the machine gun—loud, sharp—and he saw again Delano's body being lifted in the air. He remembered the sound of Delano's body hitting the ground, a single dull thud, like someone dropping a heavy sack. He remembered thinking as he lifted his grenade launcher that a body without life was heavier than a body with life.

He had always intended to drive to Selma and visit with Delano's family, but he had delayed the trip, and then it had been too late to go, and he had forgotten it.

"Maybe I will go," he thought. "Maybe that's what I'll do." Drive down there one Saturday morning—leave early—and look up his family and tell them what kind of man Delano was. Maybe now they could hear of his dying and accept it as a soldier's work.

Or maybe they wouldn't want to talk of him.

Maybe the best thing to do would be to drive to Washington, D.C., and visit the Vietnam Memorial. Evelyn had said she would like to see it one day.

"Yes," Clifford thought, "that would be better." Go there. Find Delano's name. And Frank Harris. And Cody Nations. And Marty Darby. Find all of them. Put a flower for each of them at the base of the memorial, as he had seen other people do on television.

"Jesus," he thought. Why is all this coming back?

He pulled the truck into the driveway of his trailer and got out. He could see the lights in Shelia's trailer. The new propane tank was on its new standards. He wondered if Shelia and her woman lover were huddled in bed. He shook his head sadly and opened the door. From Verdale's trailer, he could hear Elvis Presley singing *The Battle Hymn of the Republic.*

"Well?" Evelyn asked.

Clifford shrugged.

"What'd you think?"

"I don't know," Clifford answered. "I honest-to-God don't know."

"You look worried," Evelyn said.

Clifford shrugged again.

"Is that what's wrong with you?"

Clifford sat heavily in his armchair. He said, "How long's it been since we took a vacation?"

Evelyn laughed lightly. "We ever took one?"

"Yeah. We took the kids over to Cherokee, North Carolina, that summer."

"Clifford, they was babies. We got some pictures somewhere around here of them standing with some Indians. They was just babies. Don't either one of them remember it."

"Well, I think it's time we took us another one," Clifford said.

"Vacation?"

"Yeah."

"Where to?" Evelyn asked.

Clifford tilted his head back against the headrest of the chair and looked at the ceiling of the trailer. He said, after a long moment, "Washington, D.C."

5

"Nancy, for crying out loud, quit squirming."

"You're getting water in my ears, like you always do."

"I wouldn't, if you'd quit squirming."

"I wouldn't be squirming if you didn't get water in my ears."

"Don't be such a baby. The soap's almost out."

Becky turned the swivel head of the faucet in the kitchen sink away from Nancy's hair and handed her a towel. "You're such a baby," she said and giggled.

"You remember when you told me you wanted to be one of them people that help out in a dentist's office?" Nancy grumbled.

"Yeah. That was a long time ago," Becky said. "I used to like it when Dr. Bradley's assistant rinsed out my mouth. She always wore this great perfume and her fingernails were always polished like a new car."

"Well, I hope to God you don't go into that," Nancy said, rubbing the towel through her hair.

"Why?"

"Because you'd wind up drowning somebody," Nancy told her.

"It's a wonder my brain ain't waterlogged after all these years of you washing my hair."

Becky laughed and hugged Nancy quickly.

"Bitch, bitch, bitch," Becky whispered.

Nancy threw her head back, fingering the wet hair away from her face. "Yeah," she said. She smiled. Since she had talked with Becky about her baby, they had become closer than ever, and the small things—the bedroom talks with stuffed animals cuddled in their laps, the ritual of hair-washing, the early-morning walks to the school bus—had become more important. Soon it would all change, and both of them understood. Being together now was a tender, desperate need.

"Want me to roll it?" Becky asked."

"Sure. I've got some of those big rollers in my . . ."

Nancy did not finish the sentence. The door to the trailer opened and Verdale stumbled inside, helped by Lloyd Pinkerton.

"Oh, shit . . ." Nancy muttered. She knew her mother was drunk.

"Ah—hello, girls," Lloyd said, blushing. He was trying to balance Verdale in a standing position.

Nancy stepped toward her mother. "Mama, you're drunk," she said sadly.

"She's had a little too much, I'm afraid," Lloyd replied.

Nancy's face flared in anger. She looked hard at Lloyd. "Why'd you let her drink so much?" she snapped.

Verdale laughed. She grabbed Lloyd by the arm and began to pull him toward her bedroom.

"You don't *let* your mama do nothing, Nancy. You know that," Lloyd sighed. "She does as she pleases."

"I'm a grown woman, goddamnit," Verdale sputtered. "If I want to take a drink, I'll take me a damn drink." She laughed and twisted toward Lloyd. "C'mon, Lloyd, back here. I wanna tell you something."

Lloyd pulled his arm away from Verdale. "No," he said emphatically. "I got to get home." He looked nervously at Nancy and then Becky. Becky blushed. She stepped back slightly.

"My ass," Verdale bellowed. "You ain't leaving me now."

"Mama, you're drunk," Nancy said softly, touching Verdale's arm. "Just go on to bed and let Lloyd go on home to his wife."

Verdale jerked away. She shouted, "You shut your smart mouth. This is my damn house, and if you don't like what goes on here, you can get out."

"I'll see you later," Lloyd whispered. He turned to leave and Verdale stumbled to follow him.

"Lloyd, come back here," Verdale ordered. "You ain't gotta leave. Lloyd Pinkerton, get your ass back here. Lloyd I'm warning you. Lloyd? You bastard." Verdale stood on the metal stoop shouting.

"Mama, get in here and stop yelling," Nancy begged. "It's late. Ever'body in the park can hear you." She caught Verdale by the shoulders and began to pull her back from the door.

"I don't give a shit," Verdale screamed. She stuck her head through the door, toward Lloyd, who was quickly crossing the lawn to his car. "I fucked Lloyd Pinkerton!" she cried. "I fucked Lloyd Pinkerton! Ever'body hear me? I fucked Lloyd Pinkerton!"

Nancy pulled hard at her mother and closed the door. "Shut up, Mama! What're you doing? Stop it!" she said. She turned to Becky. "Help me take—'

Verdale rolled out of Nancy's grasp and pushed past Becky to the kitchen. She began opening cabinets, spilling glasses and dishes. "Son of a bitch!" she yelled. "That son of a bitch!" She found a bottle of bourbon and opened it and began pouring it into a coffee cup. Her hand trembled.

Nancy crossed to her mother. "Come on, Mama. You don't need any more to drink."

"Let me alone!" Verdale snapped. She drank from the cup. "Don't you touch me. Neither of you." The cup fell from her hand and rolled across the kitchen floor, leaving a trail of bourbon. She looked at the cup and then back to Nancy. "You know what today is?" she asked. "Would have been," she corrected. "Is . . . hell, it is. My anniversary." There were tears in her eyes.

"Mama, your anniversary's in September," Nancy said quietly. "Come on, quit drinking and go lay down. I'll fix you something to eat."

"I'm not gonna do it," argued Verdale. "I'm not talking about my wedding anniversary, Miss Know-It-All." She staggered from the kitchen into the living room and stopped at an end table covered with pictures. "Not my goddamn wedding," she muttered. She picked up a framed photo of her and her ex-husband. Her tears fell onto the glass. Then suddenly she raised her hand and smashed the picture against the corner of the table, shattering the glass and frame. "I'm talking about—about the first time I was with your daddy." She swept her hand over the other pictures on the end table, scattering them across the floor. "I was fifteen years old." She looked at Nancy. "Did you know that?" She turned to Becky and nodded. "I was just sixteen when Nancy was born. Did you know that, Becky?"

"Mama!" Nancy exclaimed.

The door opened and Wesley looked in.

"What's going on over here?" Wesley asked. "Sounds like World War III." He looked at Nancy. "You all right?"

"I'm fine, Wesley," Nancy said. "Go home."

Verdale ignored Wesley. She leaned toward Nancy. "And now Lloyd's gone home. I needed somebody on my anniversary, but you run him off. Just like you run your daddy off. You hate Lloyd, don't you?"

"No, Mama, I don't hate Lloyd," Nancy said quietly.

"You don't want me to be happy," Verdale complained. "What am I supposed to do—be without? I need a man sometimes. I need somebody to love me, too. If it hadn't been for you, your daddy would still be here."

"Mama, stop it."

"You're the reason he left and you know it."

"Mama, stop it. Just shut up."

"If your Daddy could of kept his hands off of you, I wouldn't have had to run him off. You're the reason he left."

"Mama, please. Shut up," Nancy cried. She grabbed for Verdale and began to slap her. "Shut up! Just shut up!" she bellowed.

Wesley crossed the room and caught Nancy by the waist and pulled her away and then stepped between the two women. "Y'all stop it," he ordered.

Nancy whirled from Wesley's grip and ran out of the open door. Verdale staggered after her.

"I wish you'd left instead of your daddy," Verdale shouted into the night. "You little bitch. I wish you'd left." She turned and stumbled down the hallway. "I wish you'd left," her words softened by her crying. "I wish you'd left," she repeated.

"Shit," Wesley mumbled. He stepped out of the door and Becky followed.

They found Nancy at a picnic table near the river, sobbing uncontrollably.

"Nancy," Becky said softly.

Nancy looked up. Her wet hair glistened in the moonlight. Her face was swollen with crying.

"I—" Nancy began.

"Hush," Wesley said. He sat beside her and put his arms around her and pulled her face to his shoulder. "It's all right. Just go on and cry it out. It's all right."

Becky stood back watching for a long moment then turned and headed to her trailer.

6

To Jimmie Clifford Sewell, it was like having a family portrait made at the mall. He was sitting in the middle of the sofa with his father and mother beside him, crowding him. His sister was standing at the edge of the sofa, smiling. They were all dressed in Sunday clothes and they were listening to a tall, intense man named Dick Harris, who paced the living room.

"Not only do we feel the University of Tennessee can offer Jimmie a quality education," Dick Harris was saying, "but I personally think with his talent, Jimmie will see a lot of playing time his freshman year."

"Jimmie Clifford," corrected Jimmie.

Dick nodded seriously. He turned to look at Becky's portrait of Evelyn and Jesus that hung above the television. "Nice . . . picture," he said. "Is that you, Mrs. Sewell?" Evelyn smiled and nodded.

"That ain't me," Clifford added with an embarrassed laugh.

"Jimmie Clifford." Dick began again, his eyes scanning the room. Everywhere he looked he saw Jesus, and he remembered what he had been taught by a veteran recruiter about "reading" a room.

"What Jimmie Clifford's got is straight from God," Dick Harris intoned. "No question about it. It's like he was chosen to be one of God's warriors on the football field. That's why I think he could see a lot of playing time his freshman year. God-given talent." He turned to smile at Evelyn. "You see, we've got a fine group of Christian young boys coming back from this year's team, but we're gonna be a little light at linebacker." He thought quickly, and added, "One of our boys felt the calling, and he left the team to go into the mission field." He beamed a smile. "Now we'll miss him, but we wish him luck out there in God's game."

"Who was that?" Clifford asked. "I know most of them boys from reading the paper."

Dick Harris swallowed. "A kid from Pennsylvania," he lied.

"Uh-huh," Clifford replied. Then: "Well, how much?"

"I beg your pardon," Dick Harris said.

"How much is all this gonna cost me?" asked Clifford.

Dick Harris smiled again. Poor, dumb SOB, he thought. He said, politely, "Well, it won't cost you anything, Mr. Sewell. Not one red cent. Tennessee's prepared to offer Jimmie Clifford a full scholarship."

Clifford's eyes widened in surprise. "Nothing?" he said.

"Nothing."

"Not a penny?"

"No sir, not a penny," Dick Harris emphasized. "Tuition, room, board—everything's taken care of by the university, provided Jimmie Clifford maintains the required grade-point average."

Clifford turned to glance at Evelyn. Evelyn frowned.

"But," Dick Harris added quickly, "we provide tutors to work with the student athletes. I don't see any problems with the academics."

"Have you looked at his grades?" Evelyn asked.

Dick Harris shrugged an uncomfortable yes. He looked at Becky and tried a smile. "As I said—" He looked back at Evelyn "—I don't think we'll have any problems. We have some truly dedicated people at Tennessee."

Clifford slapped his hands on his knees. "Well, I don't see a problem," he announced. He leaned forward to look around Jimmie. "You see a problem, Evelyn?" He slapped Jimmie on the shoulder. "What you think, boy?"

Jimmie rolled his head. "I don't know," he muttered.

"Don't know?" Clifford responded. "This is a good opportunity, son. Dick here is offering you a chance to go on to college. For free. You can't just shrug it off like that. 'I don't know.' What kind of answer is that?"

"Clifford," Evelyn said evenly, but with warning.

"No," Clifford said. He stood and looked down at Jimmie. "Wait a minute. What's going on here? You like football, don't you? And those college girls. Hey. Lots of college girls. Right, Dick?"

Dick Harris started to nod, but stopped. He glanced at the portrait of Jesus and Evelyn.

Jimmie pushed his shoulders back into the sofa. He mumbled, "I don't know, Daddy. All right? Shit."

"Jimmie Clifford." Evelyn's voice was tense. "We don't talk like that."

"Well, it's a big decision," Dick Harris said warmly. "Let's let him think it over for a while. I'm sure he's got a lot on his mind right now, and I know we're not the only ones that would like to have him playing football."

"I don't believe it," Clifford mumbled.

"You're a talented young man," Dick Harris said, extending his hand to Jimmie. "We'd love to have you at Tennessee. Remember, this is your home state." He nodded to Evelyn and Becky and picked up his briefcase and started for the door. Clifford followed.

"I don't know what's the matter with him," Clifford said at the door.

"It's a big decision, like I said," Dick Harris replied. He handed Clifford a business card. "You can reach me at this number when you've talked it over. What he wants is what's really important here. We don't want to rush these young men into a decision that they would regret later."

"Thank you, Mr. Harris," Evelyn said from the sofa. "We'll call you when he's made up his mind."

"Yes, ma'am," Dick Harris said.

"But there won't be a problem," Clifford added. He laughed. "Hey. Go Big Orange. Right?"

Dick Harris smiled and walked out of the door.

Clifford closed the door and turned to Jimmie.

"What the hell's the matter with you?" demanded Clifford. "A man comes to our house and offers us a chance of a lifetime and you sit there like a stump on a log."

Jimmie shrugged. He glanced back at Becky. There was a small boy's look of confusion in his eyes.

"Daddy, maybe—" Becky began.

"Damn it, Becky, I ain't talking to you. I'm talking to Jimmie Clifford," He snapped.

Jimmie pulled forward on the sofa, balancing his elbows on his knees. He said, "I don't know, Daddy. I don't wanna go to school for four more years. I don't like it that much."

Clifford threw his head back and sighed. He said, in a mocking voice, "I don't wanna go to school four more years, Daddy." He looked at his son. "Nobody in this family has ever gone to college," he said in a hard voice. "You're offered a chance to go for free, and all you can say is you don't like it that much. You like playing football, and you're damn good at it. Hell, you might even go on and play pro ball, make something of yourself, make some real money instead of beer change. But, naw, you don't like it that much."

"Clifford, that's enough," Evelyn said sternly.

"You damn straight that's enough," Clifford shot back. "I don't believe I can take it anymore." He paused, glared at Jimmie. "All right. What is it you wanna do?"

The voice from Jimmie was surprisingly quiet: "I don't know. I was thinking—I was thinking about maybe joining the Navy, like

Kenny Snow did. Or maybe working over at the plant with you—
buy me a car."

Clifford shook his head in disbelief. A strange, tired laugh
rolled in his throat. "You want to wind up working over at that
damn plant, living in a gotdamned house trailer the rest of your
life? Do you know how important a college education is this day
and time? Come on, son, use your head for something besides a
hat rack."

Jimmie looked up. His eyes were moist. He said nothing. He
got up from the sofa and walked past his father and out of the
trailer, slamming the door behind him.

"You satisfied, Clifford?" Evelyn scolded.

"No, I ain't satisfied, Evelyn. I'm just gotdamned confused."
He dropped into his recliner, picked up the paper and snapped it
open to the sports section.

Becky found Jimmy beside the river, skipping flat rocks across
the water. She watched him for a moment, then moved to him.
She picked up a rock and threw it and watched it skitter over the
surface, then plunge into the current.

"I'm proud of you, Jimmie Clifford," Becky said after a moment.

"I didn't do nothing," Jimmie replied.

"Yeah, you did."

Jimmie looked at her and smiled, then looked back at the river. A large paper cup bobbed on the moving surface.

"See that cup out there," Jimmie said. "Bet a beer I can hit it
first."

Becky scooped to pick up a rock. "Bet you can't," she said.
"But, as you know, I quit drinking."

Jimmy laughed.

They began to throw rocks at the cup, watching it drift toward
the late-day sun.

From the front door of the trailer, Evelyn watched her children—two silhouettes against the sun, playing a child's game.
She smiled proudly.

7

The vibration of the plant that he could only sense in his office hummed around Richard Moss as he opened the corridor door and stepped inside. He stopped for a moment to listen, to feel. Being there in the plant was like standing in the vigorous heartbeat of some giant, living thing.

And it was ironic that the plant reminded him of life, Richard thought. Especially now.

He knew that faces turned to him and then away as the workers bent to their work, mechanically going through the motions of labor, and he remembered the summer that he had worked in the plant, delivering supplies from station to station. He had been sixteen and the heir to the corporate throne, but it had been his most cherished time at the Big Sandy Auto Accessories—there, among the people who took the nothing of materials and made the something of products. He had liked them, had wanted to be more like them. Yet, he had also understood that being among them was only temporary, a kind of necessary apprenticeship for the larger duty waiting for him.

He saw Harvey Williams and motioned for him. Harvey crossed the floor.

"What's going on?" Clifford shouted to Jerry above the roar of machinery.

Jerry glanced up to see Harvey and Richard huddling. "Got me," Jerry shrugged. "Another cutback, maybe."

"Yeah, well, shit, we cut back any more, we just gonna be sucking wind," Clifford complained. He pushed his hands into the small of his back and stretched and watched Harvey wave for Joe Burnette.

"Wonder what they want with Daddy," Jerry said

Clifford rolled his shoulders; a look of concern crossed his face.

The two men watched as Joe stepped close to Richard. They saw Richard put his hand on Joe's shoulder and speak, and then they saw Joe slump away and sit on a nearby crate, his head lowered.

"Jesus," Jerry whispered. He saw his father look up, finding him across the floor of the plant. "Jesus," Jerry said again. "It's

Mama." The tears began to stream from his eyes. He rushed toward his father.

"Jerry—" Clifford called, following him.

Richard stood back and watched as Joe and Jerry embraced. He looked at Clifford and nodded, and then he turned and walked away, through the heartbeat of the giant living thing that was Big Sandy Auto Accessories. At the doorway to the corridor, he stopped and looked back. He could see the workers slowly approaching Joe and Jerry, circling them, reaching for them with weary hands. He swallowed hard and walked out the door.

8

Clifford sat midway in the church, with Becky and Jimmie beside him, and listened to the quartet singing "Precious Memories," announced by the preacher as one of Louise Burnette's favorite hymns. Evelyn was one of the singers. Her face glowed with the tenderness of the words. Her eyes were glistening with the mingling of sadness and happiness. To Clifford, she looked like one of the singers caught in the frenzied blithering of a television evangelist, their voices locked on the pleading words of *Just As I Am* as the evangelist pried more money from his listening audience. *"Just as you are, dear friends. Just as you are. Somebody out there in Television Land is still hurting, still wanting to get up from where they're sitting and take their checkbook and write out a love offering for God's work. Oh, yes, just as you are. All God wants is you. Don't matter if you're rich or poor or in-between. Do it now, friend. Just listen to God calling—just as you are—get up and pick up that checkbook and do it. You'll be blessed ten times over, yes you will . . ."*

Evelyn loved the singers on television, Clifford realized. She was even swaying slightly, letting the words tremble in her soul.

He had been to too many funerals, he thought. Too many. He turned his eyes from the singers and looked at the gathered row of family sitting at the front of the church—Joe, his head bent in sorrow; beside him, Jerry and Ray and Ray's wife, Donna, and their children, home from Detroit. He scanned the congregation: workers from Big Sandy Auto Accessories, neighbors, friends. He saw Richard Moss sitting near the back of the small church. His eyes blinked in surprise. Behind Richard, he saw the black girl from the Dew Drop Inn—Janice. And with Janice, sitting uncomfortably, were a half-dozen other blacks from the plant. He remembered going to a funeral in a black church—Jeb Harlow's funeral—and how uncomfortable he had been and how he had thought that it was odd that death could bring people together. Living ought to be able to do that, he had thought. Living, not dying.

Somewhere in the congregation, someone cried softly.

At the graveside, after the final words had been spoken and

the crowd had stepped back appropriately to allow the family a final few moments with the closed coffin, Clifford stood with Evelyn and watched Joe and his sons standing reverently, quietly.

Verdale crept close to Evelyn. She whispered, "You done such
a good job with her hair, Evelyn. It looked so natural."

Evelyn looked up an nodded a thank you.

"It had so much shine," Verdale continued. "What did you put
on it?"

"Just a dab of Vaseline," Evelyn answered. She looked away
from Verdale irritably.

Joe turned away from the coffin and walked numbly into a circle of friends. Evelyn tugged at Clifford to follow. She crossed to
Joe and embraced him tenderly.

"I don't know when I've seen such pretty flowers, Joe. Louise
would of loved them," Eveyln said kindly.

Joe nodded. He turned back to look at the flowers surrounding
the graveside and watched as the funeral director pulled the blanket of roses from the coffin. He said, "You know what's funny? I
never gave her flowers 'til now."

"How's Jerry?" asked Clifford.

"Taking it hard, Clifford," Joe said. "His mama was real special to him."

Jerry stood alone at the coffin, his eyes locked on it as though
he could see into it. Ray stepped close to him.

"At least Mama ain't suffering no more," Ray whispered.

Jerry turned to look at him.

"Mama really loved you, Jerry. She always liked you because—
well, you was always real good to her. I never was. I'm sorry."

A long moment passed as the two men looked at one another,
and then they moved into an embrace—hard, strong, affirming.

"Praise Jesus," whispered Evelyn. She looked at Joe. His eyes
were filled with tears.

"Lots of people come out," Joe said. "You see Richard Moss?"

"I saw him," Clifford replied.

"And all the rest of 'em," Joe said. "People thought a lot of her.
She was a good woman."

"She was," Clifford said.

He took Joe by the arm and started to lead him away, but Joe
stopped and looked across the crowd of faces around him. He
touched Clifford on the arm. "She's here," he said quietly.

"Who?"

"Wanda," Joe said.

Clifford saw her moving reluctantly through the crowd, toward Jerry and Ray. She was wearing a plain black dress and

holding a single rose. First time I've ever seen her dressed where she wasn't showing off her titties, Clifford thought.

"I hope she don't cause a scene," Evelyn whispered.

Wanda walked cautiously to the brothers. She placed the rose on the casket then said, softly, "I'm sorry. I'm so sorry." She reached for Ray and hugged him lightly and kissed him on the cheek, then she turned to Jerry. Tears began to flow from her eyes. She embraced him, clinging to him, sobbing. Slowly, Jerry returned the embrace. "I'm sorry, Jerry. For everything. I'm so sorry. I love you."

Ray stepped quietly away and crossed to Joe. Donna moved beside him.

"Ray?" Donna said.

"It's all right," Ray answered. "Ever'thing's fine."

They watched as Wanda took Jerry's hand and led him away, across the cemetery to the heart-shaped marker of their son.

"Ever'thing's fine," Ray said again. His eyes were moist. "Mama's happy," he added. "Finally she's happy."

9

Nancy was the first to see it.

"Who's here?" she asked.

"What're you talking about?" Becky said.

And then Becky saw the car. It was in the driveway of her trailer home.

"What's that on it?" Nancy said. She pressed her nose against the window of the school bus.

"You got me," Becky replied.

The school bus stopped and they rushed off, pushing among the smaller children of the Captain's Point trailer Park. They crossed the road and down the hill to the car. The car—a bright orange Camaro Z-28—had a ribbon taped to the roof.

"Oh, my God," Becky squealed. She dropped her books. "I don't believe it."

"Believe what?" Nancy asked.

Becky touched the car, circled it. A girlish, giddy laugh spilled from her. "My Daddy is just the best thing there is," she cooed.

"Is this yours?" Nancy asked in surprise.

"It's gotta be," Becky said. "I've been asking forever and I bet Daddy felt so bad about not sending me down to art school this summer that he bought it for me."

She opened the door and slipped inside and inhaled the sweet smell of new leather. She squealed again and rubbed her fingers over the steering wheel. "I love it," she cried. Then, to Nancy: "Come on, get in."

Nancy opened the door to the passenger's side and slipped inside. She touched the leather seats. "It's sure pretty," she said in awe, but if your Daddy couldn't afford to send you to art school, how come he could afford to buy you a car?"

Becky shook away the question. "I don't know. My birthday is in a couple of months. Maybe that's what it is, an early birthday present. "It sure is orange," Nancy said.

"I don't care if it's purple-striped," enthused Becky. "I love it.

And once they get a union in at the plant, Daddy'll get a big raise and I'll get it painted whatever color I want." She leaned across the seat and hugged Nancy. "We're going in style from now on, girl," she said.

"Well, one of us is," Nancy replied quietly.

10

If anything bored Clifford more than grocery shopping with Evelyn, he could not think of it. Pushing a cart around Piggly Wiggly, waiting patiently as Evelyn read labels and compared prices and complained across the store to Lloyd Pinkerton, was not his idea of a relaxing afternoon off. Still, he only managed to get trapped in the duty three or four times a year, and he preferred to suffer the experience rather than hear Evelyn's grumbling about his lack of responsibility.

They had been in the store for an hour and a half before Evelyn declared that she had completed her list.

"About damn time," Clifford muttered. "You been up and down ever' one of these aisles a half-dozen times. Hell, I about got the place memorized by now."

"Good," Evelyn snapped back. "Next time, you can come do it by yourself."

"Suits me," Clifford said. "Takes about two minutes to stock up on beer and potato chips."

Evelyn glared at him and pushed the cart into Verdale's check-out line. Betty Sue Green was in the other line, managing two overflowing carts while Lloyd operated the cash register.

Clifford stood idly as Evelyn unloaded the cart on the rolling conveyor belt. He picked up a copy of the *National Enquirer* and began to thumb through it.

"Says here that Elvis was stopped for speeding in Wisconsin," he said aloud. He laughed. "Listen to this shit. 'Officer Bostick reported that the legendary singer ran from his vehicle into the woods. The officer reported that he knew it was Presley because of the rhinestone trim on his pants.' "

Lloyd chuckled. "Yeah, I read that," he said.

"Me, too," Betty Sue added. "Wadn't that something?"

"Shit, I don't know why they won't leave the poor bastard alone," Clifford said.

"He's made a lot more money dead than alive," suggested Lloyd. He held up a can of French-style green beans. "How much are these, Verdale? You remember?"

"Two for a dollar," Verdale answered.

Lloyd punched in the cost of the beans on the register. "Yeah," he continued, "ol' boy keeps raking it in—for somebody. His daughter's about the richest kid in Tennessee."

"There ain't hardly a week goes by that somebody don't see him somewhere," Verdale said. "Won't be long before he comes out of hiding and makes a new record."

Clifford closed the *National Enquirer* and put it back in the rack. "You ain't gonna stand there, and you a grown woman who votes and drives a car and ever'thing, and tell me that you think Elvis Presley is still alive," he said to Verdale.

"You just read it for yourself, didn't you?" Verdale responded. "A policeman spotted him. He ain't got no reason to lie about it that I can think of."

Betty Sue laughed. She said, "Y'all don't get her started on that, now. Lord knows, ain't nobody on earth knows more about Elvis Presley than Verdale."

"Betty Sue's right," Lloyd said. "I'll have to listen to it the rest of the day if you get her started." He chuckled and winked at Verdale.

"No, now wait a minute," Clifford insisted. He leaned toward Verdale. "Why does ever'body else think he's dead but you? They had a funeral for him. They buried him, Verdale. I watched it on the news."

Verdale huffed a cynical laugh. She held up a box of Kotex. "Did you get the right ones, Evelyn?"

"They're for Becky," Evelyn said.

"Just wanted to make sure," Verdale said.

"Just ring the damn thing up, Verdale," Clifford mumbled. "Now, what about it? They buried the boy in the backyard like a pet dog."

Verdale punched in the cost of the Kotex and slipped them down the counter. "That was all a fake," she declared to Clifford. "He wanted people to think he was dead so he'd be left alone. He couldn't go nowhere without people worrying him nearly to death about something. Wanting his autograph. Wanting to give him a song to sing. Wanting him to show up at some barbecue fundraiser or something such as that. He couldn't get no peace at all."

"Can't argue that," Clifford said. "He didn't exactly blend into a crowd real well."

Betty Sue lifted a six-pack of Coors to the counter. She said, "Verdale, the man died sitting on the pot. Don't you think if he'd been faking it, he'd have come up with something a little better than that?"

"The man's dead as a doornail, but you can't tell her nothing," Lloyd intoned.

"Well, I got to give him this," Betty Sue continued, "he was a flat-out good-looking thing until he got hooked on drugs and got fat."

"He was, wadn't he?" Evelyn said. "I had the biggest crush on him, God bless his heart."

"Hell, he eat fried banana sandwiches 'til he nearly exploded," Clifford suggested.

"Ya'll don't know what you're talking about," Verdale argued. "They blowed that story all out of proportion. Them was prescription drugs he was taking, not dope."

"Same thing, if you ask me," countered Clifford.

"Well, nobody asked you," Verdale snapped. "But for your information, there's tons of difference between the two."

"That may be," Lloyd said, "but I'll tell you the truth, they're gonna have to find a way to keep 'em from bringing all that dope into this country. We're about to ruin the moral fiber of our young people."

"Good God," Verdale whispered. She punched the cost of a five-pound bag of Dixie Crystal sugar into the register.

"Well, I don't know what killed him," Betty Sue suggested, "but I believe he's as dead as he's ever gonna be."

Verdale was now angry. She slapped her hand on the top of the counter. "Well, let me ask this," she hissed: "Did any of y'all ever see him dead?"

Betty Sue looked up in surprise. She batted her eyelashes and smiled sweetly across the aisle. "Well, no, Verdale, I ain't," she said, "I never saw President Kennedy dead neither, but I'm pretty sure he's no longer with us."

11

Clifford cut the truck motor and sat for a moment looking at the car in his driveway. The bright orange of the setting sun spilled over the bright orange of the car.

"By, God, I'm proud of that," he said to Evelyn.

"Well, I just hope it was worth it," Evelyn said.

"It was. You wait and see," Clifford replied.

They got out of the truck and began to unload the sacks of groceries. Clifford hated taking groceries into the trailer worse than he hated shopping for them."

"We got too gotdamned much stuff—again," he grumbled.

"We got to eat, Clifford."

"Well, we ain't got to eat so damn much," he argued.

He followed Evelyn to the door of the trailer and waited for her to open it. Then they stepped inside and stopped abruptly.

"Jesus," Clifford whispered.

Their eyes scanned the trailer. It was immaculately clean. The smell of food steamed from the kitchen. A banner hung across the back of the wall, behind the dining room table. It was a picture of Becky sitting in a hastily sketched version of the Z-28. Underneath the drawing were the words:

THANK YOU, MOTHER AND DADDY. I LOVE YOU!

Evelyn stared at the sign. She sighed, "Oh, no . . ."

"What the hell's going on in here?" Clifford said. "Good, God, Evelyn, look at this place. I ain't never seen it this clean."

Becky popped from the kitchen, with Nancy behind her. Becky's face was glowing.

"I just want to show you how much I love you and say thanks," Becky bubbled. She looked around the room with pride. "Nancy helped," she added. "I told her she could stay for supper—if it's all right."

Evelyn bit her lip to stop the tears. She nodded yes.

Clifford bent over to examine the carpet. He said, "Damn. I'd almost forgot what color that carpet was." He looked up at Becky. "Thank us for what?" he asked.

The smile left Becky's face. Nancy stepped back into the kitchen.

"Well," Becky said tentatively, "the car, of course."

Clifford laughed. "Hell, honey, that ain't your car. It's Jimmie Clifford's car. He ain't here, is he? I wanted to surprise him."

"What?" Becky whispered.

Evelyn crossed to her. "It's your brother's car, honey, I'm sorry. I didn't think to tell you."

Clifford moved to the table and looked over the food. "Did you cook this?" he asked. He put down a bag of groceries and picked up a piece of fried okra and tasted it.

"But, why . . . ?" Becky said.

Outside, a voice cried: "Yeeeeehaaa!"

Clifford turned and raced to the door. "It's Jimmie Clifford," he said, smiling proudly. "He loves it. I told you, Evelyn. I knew he'd like it." He put down the other bag of groceries and rushed outside.

Evelyn could hear their voices through the opened door:

"Go, Big Orange! You like it, boy?"

"Hell, yeah! Are you kidding?"

Evelyn closed the door and turned to Becky.

"Jimmie Clifford agreed to go play football at Tennessee if we bought him a new car," she explained gently.

"Why?" Becky said in a pained voice. "He's already got a car."

"No," Evelyn answered. "Not now. You know your daddy had to take that truck back when his car got burned up by the propane tank. You know that, Becky. He bought this car with the insurance money."

Becky swallowed to control her anger and tears. The door opened and Clifford and Jimmie entered the trailer.

"It's great, Daddy. I mean, really great," Jimmie said. His smile covered his face.

"That's the only Big Orange Z-28 in west Tennessee," Clifford bragged. "Hell, had to send over to Dyersburg to find it."

Jimmie sniffed the air. "What's for supper?"

Evelyn knew what was about to happen. She put her groceries on the floor beside the table and moved to Becky. Becky's eyes filled with tears. She pulled away from her mother and started for her room, then stopped and ripped down the sign she had painted.

"What the hell's going on here?" demanded Clifford. "I done told you, Becky, that I wadn't gonna buy you no car. Now cut it out. Let's eat."

Becky glared at her father and ran from the room, down the hallway. The sound of her door slamming echoed in the trailer.

"Well, hell's bells," mumbled Clifford. He sat at the table. Jimmie sat opposite him.

"Clifford, don't you dare eat a bite of that food," warned Evelyn. "Not one bite."

Clifford looked up, surprised by the tone of Evelyn's voice. He saw Nancy slip around Evelyn.

"I better go." Nancy said. She crossed the room quickly and left through the front door.

Evelyn moved toward Clifford. Her voice quivered with anger. "You ever hear of the word *tact?*"

"Yeah," Clifford answered bluntly. "I've heard of the word, Evelyn. I went as far in school as you did."

"Then why don't you try using some sometime?" Evelyn snapped.

"I said I'd heard of it," Clifford responded. "I didn't say I knew what it meant."

There were some things that were impossible to understand, Clifford believed, but nothing as confusing as the behavior of women.

The fuss over the car had been ridiculous. It had to be as plain as the nose on your face that the car would be for Jimmie Clifford. How in the name of God and Jesus could anyone blame him for hurt feelings?

But there were hurt feelings.

Evelyn refusing to eat, sitting in her chair, reading from *The Upper Room*, sniffing tears of such deep pain she seemed to be bleeding inside.

Becky locked in her room, the wail of sobbing escaping through the thin walls.

It was all right as long as Jimmie Clifford was there and there was someone to talk to about football and how his car would look on campus. But Jimmie Clifford had gone out to show off his new car, and Evelyn would not talk to him until he apologized to Becky.

"Well, honey you know damn good and well I didn't mean to hurt Becky's feelings," he had argued quietly, and uselessly. And, finally, he had said, "All right. I'll go talk to her."

Clifford had never been comfortable with one-on-one talks with his daughter. She was like his wife in so many ways. Disarming ways. He could never win in a contest of feelings, and he knew it.

He knocked on Becky's door, "Can I see you a minute?"

There was a pause, and then a small, aching voice, "It's open."

Clifford opened the door and stepped inside. Becky was huddled in the middle of her bed, hugging a teddy bear she had gotten for Christmas when she was only a child. Her face was streaked with tears, her eyes swollen, her hair pulled severely to the back of her head. "Uh, honey," Clifford began, "that, ah, that was a good supper you made."

Becky did not answer. She inhaled a sob.

Clifford moved closer to her bed.

"You make fried okra better'n your mama," he said.

"I didn't make it," Becky said in a small voice. "Nancy did."

"Well, Nancy makes it better'n your mama," Clifford replied. He cleared his throat and sat on the edge of the bed.

"Look, baby," he said, "your mama and me don't want you to think that just because we do a lot more for Jimmie Clifford, that we love him more'n we do you."

Becky's eyes flashed open in a glare over her teddy bear.

"It's, ah, just that he's the oldest, you know," Clifford continued. "And he's got this chance to go to college and make something out of himself." He looked hopefully to Becky. The glare was still holding. "You know Jimmie Clifford will be the first person on either side of the family who ever went to college." Another hopeful look. The glare increased. "Who knows? He might go on to play pro football. Make us all proud."

Becky ducked her head into her teddy bear. She began to sob again.

Jesus, thought Clifford. What'd I say?

"Honey—"

Becky's face flew up. The tears were springing from her face. She cried, "I want to make us all proud, too Daddy."

Clifford opened his mouth to speak, but the words failed him. He heard the door open and he turned to see Evelyn standing in the doorway. He reached and touched Becky on the shoulder and patted it, then he got up and left the room. Evelyn stood for a moment looking at her daughter, then she closed the door.

"Gotdamnit," Clifford muttered as he ambled down the hallway. "I can't never win."

12

It was, according to Benny's wife Fat Ethel, an omen.

"Ain't the right day," Benny complained to Clifford. "We ought to put off the vote. Ethel says so."

"Jesus, Benny, we can't go changing the vote just because we got some clouds outside," Clifford said in exasperation.

"Ain't just clouds," Benny replied. "Them's hanging, gray clouds. They ain't moving at all. Not a smidgen. Not the kind of day to do nothing new. I'm telling you. Bad sign, Clifford, bad sign. Ethel can read the weather, you know?"

Clifford muttered "Bullshit," and strolled away from Benny, trying to look confident. Still, his eyes wandered to one of the small, high windows of the plant. Outside, it was cloudy and the clouds were not moving. They were like a blanket—a cold, damp blanket—holding over the Big Sandy valley. Clifford felt a chill race through him. He shuddered involuntarily.

"Hey, Clifford," yelled Jack from across the plant, "we about to get started. C'mon."

Clifford glanced at the window again. "Bullshit," he whispered.

A line was gathering outside the breakroom for the union vote as Clifford entered the corridor. He ambled down the hall, toward the door, stopping to glad-hand, to encourage, to listen to the eager and suspicious voices of his co-workers.

"Don't let 'em get to you," he said, forcing energy in his voice. "They gonna try to stare you down, but it ain't nothing but a stare. We got a right. Remember that: we got a right."

"We're with you, Clifford."

"Go kick some ass, Clifford."

"How many times can I vote, Clifford?"

"We got it knocked, Clifford."

He waited at the door of the breakroom until Richard Moss opened it with his key. Jack and Ed and a union official named David Shelby were whispering in a corner. Gerald Moss sat stoically behind the desk where the ballot boxes had been placed.

"Good morning, Clifford," Richard said pleasantly.

Clifford nodded. David Shelby had said to avoid being buddy-buddy with Richard or his father. He stepped into the room.

"Well," Richard announced, looking at his watch, "I think it's time we got started." He looked across the room. "You concur, Mr. Shelby?"

"Anytime," David Shelby answered.

"Any last-minute details we need to discuss?" Richard asked.

"None I can think of," David replied.

"Daddy?" Richard said.

"Open the door," Gerald Moss ordered.

And the voting for a union in the Big Sandy Auto Accessories plant began.

Outside, it was cloudy. None of the clouds were moving.

"Bad sign, Clifford, bad sign," Benny had warned.

And the words echoed in Clifford's mind as he watched the slow traffic of voters flow in and out of the breakroom.

13

It was late afternoon and the clouds were still holding over the valley, holding like an oppression.

Wesley sat on the tailgate of his truck cleaning his deer rifle, his face furrowed in thought. He did not hear Nancy approach.

"Hey, Wesley," Nancy said brightly.

Wesley looked up and smiled. "Hey, yourself."

"What you doing home so early?" Nancy asked.

"Took off," Wesley answered. "Hell, wadn't nothing going on down at the plant, not with the vote going on today. Told them I felt a cold coming on."

Nancy giggled and pulled herself up on the tailgate beside him. "I can't believe you'd just out-and-out lie like that."

"Why not? I've lied about a lot worse. Besides ain't a lie," defended Wesley. "I had a sniff or two this morning when I woke up."

"That ain't exactly walking pneumonia," Nancy laughed. "How'd the vote go?"

Wesley shook his hand and rubbed his polishing rag over the stock of the gun. "Won't know until tonight, I guess. Way ever'body was talking, it'll pass without much trouble."

"You think it's a good thing, Wesley? The union?"

"Hell, I don't know," Wesley said honestly. "Tell you the truth, I ain't never been much for 'em, but, shit, we can't get old man Moss or his boy to do what ought to be done. Not much choice but to get some muscle in things down there."

"My daddy never believed in them," Nancy said after a moment. "Not that I remember a lot about what he did or didn't believe in," she added quickly, "but I do remember him raising hell about the unions. Said they was as bad as the bosses in the long run."

"Your daddy may of been right," Wesley replied. "Don't much matter to me, one way or the other. I'm gonna get me a truck-driving license—a class-five—and get out of there, anyhow."

Nancy rolled her eyes. Not that class-five story again, Wesley. I heard it enough she thought. She looked at him. "I know what you mean about getting outta here. I'd like to get away my-own-self."

"You damn right. Make me some money before I cash it in," Wesley said, smiling. He turned to gaze at the Tennessee River rolling ceaselessly below him. "You see that river? Well, one of these days, I want to see where it winds up."

Nancy stared at the river. She said, softly, "Yeah, I know. Sometimes, I come out here and sit and I'll see something floating by—you know, a can or a piece of wood, or something—and I get to thinking I'd like to hop on whatever it is and just float away, and wherever it stops, that's where I'd stop and start over."

"You might wind up on a sandbar between here and nowhere," Wesley smiled.

"Feels like that's where I am now," Nancy told him.

Wesley held up his gun, admiring it.

"Why you hunt deer, Wesley?"

"I like it. It's fun."

"You think it's fun to kill defenseless animals?"

"Uh-huh."

"Would you go hunting if deer had guns?"

"Nope."

"Why not?"

"Wouldn't be no fun," Wesley said seriously.

14

Toby Johnson was sitting in a rocker on the front porch of his shack. The rocker had a broken bottom that had been repaired with two sagging boards nailed across the frame and a stained cushion. In the yard nearby, Sudie pedaled her tricycle across a mound of sand that Toby had laboriously scooped up and hauled to the yard. He was smiling peacefully. Watching his great-granddaughter was his most pleasurable occupation.

He looked up when Jerry's car pulled into the driveway. His smile faded, then returned when Jerry opened the car door.

"Hey, Sudie," Jerry said. He crossed to the child, scooped her from the tricycle, and lifted her above his head. "How you doing, Sudie?"

The child squealed in delight and Jerry cuddled her and moved to the porch.

"Afternoon, Mr. Johnson," Jerry said.

"Uh-huh. How you?" Toby replied.

"Fine," Jerry said. "Just got off."

"They gon' get 'em a union over to the factory?" asked Toby.

"Don't know, Mr. Johnson," Jerry answered. "We voted today. They might. Lot of talk for it, but I think it's gonna be close."

The door opened and Janice walked outside. She nodded to Jerry but did not speak.

"I think people oughta try and do better," Toby philosophized. "I believe that, I truly do, but sometimes it's harder to do the right thing than it is to follow along with what the rest of 'em's doing. You see my meaning?"

"Yes sir, I think I do," Jerry told him. Sudie wiggled from his arms and scurried back to her tricycle.

"Gon' be a lot of changes around here, son," Toby continued. He cackled a laugh. "People don't know how good they got it sometimes. No, they don't."

Jerry looked up at Janice. "Can't disagree with that, Mr. Johnson," he said quietly. "Janice, can we talk a minute?"

She nodded and opened the door to step inside.

"How about we take a walk?" Jerry suggested. "Pretty out today."

"All right," Janice said. She looked at her grandfather.

"Go on," Toby said, waving his bony hand. "Me 'n' the girl'll be just fine. Yes, we will."

Janice stepped from the porch and began to cross the yard. Her arms were folded against her chest.

"Won't be long, Mr. Johnson," Jerry said.

"Uh-huh," Toby muttered. There was sadness in his voice and in his eyes.

Jerry turned beside Janice and they began to walk the field leading to the river. He did not speak until they were near the edge of the woods.

"You all right?" he asked.

"I'm all right," Janice said quietly. "You?"

He took four more steps before he answered. "Yeah." he paused. "I think."

"What you got to tell me, Jerry?" Janice asked suddenly.

"I think you know." he answered.

"I hear the talk," Janice replied. "In the bar. People say you and Wanda back together now."

Jerry stopped and looked toward the river. "That's right," he said after a long moment.

"You won't be seeing me no more, will you?" Janice asked quietly.

Jerry turned to her, looked at her face. Her eyes blinked rapidly against the moisture. "No," he answered.

Janice ducked her head and nodded. She hugged her arms closer to her chest and fingered Jerry's gift of the heart around her neck.

"All right," she whispered. Then she turned and started back toward the house.

"Janice—"

She turned to Jerry. She said, "I know you got one more question to ask. And the answer's no. No, Sudie's not your baby, and it don't matter that she's light-skinned. She's not yours."

"I—"

"You don't have to say it, Jerry. I know you love her. I'm glad for that."

"And I love you, too, Janice," Jerry said, the words rising in his mouth naturally and honestly.

"I know that," Janice replied. "It just wadn't meant to be."

She walked away.

15

Furman Mason knew it was a gamble, but he had decided to take it: Family Night.

And it was not without coincidence that Family Night at the Dew Drop Inn was on the same date the union vote would be taken and counted at the Big Sandy Auto Accessories plant.

For Furman, it would be a night of celebration or despair. The oddsmakers who had staggered in and out of the Dew Drop—the regulars from the plant—had made it celebration, five-to-one, and Furman trusted bar-talk as much as he trusted pulpit-talk. Maybe more.

He had moved the pool tables into the back room to bring in more dining tables, and he had hired a live band—Howie Epps and the Dirt Road Band—to perform. He advertised all-the-way hamburgers for $1.50 and barbecue plates cooked by Dub Mallard for $6.99. He knew he would be marginal on the meals, but he would make out like a bandit on the beer.

And, more important to Furman, he wanted the Inn to be known as the one place in the Big Sandy valley that catered to change. It was simple mathematics to Furman: the union would provide more spending money, and if there was more spending money, he wanted it to be spent in the Inn.

"Shit," he had said to Clifford privately, "it don't take no scientist to figure that out."

The signs that he had posted on the front door of the Inn and in the bathrooms and on the pillars behind the bar had advertised:

VOTE UNION

At the bottom of the sign, in smaller print, was the announcement of Family Night and the band and the specials.

"Fucking Furman. He don't miss a trick, does he?" the men chuckled. "Still got his first dollar."

By six-thirty, the Dew Drop Inn was crowded and Furman stood behind the cash register, a cigar jabbed into his mouth, and beamed. "Shit," Wesley said to Furman as he shoved his way to the bar for more drinks, "you done found the pot at the end of the rainbow."

"Looks that way, don't it?" Furman replied proudly. "Damn good thing I put on some extra help."

"Barbecue smells good in here, Furman," Wesley said.

"A little heavy, if you ask me," Furman judged.

"Good Lord, Furman, it covers up the sour smell of spilt beer," Wesley argued.

Furman nodded. "Now that you mention it, you're right. Heard anything about how the vote's going?"

Wesley shrugged. "Who the hell knows? It'll pass." He picked up his beer and a Coke and wiggled back through the crowd to a table where Nancy was sitting with Becky and Cecil.

"Here you go," he said to Nancy, pushing the Coke in front of her.

"I'd rather have a sip of what you're drinking," Nancy said.

Wesley noticed Becky and Cecil examining their class rings. He saw Nancy didn't have one.

"How come you didn't get no senior ring like ever'body else?" Wesley asked.

Nancy flipped her hair casually. She looked away to the couples on the dance floor. "I don't know," she said after a moment.

"Well, by God, it ain't right," Wesley exclaimed.

"What?"

Wesley pulled his class ring from his finger and took Nancy's hand.

"Ever'body ought to have a senior ring," he said. He slipped the ring onto Nancy's ring finger. "I know it's a little big right now, but you can put a wad of wax in there and it'll fit."

"Wesley—"

"Don't say nothing, Nancy," Wesley said. "Hell, I didn't do enough in school to earn the damn thing, anyhow." He squeezed her hand. "You wanna dance?"

Nancy nodded. "Yeah. That'd be nice."

"I ain't much at it, but I'll try," Wesley warned.

"That's all right."

Wesley pulled Nancy to the floor and caught her and they began to slide awkwardly among the spinning bodies of other couples. Wesley had not lied: he was not a dancer. To Nancy, it did not matter. She could feel the gift of his ring dangling from her finger.

"Way to go, Wesley," Clifford called as Wesley and Nancy turned stiffly in front of the table where Clifford and Evelyn were sitting, eating barbecue.

Wesley smiled and winked.

"Don't you go stepping on my daughter's toes, Wesley Tubbs." Verdale shouted.

"I won't," Wesley called back. Then, to Nancy: "Who's that man your mama's with?"

Nancy lifted her head over Wesley's shoulder and giggled. She could see her mother and her mother's date—a man with a full head of jet-black hair, swirled up in front, tapering into three-inch sideburns. He looked like a B-movie version of Elvis Presley.

"Oh, that's Ernie," Nancy replied.

"Where'd your mama come up with him?" asked Wesley.

"He drives a produce truck, delivers to the store," Nancy told him. She glanced back at her mother and Ernie. Ernie was posturing like an Elvis imitator. "At least he's not married," she added. She paused, sighed. "Or I don't think he is."

The waitress put another beer in front of Clifford. She leaned to him and said, "I don't think them kids oughta be drinking in here."

"They ain't," Clifford replied.

The waitress motioned with her head toward the bar. "Jimmie Clifford is," she sniffed.

Clifford glanced toward the bar. Jimmie was standing with members of the football team, drinking a beer from the bottle.

"Then you go tell him to stop," Clifford said to the waitress. "Hell, he's bigger'n me."

The waitress glared at Clifford, spun and walked away.

"Well, I'll go tell him," declared Evelyn. She stood. "I ain't gonna have—"

Clifford sprang to his feet and caught Evelyn's hand. "Aw, leave him alone," he said. "C'mon, let's show 'em how it's done."

Evelyn stared at him with bewilderment, but allowed herself to be led to the dance floor. "Clifford—"

"Aw, shit, Evelyn, have some fun once in a while," Clifford said. He pulled her to him and led her into the two-step. A howl of approval rose from the crowd.

"Look at your mama and daddy," Cecil said to Becky. "What's that step they doing?"

Becky blushed, then smiled. "It's supposed to be the two-step, but I never saw anybody do it to this kind of music."

"You look like Ginger Rogers, Evelyn," shouted Ernestine.

"But that ain't no Fred Astaire you're with," countered Benny.

The gaiety was high-pitched when Ed and Jack and David Shelby entered the Inn. Joe saw them first. He was sitting at a table near the door with Jerry and Wanda.

"Well, here they are," Joe said to Jerry. "We oughta know something pretty quick."

Jerry wagged his head in doubt. "This is either gonna be the happiest bunch of people you ever saw, or the saddest."

"Yeah," his father mumbled.

The recognition of Ed and Jack and David rolled across the floor behind them as they crossed to the stage where the band played.

"Cross your fingers," Wesley said to Clifford.

"Boy, I got everything I own crossed," Clifford replied, "and that ain't easy to do."

Howie Epps took the signal to stop playing from Furman and gave a swipe on his guitar to end the song.

"I think this is what you all have been waiting for," Howie crooned into the microphone. He moved back and Jack stepped in front of the mike. There was a serious frown on his face. He waved down the applause.

"First off, let me say that—ah, we've all got a lot to be proud of," Jack said solemnly. "We worked hard, and we gave it our best shot. I want you to know as far as I'm concerned, we got nothing to be ashamed of."

A loud moan rose from the crowd.

"Holy shit," Clifford whispered.

"Clifford!" Evelyn said.

"Now, now wait a minute," Jack continued. He shoved his palms toward the audience for silence. "You've got nothing to hang your head about 'cause—" He paused. A smile began to break over his face. "What you may not know is that we won an overwhelming victory over management with an astounding ninety-five percent *yes* vote! We got ourselves a union."

There was a beat, an eternity-long second. The echo of Jack's words rang over the Inn. And then an explosion of applause and shouting sprang from the audience.

"Jack," Clifford yelled above the noise, "you sumbitch!" You almost nearly gave me a stroke." He hugged Evelyn, then Benny, then Wesley, then Nancy.

Jack laughed and stepped away from the microphone and let the celebration flow. After a minute, he leaned again to the mike. He said, "Listen up. Listen up." The crowd began to grow quiet. "We're gonna have our first union meeting next Thursday night over at the Elks Lodge. We'll air our grievances and get 'em ready to take to management." He turned and beckoned Ed forward.

"I just wish we'd of done this ten years ago," Ed said. "Every one of us would of been better off than we are now." He looked at Benny. "Benny, let me have that pitcher of beer on the table there." Benny handed him the beer and Ed raised it. "To the union!" he shouted and then drank in large gulps.

"To the union!" the crowd answered. A dull sound of bottles and glasses clicking together rolled over the Inn.

Jack tapped on the microphone for attention. He said, "We all worked real hard to get this thing put through, but I think we owe a special thanks to Clifford Sewell. He worked his butt off to get this union in here." Jack looked at Clifford. "We couldn't of done it without you, buddy. Shouts of "Damn right" fell over Clifford. He could feel hands pounding on his back. A blush colored his face.

"I say we make Clifford our first shop steward on day shift," Ed called.

Again, a chorus of voices praised Clifford, anointing him with approval. Evelyn smiled proudly.

"Come on, Clifford, get up here," Jack urged, waving his hand.

"Yeah, Clifford," the crowd shouted.

"Speech, Clifford! Speech!"

He could feel hands pushing him forward.

"Go on, honey," Evelyn whispered. "They want you to."

Clifford shook his head in embarassment, then moved through the crowd to the stage. Jack gestured him to the microphone.

"Thank you," Clifford said awkwardly. "Y'all—" He paused and laughed nervously. "Well, hell, I appreciate that. And thank you, Jack Wimberly and Ed Stone. Y'all are the ones that really pulled it off. And David Shelby over there, from the union." He paused again and searched for words. "We can all be pretty damn proud of ourselves. I'll tell you one thing: if I'm shop steward, we're gonna cut out this practice of hiring people ahead of others just because they went to college, and we're gonna get it back to the way it oughta be—by seniority."

More cheering of agreement from the audience. At his table near the door, Jerry shook his head slowly. He looked at his father. Joe only shrugged and turned back to Clifford.

"There's gonna be some changes around that plant," Clifford continued, "and I mean pretty damn quick. They think we're a bunch of dumbasses over there. Well, by God, we may be dumb, but we ain't stupid."

"You tell 'em, Clifford," a voice shouted from the back of the room.

"Yeah, Clifford, you tell 'em," another voice added.

And the cry became a song of bravery.

"You tell 'em, Clifford . . ."

"You tell 'em, Clifford . . ."

"You tell 'em, Clifford . . ."

16

Bailey Hart tugged at his police hat, pulling it down tight on his forehead. He kicked at a rock on the ground, toed it with the spit-shine shoe. He did not want to look up into the faces of the men and women who stood silently at the chain-locked door of the Big Sandy Auto Accessories plant. There were days he hated being Sheriff of Big Sandy, Tennessee.

It was a numbed crowd, speechless. A dangerous crowd, Bailey believed. One hothead and all hell could break loose. He glanced to both sides, assuring himself that his deputies were still there. If anybody tried to storm the door there would be a riot, and it would be impossible for them to stop it. And Bailey wasn't sure he would want to stop them. Let them break down the door, let them spill inside and wreck the place. His father had worked at the plant. There were cousins standing across from him holding their lunchpails, numbed by the sign on the door:

CLOSED

The silence was finally broken by Clifford. He said, "Bailey, one of us has just naturally got to kick the shit out of that lock. Just so we can say we did it."

Bailey looked at the lock dangled to the chain. "Just one of you, Clifford?"

"I reckon one of us will do," Clifford answered.

"All right with me," Bailey said. "Just so it don't start nothing."

"It won't," Clifford assured him.

"Which one of y'all want to do it?" Bailey asked.

"Well, gotdamn, Bailey, ever' last one of us *want* to," Clifford exclaimed.

"You do it, Clifford," Benny said in an empty voice. "I ain't got the strength for it."

"Yeah, Clifford," someone else said.

A few other voices mumbled approval.

"Looks like you been elected, Clifford," Jerry said. He added, "Again."

Clifford looked coldly at Jerry. "All right, by God, I will," he said. He stepped forward and raised his foot and kicked the lock. It banged against the door. The he raised his face toward the office high above the crowd. He could see two figures standing at the window. "You sumbitch," he growled.

From the window, watching the unmoving, silent crowd, Richard Moss shook his head.

"Look at that," Richard said. "It looks like a wake."

"It is," Gerald Moss said. "Mine."

"Yours?"

"Mine," Gerald repeated. Then: "Greed. That's what's wrong with this country today."

"I don't know, Daddy," Richard said. "They're just like everybody else. They just want to make a better living for their families."

Gerald Moss scoffed. "If we let it get started here, it's just a matter of time before it'll spread to our other plants. Put this company out of business in a year." He paused, watching. "One thing I've never been able to understand," he continued. "We start a company. We take the financial risks. If the company fails, we are the ones who lose. We create jobs for people who don't have any jobs. Hell, I've never made anybody work for me. Then one day, you're the enemy. You're not treating them right. Not enough paid time off. No Christmas bonus. Need more candy machines in the breakroom. Need a bigger breakroom. They get this notion: You're making money; why shouldn't we get more of it?"

"I think they've got a legitimate argument, Daddy," Richard said softly.

Gerald turned to study his son. His son was too weak to run a company. "Where were they when I was scraping together the money to start this company? Busting my butt twenty hours a day, seven days a week? And all of it for free. Had to borrow money from my brother to keep food on the table and a roof over our heads. And he's never let me forget it."

Richard laughed easily. It was an old story, and a true one.

"I always treated the people who work for us fair, and you know that," Gerald said. "But I took the risks. It cost me my marriage to your mother and a quadruple bypass."

Below them, the crowd began to move away from the entrance to the plant and huddle in groups. They moved slowly, like old people—like tired, old people.

"I've seen it too many times, son," Gerald said. "The unions prey on these kind of people. Unskilled, uneducated, living hand-to-mouth. They'll believe anything anybody tells them, except for the ones that are paying them. The grass is always greener on the other side of the picket line. Now, look at 'em. What are they gonna do? It's greed, son. And these unions are about to kill the manufacturing business with it."

Clifford's foot was aching from kicking the lock on the door of the Big Sandy Auto Accessories plant. He hobbled to his truck and pulled himself up on the tailgate and sat. Wesley and Jerry trailed him. The three men lit cigarettes in unison.

"You know, I started working here right after I come back from Vietnam," Clifford said. "Right after me 'n' Evelyn got married. Hell, we didn't even get a honeymoon, 'cause I had to go to work the next day." He shook his head. "All them years down the drain, and I still ain't got a pot to piss in or a window to pour it out of." He fingered the employee badge that was pinned to his shirt. "Ain't got nothing left, but this thing."

"Hell of a lot of good that thing does us now," Wesley said sourly.

"You're right," Jerry said. He unpinned his badge. "It's worthless." He turned to walk back toward the chain-link fence surrounding the plant.

"Where you going?" asked Wesley.

Jerry did not reply. He walked to the fence and thrust the needle arm of the pin around a wire and snapped it closed, leaving his badge caught on the fence.

"Well, by God," whispered Wesley. He pulled off his badge and followed Jerry, pinning it to the fence. He stepped back and looked at the badge. His face, in a picture the size of a thumbnail, stared back at him. His name was printed beneath in bold capital letters. "Let'em keep the goddamn thing," he muttered.

Clifford slipped from the truck and crossed to Wesley and pinned his badge to the fence. He looked up at the sign hanging above the entrance: "Through These Doors Pass the Happiest People in Tennessee." "Y'all remember this day," he called in a clear, strong voice. "Don't never forget it."

And then they all moved forward, silently, leaving their badges dangling in the soft morning breeze. And they turned and got into their cars and trucks and drove away.

Bailey Hart stared at the fence. "God-o-mighty," he said quietly to a deputy. "It looks like some sorta memorial."

17

Working on Sally Dewberry's hair was never easy, even when Sally was in a good mood, which was seldom. The hair was thin and blue-grey and Sally yammered constantly to Evelyn about how short it should be, and how she wanted the curl.

"Last time, you almost ruined it, Evelyn," Sally said irritably. "Carl said it looked like I was trying to be seventy years old."

"I thought you liked it," Evelyn said sweetly. "You said you did."

"Well, honey, that was before I got home and got a real look," Sally complained. "You know how it is in beauty-shop light. You can't tell nothing about it."

"You just tell me how you want it, and that's how I'll do it," Evelyn said patiently.

The phone rang and Juanita answered it. "Juanita's Clip and Curl," she said. A pause. "Uh-huh." Another pause. "When?" Another pause. "Okay." She hung up the phone and turned to Evelyn.

"What's the matter, honey?" asked Evelyn.

"They've closed the plant," Juanita said.

A gasp caught in Evelyn's throat. She stood for a moment, staring at Juanita, then she pulled off her apron and grabbed her purse from a shelf and rushed through the door.

"Is she coming back?" Sally demanded from her chair.

Evelyn found him sitting at the kitchen table in the trailer, sitting as though he had fallen suddenly ill. He held a burning cigarette in his hand and his hand trembled.

"Clifford," she said.

He looked up. "What're we gonna do, Evelyn?"

She moved to him, knelt before him, took the cigarette, and crushed it out in the ashtray. She said, "We'll manage. We always have."

"What the hell's wrong with me, Evelyn?" Clifford said, swallowing a sob. "I always got to act like I know ever' gotdamn thing there is, when the truth is, I don't know shit."

"It wadn't your fault, Clifford."

"Then whose fault was it?" he asked.

"It just happened," Evelyn said. "It's okay, honey. You was looking for work when you got this job. We'll be allright."

"I don't know why you put up with my sorry ass," Clifford said quietly. "I don't know why you don't just run me off."

Evelyn began to stroke his hair. "I don't want to hear that, Clifford. This ain't the end of the world. We've got each other, we've got the kids. That's all that matters.

Clifford nodded. A tear bubbled in his eye and he wiped at it with his hand.

"Listen to me," Evelyn continued. "I love you. I wouldn't want to be anywhere else in the world, but right here with you." She reached to pull his face to her. She could feel the trembling in his body. "We'll manage," she said again. "We always have."

Clifford buried his face in Evelyn's blouse. He wrapped his arms around her waist. Evelyn stroked his hair again. "We'll manage." She looked out the window, down to the river. A barge moved slowly south.

18

N ancy saw him from the school bus, sitting beside the river idly tossing rocks into the water. She said to Becky, "There's Wesley. God, he must feel bad."

"Ever'body does," Becky said. "I'm worried about Daddy."

The bus stopped and the children of the Captain's Point Trailer Park filed noiselessly off. News of the plant's closing had invaded the school like a disease, leaving the chidren of the workers fearful and uncertain. It was in the messages of their eyes— scared, confused, suspicious.

"See you," Becky said to Nancy, and Nancy understood. Becky needed to be with her father.

"Sure," she said. She stood, watching Becky hurry to her trailer. She envied Becky. At least she had a father to worry about. She turned and crossed the road and walked toward the river, toward Wesley. He glanced at her when she approached.

"Hi," Nancy said.

"Hi, yourself," Wesley replied. He faked a smile. "How was school?"

"So-so," Nancy answered. She sat near him. "I heard about the plant closing. You all right?"

Wesley lofted a rock into the water, watched it splash and disappear beneath the ripples. He clucked lightly. "Yeah," he said softly. "Yeah, I'm all right. Shit, can't do nothing about it, can I?"

What're you going to do? Nancy asked.

He shrugged, picked up another rock. "I don't know. I got a little money put away. Maybe it's time I headed over to Nashville and got me my—"

"Number-five license," Nancy said.

Wesley smiled. "Yeah. My number five."

"Why don't you?"

"Maybe I will," Wesley said. "You remember what we was talking about before?" He motioned toward the river.

"What?" asked Nancy.

"Getting on the river and floating off," Wesley said. "That's what I been doing. Sitting here, watching the barges. Even thought about stripping down butt-naked and jumping in the river and swimming out to one, and getting on board, and just keeping on going."

"I don't know," Nancy mused. "I think if they fished you out butt-naked, they'd take one look and throw you back in."

Wesley laughed. "Yeah, I guess so."

Where'd you want to go, Wesley?"

"Anywhere," Wesley said. "I don't know. Somewheres else."

The whistle of a barge cried over the river.

"Yeah, me too," Nancy said wistfully.

Wesley stood and reached out his hand, and Nancy took it and let him pull her up. He started to walk down toward the river, still holding her hand.

"Wesley."

"Uh-huh," Wesley said.

"I'm pregnant."

"I know," Wesley replied gently.

19

The mood in the Dew Drop Inn was as somber as the slow, dragging ballad of lost love that blared from the jukebox. Clifford sat alone at the bar, nursing his fourth beer of the night. Behind him, Wesley and Benny were shooting pool but not talking or arguing as they normally did. At a table near the bandstand, Ed and Jack and several other men from the plant sat and talked in angry, anxious voices.

Clifford had waved off their invitation to join them. "Just wanna have a couple of beers," he had said. "I ain't up to talking." And the men had understood.

But Clifford could hear them, and listening was as bad as sitting among them.

"They can't do it," Ed complained bitterly. "It's against the damn law. I talked to David Shelby about it."

"Union'll file a damn law suit in Nashville against old man Moss if we raise enough hell about it."

"Lot of good that's gonna do," one of the men suggested. "It's his damn plant. He wants to close it, well, by God, I guess that's what he'll do. I don't like the sumbitch, but I got to give him that. Hell, if it was my place and I wanted to burn the goddamn thing to the ground, I'd do it."

"Ain't nobody arguing that," Jack said. "But to close it because they was a union voted in, that's against the law, by God."

"Well, what the hell you think can be done about it?" the man asked.

Ed's fist slapped the table. "I'll tell you what the hell I'm gonna do," he snapped. He stood. "Hey, ever'body, listen up," he called across the room. "We ain't gonna take this bullshit lying down. We're tax-paying Americans and we got just as many rights as Gerald Moss does." He began striding toward the bar. "Janice, give me a piece of paper. We'll get up a damn petition."

A flush of excitement quivered in Jack. He stood. "Hell, yes," he shouted. "We'll take their asses to court."

"To the damn Supreme Court if we have to," Ed bellowed. "We'll sue the son of a bitch. He'll find out right quick who the hell he's dealing with." Janice handed him a sheet of paper and a pen.

"Damn government won't let him do this to us. We'll get that plant opened back up, and we'll run the son of a bitch off." He crossed to Clifford. "Here, Clifford, help me write this thing and then be one of the first to put your name on it. You sign up, and the rest of 'em will feel better about signing it."

Clifford shook his head in disbelief. He shifted on the bar stool to control his anger.

"C'mon, Clifford," Ed urged. "You ain't gonna let 'em treat us like this, are you?"

Clifford slipped suddenly from the bar stool, caught Ed by his shirt, and drove him across the room into the jukebox. The record was stuck on the same line, playing it over and over. Clifford drew back his fist to hit Ed in the face, but his arm locked. Wesley and Jack rushed to Clifford, grabbing him and trying to pull him off of Ed, but Clifford stood rock solid. His cocked arm began to tremble.

Ed looked at Clifford in astonishment. He said, "What the hell's wrong with you, Clifford? You did as much as anybody to get that plant closed down."

Clifford jerked free of the men holding him. "He's right," he thought. "It was as much me as anybody." He reached out and caught Ed on the shoulder and squeezed an apology, then turned and left the Inn.

the more things change
the more they stay
the same

1

Jerry was weary. He had made applications for jobs at four places where no jobs existed, and he had interviewed with Curly Edison at the hardware store. Curly had said "maybe," but Jerry knew it was only kindness. With the closing of the plant, Curly's business would suffer; he would have no need for help—even part-time.

It was dark when he pulled into his driveway. He turned off the motor and got out and stared curiously at the trailer. A dark, eerie glow flickered from the window. He frowned a question and walked up the steps and opened the door and went inside.

There were no lights burning. Only candles. On the kitchen table he saw a styrofoam cooler filled with ice and beer. He turned in the room to study it. On the top of the television, he saw the framed picture of himself and Wanda and Clayton—the picture that had been put away on the day of Clayton's death. He crossed to it and picked it up.

"Jerry?"

It was Wanda. He looked up. She was standing in the hallway, silhouetted against the dim light of candles coming from the bedroom. She was wearing a see-through nightie.

"I read about this in a magazine," Wanda said hesitantly.

Jerry put the picture back on the top of the television. "Well, don't ever cancel that subscription," he said softly.

Wanda smiled. In the candlelight, she was as beautiful as any woman he had ever seen. He moved to her and cupped her face gently in his hands and kissed her. A purr, like a sigh, rose in her throat. She embraced him and thrust against him passionately. With her hands, she began to rip away his shirt. He lifted her and carried her down the hallway to the bedroom, into the shadowed light of the candles.

"God, I'm glad you're here," Wanda whispered.

"Me, too," Jerry said, then paused. "Wait a minute."

"What?"

"I forgot the beer," he said. He turned and raced down the hallway to the kitchen table and grabbed the styrofoam bucket. He could hear her laughing from the bedroom.

2

Evelyn could feel the tension building in her stomach. Her fingers were damp with perspiration, and they trembled slightly as she pulled Brenda Avery's thick dark hair up and snipped it with her scissors.

"Not too short, now," Brenda advised, frowning into the mirror.

"I won't," Evelyn. She held the hair in her fingers. It was too short and she knew Brenda would complain later. She felt a flutter in her heart. She thought, Mama was right. Her mother had told her there would be times in her marriage when she would have to be the strong one, the one to keep the spirit alive and thriving. Today was such a time.

The door opened and the spring-bell on the top of the door frame jingled. Evelyn glanced at the door. It was Clifford. His face was furrowed.

"Hi, honey," Evelyn said.

Clifford nodded.

"How you doing today, Cliff?" asked Juanita.

"I'm all right," Clifford answered. "Why?"

"Just take a seat, honey," Evelyn told him. "I'll be finished in a few minutes."

Clifford sat in a chair, picked up a magazine of hairstyles, and began leafing through it. He paused at a page showing men's styles from California. He thought: "Bunch of queers." He turned the page. A woman whose face looked porcelain glared at him. Her hair was crew-cut. He closed the magazine and put it down.

"All right if I smoke, Juanita?" he asked.

"All right with me," Juanita said. "I do."

Clifford tapped a cigarette from its pack and lit it. He watched Evelyn's hands lifting and snipping Brenda's hair. One good thing about being married to Evelyn, he never had to pay for a haircut.

Evelyn had finished Brenda's cut by the time Clifford crushed his cigarette in an ashtray. He could hear Brenda's irritated question: "Don't you think it's a little short, Evelyn? I didn't want it this short. Look here, Juanita."

"Honey, it looks great," Juanita said. "Shows off your face just like God meant for it to."

"Oh, I like it," Evelyn cooed.

Brenda shrugged and reached for her pocketbook.

"Damn," thought Clifford, "no wonder women make the rules; they take up for one another like a bunch of trapped animals."

Brenda left the shop in a huff.

"I'll be back in a little while, Juanita," Evelyn said, slipping on her coat. She added, "We're gonna run over to the unemployment offi–"

"She'll be right back," Clifford interrupted.

"That's all right," Juanita said. "We're not busy." She looked at Clifford and smiled weakly.

Outside the beauty shop, Clifford snarled, "Jesus Christ, Evelyn, ain't it bad enough we got to ask for welfare without you having to tell ever'body?"

"Clifford, it ain't welfare," Evelyn replied gently. "It's unemployment. You've earned it."

"I don't give a damn what you call it, it's a handout and I don't want ever'body in town to know about it."

They turned the corner at Woolworth's and continued down the sidewalk.

Evelyn said, "You know, we could get—" She paused, searched for the right words.

"What?" demanded Clifford.

"Help," Evelyn answered. "From the government. You know . . . stamps."

Clifford stopped and glared at her. "Food stamps? Have you lost your mind?"

"Now, wait a minute," Evelyn replied. Betty Sue told me that we could qualify now that the plant's closed. Her and James applied for 'em."

"Gotdamnit, Evelyn," Clifford snapped. "Did you tell ever'body in the whole gotdamn town how bad a shape we're in? Betty Sue Green! Shit! Why didn't you just take out an ad in the gotdamn newspaper? That way you'd be sure and not miss anybody."

"Clifford, you ain't the only person in this town that got laid off, remember that."

"That may be true, but we ain't got to broadcast it, and we ain't taking no food stamps, neither. I'll wipe people's asses for a living before I take food stamps."

Evelyn sighed. She stared at the traffic light, watching it blink from red to yellow to green, and stepped into the street with Clifford beside her.

"Betty said we could—" Evelyn began at the center line of the street.

"No," Clifford snapped.

They were at the sidewalk.

"Betty said we could get cheese and—"

"No. I don't wanna hear it," Clifford said.

"—milk and stuff like that. Government surplus." She raised her voice, determined to be heard.

"Food stamps and government handouts. We ain't living like a bunch of damn niggers, so forget it," Clifford ordered. "Something'll come up."

"Clifford, I ain't gonna let this family starve because of your bullheadedness," argued Evelyn.

Clifford whirled toward her. His face burned red with anger. His fist opened and closed, opened and closed.

"Don't you dare look at me that way," Evelyn said evenly.

A voice rolled from across the street: "Clifford. Hey, Cliff."

Clifford glanced toward the voice. It was Harvey Williams. He was standing on the sidewalk across from them, checking the traffic.

"Shit," Clifford muttered to Evelyn, "let's just keep on walking like we don't see him."

"I don't believe you," Evelyn hissed. "Since when did you start treating people like that?"

"Since I don't want to talk to that black sumbitch," Clifford growled. "That's when. Now let's go."

Harvey's voice grew stronger: "Hey, Clifford, wait up." He rushed across the street, dodging Benny's truck. Benny glared at him from the window, then pressed on the horn until his wife, Fat Ethel, slapped him on the back of the head.

"Shit," Clifford muttered. He stopped and waited.

"Hey" Clifford, I've been looking all over for you," Harvey said pleasantly. "Called your house and your boy said you were up at the beauty shop, so I called up there and they told me you were going over to the unemployment office."

Clifford turned to glare at Evelyn.

"Morning, Mrs. Sewell," Harvey said.

"It's Evelyn, Harvey," Evelyn replied. "How are you? How's them kids?"

"Pretty good," Harvey answered. "The littlest one's been down with the earache, but everybody's doing pretty—"

Clifford interrupted: "You found me, Williams. What'chu want?"

Harvey smiled. "I want to offer you a job."

Clifford's face blinked in surprise. "Come again?"

"You know my brother-in-law, Clement, owns that septic tank business," Harvey said. "He's looking to put on a couple of people, and I told him about you. You always was the hardest-working son of a gun I ever saw."

Clifford shook his head as if confused. Evelyn smiled.

"Harvey, bless your heart," Evelyn said.

"Now, it don't pay what we was making at the plant," Harvey warned, "but it's a job."

"You want *me* to come to work for *you?*" Clifford asked suspiciously.

Harvey laughed easily. "Naw. Not for me. For my brother-in-law. Starting Monday, if you want it."

Clifford stared at Harvey, the question still frozen in his face.

"Well, that's great," Evelyn said. She touched Clifford on the arm, then forced his arm out toward Harvey. "Clifford?" she said. She looked up at Harvey. "He'll take it."

Clifford's grip was the grip of a dead man.

"That's great, Cliff," Harvey said, pumping Clifford's hand. "Glad to be working with you again. You want me to pick you up at your house on Monday morning?"

Clifford blinked his eyes and wagged his head vigorously. He said, "No. Ah . . . no. That's all right. I know where the place is. I'll just drive."

Harvey stepped back. "Okay," he said. "I'll see you at six o'clock sharp Monday morning."

Clifford nodded. He watched as Harvey turned to cross the street. He glanced at Evelyn. She was watching Harvey as though Harvey was a messenger of God. A peaceful, thankful smile rested in her face. He looked back to Harvey and called, "Hey, Harvey. Why don't you just give me a ride?"

Harvey acknowledged with a wave. He disappeared across the street. Evelyn stepped close to Clifford and put her hand through the crook of his arm.

"You know," Clifford said philosophically, "I always did think a lot of him."

3

Jimmie had spent an hour punching holes into the top of the tin cans and running a nylon cord through them. There were five strings of cans, with six cans on each string. The strings were ten feet long.

"Wesley's gonna kick your ass, son," Clifford told him, a wide, proud smile creasing his face.

He stood up from the back of Wesley's truck and admired his work: a net of cans and string tied to the bumper.

"Gonna raise some racket," Jerry said. He laughed. "When we gonna put the shaving cream on?"

From the doorway leading into the church, they could hear Evelyn's command: "Clifford, Jimmie Clifford, y'all get in here!" There was a pause. "You too, Jerry. Wanda's looking all over for you. You supposed to be in here with Wesley."

The three men shrugged, inspected the truck once again, then trudged up the walkway leading to the church. Clifford began giggling. "We should of blown up some rubbers and tied 'em to the antenna," he said.

The wedding of Wesley Alvin Tubbs, age thirty-three, and Nancy Jean Calloway, age seventeen, in the Big Sandy Pentecostal, First Covenant, Assembly of God was both festive and speculative, and the speculation had the white heat of good, full-bodied gossip.

"She's as big as the side of a barn."

"You don't reckon that's really Wesley's baby, do you?"

"He's such a sweet boy. His mama and daddy are the finest people you'll ever want to meet, the way they watch after that girl of theirs—that Susie. She's retarded you know."

"Lord, it's a wonder half the girls around here don't get pregnant, the way these boys carry on."

"Can't blame Nancy. Her mama's crazy as they come. All she wants to do is get out from under that mess."

"I'll bet Lloyd Pinkerton moves in over there. It's a sin how he carries on, and his wife suffering like she does."

"Won't be Lloyd, from what I hear tell. It's that new man. Ernie Something-or-Other."

"I hear tell half the women in Big Sandy are crying because of Wesley going out of circulation, and the other half's celebrating because they won't have him aggravating them all the time."

"That boy don't know what he's in for."

"God bless Nancy. She's gonna need all the help she can get."

"I wouldn't miss that wedding for nothing."

The church was packed with friends of the bride and friends of the groom and the curious. Becky was Nancy's one bridesmaid, and Jerry was Wesley's best man. Clifford was selected to give the bride away, and he did it in Clifford-style, encouraged by a six-pack of beer that he had consumed since mid-morning.

Clifford said: "Well, I ain't her daddy, but I'm a pretty close second, since I been seeing her since she was no bigger'n a doll, so I'm proud to be a stand-in, and tell ever'body here that giving her away to my good friend Wesley Tubbs, makes me about as proud as if she was my own flesh and blood." He turned to Evelyn, who was seated beside a tearful Verdale. "Ain't that right, Evelyn?"

A snicker rolled across the church.

Clifford sat, smiling, ignoring the horrified stare of Evelyn.

"That was sweet, Clifford," Verdale whispered, reaching across Evelyn to pat Clifford on the arm.

And the wedding of Wesley and Nancy was over in eight minutes.

"You can kiss the bride now, Wesley." Brother Ruffin said, beaming.

"You don't have to tell me twice," Wesley said. He embraced Nancy and kissed her.

"Don't squeeze so hard," Nancy said.

"You all right?" Wesley asked. He stepped back to get a good look at her.

Nancy frowned. "Yeah," she mumbled.

"You look like you're hurting," Wesley whispered.

"Let's just go," Nancy said.

They stood at the front of the church and waited until the congreation had filed out, forming a rice-line.

"They're ready now," the Preacher urged.

"Good," Nancy said. She caught Wesley by the hand and started down the aisle toward the door of the church. He could feel her grip tighten on his hand.

Outside, the crowd poured rice into their palms from Uncle Ben's converted rice boxes. They were laughing, loud-talking.

"Damn! You hear Clifford?"

"I thought he was gonna start into a sermon or something."

"She looks beautiful."

"She looks pregnant."

"Ol' Wesley cleans up good, don't he?"

"You see what Jimmie Clifford wrote on Wesley's truck with that can of shaving cream?"

"Here they come," Verdale shouted.

The church doors swung open, and Wesley and Nancy started down the steps, ducking a shower of rice.

"You looking good, Wesley," Benny shouted.

And then Nancy stopped and slumped over in pain. Wesley caught her.

"What's the matter, baby?" he asked.

"I—I think—"

"Holy goodness, she's in labor," Fat Ethel proclaimed.

"That it, honey?" asked Verdale. She was holding Nancy's arm, squeezing it.

Nancy nodded. "I—I think so," she whispered. She looked up. "Where's Becky?"

"Right here," Becky said, pushing through the crowd.

"Don't you leave me," Nancy said. Her face flashed pain.

"I won't," Becky promised.

"Your water break, honey?" Fat Ethel said.

"I—" She could feel the dampness on her legs.

"Well, Wesley, don't just stand there like a bump on a log," demanded Fat Ethel. "Get her down to the hospital before she gives birth right here."

Wesley and Becky led Nancy to the truck, with Verdale and Evelyn and Fat Ethel and the wedding crowd following. The windows of the truck were coated in drying shaving cream: "Watch Big Sandy Grow!" and "The End of Wesley Tubbs!" and "She got him today, but he'll get her tonight!" Then someone wrote with finger in the smeared shaving cream, *Not in her condition.*

"Damn," Clifford exclaimed as Wesley roared away with Nancy and Becky in the front seat of the truck beside him, the tin cans dancing wildly over the pavement. "Now that, by God, was what a wedding ought to be."

"Clifford, just shut up," Evelyn said. "Just shut up."

4

Evelyn awoke as always, with the image of God looking down on the Captain's Point Trailer Park blinking in her dark, inner eye.

God's face was sad.

What God saw was not a full nest of trailer eggs in the green Tennessee trees—only a few frosted tops, looking oddly cold and lonely.

God saw the brown spots also. Ugly, empty brown spots. Brown spots where trailers had been but were now missing, leaving only a dead patch of ground scarred by discarded junk and sewage hook-ups and the pale markings of gravel driveways.

One by one the trailers had been jacked up, refitted with wheels, and pulled away by trucks taking them to new parks, and new towns, where new jobs awaited the residents of Captain's Point Trailer Park.

And today another would leave, Evelyn thought as she waited for the ringing of the alarm clock.

Jerry and Wanda were moving.

Evelyn stirred in the bed and sighed. She turned to Clifford in the murky dark of the bedroom, then sat up. Clifford was not in bed. She could smell the thick odor of coffee seeping like a narcotic through the trailer and, mixed with the coffee, the smoke of a fresh cigarette.

She threw the cover from her and looked at the see-in-the-dark face of the clock. It was 5:14. Her mind raced with worry. Was Clifford sick? Why had she not heard him leave the bed? She pushed the clock alarm off and slipped into her gown and went into the kitchen. Clifford was sitting at the table, sipping coffee, smoking, staring out of the opened front door.

"What's wrong?" Evelyn asked anxiously.

Clifford's head moved to look at her. "Nothing." he said quietly. "Just couldn't sleep."

Evelyn stepped closer to him, examining his face.

"Gotdamn it, Evelyn, don't start looking at me like that," Clifford said irritably. He drew again on the cigarette—deep, hard, then crushed it out. "There's some more coffee in there if you want some."

Evelyn eased her way to the kitchen for the coffee, but her eyes stayed on him. It was not like Clifford to be up before the alarm. She could not remember when Clifford had made coffee. Never, maybe. She poured the coffee and tasted it. It was surprisingly good. Not bitter. Not weak. She went back to the table and sat opposite him.

"Why's the door open?" Evelyn asked.

"Just letting some air in and the smoke out," Clilfford said.

"You got to go in early?"

Clifford shook his head. "Ain't going in until after lunch," he replied. "Promised Jerry I'd help him get ever'thing locked down with the trailer before they left."

Evelyn sipped from her coffee. She looked out of the doorway. She could see the bedroom light in Verdale's trailer. "Baby must be awake," she thought. She wondered if Wesley had awakened at the baby's cry, or if Nancy and Verdale were up, quarreling over the feeding. Far off, across the river, she could hear a rooster crowing, and on the river, even farther away, she could hear the horn of a barge.

"Won't be the same around here without Jerry and Wanda," Evelyn said. She added, "Now that they got things all patched up."

"He's a good man," Clifford said suddenly. Evelyn recognized the catch in his voice.

"Yes, he is," she agreed.

"I was thinking," Clifford said, "that—" he paused.

"What?"

"Well, since we both up, that maybe we could cook up some breakfast for 'em, have 'em over," Clifford suggested. "I know they packed all their cooking stuff last night."

Evelyn smiled. She thought of God listening, as he always listened early in the morning. God would be pleased with Clifford.

"I think that's a good idea," she said. "Let me get dressed."

Clifford nodded. A satisfied look settled into his eyes. He lit another cigarette.

The breakfast for Jerry and Wanda became a feast, with pots of coffee and biscuits and sausage and scrambled eggs and cheese grits and drop-in neighbors bringing fried salmon patties and tea cakes—Wesley and Nancy and Wesley Jr., Benny and Fat Ethel, Verdale and Ernie and Shelia. It was as though someone had pounded a hammer against a dinner bell and called the remaining residents of Captain's Point Trailer Park to Clifford and Evelyn Sewell's trailer.

"This is so nice," Wanda repeated again and again. "So nice."
"Yes, it is," everyone agreed. "We oughta do this more often."
"I won't never forget this," Wanda said. "Never."
The breakfast lasted until mid-morning, until the workmen announced that Jerry's trailer was ready to move.
"Well," Jerry said, forcing his voice to be bright, "I guess we better get on the road."
"We're gonna miss you, man," Wesley told him. He took Jerry's hand, pumped it once, pulled Jerry to him in an embrace. He whispered, "You ol' sumbitch, now who am I gonna hunt with?"
Jerry laughed and swallowed. "You know how it is. Gotta go where the work is. I love ya, man."
"Starting out as line foreman, you can't beat that," Wesley kidded, "even if it is working for old man Moss."
Clifford offered his hand to Jerry. He said, "Don't you let that sumbitch give you any shit over there. We closed this plant down, we'll close all six of them plants. Shit, we can close ever' last one of 'em, if that old bastard gets out of line. You just give me a call."
Jerry laughed. "Last thing I need is that," he said. "I can't afford to move ever' few weeks."
Clifford's eyes misted. He said quietly, "Gotdamnit, I hate to see you go."
Jerry nodded vigorously, forcing the building emotion to stay in him. "Yeah," he whispered. "I hate to go, too." He looked at Wanda. She was standing among the women, holding Nancy's baby. "But it might do us some good to get away."
"Hope so," Clifford said. "But you always got a spot here if it don't work out."
Jerry did not reply. He turned to look at the trailer, then turned back to Wanda. "We better go," he called.
Wanda handed the baby back to Nancy and began embracing the women.
"I'm gonna miss y'all," Wanda cooed. "And, Evelyn, thank you so much for breakfast. I think it was one of the best times I ever had here."
"Now, y'all be careful," advised Evelyn. "I know y'all are going to like Dyersburg. My sister used to live there, and she just loved it."
"Damn, Wanda, let's go," Jerry exclaimed. "All this goodbye stuff's about to make me blubber like a baby."
And they were gone, following the trailer—another of God's frosted top eggs being pulled away from its nest of Tennessee trees.
"I got to go in and cry," Evelyn said to Clifford.

And those who were left in the Captain's Point Trailer Park began to wander away, back to their own homes.

"Come on back to the trailer with me," Nancy said to Becky. "Just for a few minutes."

"I will if I can carry little Wes," Becky said.

"Be my guest," Nancy offered, handing the baby to Becky. "He feels like he weighs a ton by the middle of the afternoon."

They crossed the yard in silence. Then: "Mama said if I wanted to finish high school she'd help with little Wesley," Nancy said. "But I think I want to go to the vo-tech school and learn how to do hair. What'd you think?"

"You'd be good at that," Becky encouraged.

"You know Lloyd gave Wesley a job bagging groceries down at the Piggly Wiggly," Nancy said. "It's not much, but it's something."

"It's just a start, Nancy. That's what you've got to think," Becky told her.

"What I keep telling Wesley," agreed Nancy. "First chance he gets, he's going over to Nashville to that truck-driving school." She laughed. "Lord, I hope he gets to do that. He'll drive me crazy talking about it if he don't, and if he don't drive me crazy, Mama will. I know one thing: we've got to get our own place."

"He'll go," assured Becky.

Nancy stopped. She ran her fingers gently through the thin hair of her baby. "Becky?"

"What?"

"You reckon it'll be any better for him?"

"Who? Little Wes?"

"Yeah."

"It'll be better, Nancy. I know it will."

"I don't know," Nancy whispered. "I want to believe that, but I think my mama wanted to believe it, too. I just hate to think he's got to grow up the same way . . . in this same place."

The baby reached instinctively for Nancy and she took him from Becky's arms.

"Hey, Nancy, I'm gonna help Benny out for a few minutes," Wesley called.

Nancy turned to him. He was bending over an engine that Benny had pulled from his car and had lowered onto the ground. Fat Ethel was at the clothesline folding clothes. Her children swirled about her legs like flies.

"All right, honey," Nancy said in an empty voice.

"Yep, it's gonna be great," Becky added. "You know what? I'm gonna paint clouds and angels on the baby's ceiling."

Nancy smiled, lost in the thought of waking up every morning looking at a beautiful blue sky filled with cotton clouds and cherubs. She kissed the baby on the forehead, then stopped in her tracks.

"The baby sleeps in our room." Nancy rolled her eyes up as if looking at the imaginary ceiling. "Could you put one of those angels in a big rig truck for Wesley?"

"Sure," Becky laughed. "I'll give 'em a class-five license too."

The girls giggled as they moved toward Nancy, Verdale, and now Wesley's trailer.

5

Clifford was sitting on the steps of the trailer, dressed in his work uniform, when Becky returned from her visit with Nancy. He was drinking his eleventh cup of coffee and having his fourteenth cigarette.

"What're you doing, Daddy?" asked Becky.

"Waiting for you," replied Clifford.

"What for?"

"Need you to go with me into town for a few minutes," Clifford said.

"Where?"

"What difference does it make? Just go put your butt in the truck," Clifford ordered.

Becky could not remember seeing her father in such a mood— Well a good mood for him. The radio in his septic tank truck played loud country music, and he tapped out the rhythm on the steering wheel with his finger.

"Why you so happy, Daddy?" Becky asked.

"Who said I was happy?" Clifford answered. "I ain't been happy since God was in boot camp."

"Well, you sure are acting funny," Becky told him.

Clifford nodded. He said, "So, tell me who your boyfriend is these days. You got one?"

"Daddy!"

"No, I mean it," Clifford insisted easily. "Seems to me like your old man ought to know who's trying to take his little girl away from him. Lloyd Pinkerton's boy?" What's his name? Cecil?"

Becky blushed. "He's nice. We went to the Junior-Senior together."

"Uh-huh," Clifford mumbled. "Yeah, I remember. Boy looked like he'd gone to Nashville and had one of them fag cowboy places dress him up."

Becky turned to him in disbelief. "Daddy! He did not! He looked nice. It was a western theme."

"Well, call it that if you want to," Clifford mused. He added, "He seemed kind of shy. A shy queer Gene Autry."

"A little."

"Jimmie Clifford was saying you had to force him into asking you to go to that Junior-Senior."

"Jimmie Clifford ought to mind his own business."

"Did you?"

"What, Daddy?"

"Did you have to ask him to take you?"

Becky smiled. She remembered the awkward conversation with Cecil. "Yes," she thought, "I did make him ask me."

"No," she said to her father. "It was up to him if he wanted to go with me."

"Lord, baby, all you women are just exactly alike," Clifford roared. "A man ain't got a chance. Not one."

Clifford slowed the truck in front of a tall wood structure with a sign that read TAYLOR SIGN COMPANY. He pulled into a parking space and stopped.

"What're we doing here?" asked Becky.

"Come on," Clifford answered. "You're just like your mother. Always gotta know everything."

Becky shrugged. She got out of the truck and followed her father into the building and down a hallway where workers were busy designing and painting signs. She could smell the heavy fumes of the paints and hear the echoing chatter of the painters' voices. A chill struck her. She had never been in a place where artists were working. Not working and getting paid.

"There he is," Clifford said.

"Who?"

"Earl Taylor," Clifford answered. He walked briskly down the corridor to a man standing at a doorway, studying a large drawing on the wooden boards. Becky hurried to catch up with him.

"Hey, Earl, looks like y'all staying pretty busy," Clifford said cheerfully.

Earl Taylor looked up and smiled. "Got more to do than we can handle, thank goodness," he replied. "This Becky?"

"In the flesh," Clifford said. Then, to Becky, "Honey, this is Earl Taylor. He owns the place."

"Hi," Becky said tentatively. She looked to the loft as she shuffled her feet.

"Well, hello," Earl responded pleasantly. "I think you know my niece, Susan, Susan Taylor."

"Ah, yes, sir," Becky answered. "She's—she's a friend of mine."

Earl nodded. "Clifford told me you painted all of them signs for the football team. I gotta tell you, there's nobody working here who could have done a better job."

"Thank you," Becky whispered. She looked at Clifford, who winked at her.

"Your daddy tells me you're looking to go to art school," Earl said.

Becky glanced up in surprise at her father. Clifford smiled smugly.

"I might have a deal for you that could benefit both of us," Earl continued. "You go to school, and you do well, I'll pay for it."

"Sir?"

"I'll send you to art school," Earl explained. "Then when you finish, you come back here and work for me until you've paid me back. If you want to move on to something else after that, then you'd have my blessing to go. But I'd hope you'd stay here with us."

Becky said, "Really?"

"How you like that?" Clifford asked. "Remember this. It's who you know."

"When could I start?" Becky said.

"Next weekend," Earl answered. "We'll start you touching up some signs. Then you'll work full time in a few weeks."

There was a pause. Becky's eyes were damp with excitement. "Thank you, Mr. Taylor," she said. "I'll work hard."

"I know you will," Earl replied. "We're all proud of Jimmie Clifford getting the scholarship to play football at Tennessee, but Becky, I'm just as proud to have you working here."

"Me too," Clifford said with a toothy grin.

Becky could not contain her excitement. She opened the door to the truck and jumped from it before Clifford had braked to a stop.

"Jesus, Becky," Clifford snapped. "You gonna kill yourself."

Becky did not hear him. She saw Jimmie washing his car, and in the backyard, she saw Evelyn hanging wet sheets on the clothesline.

"Mama! Mama!" Becky screamed. She sprinted across the yard and threw herself into her mother's arms. "You knew about it, didn't you?" Becky cried happily out of breath.

"Yes, honey, I knew," Evelyn told her.

"It's the best thing that ever happened to me in my whole life," Becky declared. "Oh, Mama, I love you and Daddy so much. I won't ever ask for anything else."

"Don't say that, honey," Eveyln said. "Your day's just getting started."

Becky laughed and danced away from her mother. "I couldn't take anything else," she enthused. "I'm about to bust as it is."

Clifford and Jimmie strolled up. Clifford was smoking a cigarette. He tapped the ash from the tip and shook his head. "Good God, calm down, Becky, you're acting like you ain't got good sense."

"She ain't," Jimmie said.

"I don't care what you say or do, Jimmie Clifford, you can't make me mad—not today," Becky replied gleefully.

"Well, maybe—like your mama said—your day's just getting started," Clifford offered.

Becky stopped and gazed at her father. "What's that supposed to mean?"

Clifford turned to Jimmie. "You gonna tell her?"

"Tell me what?" Becky demanded.

A smile—a boy-man smile—broke on Jimmie's face. He said, "You care anything about using that car back there?"

"What?"

"You got turds in your ears?" Jimmie asked. "I said, do you want to use my car your senior year?"

Becky's face furrowed in suspicion. "Yeah, sure," she said. "Okay. What's the catch?"

"Catch?" Jimmie said. "There ain't no catch." He turned to walk away. "Hell, just forget it, then."

"Jimmie Clifford," Evelyn said sharply.

"Yeah, boy, c'mon, now," Clifford mumbled. "Ain't no reason to get testy." He looked at Becky. "The coaches up at Tennessee won't let freshmen players have a car the first year."

"Jimmie Clifford thought maybe you might drive it your senior year, and then he'd get it back," added Evelyn.

Becky's eyes flashed. "You're kidding?" She stared at Jimmie. He wagged his head and smiled. "Yes! Yes! *Yes!*" Becky screamed. She rushed to Jimmie and jumped up, wrapping her arms around his powerful neck. "I love you, Jimmie Clifford. Thank you, thank you, thank you."

Jimmie pried her loose. "Well, damn, Becky, you don't have to choke me to death," he said. "Wadn't my idea, anyhow. It was Daddy's."

Becky bolted for her father. He threw down his cigarette and ran back to the car, grabbing the water hose. "Don't you come near me," he called playfully. Becky charged him and he squeezed the nozzle and began spraying her.

"Clifford!" Evelyn commanded.

Clifford turned the hose on Evelyn.

"Clifford!"

"Watch out, Daddy," Becky yelled.

It was too late. The bucket of soapy water that Jimmie had been using to wash the car was already aimed and dumped. The water slapped against Clifford's back.

"Hey, you're gonna get the interior of my car wet," Becky shouted.

"Whose car?" Jimmie questioned as he stopped and turned toward Becky.

"Your car. But I'm gonna take real good care of it," Becky promised.

"You damn straight you are." Jimmie warned. "And if you gonna drive it, you're gonna wash it,"

"You know something, Clifford, I'm happy." Evelyn said.

"Yeah?" Clifford mumbled. "That's good."

They were sitting on the steps of the trailer, their clothes soaked, watching their children wash the orange car.

"Dammit, Becky, you're missing half the dirt," complained Jimmie.

"It's not me; it's you," Becky argued.

"Yeah," Evelyn said again as she shook off a chill. "I'm really—really happy."

"Well. Life goes on," Clifford added philosophically. "Life goes on."

6

"They's heathens ever'where . . ."

Clifford looked up from his paper. He thought: "That dumb sumbitch ought to be in jail with Jim Bakker."

"They's heathens—ah—where you go to work—ah. They's heathens where you—ah—shop. They's heathens—ah—where you get your hair cut. Oh, yes! Help me, sweet Jesus! Ah—they's heathens in your—ah—own church. They's—ah—heathens—ah in your own—ah—home . . ."

Clifford folded his paper. "Jesus H. Christ, Evelyn," he shouted. "I'm getting real tired of listening to this shit all the time!"

"Clifford," Evelyn said from the kitchen. "You just hush. Supper'll be ready in a couple of minutes."

"Look at this poor bastard!" Clifford ordered irritably. "He's about to have a asthmatic fit right there on television."

"Clifford!"

"But, yes, oh, help me, Sweet Jesus—ah. They's help . . . ah, yes, they's help, ah. Washed in the blood—ah—of our sweet savior, Jesus—ah . . ."

"God-o-mighty," Clifford whispered to himself. He watched the preacher on television. The preacher was leaping about the stage, dragging one leg in a holy-seizure dance step. His long blond hair, puffed up by a hair dryer sprayed thick, bounced on his head like a hat in the wind. His shoulders twitched. His mouth twitched. His eyes twitched. His hands twitched.

Evelyn put a bowl of beans with steam curling from the top on the table and paused to look at the preacher. Then she glanced toward the hallway leading to the bedroom. "Becky, come to supper," she yelled.

From the back of the trailer, Becky answered harshly: "Mama, I'm busy. I'll be there in a minute. Okay?"

Evelyn turned to Clifford. "Clifford, did you hear that?"

"Becky, get in here." Clifford bellowed.

A toilet flushed.

"Damn it, Evelyn," Clifford grumbled. "She was taking a crap. You won't let anybody in this place have any peace, will you?"

Evelyn turned to go back into the kitchen. "Shut up, Clifford," she said.

Becky came up the hallway, tucking her blouse into her jeans. "All right," she said, "I'm here. What's the big emergency?"

"Don't get smart with me, young lady," Evelyn answered from the kitchen. "I just want us to sit down to supper together like a family, is that too much to ask?"

"Then where's Jimmie Clifford?" Becky said.

Clifford threw his newspaper to the floor and pulled himself from his chair. "Don't start with that bullshit again." He strolled to the table and inspected it.

"That's what I figured," Becky grumbled. "When you say us, you mean me."

Clifford sat at the table. In the background, from the television, the preacher was praising the miracle cure of strips of a prayer cloth. He shook his head. He reached for the salt shaker, paused, pulled his hand back.

"What's this?" Clifford demanded.

"What's what?" Evelyn asked, putting the plate of cornbread on the table.

Clifford lifted the salt shaker. "This, gotdamnit. This!" He picked the pepper shaker up. "This."

"What's it look like?" It's a salt shaker and pepper shaker, for goodness sake."

"I know it's a salt and pepper shaker, Evelyn. I can see the little holes in 'em. But what is it?"

Evelyn sat at the table and spread a paper towel in her lap. "The white one's Jesus and it represents good, and the red one's the Devil and it represents evil," she answered.

"What's it doing on this table?" Clifford demanded.

"Good grief, Clifford—"

"Listen to me one more time, Evelyn," Clifford growled. "I don't want good and evil on my kitchen table, gotdamnit. I want—"

"Clifford, stop taking the Lord's name in vain in this house."

"I want regular salt and pepper shakers on my table. Is that too much to ask? I work my ass off seven days a gotdamn week and—"

"Y'all hush," Becky said rolling her eyes. "Anybody listening to y'all, would think we were a bunch of retards."

"Where'd you get 'em, Evelyn? Did you order 'em?"

"Don't start with me tonight, Clifford. I've got cramps. I don't want to hear it."

Clifford sprang from his chair and marched to the television set and yanked the cord from the outlet. "I told you what I'd do if I

caught you ordering anything else from that sumbitch," he
snapped.

"Clifford, put that TV down."

"You watch me. It's going out that damn window."

"Daddy, put the TV down," Becky said. *Wheel of Fortune*'s
. coming on in a few minutes."

"Jesus H. Christ. I don't believe it," Clifford sighed as he carried the television set from window to window until it was too
heavy to carry any longer. He did not throw the television through
the window as he had threatened. He put it back in its place, then
left the trailer in a hot silence and went to the Dew Drop Inn for a
beer and a ham sandwich. Evelyn and Becky ate, then watched
Wheel of Fortune.

Evelyn crawled into bed beside Clifford. She could hear his
heavy breathing, his prelude to sleep. She reached and patted his
arm, then turned away from him.

"Well, God," Evelyn thought, "I thank you for this day. Maybe
the best day I've had in years."

She smiled and imagined God pausing above her, his great
cosmic eyes sweeping across Captain's Point Trailer Park. God
seeing everything. The frosted tops of the trailers shimmering in
the spotlight of the round, clear, bright moon. The silver of the
street lights. The headbeams from Shelia's car. The bathroom
light left glowing in Benny and Fat Ethel's trailer. The dim night-
light for Wesley Alvin Tubb, Jr.

"I'm glad you look in on us, God," Eveyln prayed. "Even if I'm
the only one who really knows you're doing it.

"I hope you're hearing me, God.

"But of course you are. I know it. You hear everything."

The sweet voice of Elvis singing "Just a Closer Walk With
Thee" floated across the night, from Verdale's trailer.

"Thank you God. Thank you for blessing our family and our
friends," Evelyn said in the silence of her soul, throwing the
thought upward through the trailer, straight to heaven.

"Thank you, God. You made it right today. Thank you for Clifford. I love him so. He's really a good man, but you know that."

Evelyn rolled to Clifford. She watched him sleep. She kissed
him on the cheek.

"Clifford," she whispered.

"Clifford," she said louder.

"Clifford!"

She punched him in the side with her elbow.

"Wha—what?" Clifford muttered sleepily. He rolled over and squinted at Evelyn.

"Wadn't it a good day today, honey?"

Clifford raised up on one arm and glared at her for an unbelieving moment. "You woke me up to ask me that? Evelyn, I got to get up and go to work in the morning." He fell back pulling the quilt over his head. "Turn that gotdamn light out and go to sleep."

"Clifford! Don't you take the Lord's name in vain in this house."

The light in the Sewell trailer went out.

God smiled.

He gently blew a breath of warm wind across the river and into the trailer park, causing the thin curtains in the opened windows to quiver. Then he blinked his eyes and waited for morning.

the end

If you would like to be on the *poor white trash* mailing list just drop us a note at:

pwt productions, inc.
P.O. Box 120595
Nashville, TN 37212

We'd love to hear from ya!